IN THE ENEMY'S CAMP

BY
LISA REANEY

DEDICATION

For Brian,
My True North, my soul mate, the air I breathe,
You showed me the meaning of true love,
and what it means to truly grieve.
Until we meet again, a ghrá.
I love you more.

For Mom,
Who never stopped believing,
and who never gave up.
You have always been the wind beneath my
wings. Thank you for being the best mother I could
have hoped for. I love you.

and

For Grandad,
Who encouraged me and saw my potential,
even as a little girl.

Author's Note

In this time of growing cultural awareness, it is more important than ever to acknowledge and respect the individuality in cultures different from our own. Although I grew up in Alberta, Canada, and was fortunate enough to experience much of the First Nations culture first-hand, I know I can't truly understand who they are, or their history. All I can do is try to portray it here in a way that is as respectful and as authentic as an outsider can make it.

Any mistakes or misunderstandings of the history or culture of these incredible people are my own, and completely unintended.

In the end, I hope that my admiration and deep respect for the First Nations people of North America shines through.

"Grief is the price we pay for love."

Elizabeth II

&

"Here is the truth about grief. Loss gets integrated, not overcome."

Megan Devine, author of *It's OK that You're Not OK*

PROLOGUE

Spring, 1763

The young warrior sank to the ground on the bank of the river, gasping for breath, mud oozing between his bare knees. The water churned before him, grey and swollen from spring rains. He didn't know how long he'd been running, only that he hadn't stopped since seeing the bodies.

Flinging a filthy, dripping strand of black hair away from his face, he opened his fist and ran his thumb over a sweat-covered, clear purple stone. Lifting his face to the sun just beginning to set over distant mountain peaks, his features twisted in pain.

His chin dropped to his chest and he allowed himself to give in to his grief, finally. Hunched over, his shoulders shook as tears of rage and shame streamed down his face while sobs shook his body.

What had been, hours earlier, a bold and imposing display of red clay and yellow ochre stripes criss-crossing his chest, was now a heaving mess of streaked paint, sweat and blood.

Their blood. Hers.

He could still see them, the women he loved, one old and one young, their bodies broken. They lay twisted together as if trying to protect each other, comfort one another, even as they had died. Dried tears left trails through the blood and dirt on their faces. Lips forever frozen in silent screams for help.

1

But help had come too late.

He had come too late.

He could not get the image out of his mind. Deerskin dresses filthy, bodies lifeless. And blood. So much blood. And this stone, laying cold between his young bride's breasts, as cold as her own flesh.

He let out a scream of rage that seemed to echo off silent peaks.

His fault.

It was his fault!

His people had told him what happened. He could not face their accusing stares as they recounted what the enemy raiding party had done, how the enemy warriors had been able to wreak havoc undeterred, stealing horses and brutally killing the two women who had tried to stop them. How there had been no one there to protect them, because *he* had gone off with his small raiding party when he was supposed to be protecting the camp. He failed them.

All he could do was run, to try to escape the truth, to escape the fury and accusation he saw in the faces all around him. The fury and accusation - the disgust - he felt for himself.

How could he ever forgive himself?

Opening his clenched fist again, he stared at the polished stone. He'd given it to her as a gift, just before they married.

Yet another shudder tore through him and he tried to force the image of the broken bodies from his mind. *She was so young. . . so young.*

"No!"

His cries echoed off the jagged peaks that surrounded the clearing.

"Why? Why!"

But the mountains stayed silent, mocked him with stony faces.

Condemned him for his crimes.

His fault, for being so impetuous, so defiant. For disobeying his father's orders – his chief's orders - and leaving them alone, unprotected, to die.

Because he had failed.

Against his will, his eyes were drawn again to the glittering stone in his hand. Never in his life had he spent so much time making a gift for anyone. He'd spent hours searching for the perfect stone, stunning in its glittering translucence. Months rubbing it smooth with sand until all the jagged edges were gone. The stone had been a promise, a promise of love. A promise of a lifetime together. Of his protection and care.

A promise that he hadn't kept.

He had failed her.

But she was not the only one he had failed. He had failed his mother. His father. He had failed his people.

He did not deserve forgiveness.

An anguished moan escaped him. He hurled the stone into the river and collapsed onto the ground, laid in a crumpled heap, and wept.

Finally, exhausted, he grew still.

Barely discernible over the sound of rushing water, a twig snapped in the mountain clearing. The warrior lifted his head and turned toward the sound, looked death in the face, acknowledged it. Welcomed it.

A massive wolf crept forward from the darkness of towering pine trees, an inky shadow in the fading sun. It slunk toward him, body low, ears laid back flat against its head. The young warrior turned away and squeezed his eyes shut, willing death to come quickly. The wolf sniffed at the man and whined, nudged his arm with its nose, and whined again, then laid down and placed its head on the warrior's leg.

CHAPTER ONE

Late Autumn, 1766

Flames consumed the village.

Kimana knelt on the ground, lifted the teepee flap, and stared out on what had been - just hours before - a peaceful Cree encampment joyously making last-minute preparations for her wedding. Now, war cries and women's screams pierced the night. The air reeked of burning hides, of urine, of vomit. Of death.

She struggled not to gag.

Clasping her hands against her belly, she tried to stop the sick feeling that threatened to overwhelm her. Bile clogged her throat. Swallowing it back, she glanced over her shoulder at her young cousin. He must be terrified. Somehow, she had to find a way to control her own fear. She wouldn't be any good to him, to any of them, otherwise.

She looked back through the flap and ground her teeth together, hating the enemy more than she ever had. Dogs! A stampede of frantic buffalo would be less destructive than these Blackfoot warriors.

"Kimana?"

"Shush," she told her cousin, waving a hand behind her. "Someone will hear."

She tried to ignore the sound of weeping. But it was not her little cousin who cried. It was her mother, crying and moaning and babbling as if she'd finally lost what little had been left of her mind. Little Otter was braver than that. He might be only six summers old, but he had more sense than Grey Owl.

"Mother, please be quiet," she begged. She searched the darkness with her eyes, terrified that, at any moment, a Blackfoot warrior would burst into their teepee and murder them all.

The crying continued. Curse that woman, she was going to get them all killed.

"Mother! Please! Be quiet, I beg you."

Never had her mother frustrated her more than at that moment. The woman had been prone to hysterics and selfishness as long as Kimana could remember. She spared another glance over her shoulder. Grey Owl crouched before the embers of their fire pit, buttocks flattened against her heels. She rocked on her toes, back and forth, back and forth, back and forth, her lips twisted into a demented grin. Tears flowed down her cheeks. Then, bizarrely, she cackled. And cackled again.

She was mad.

Kimana shuddered. Nausea surged inside her belly once again.

Damn the Blackfoot. They had no souls. No decency. They laid waste to everything in their path. No thought for what they destroyed. For those they butchered in the night.

Or for those they drove insane.

If her mother didn't stop soon, she wouldn't be the only one who went crazy. Kimana wanted to block out the sound of her mother's moaning, but it was pointless.

She brushed tears from her cheeks, allowed herself a moment of self-pity. Tomorrow, she would have been wed. Tonight, she would probably die.

They would all die.

She dropped the flap and held her breath a moment as someone ran past, yipping and yelping like a starving dog. Taking a deep breath, she counted in her head as the footsteps and shrieking blended into the din. It had been like this since the moment the enemy stormed their camp.

"Kimana?"

"Little Otter, hush now."

Cracking opening the buffalo hide no more than a hand's breadth, she looked out again, self-pity forgotten. Her father was out there somewhere, amidst all that chaos. She had to believe he was still alive. That he would rally their men and send these Blackfoot dogs scurrying home, too ashamed to write a song about the battle.

Battle. It was no battle. That would have been honourable. This was a massacre. These warriors had no honour, attacking in the night. Killing innocent people. Women. Children. Old men.

She choked back a sob. It didn't look like enough of her people were alive to send the enemy running.

She had to do something.

She had to find her father.

When the first war cries had torn them from sleep, he ordered his family to stay inside their lodge. It seemed like so long ago. Had Manitou, the Great Spirit, stopped time to watch the battle? Morning should be here soon. And with it, she hoped, enough light to scare away the evil invaders.

It was impossible to see anyone clearly through the dust and ochre-tinted smoke that clogged the air outside the lodge and filled her mouth with grit. All she could make out were bodies, twisting shadows in the light of the fires of dozens of burning teepees.

She had to do something before someone burned down her lodge and her family with it.

Kimana pushed herself back from the entrance and turned to face her mother. Grey Owl still moaned, rocking back and forth on her knees, shaking her head from side to side, muttering and cackling in turn. Kimana's stomach heaved. Had the old woman finally gone completely mad? Had the attack been the thing to push her beyond this world, and into the realm of the trickster spirits?

"Mother!"

Grey Owl looked up, locked wild eyes with her daughter, put her hands on either side of her cheeks, and screamed. Kimana's stomach lurched and she whirled back to the opening, expecting to see someone behind her, one of the enemy warriors coming through the flap, brandishing a blade. She had no weapon, nothing to protect them.

But there was no one there.

Light from the fires outside made it look like spirits danced on the walls around them - mocking, taunting, shrieking with silent laughter as they closed in to steal Grey Owl's soul.

Kimana crawled forward and grabbed her mother's upper arms, shaking until the woman's head flopped onto her shoulders and for a moment, the old woman's eyes focused, just a little bit.

"Mother, stop this! I have to go. I have to find Father. You need to stay with Little Otter. He needs you. Mother, listen to me. Listen!"

Grey Owl screamed again. She yanked her arms out of Kimana's grip. Gnarled hands twisted and tore at her own hair.

Not knowing what else to do, but desperate to silence her lest her screams draw attention, Kimana slapped her. Immediately, a welt welled up on the worn face as she stared at her daughter in shock. For less than a heartbeat, they both sat back on their heels, stunned at the impertinence. Then Grey Owl cackled. Moaned as she fingered her cheek with an expression of wonder. Cackled again.

The brief hint of awareness and sanity was gone.

Kimana dropped her hands into her lap.

Knowing there was nothing she could do to reach her mother, she turned to her cousin. He sat, huddled on a sleeping mat, a hide pulled tight around his body. Huge eyes stared at her.

He must be terrified.

Understanding how he felt – not knowing where his parents were and if they were okay - she tried to reassure him.

"It's okay, little man. I'm going to find your mother and father. I'll be right back."

"You promised. You said you wouldn't leave me." His eyes were bright with fear.

"I know. I'm sorry. I have no choice. I won't be long, I promise you. I've got to find them and bring them back so we can all get away. All right?"

There was no way she could take him with her. He'd be safer where he was, and one way or another, she wouldn't be very long. She crawled over as he nodded and rubbed her hands against his arms. "Be very quiet, now. Don't make a sound. Understand?"

He nodded, but his eyes glistened with tears.

"If someone comes, or brings fire to the lodge, you have to run. Crawl under the wall and run. I'll loosen a peg, look, right here. See? If someone comes, run out onto the prairie as fast as your legs can carry you. Look for some tall grass, someplace to hide until I come to find you, like we do sometimes when we play. Do you hear me?"

He nodded again.

"All right. I won't be gone long. I love you."

Little Otter nodded.

Glancing once more at Grey Owl, she staggered to her feet and inched through the teepee's flap.

"Oh, Manitou," she prayed, grasping a hide-covered pole for support as she looked over the camp. "Great Spirit. Why have you let this happen?"

She stepped out into the madness.

***

Running Wolf reined in his horse and grimaced. On the ground before him lay the old Cree chief, a spear lodged deep in his back. Blood stained the earth around him. Although some of the Blackfoot had acquired fire-sticks several years ago, his people still preferred fighting with a blade, a bow. A spear.

Or their hands.

It was more honourable.

And far more satisfying.

Not that honourable fighting mattered when your enemies preferred fire-sticks. That was all the reason they had needed to justify the night-time attack he had announced earlier that evening after spying out the village. In the hour he spent watching the idyllic scene before him, the obvious preparations for some sort of celebration, his rage reached its height. It took all he had to reach backward with his arm and gave a silent signal for retreat to the warriors who lay flat in the tall grass behind him. The tiniest whisper of sound marked their passing as they backed away, melting into the aspens. He allowed himself to watch the village for a minute longer. He wanted to rush right in, in full daylight, but he held himself back. He knew from experience the price that could be paid for rushing in without thought or planning. These vermin deserved to have their own dishonourable tactics used against them. Besides, he had already waited more than three summers.

Waiting a few more hours was nothing.

And now, just a few hours later, Running Wolf gave a small

grunt of satisfaction as he looked again at the fallen chief. Three summers had indeed been a long time to wait. But revenge was as sweet as fresh, warm honey. He could finally let go of the grief that had consumed him all these years.

It was almost embarrassing how easy the village had been to take. Their enemies were well asleep when they attacked. Even those few who had time to grab a weapon and charge through their teepee flaps were stopped in their tracks by lances or arrows in their foreheads or chests.

Blinking, Running Wolf tried in vain to soothe his burning eyes. The air was thick with smoke, and the acrid taste of it nearly made him gag. The stench of blood and piss flared his nostrils.

It would have been so easy to kill them all. Women, children, it didn't matter. His hands still ached to feel the warmth of his enemies' blood on his fingers. They all deserved to die. They were like wolverines that preyed on the weak without mercy or honour.

Murderers.

Filthy, stinking animals. Yes, they should all die.

He felt a moment of unease. Teeth ground together as he thought about his father's reaction. Stealing horses was one thing. Killing Cree warriors? Expected. But completely destroying their village? He may have gone too far, but he didn't care. It was no matter. If there was a penalty to be paid for his revenge, he would gladly pay it, a thousand times over. But he would not be the only one to pay. Even now, the sins of the murderous Cree were being paid with the lives of their men.

Soon, their sins would be paid again.

By their wives and daughters. Mothers and sisters. Their children. Paid, perhaps not with their lives, but certainly with their freedom.

Even then, he knew it was not enough. Could never be enough. But it would have to suffice for now.

All around him, Cree women knelt crying beside the bodies of their men. Some of them looked up at his warriors, arms outstretched, begging them to stop. Pleading for mercy, for their lives.

He shook his head. No mercy. No sympathy.

These were the enemy. They would not be killed, but all the women and children would be sold at next summer's gathering. A smile touched the corner of his lips. The captives would bring a good price, but the horses were better still. They were some of the finest he had ever seen.

The horses would not be sold.

They would be added to the Blackfoot herd and bred, producing, he hoped, some of the most sure-footed beasts to ever graze in the mountains or gallop over the western plains. That should soothe his father's anger.

He raised his arm into the air, waving a blade toward a crescent moon that tried in vain to appear from behind heavy rain clouds. "Tonight, you have heard the war cries of the Blackfoot! The wind will carry the sound of your weeping and wailing to the four corners of the earth," he promised his enemy, as he had sworn he would do, almost four years past. "None will forget the name of Running Wolf. All will know and fear the vengeance of the black-footed people!"

His stallion shifted nervously. Tightening his knees against the beast's belly, Running Wolf fought back an unexpected wave of queasiness. He straightened his spine. He had done what was necessary. Better to kill the enemy before they wreaked even more havoc in his world. With the slightest pressure into the side of his mount, he spun toward the centre of the village.

It was time to give the order to his men to begin rounding up the captives.

***

The village was laid waste. Everywhere she looked, there were fires. And bodies.

The bodies of their men.

Kimana closed her eyes and tried not to weep. There was no time for tears.

Women screamed as she ran past, groaned, tore at their dresses, exposing heaving breasts. A few held knives to their throats and slashed themselves, their lifeless bodies collapsing on top of dead husbands and sons.

She prayed her family was not among them.

Kimana stopped to catch her breath. The enemy swarmed through the camp like hornets around a bewildered bear. As she looked, her nausea surged again as she realized how unlikely it would be to find her father alive.

Unwilling to give up until she knew for sure, she ran through the rubble, dodging enemy horses. Shreds of blazing hides singed the soles of her feet. Thunder boomed and crashed, blending with the sound of pounding hooves. She spun around, terrified, closed her eyes and covered her ears with shaking hands. A scream lurked at the base of her throat.

"I'm okay. I'm okay," she whispered aloud.

Taking a deep breath, she opened her eyes as icy rain began to pummel the earth. So, Manitou had finally broken his silence. The Great Spirit wept for his children. Fires sizzled and hissed as the great drops fell. More bitter smoke filled the air, and she coughed, choking. Somewhere in the dark, dogs howled. She looked up at the sky, terrified they would bring the evil spirits.

But no. The evil spirits were there already. They had come with the raiding party.

She needed to find her father. Straightening her shoulders, she surged forward, ignoring the ever-present pain in her leg.

She found him at the edge of the camp, a lance protruding from his back. He had fallen facedown. Mud oozed from between outstretched fingers.

"No!"

She fell to her knees, lifted his head onto her lap, turned it so she could see his eyes, open and staring vacantly. Smoothing the wet hair from his forehead, she leaned over his beloved face. Her tears joined the rain, washed the mud from his skin. She held him, weeping, crying out to the Great Spirit. She needed an answer for what had happened.

But Manitou was silent.

Time seemed to stand still. An eerie hush settled over the camp. Kimana gently eased her father's head onto the ground and struggled to her feet. Running back to her lodge, she wiped viciously at the tears stinging her eyes. There was no time for tears. No time to waste feeling sorry for herself. She had to get Little Otter and her mother and escape before someone found them.

As quickly as the silence had fallen, it ended. The Blackfoot warriors started screaming their war cries again. She covered her ears, trying to block out the terrifying sound.

Opening the flap of their teepee, she looked with horror on her

11

mother's body. Grey Owl lay on the ground, her legs twisted beneath her, a knife in her outstretched hand, dripping with blood. Her throat lay open like the carcass of a badly slain deer.

Little Otter was gone.

Kimana gagged.

Staggering outside, she fell to her knees and vomited in the mud.

***

"Woman!"

The word came to her from a distance. She was swimming upwards through a great cold lake, tearing at the weeds, trying to break through the icy surface of her pain to answer the persistent voice.

"Woman! I'm speaking to you!"

Kimana looked up into the angry face of a Blackfoot warrior. He towered above her, his scowl creasing his war paint. Blood covered his arms and hands. His chest. Fearing a blow, she covered her head with her arms. Would he strike her down, too? For a moment, terror and despair overwhelmed her.

Let him be quick, Great Spirit. Take me to the place of my people, to the great campfire, where I can listen to my father tell the stories again.

The man grabbed her arm and pulled her to her feet. She gasped as pain seared through her shoulder and down into her arm. For a moment, he hesitated, his expression stunned as his eyes met hers. Was it regret she saw there? Just for a moment? Any hint that he might have any compassion at all vanished when he dragged her toward a horse. She tried to twist out of his grasp, but he was too strong, the pain too intense. Other women and children, their heads bowed, shoulders slumped in defeat, sat bound and mounted in front of the enemy warriors. The one who held her grabbed a cord of buffalo sinew from another man and roughly tied her wrists together.

"No!" she finally screamed and tried to hit him with her arms. Grabbing her by the hair, he tilted her face up to his.

"Enough!"

From somewhere deep within her, a spark of rage and defiance broke through her fear.

She spat in his face.

For a moment, they stared at each other in shock.

Suddenly aware of what she had done, wondering if he would slice her throat wide open and leave her there to slowly die, she tried again to wrench free of his grasp, but his face broke into a wry smirk, and he simply picked her up and tossed her over his shoulder. Hoisting her effortlessly onto his mount, he swung up behind her, then nudged his horse into motion.

Kimana watched as her village faded into the night, fires staining the night sky. The rain had stopped, and a chill was in the air. Already, a frost painted the ground, and would soon make ghosts of the corpses.

She thought of her father, of the stories he would never tell on this earth again. She thought of her little cousin. Had he managed to get away? And even if he had, what would happen to him now, alone on the prairies with no one to protect him? She thought of her mother and could not help but feel a bit of relief that her battle with madness was finally over. And she thought of the brave warrior she was supposed to have wed. Two Hawks. Tomorrow she would have been sharing a mat with him, living in her own lodge. Starting a new life. But that would never happen now, and the Blackfoot dog who held her pinned in his iron grip was responsible for each and every loss.

CHAPTER TWO

K imana shifted her weight on the blanketed horse and tried to get comfortable. Her buttocks ached from hours of sitting motionless, trying not to touch the warrior behind her. Her arms were numb from being tied. Despite her discomfort and sorrow, it was impossible not to appreciate the display the Great Spirit was putting on this morning. The sky was awash in colour; inky blues, vibrant orange, and countless shades of pink and purple. In the distance, she could just now make out the shapes of what she could only assume were the mountains. Even as she watched, they seemed to glow, as if lit from within, set on fire by the magnificent sunrise to the east.

She'd never been there before, to the mountains, but she knew they were filled with all sorts of strange spirits. She was honestly more curious than afraid of what secrets they might hold. She'd never been the type of person to fear the unknown. Her parents had often scolded her for rushing into things without thought or planning. Reckless, they called her. Impetuous. When said by her mother, the words and tone were filled with scorn and anger, impatience. But when said by her father, it was impossible not to see and hear his barely suppressed amusement and pride.

It would take two or three days to reach their destination, unless something had changed since their scouts last reported the locations of the countless Blackfoot villages that dotted the eastern slopes of the mountains and foothills.

It hadn't been long since they'd left her village. The sky had started to lighten almost immediately, giving them ample light to see by as they raced westward. An icy wind chased them off the prairies, nipping and scratching at her exposed skin like an angry wild cat. Her flesh was covered in tiny bumps. Anger surged as she thought about the warm fur wraps burning in the fires these men had left behind. She looked down at the corded arms that imprisoned her and wondered if the warrior even felt the cold. He didn't appear to notice.

She still hadn't seen Little Otter, but her aunt, Utina, was riding just ahead and to her right. She was surprised at how many women and children rode in front of the enemy warriors. By the looks of it, very few of the village's women had died in the attack, certainly less than she had originally thought. And hopefully, none of the children.

But where was Little Otter?

She twisted her body to see behind her and received a warning grunt from her captor. By all the spirits! Her back was stiff from trying not to touch him.

But her back was the only part of her that was warm.

Kimana could feel the heat radiating from the forbidding body that was uncomfortably close to hers. He urged the horse faster, and her hair whipped around and slapped against her face.

Was it hitting him, too?

She hoped it hurt.

Her eyes burned from the wind and the pain of forcing back angry tears. Although she wanted to ignore him, she knew it was better to focus her thoughts on the man who held her trapped between his arms than to think of her family, her loss.

He breathed down her neck like an angry buffalo, his muscled arms squeezed against hers. The reins were held tightly clenched within hands that were crusted with flaking blood.

She quickly shut her eyes and forced herself to focus on him, not on the blood and the images it threatened to bring to mind.

What kind of warrior was he, anyway?

He didn't seem to have much confidence in his ability to keep her from escaping. She glanced over her shoulder, wanting him to see the mocking look in her eyes. Was he afraid she'd escape? Afraid he would lose his precious prize? He ignored her look, staring forward with a hooded gaze. Facing forward, she allowed

15

herself a scowl. Blasted man wouldn't give her the satisfaction of seeing his reaction. She wriggled her wrists, trying to loosen the cords that held her.

Too tight. The effort turned the skin red and sore.

A soft growl rumbled against her back as he pressed his chest against her and warned her without words not to bother attempting to free herself.

Well, he didn't need to worry about her escaping.

Yet.

Her aunt Utina's captor slowed his horse so they were riding side-by-side. The two men exchanged a few words, giving her time to try to get her aunt's attention. But Utina sat tightly enclosed in the fierce looking warrior's arms, her head hanging toward her chest. Long black hair was matted and bloody, and her shoulders shook with tears that Kimana herself could not, would not, shed. She felt a surge of anger toward the woman who was just a few years older than her, and immediately felt guilty.

Utina was probably thinking about her husband, his body left to be devoured by animals - not even given a proper burial.

Kimana looked around at the faces of the other captives.

Women.

Children.

Each one, silent. Afraid. Defeated.

Their lack of spirit frightened her. Had they all given up completely? Would they allow themselves to be conquered without even trying? Such weakness was unforgivable. She couldn't allow herself to give up. She had to be strong for her people. Her father would expect no less. It was her duty.

Twisting her wrists again, determined to loosen her bonds, she bit her lip to keep from crying out. Blood trickled onto her hands, warm and sticky.

It was pointless.

She was surrounded by dozens of warriors, and even if this one, the arrogant one who held her, couldn't catch her, the rest of them combined certainly could. But she could never leave her people. Her only hope was to find a way for them to escape after they reached the enemy camp.

Maybe everyone else had given up, but she would not. She lifted her chin. The daughter of a chief did not give up.

Another warrior urged his horse forward on the left side and spoke with her captor. She glanced at the child held in his arms and felt her breath catch in her throat. Little Otter! Thank the spirits. He looked at her with eyes round like the moon, his lips quivering. She smiled, trying to reassure him. He wasn't crying but she could tell he was terrified. He might be afraid, but he was alive. As long as they lived, there was hope. His horse dropped back again, and she couldn't see him anymore without twisting completely around.

This Blackfoot dog who held her in his arms obviously wouldn't allow that.

At least she knew her cousin was alive, and not alone out on the cold prairie. Two Hawks probably would have found him in the morning when he returned from his spirit journey, but perhaps it was better he was captured too, rather than the risk of falling prey to an animal while hiding. There may not be many bears or wild cats on the plains, but there certainly were a lot of wolves. And other predators. Even a small pack of coyotes could be dangerous if they were hungry, especially to a child.

Little Otter was safe for now.

Safe. She let loose a disdainful snort. None of them were safe. She didn't know what their future held, but she was reasonably sure they weren't going to be killed. Why take on the burden of captives only to kill them later?

Unless torture was intended.

No, she wouldn't think about that.

Two Hawks. She'd think about Two Hawks. She had been worried about him while he was gone on his vision quest. He had gone down to the sacred place, *AisinaiPi* - Where the Drawings Are. It was always a risk heading deep into Blackfoot territory, but there was no place more spiritual, and it was the first choice of many a young man for his vision quest. At this time of year, the Blackfoot would be closer to the mountains – where they were headed now. There was no reason to think Two Hawks would have encountered any problems.

He certainly wouldn't expect to come back to the destruction of their home. No, he had expected to return to an excited bride. To preparations for their wedding ceremony and feast. Now all he'd find was devastation and death. Would he realize they'd been taken captive? Would he follow? Of course, he would. He was honourable.

But what could one man do against so many?

She closed her eyes for a moment. Her wedding dress. It was probably destroyed by the fire. And she'd spent so much time on it, even though she hated beadwork and sewing. After months of work, it had finally been finished yesterday afternoon. Her father had been so proud. The flap of the teepee had lifted while she knelt on a sleeping mat and put the finishing touches on soft hide. Kimana had looked up and smiled. Her dress fell to the ground as she scrambled to her feet. Chief Three Bears stood at the entrance and watched her with quiet laughter in his eyes.

"Is that how you treat your wedding dress, daughter? If I had known you would be so careless, I would have found a less perfect deer."

A blush warmed her cheeks and she looked down at the soft hide lying in a pool at her feet. The months of work had been worth the effort. She'd spent hours soaking the hide in water and ashes and scraping it to remove every last trace of hair. Then she had chewed it for endless hours to soften it.

The final step in preparing the skin had been finished several weeks ago, and she was glad it was over. Although she'd seen it done, it had never been necessary for her to soak her own hides in urine to lighten them.

It was a tradition for the women in her tribe to wear the palest colour possible at their wedding, to symbolize peace and happiness, so the only time the practice of lightening hides was common was when a maiden was preparing her wedding dress.

It was disgusting work, but the end result was always worth it.

The deerskin dress was soft, supple, and nearly as pale as a snowshoe hare in winter.

"Let me see if your beadwork is worthy of such a fine hide," her father said.

She felt her delighted blush grow deeper and she picked up the dress and presented it for his examination. He studied the coloured wooden beads and dyed porcupine quills with a careful eye, then grunted his approval.

Reaching out a hand he turned her face to his and looked into her eyes.

"You will make a beautiful bride, daughter. May Manitou grant you much happiness."

These last words were choked out.

Kimana searched her father's face.

He'd never been one to show deep emotion. Such things were for women, he always said. She turned her cheek into his hand as he stroked her skin. Absently, she reached up and touched the pink quartz stone that hung from her neck. Two Hawks had given it to her just before her left on his vision quest. Remember me, he'd said.

"Oh!" she said, and her eyes grew wide as she remembered the treasure she'd found at the river earlier that morning. "Look what I found, father. It's an omen from the Great Spirit."

She pulled the eagle feather from her belt and held it out to him. She knew he would be delighted. Every young maiden hoped for a sign before her marriage, but few got one as important as this, she was sure.

He took the feather from her and gently held it between his fingers, careful not to damage the delicate shafts. His smile faded and his face grew serious.

"What is it? Isn't it a good sign?" Suddenly feeling anxious, she waited for his verdict.

He ran a fingertip down the spine. "When someone finds an eagle's feather, it means they are about to leave on a journey to a new and strange land."

She shook her head in confusion.

"But I am not going anywhere."

Her father looked at her, his eyes sad. "Why else would the eagle give his feather, if not to speed you on your way?"

She touched his arm, feeling his sorrow, but not knowing how to reassure him.

He was wrong about the journey, she had been so sure of that, but he'd been so sad. Maybe the idea of losing her, of having his little girl finally marry and move into another lodge, was harder for him to accept than she had expected.

They had an unusual relationship for a father and daughter.

They walked together, rode their horses, talked for hours.

Sometimes, he even took her hunting and fishing. He gave her freedoms a girl did not normally have. She often wondered if Two

19

Hawks shared her father's unorthodox views on women. He didn't seem to but spending so much time with her father as he grew up, he was bound to share something of his views.

Feeling weepy suddenly, and strangely insecure, she held out her arms and her father gathered her into his, pulling her close to his familiar body.

"You have always been my special child. I will miss you when you take your own lodge. Now who will laugh at my stories?"

She pulled away, and tried to grin up at him, "Little Otter loves to listen. But I promise I'll come every night and beg you for the stories, and you'll get sick of me and send me away. Maybe that's the journey I'm going on. I just hope I'm a worthy wife for Two Hawks. He deserves someone beautiful, not someone disfigured like me."

He snorted.

"You are more than worthy. You are my daughter. And daughter? The greatest beauty comes from within. Your scars only make you more interesting."

She felt her face warm again and she turned away.

"I know. Please leave me now, father. I have much to do, and there is little sunlight left. Two Hawks will be home from his vision quest in the morning, and I would have myself ready for his return."

His laughter had echoed in her mind long after he left the teepee.

It still echoed now, over the pounding of her heart and the sound of the horse's hooves.

Don't think about it, she told herself.

She shifted her buttocks and tried to find a more comfortable way to sit. She wasn't used to sharing a mount, and her position was awkward, being so much closer to the animal's neck.

Everything ached.

Even moving a little bit hurt. She certainly didn't want the warrior to see weakness in her, so she tried not to squirm.

Something cold touched her cheek and she glanced up at the sky. Snow. Wonderful. It didn't take long for her breath to come out in frosty clouds. Her shoulders slumped. With every hour that passed, the chances of Two Hawks finding them were reduced. Before long, the thick flakes would completely cover their tracks.

The horse's chest heaved from the exertion. Flecks of foam speckled his black coat.

Kimana wondered again how long it would be before they finally reached the enemy's camp, and whether or not they would stop soon for some rest. They had hardly slowed since leaving the Cree village. She knew they couldn't possibly keep up this pace for long.

The horses would need time to rest and recover from their exertion.

The warrior shifted behind her, pressing himself against her. She twisted around to stare at him, her eyes wide with shock and outrage. He squeezed her with his elbows and gave a warning growl. She glared at him, her eyes flashing a promise of vengeance, but he only smiled.

But there was no warmth in his smile. He looked angry, his eyes cold. For two pheasants she would shoot an arrow straight through his heart. No, she would do it just for the pleasure of seeing his hated blood stain the earth.

At least now that it was daylight, she had a better idea what he looked like, though knowing didn't make it easier.

His black hair was waist-long, and twisted into a single thick braid, which hung forward over his shoulder. His face was strong under the war paint that streaked his cheeks and forehead. In other circumstances she would have thought him attractive. Eagle feathers dangled from the top of his head. Would he be so arrogant as to add another one once they reached his home camp?

She sneered. He would not dare to honour himself that way. She'd tear it from his head. Rip it, and his blasted hair, right out of his skull. See if he still smirked at her then!

She turned to scowl at another warrior who had edged closer. He said nothing, but he cast an appreciative glance at her and grinned at the warrior who held her.

"A little wild cat, eh, Running Wolf?"

The warrior only grunted in response. Lucky for him, or he'd have had an elbow in his gut.

She stared the younger warrior down, her eyes shooting arrows her hands could not.

He grinned.

"I'll let the men know to steer clear. She looks like she has sharp little claws. Glad she's your problem."

"Quiet, Stands Alone, or I'll dump her in your lap and take that little old lady instead," Running Wolf growled.

Stands Alone laughed.

"I'd take her. Looks like she'd be a wild cat on her back, too. Wouldn't mind taking her for a ride."

Kimana stiffened and shot him a nasty look.

"Your mouth is going to land you in trouble," Running Wolf said. "You forget we speak a similar tongue. I wouldn't be surprised if she launched herself right off my mount and clawed your pretty young face."

Stands Alone glanced back at Kimana. His grin grew wider, but he inched his horse farther away.

Smarter than he looked, she thought sarcastically.

Deliberately, she looked away. She wasn't sure where they were now. They'd ridden into a deep ravine and were approaching a wide, fast river. She had never been this far west herself, never been so close to the mountains before. Her life had been spent on the open prairies where food was plentiful, and the winter snows bearable due to the constant wind blowing them away.

She was thirsty.

And tired.

Many times over the long night, she'd been tempted to close her eyes, just for a moment, but each time her lids had fluttered shut, her body had slumped backwards into his hard chest, and she jerked forward, wide awake. The low, mocking chuckles coming from deep in his throat did nothing to soothe her fraying nerves. Her back throbbed from the effort of sitting so straight, and her eyes ached from fatigue. All she wanted was a place to sleep and some peace from the images that tormented her. All she wanted was the time and privacy to mourn her father. She squeezed her eyes shut, willing the tears not to fall. Not here, not now, not in front of these men who were responsible for so much sorrow and loss.

***

They stopped after fording the river, to let the horses rest and drink from the icy water.

Running Wolf pulled her from the horse's back and dumped her on the ground like a sack full of meat, ignoring her cry of pain as her ankle twisted. She rolled over and glared at his retreating back, but he didn't give her a single backward glance.

The horses' hooves had churned up the ground, and the earth beneath her was thick with snow and mud as she attempted to sit with some dignity. Stands Alone approached and crouched before her. He gave her a tentative smile, and then took a quick glance around. His eyes settled on Running Wolf. The tall warrior was busy speaking with another of the men. The young man looked back at her and smiled again.

"I am called Stands Alone."

"I have ears. I'm not stupid."

His smile spread into a grin.

"Sorry for earlier. I was teasing him more than you. Look, I thought you might be thirsty."

He held out a skin filled with water. Deliberately - with as much scorn as she could - she turned her face away, rejecting the offer. She would rather die than take anything from these animals. He shrugged and poured the liquid out onto the earth, splashing her already filthy dress. She bit her lips to keep from crying out and watched the water she so desperately wanted disappear into the sloppy ground.

Stands Alone stood up and looked down at her, his face a strange mixture of pity and admiration.

She wished she hadn't been so rude.

He was her enemy, but he was trying to be kind. He probably wasn't old enough yet to have the same viciousness as the rest of the warriors. Just as she was about to apologize, he turned away.

"Wait!"

Stands Alone looked back, his eyebrows raised.

"What river is this?"

"We call it the Old Man. After Napi, the creator."

"Manitou is the creator," she said, her voice filled with scorn.

"Same thing."

He waited to see if she would say anything else, but she clamped her mouth shut. He walked away and refilled the skin, then went to each woman and child in turn. The others eagerly took the offering, and she scowled, silently warning them against accepting any show of kindness, but they looked away and ignored her.

23

She had given up hope for Little Otter's mother. She was definitely not amongst the captives. Kimana let her gaze drift over the river and up the steep cliffs on either side of it.

She wanted to cry, needed to, but the tears would not come.

When the horses had rested, Running Wolf reached down and picked her up, tossing her face first onto the back of his stallion. Her breath whooshed out as her belly made contact. She lay across the blanket, the horse nervously sidestepping beneath her. Her face burned with shame as he swung up behind her, then landed a single, firm slap on her behind.

She shrieked. How dare he touch her?

He chortled but made no move to help her shift into a seated position. He seemed to be waiting for something. Did he expect her to ask? To beg? Her teeth ground together. She'd be damned first. He would allow her to sit properly, or he would wish he had.

"If you can do nothing else, at least give me the dignity of sitting like a human being instead of being tossed over your horse like a deer's carcass."

He chuckled again and shifted her into a sitting position.

Everything he did seemed intended to humiliate her.

***

Night fell once again, and she scolded herself for refusing the water. How could she be so foolish? Her mouth was dry and she felt light-headed. Her father would have been so disappointed. She could almost hear his voice telling her that pride was useless without wisdom. And hadn't she grown out of her fits of temper? Knowing that she would have shamed the man she loved so much, she hung her head as silent tears finally flowed down her cheeks.

***

Running Wolf glanced down at the woman in front of him. For the first time since her capture, she appeared vulnerable. Her defiant shoulders sagged and shook with silent tears, and he felt a twinge of regret.

She might be more trouble than she was worth, but she had spirit. And lots of it. He admired that, even in a woman. Maybe especially in a woman. His mother had been like that, full of pride and fire.

But now the same spirit he admired in his mother, and recognized in this Cree woman, was crumbling into tears.

He didn't want to feel sorry for her, but it was almost impossible. He couldn't imagine what it was like to lose a family, a whole tribe, a home, in a few short hours. It wasn't really her fault their people were at war. The Cree had been his enemy for more years than he could remember.

But he had a far deeper, more personal debt to collect, and no time for pity or mercy.

It had felt so good when he gave the signal to attack. He had no time for sympathy or second thoughts. He'd waited a long time, too long, for that moment. But when it was over and he looked at the carnage, he could not deny the sick feeling that came over him, or the way his stomach turned as he watched some of the women take their own lives. And when he had seen this one, this prideful beauty kneeling in the dirt, her long dark hair matted and her cheeks streaked with ashes and tears, he felt something stir inside of him. Was it regret? No, more than likely it was just pity.

He didn't want to feel sorry for these people. They didn't deserve it.

Woman or no, she was the enemy. And typical of the headstrong Cree, she had stubbornly refused Stands Alone's offer of water, which proved only that she was foolish as well.

It was her own fault if she died of thirst.

She and her people wouldn't see any sympathy from him.

If it took his whole life, they would pay for what they had done. He straightened on his stallion's back, and his eyes hardened.

Yes, they would pay. Again and again.

After a while, her body slumped against him. Finally, it seemed, she slept. He fought back the urge to pull her closer toward him, and the equally strong urge to shove her away.

Let her rest. She would need her strength. He barely noticed his thumb gently stroking her arm.

CHAPTER THREE

He had never felt such anguish. Or such fury. Two Hawks stood in the middle of the encampment and stared at the carnage. So many, dead. Dogs slunk around the camp and whined. Some of the teepees still smouldered. Most were burned to the ground, their supporting poles charred black, but a few still stood. Bodies were strewn about like leftover fish tossed to the dogs. He closed his eyes and tried to control the anger raging inside of him.

He had to control it.

He looked over toward the chief's lodge, one of few that had escaped the devastation of flames. There was almost no point in looking for her. If she were here at all, she would already be dead, and he could not face looking upon her body, knowing his dream of a life together was over.

It didn't matter. He had to know.

Pushing aside the flap, he stared at Grey Owl's corpse in shock. Taking a moment to steady himself, he stepped inside, crouched beside her body and touched the back of his hand against her cheek. Her flesh was cold to his touch. Closing his eyes for what seemed like a single, hard heartbeat, he allowed the pain to sweep over him. The old woman had treated him like a son since he had been a small boy. She'd treated him better than she had treated her own daughter. If only he had been there, maybe he could have saved her.

"I'm sorry."

The whispered words seemed to come from far away.

He rose from the ground and looked around. A pale hide lay neatly folded on top of a pile of thick furs. He knew what it was, though he had never laid eyes on it until this moment. Grief shot through him again and almost forced him to his knees. He crossed to Kimana's mat and picked it up.

Her wedding dress.

The beads and porcupine quills shivered and danced as the dress unfolded in his hands and draped softly to the ground like something out of a dream. He lifted it up and buried his face in the velvety hide. Closing his eyes, he let her scent wash over him.

Kimana.

Gently folding the dress, careful not to bend any of the quills, he tucked it reverently into the pack that was tied around his waist.

He took one last look around. She wasn't there. Somehow, he hadn't expected her to be. She was far too lovely. No man in his right mind would kill her. She might have some scars on her face, and she might walk with an obvious limp, but she was still lovely. Her hair alone made her worth a fortune. Its coppery streaks were unusual and gave her a striking beauty few could match. No, they had likely stolen her to be sold as a slave. She would bring a high price.

No! He scowled. She was his. Whoever was responsible for this would die.

In two strides, he was outside. He called out, hoping someone was still alive. Someone who could tell him what had happened here. Someone who could tell him who had done this.

But no one answered.

The horses were gone. Most of the women and children were gone, except for those who lay in bloody heaps on the ground next to the bodies of the warriors. He felt the rage that burned through him turn slowly to ice.

He looked up at the sun and judged it to be halfway to its zenith. He knew from the tracks on the ground that there had been dozens in the raiding party. There was no way he could take them on alone, but he had to find out where they had gone. Somehow, he would get her back.

The slap of the wind on his face reminded him that time was

short. The snow was coming and soon the tracks would be buried. He had to find Kimana.

But how would he catch them? He had no horse. A week earlier he had left on the traditional short vision quest before his marriage. It was customary to walk.

For a moment he felt hopelessness overtake him and he closed his eyes. It didn't matter. Even if he had to walk the whole way, he would. He would find her.

Sprinting to the edge of the camp, he knelt down to study the tracks. He lifted his face to the west, his brows drawing together. Shoshone? Blackfoot? Whoever it was, he would find them. No one could steal his woman. No one could destroy his people and expect to get away with it. Yes, he would find them. And then he would destroy them.

CHAPTER FOUR

K imana's eyes snapped open as the horse slowed beneath them. The sun was high in the sky, and though it warmed her skin, the wind still bit into her flesh. How long had they been riding? Two days? Three? She couldn't remember. The days and nights blurred together.

She was exhausted. Not hungry, though, and not thirsty, thank the spirits. After her stubborn refusal of water from Stands Alone, she forced herself to accept further offerings with a nod and a slight smile of thanks.

Pride was one thing. Survival was another.

And common courtesy probably wouldn't hurt, either. She hated to admit to being witness to random acts of kindness and respect from some of these warriors toward her people over the last couple of days.

The Blackfoot had ridden hard, but they also stopped for frequent breaks, each time treating the prisoners well. Most of the women weren't even bound anymore, and none of the children had restraints. It surprised her that they were showing mercy and surprised her even more to see kindness and empathy. It contradicted everything she thought she knew about the Blackfoot.

She looked uneasily up at the mountain peaks around her. She'd grown up on stories of the spirits who lived in the mountains, and the warnings not to venture too near. It was said that if a person went alone into the mountain passes, they would never return.

Her eyes widened with terror as a shriek pierced the air.

Another shriek.

Laughter.

She looked around wildly, her heart thumping in her chest, but the warriors didn't seem concerned.

They were grinning.

Something moved to her left and she shrunk back into Running Wolf's chest, squeezing her eyes shut. Enemy, be damned. Right now, he was the only hope for survival she had.

Feeling foolish even before she opened her eyes, she forced herself to take a look and watched in stunned surprise as throngs of women and children poured out from amongst the aspens.

Not spirits after all.

She didn't know whether to thank Manitou or not.

They had finally reached the enemy's camp.

Throngs of children rushed forward. They reached up and grabbed at her legs and the legs of the other prisoners, then collapsed on the ground in fits of delighted giggles. The women of the camp watched their approach with eyes that revealed nothing. They looked neither welcoming nor hostile, simply curious. Their clothes were similar to the Cree people's, but perhaps with somewhat less beadwork. Her eyes opened a little wider as she noticed that many of the women wore feathers. In her tribe, only the men were permitted to wear feathers, a sign of great courage.

The women shouted questions at the returning warriors, but the men answered only with silent grins, obviously enjoying the adoration of their people and the suspense of keeping their tale for a time of their own choosing.

Kimana turned her face away in disgust.

With a grunt, Running Wolf reined his horse to a stop and dismounted, dragging her unceremoniously from the horse's back. Ignoring both her glare and her struggles, he pushed her, not quite roughly, toward the waiting women. Several pairs of hands reached out and grabbed her.

Like Running Wolf, they too ignored the vicious looks she shot at them. They merely clucked their tongues and shook their heads as if they thought she was a naughty child.

They pulled her through the trees to a large village in a

clearing. The other Cree women were similarly brought to the centre of the camp. The children were coaxed forward gently, with encouraging smiles and nods from those who led them.

Teepees stood in two large rings, one ring inside the other, their entrances facing east. In the centre, a fire blazed in a circle of stones. Nearby drying racks held strips of meat. It was impossible to ignore the excited shouts of the men, victorious in their return from battle. Old men shuffled out of teepees and sat cross-legged on the ground; their faces impassive but their eyes lit with curiosity. The young warriors also sat.

Someone forced Kimana to her knees.

Her head started to throb as she listened to the excited chattering of the Blackfoot people.

Suddenly, all eyes turned toward a large teepee near the middle of the centre ring, and a respectful silence fell. Her heart pounded as she watched the most impressive man she had ever seen emerging from it. He was tall, like Running Wolf, but his hair was hidden beneath a ceremonial headdress covered in feathers and porcupine quills. He walked slowly, but with a confidence and power she could easily see, even from the other side of the fire. He looked so much like her father - without question a leader.

She snorted at her ridiculous musings. Her father was kind and good. He was not an animal.

She shuddered as she remembered the stories of the Blackfoot's treatment of prisoners.

Horrible stories.

Unbelievable stories.

Stories of captives being forced to run through a corridor of people with sticks, being beaten, often killed, before they could make it to the end.

And it was this man who would decide their fate.

He walked to the centre of the camp and faced Running Wolf, the only one who still stood.

"My son. You have returned home in victory."

His son. She sneered. Why did that not surprise her?

She watched as they stood face to face. The chief hadn't asked his question, rather, it was a simple statement of fact. Obviously, he'd expected nothing less than victory.

"You brought us prisoners."

31

His voice was deep and sure, and his eyes roamed over the captives with interest before glancing at the stolen horses.

"And many horses. It is good."

Kimana felt his eyes light on her face, and she straightened her back and turned her head away so he wouldn't see the fear in her eyes. *Great Spirit, give me strength. Give me courage. Help me to bring honour to my people.* With an effort she knew he couldn't possibly detect, she deliberately looked back at the Blackfoot chief and met his eyes in defiance. She lifted her chin and stared at him with the same intensity that he looked at her.

He might be the chief here, but she was a chief's daughter. She would not tremble at his feet. And she certainly wasn't about to show fear.

***

Running Wolf watched his father, and knew he was enraged. Horses were one thing, in fact, expected. But prisoners were another thing altogether. It was many moons until the summer gathering. And in that time, they would have to feed and care for these people, not to mention deal with their hostility and anger, and potentially even their rebellion.

He knew his father would be even angrier when he heard the whole story. Running Wolf could see the questions burning in his eyes but knew he would wait to ask until they were alone. His father's eyes swept over the captives and came to rest on the fiery young woman he had ridden with. Black Eagle lifted a brow as he observed her insolent stare, but Running Wolf knew that no one else would have noticed his surprise. The chief hid his thoughts and feelings well.

His father watched the girl for a few moments before letting his eyes drift once again over the other prisoners. With a nod and a soft grunt, he turned toward his lodge. He did not beckon his son to follow, he obviously knew he did not need to. When he disappeared inside his teepee, the people released a collective breath and stood as one. Women scurried about, preparing for the victory feast they would share that night, when they would finally hear the stories of the battle. The men would rest, clean and repair their weapons, and pretend to ignore the children that would swarm around them like intoxicated bees over sweetgrass.

Running Wolf glanced toward the prisoners and watched as an

old woman led them to a place on the edge of the camp where they could watch them, but still prepare the meal.

He looked again at the defiant young woman, her back straight and proud as she lowered herself to the ground and crossed her legs. Glancing up, she saw his gaze. She stared at him with eyes that held more insolence and fury than fear, then tossed her head and dismissed him.

He took a step toward her, his anger churning within him. A grunt caught his attention, and he turned back to his father who stood at the door of the teepee, watching him with eyes as hard as quartz.

***

Running Wolf sat next to the fire and watched the reflections flicker and dance over his father's face. As he recounted the tale of the raid his father said little.

Now they sat in tense silence.

His father's lack of comment spoke more to Running Wolf than a reproach ever could. The prospect of feeding extra mouths in a winter that promised to be long and hard was justification for his fury. Hopefully, they wouldn't have to wait for the summer gathering to sell them and recover some of the losses they would incur in feeding them.

"Who is the girl, the one who stands proud like a warrior?" Black Eagle asked.

Running Wolf stared, feeling uneasy. "I think she's the daughter of their chief. I saw her with him after he fell."

"Whose arrow took him down?"

Running Wolf was startled by the unexpected question. "It was a lance."

Black Eagle's eyes blazed. "Do not think to run in circles around me with your words. I ask again, who killed the chief?"

"I don't know."

"You should know! Did you not lead them?"

Running Wolf looked his father directly in the eyes and said nothing. He alone would be held responsible. He had expected that. But still, his father's disapproval stung.

"I thought you had learned something these last few years. But now I see you are just as reckless as ever." The chief grunted and waved his hand dismissively. "The prisoners will be adopted into

33

whichever families wish to take them. They will be expected to contribute to this camp. They are not to be treated as slaves."

Running Wolf tried to hide the sudden flare of anger that lit his eyes. "But…"

His father gave him a hard stare. Arguing was pointless.

"It will be as you say."

"They are to be treated well. I will tolerate nothing less. See that the people know this."

Running Wolf gave a single, curt nod and tried to hide his resentment. He'd expected to sell the captives, not have them live with them like honoured guests. He wasn't happy that their enemies would be treated as members of the community, but he accepted his father's decision. It had been a foolish thing to do, to leave them with no providers, and now, his people would be responsible for them. He stared into the fire and wondered how he had yet again been so stupid as to let his emotions take over. Once again, his people had reason to be angry with him. For a year after the attack that saw his mother and young bride killed, many had shunned him, blaming him for the deaths. He had let them down. Disobeyed orders. Failed in his responsibility to protect his people while the older warriors had been away. The humiliation and loneliness of that time had been unbearable. Not to mention dealing with the grief of losing those he loved. He could still remember how it felt, to be part of the tribe, but never really a part of it. The time it took before he finally earned his way back into the people's good graces was the longest year of his life. He'd learned a lot about self-control and discipline. And now, here he was, once again. Responsible for his own impulsiveness. He looked up and saw his father watching him. The old chief said nothing for a while, he merely nodded slowly.

"Since your mother and Laughing Brook left us for the Place of the Spirits, we have depended upon the grace of the women of this camp to tend to our needs. The girl, the proud one, will live with us. She has a limp, but it does not seem to affect her much. She will know how to care for the lodge of a chief and should not require much instruction."

Running Wolf fought to hide his shock. He hadn't noticed any limp, not that it mattered. It was bad enough to have the enemy in this camp, treated as guests rather than prisoners, but to have one living in his own lodge was unthinkable. Especially one with such an attitude.

Black Eagle stared at him, his hooded eyes probing his son's face.

"You should have given thought to the result of your actions. Vengeance can eat at a man's soul, my son. There is still much for you to learn. One day the Great Spirit will call me home, to sit at the great campfire, smoke the willow bark, and share the ancient stories with our ancestors. The people will need a man to lead them, one who can make decisions based on what is right, not on what he feels. It is not an easy thing to do. You will learn. You are strong and brave. The only thing you lack is wisdom."

A small smile turned up the corners of his mouth, softening his gruff expression for a moment as he gazed at his son, then his eyes hardened once more.

"There will be no discussion. Tell the people my words. The captives will be given new homes at the feast tonight."

Black Eagle turned his face from his son in obvious dismissal and stared into the dancing flames.

It was the closest his father had come to a reproach, and it twisted in his stomach like rancid bear fat.

CHAPTER FIVE

The sun set, the air chilled, and the feasting and dancing began. Drumbeats shook the ground and echoed through the night, throbbing in time with the heart of the great Earth Mother.

The sound was hypnotic, primal.

With each beat of the drum, Kimana's own heart pounded. She wasn't sure if it was fear of what was yet to come, or her ever-present grief over her father's death. It was like crashing again and again into a reality that could not possibly be real.

And yet it was.

Impossibly real.

She wanted to curl up and let the tears come, escape into the pain of her loss, just for a while. Just for a little while. He deserved that. He deserved every single tear, and it felt like she was not permitted to even give him that.

But perhaps she would find time for that later. For now, she would allow herself to be distracted by the scene playing out in front of her.

Groups of warriors whirled and danced, pounding their feet and crouching low in imitation of stalking their enemies. They thrust their arms out, made stabbing motions, all to glorify and celebrate their victory over her people. As she watched, hating every last one of them, she fingered the pink quartz stone that hung from her neck.

Stands Alone, the young warrior who had shown her kindness

more than once during their long journey, joined in the dance, every now and then looking at Kimana as she sat a short distance from the revellers. He seemed to want to impress her as he twirled around the fire with the other men, hooting and singing, occasionally tripping over his own feet, then looking at her with an embarrassed grin. The Blackfoot women stood on the periphery, swaying, and clapping their hands, and laughing in delight. Shouting encouragement.

The dance wasn't just celebratory, it was spiritual, a form of prayer and thanks to the spirits for their triumph, for returning home with their lives.

As the enemy celebrated their triumph, the ember of anger inside of her blazed up once again into a raging fire. But she was tired, so tired, of keeping her fury constantly burning in this way. She was not used to maintaining this level of rage. Her anger never lasted very long. It burned hot and fast like the wood of a pine tree but died out quickly.

Not this time.

But the effort it took to sustain it was exhausting.

After the celebration, Kimana watched with narrowed eyes as her people were taken away, one by one - lead like horses. It was a common practice to adopt prisoners into one's lodge. At least, for her people. It was, in many ways, far more merciful than killing them, but it angered her just the same. And her people seemed so grateful. Many of them had obviously expected to be killed. They had heard the same stories she had. In fact, they had told many of those stories themselves. Her eyebrows creased together as her scowl deepened. Since they had arrived, her Cree sisters had refused to look at her. Even her aunt Utina refused to meet her gaze.

Well, she wouldn't give in. She wouldn't give up. She wouldn't go happily into anyone's lodge like a widow accepting charity. In her own village she would have her own lodge, her own husband. Not been the second wife to any man. How could her people accept this insult?

Her wrists were still bound, but she noticed that not long after Running Wolf had emerged from his father's lodge, the other women had been released. The children had been allowed to run through the village and were quickly making friends.

If it was only that simple.

Little Otter hadn't hesitated to join in with the other children, though he glanced uneasily at her now and then, obviously sensing her disapproval. So, she gave him a gentle smile and encouraging nod, hoping to ease his worry. There was no point in him sharing her fear, especially since he was playing and laughing for the first time in days.

Children adapted so easily.

Kimana rolled her wrists and tried to ease the ache from being bound so long. It was interesting that she was the only one who was still tied. She glared at Running Wolf.

It could only be his doing.

He must know that she would claw his eyes out if he allowed her to be untied. Well, he couldn't keep her like this forever.

She stared at the tall warrior's back, wishing she could burn a hole with her gaze. As if sensing her gaze, he turned and gave her a lopsided smirk. She forced her face into an unreadable mask and looked away. Trying to distract herself, she glanced around the camp, awed by the bustling activity, by the sheer number of people who lived there.

Her survey came to an abrupt end as she noticed a woman standing off to the side watching her with eyes that were both curious and hostile. When the woman realized Kimana had noticed her staring, she sauntered forward. The beaded fringes of her dress swirled around honey-coloured legs, and her narrow hips swung as if she were dancing. Long, black hair billowed around her face and fell to her waist. Beads of all colours decorated her clothes, and white weasel tails swung from her hips.

Kimana was certain she'd never seen anyone so beautiful.

The woman stopped an arm's length away and looked down with a sneer that somehow managed to turn her stunning face into something almost hideous.

"I am called Silver Fox," she said, her voice dripping like sap from an old stump. "I don't think I've ever seen a woman as - ugly as you - in all my years. How did you get those scars?"

Kimana bristled, and the mouths of several at the women sitting nearby dropped open. Her scars were no one's business.

Silver Fox came closer, then crouched down so they were at eye level. The pale deer skin dress she wore stretched against her breasts and she smiled as she watched Kimana's discomfort.

Kimana lifted an eyebrow.

If this woman meant to intimidate her, it wasn't working.

Silver Fox's eyes narrowed. The women sitting nearby did not even try to hide their curiosity as they craned their necks in an obvious attempt to catch her quiet words.

"And not only ugly, but stupid as well, I think. But I'm sure you can be trained like any dog. I'll take you into my lodge. We could use a slave. And you are so ugly no one else would want you. You should be grateful that I would do this thing for you."

She smirked and reached out a hand to grab a fistful of Kimana's hair, giving it a sharp tug. Pain shot through Kimana's head. She had to restrain herself from lunging at the woman and knocking her into the dirt.

"She will not be going into your lodge, Silver Fox. She will be coming into mine."

Both women looked up in shock to see Running Wolf towering above them. He had approached so quietly neither one of them had realized he was there. Silver Fox came up from her crouch and stood with hands fisted on her hips, her eyes blazing with fury and disbelief.

"What? We don't adopt prisoners into lodges that have only men! She must go to a family, to be useful, not be someone's whore."

Running Wolf tensed, and then pasted a patient smile on his face. His eyes remained hard.

"She will come into our lodge to serve my father's needs. To care for his home. To prepare his meals. Anything else she is required to do is not your concern."

He stepped closer and pulled her to his well-muscled chest.

"You do not need to worry about this woman. She will be, as you say, nothing more than a servant."

Kimana's mouth dropped open as she watched Silver Fox grind herself against his thigh. Her face burned with embarrassment and disgust at their exchange. No proper woman would ever behave in such a way.

"Enough," he said. "Now is not the time for your games." Running Wolf pushed her away, but his eyes held a promise that neither Kimana nor Silver Fox could miss. He looked down at

Kimana with a thoughtful look in his eyes, then beckoned to an old, one-eyed woman who was seated close by, listening with great interest to the conversation. Dozens of bulging pouches of various sizes and shapes hung from her belt.

"Meda, this woman is being taken into our lodge. Please show her to it. No doubt she will need instruction on proper behaviour and perhaps even on how to prepare simple meals. My father and I ask you to supervise her, to see that she learns what she must know."

Kimana struggled to her feet and glared at him, a task made all the more difficult with her hands still tied.

"I am well aware of how to run a home!"

His black brows arched with amusement, and he looked back at the old woman. Kimana felt her face flush and she wondered what she was doing. Was she possessed of an evil spirit? What was the matter with her? She was acting like she wanted to take care of his cursed lodge.

"Meda, my father will be in your debt if you do this thing for him. The woman appears eager enough to learn."

He smirked at Kimana again and strode off. Silver Fox tossed a spiteful grin at her and followed him, hips swaying and hair swinging.

Meda looked at Kimana with a single curious eye, then reached into her belt and pulled out a knife.

"Let me cut those ropes," she said, not unkindly. "You will not be much good if you do not have your hands to work with. You are honoured to be taken into Chief Black Eagle's lodge. He is a good man, wise and brave. If you treat him well, he will treat you well also."

Meda cocked her head. Her solitary eye stared at Kimana.

"You know, if you cooperate, it will go easier for you here. Easier for your people. You must not allow your pride to override your common sense. A chief's daughter must be, above all, self-controlled."

Kimana looked at her in astonishment.

"How did you know I'm a chief's daughter?"

Meda shrugged and reached out, slicing through the cords on Kimana's wrists, and dropped them onto the dusty ground.

"I know. It is the way you walk, the fire in your eyes. It is many things."

Kimana cried out then, as the pain of a thousand wooden awls pierced her hands and wrists.

"It is just because you were tied so long," Meda said. "Rub them. The pain will go."

Kimana hesitated.

Meda reached out and took Kimana's hands in hers, examining the bloodied wrists.

"They need to be cleaned, but no damage has been done. I will give you a healing salve to rub in, so they do not get infected." She patted one of the pouches that hung from her waist. "Now come. We have much work to do."

Kimana stood stubbornly for a minute and looked down at her wrists. They hurt, but she was free. She'd waited for this moment since Running Wolf had first tied her, days ago. She took an uncertain step in the opposite direction.

"You should not. There is too much to lose."

Startled, she turned back and found Meda standing motionless, looking at her.

"The only thing I have left to lose is my life. You have stolen everything else."

"Is your life not enough? The time of the howling winds will soon be upon us. Can you not hear the spirits moaning in the mountains even now? What can one girl do? Where can she go? You think we are your enemy, and maybe this is true. But now we will be part of you, and you will change." She shrugged and smiled a crooked smile. "We will change also. You will be a part of us. It is the will of the Great Spirit. The time of growing will come soon enough, and then we will see if your heart is still so hard toward us."

"Time will not change how I feel, old woman. You are right. There is nowhere for me to go. Not now. But when the spring rains come, things will be different."

"Yes, things will be different. But maybe not the way you think. Hurry now. The moon is high above us and Chief Black Eagle will want his fire burning."

She walked toward the chief's lodge. She did not turn to see if Kimana followed her.

***

Kimana stood just inside the entrance to Chief Black Eagle's teepee. It was a huge lodge, and a great fire pit dominated the centre. The inner walls were painted with images of buffalo, deer and bears. They were brightly coloured with ochre, vermilion, and vibrant blues, which she was certain had been made from blueberries or even wildflowers. Bear and buffalo skins were scattered around the edges, and there was a lonely looking assortment of cooking pots and tools.

She wondered when they had last been used.

In spite of the opulence of the furs, the teepee seemed neglected. Not in any tangible way. The furs were clean and well-kept, and it was tidy. But it lacked warmth.

"Where is the woman of this lodge?"

Meda peered at her. Her gaze was sharp and direct. "She is gone to the Place of the Spirits, Kimana. It is best if you do not ask too many questions. For now."

Kimana took a step inside and the flap closed behind her, shutting out the light from the bonfire. Meda walked to the fire pit and looked at her impatiently.

"Come on, good-for-nothing, get the fire going here. Do not stand there gaping like a fool. You have much work to do. You may be able to deceive some with your haughty ways, but I can tell that you have cared for such things before."

A slight smile softened her words, and there was a hint of laughter in her voice. Impossibly, Kimana found herself smiling back, liking the woman despite her determination not to like anyone here. Was it possible she had found an ally? She watched Meda with new interest.

"What happened to your eye?"

"You do not know me well enough to ask such a personal question," Meda said, scowling. Then she shook her head and smiled gently. "I was born this way. My mother told me that one night while she slept, a raven flew down from the sky and into her womb. It plucked my eye right out of its socket."

"How awful!" Kimana said, wondering if such a thing could be true.

"Not so awful. It took half of my sight, but it left a gift behind. That is how the spirit world works. Tell me, what gift did the spirits give you?"

"Why would they give me a gift? I'm nothing special. Besides, they took nothing from me," Kimana answered.

"Didn't they? Well, we'll see."

Meda cackled and slapped her thigh, obviously enjoying her private joke. Kimana wondered if she should be offended but decided against it. Meda was just trying to be kind.

And now she was curious.

"What gift did the spirits leave for you?" she asked.

"They gave me the gift of sight."

Kimana shook her head, confused. If the bird had stolen her right eye, how could it have given sight?

"Second sight, Kimana. I am a seer. They also gave the gift of medicine. I am healer here, medicine woman. Perhaps now you will trust my salve for your wrists, eh?"

Kimana lowered her eyes, embarrassed that Meda had seen her scepticism of the old woman's diagnosis.

"No, do not be embarrassed. You could not know."

When Kimana's wrists were cleaned and a salve had been spread over the chafed areas, Meda showed her where to find everything she would need. Then she stood and tweaked Kimana's right cheek.

"You will do well here, little one. Who knows? Maybe Chief Black Eagle will take you as his wife. Ai-ee! That would be fine, would it not?"

She cackled good-naturedly and watched Kimana's face for a reaction.

"I will not marry any old man. In my village I would have wed a great warrior, Two Hawks. A young man, strong and brave, not some withered old man near the end of his days."

"Hmph!"

Kimana whirled at the sound and found herself staring into the face of the old chief. His black eyes bore into hers. Against her will, she could feel herself starting to shake. Running Wolf stood behind his father and looked at her with something like amusement in his eyes.

Meda cuffed Kimana softly on the head and yanked lightly on her matted hair. No doubt it appeared to hurt worse than it did. Kimana winced, trying to hold up the appearance of being thoroughly chastised.

She didn't want to like Meda, but she found she liked her more with each passing minute. The old woman was feisty, but she was kind. Kimana tried not to grin as the old woman scolded her.

"Naughty child. You should be thrashed with a willow stick! Your mouth will get you into trouble and I will not help you then. You will only have what is coming to you."

Meda smiled an apology at Black Eagle and shuffled out of the lodge with one last reproachful glance at the foolish young woman she had been put in charge of. The chief watched Meda leave, then turned his dark eyes on Kimana once again. Her humour fled, and her legs quivered beneath her like congealed buffalo fat.

She started to speak, but no words would come. Her throat felt dry and thick, and her tongue seemed to swell in her mouth.

The chief waved a dismissive hand. A smile ghosted his lips. "No, your words are not needed. You are angry, and you have a right to be so. You have lost much, and it will take time to adapt to your new life here. I will forgive your thoughtless words this one time but let me never hear you speak such things again. Besides, you are right. A young woman needs a strong young brave to share a mat with. Someone who will live to teach his sons the ways of a warrior, not a withered old man like me."

He chuckled and looked over his shoulder at his son.

Running Wolf struggled to close his mouth. His lips settled into a grimace. He looked as if he had bitten into a rotten fish. Seeing him flustered by his father's kind words was a small victory, and one she savoured. She was tempted to smirk at him but didn't want to push her luck.

The chief continued. "You may choose a mat to sleep on. Tomorrow you must take up your duties in this lodge."

Black Eagle turned from her and settled himself next to the blazing fire. He reached over and picked up a pipe, filling it with red willow bark. Running Wolf sat across from him and watched Kimana with hooded eyes. He pulled a buffalo hide over his shoulders and waited patiently for his turn with the pipe.

"Put some sweetgrass on the fire, Kimana. Fill this lodge with its perfume, and I will tell you a story."

She stood for a moment and stared at Black Eagle.

Despite his gentle words, she'd half expected the beating that Meda had recommended and was shocked that it didn't seem to be forthcoming. She'd been prepared to fight, to defend herself even if it meant giving up her life, and instead, she was being offered kindness yet again.

A story? He wanted to tell her a story?

Her father had told her many stories. The people would sit around the alder wood fire at night, smell the sage and sweetgrass burning and listen to him tell his tales.

Her father was the best storyteller in the whole tribe. His teepee was always full. When the sun went down, the people would come to bring their arguments and their requests to him. They always stayed afterwards, lingering, like the smell of smouldering sweetgrass.

She was sure their many reasons for coming were just excuses to stay and listen to him tell the stories he only told in the winter.

He never told the stories in the summer.

He said if he told the stories of the animals while the grass was green and the days long, the spirits of the animals might become angry. The spirits only roamed in the summer and slept warm in their beds in the winter. He would sit, legs crossed, and fill his pipe with willow bark. Then he stood, facing north to honour the Great Spirit, then east, south, west and north once more. He sat again and inhaled deeply on his long pipe.

The people would wait, hardly breathing, for the stories to begin, and the men waited for their turn to smoke. Each man would hold the pipe gently, almost reverently, in his own hands, and take a single long puff, nod in approval and appreciation, then pass it to the next man. The women never smoked but looked on in awe at the coloured horsehair, white weasel fur and feathers that decorated the sacred pipe. The children watched in wonder and cuddled against their mother's laps, the young boys dreaming of the day that they too would smoke the pipe. Soon they would fall asleep, listening to the sound of her father's voice as he wove the tales they waited all year to hear. It was only after each man had tasted of her father's pipe, that Chief Three Bears would begin his stories.

And once he began, they let out a collective sigh of anticipation and delight.

Now, she would never hear him tell his stories again.

Choking back tears, her throat thick, she felt as if she could barely breathe. She turned to the bag that held the braided sweetgrass, and for one brief moment, she was tempted to toss the whole thing into the fire.

Her lips twisted into a spiteful grin. She glanced back at Running Wolf. His eyes were narrowed, and he watched every move she made. He looked dark – dangerous - in the flickering firelight.

Perhaps not this time.

She tossed some of the fragrant grass onto the fire. It smoked for a minute, then turned red and glowed like the sun, crackling softly as it danced in the flames. She drew the smoke toward her face with practiced hands and the sweet scent filled the teepee. Black Eagle nodded his approval, grunted once, and inhaled deeply on his pipe.

Kimana settled on a mat as far from the two of them that she could get, tucked her knees against her chest and crossed her arms over them. Dirty hair spilled over her knees. She looked across at Running Wolf. Like a cougar watching an unsuspecting deer, his eyes glittered in the firelight as he watched her. Her own eyes narrowed with a promise of vengeance as she tried to stare him down.

Dark brows came together, and his lips turned down in a fierce scowl.

Kimana tilted her head up and looked away as if dismissing him from her very thoughts.

When she was certain he no longer watched her, she dragged her soiled fingers through her hair. The knots hurt as she tugged and yanked them without mercy. Tears of pain stung her eyes.

What she would do for a twig!

When she was finished getting the worst of the tangles out of her hair, she absently rubbed the ache in her right leg. She was only vaguely aware of the pain that had plagued her since childhood. It was simply a part of life now. And although it somewhat limited what she could do, she had learned to adapt. Most people would never know about her disfigurement if it were not for the horrible scars on her cheek.

The old man talked of *Wasakejak* and the grizzly bears, an old story she had heard many times. It was a little different than what she was used to, but similar enough to lull her into relaxation. She closed her eyes and breathed in deeply through her nose.

The smell of sweetgrass and willow bark filled her senses.

Black Eagle's quiet words were hypnotic. She half listened to him, hearing instead the raspy sound of her father's voice. After a while, her lids became heavy, and her head dropped to her chest. Black Eagle stood up and covered her with a soft fur. Her eyes flew open, but he only smiled and nodded. She lay down on the mat and watched him as he moved to the other side of the teepee and sat next to Running Wolf, whose gaze was on her still.

When she was certain he would leave her alone, she closed her eyes and tried to let the gentle drone of Black Eagle's voice lull her to sleep, but the image of his son, tall and terrifyingly bold, haunted her mind.

CHAPTER SIX

Two Hawks stood on the edge of a precipice, breathing heavily as he looked at a river far below. He bent over at the waist and laid his hands on his knees, trying desperately to slow his pounding heart and catch his breath. He'd been running for two days, stopping only for short rests, eating dried pemmican and warming snow in his hands to sip.

He didn't know how much longer he could keep this pace up.

The only thing that had kept him going this far was the thought of Kimana lying beside him, smoothing his hair, and soothing his aching muscles with her fingers.

He'd waited years to make her his, and nothing was going to stop him from turning his dreams into a reality.

Since he'd first been adopted into the Cree camp as a young boy, he'd watched her, fascinated with her bright hair and smile. Even as a little girl, he'd known Kimana was special. And although an orphan could never hope to marry a chief's daughter, he'd done everything he could to become strong and respected, so her father would accept his bid for courtship, and perhaps even name him as his successor. So many years, so much work, only to have it stolen from him the night before his dreams would have come true.

The icy wind chilled him through to the bone, but he barely felt it anymore.

He flexed his fingers, trying to bring some feeling back into them. His legs were the only things he really felt. They ached mercilessly, but he refused to allow the pain to win.

The tracks had been almost impossible to follow in the falling snow, but every now and then he saw a definite sign the group had passed this way. Feeling somewhat less winded, he let his gaze sweep over the scene before him. The cliff overlooked a wide river. All around him were signs that the group had crossed here, perhaps even spent the night. If nothing, they had certainly stopped here for a time to rest.

It would be insane to attempt to cross the fast-moving water without a horse, but he didn't have any choice. With every hour that passed, his determination to find Kimana and kill her abductors grew until it was like a madness clawing away at his mind.

He was certain now it was the Blackfoot who had attacked the camp. The Shoshone or Dakota would have veered farther south, and the Sarcee, to the North. This group was heading straight west, right toward the mountains. Another few days, and he should know exactly where they were camped. Then he would figure out a way to save the prisoners. And if he couldn't save them all, he could at least sneak in, and rescue Kimana.

He looked down again. The cliff was steep. Under normal circumstances, he would never consider making his way down with the rocks covered in snow and a thick layer of ice. But these weren't normal circumstances.

A blast of wind took his breath away and he folded his arms over his chest, trying to get warm.

For a moment he thought about abandoning his search until spring. It was pointless. The group was days ahead of him by now, and it was possible he would lose the trail before long. It had been harder to follow with each passing of the sun across the sky.

He straightened his back and fingered the pack that held Kimana's wedding dress.

No. He couldn't stop now. One way or another he had to find her. They may not yet be married, but she was his, and he was responsible for her just the same. He grimaced. It was more than that, he knew. For years, Kimana had filled his every waking thought. He'd watched her grow and develop into a woman, and his fascination with her had grown into desire, and eventually, into what could only be called obsession.

49

He knew that. But it angered and frustrated him. He was a warrior. Warriors weren't supposed to be distracted by women. But Kimana was different. Strong, brave.

Maybe even a bit hard-headed and spoiled.

He grinned.

Spoiled, yes. How could anyone not spoil her? But she wasn't vain or selfish. He knew other women who were spoiled, and he couldn't stand them. They expected to have their own way. Although Kimana often got what she wanted, she didn't have that annoying attitude so many others did. She had dignity, and strength and a gentle spirit. Not that she couldn't be stubborn and difficult.

With a renewed surge of determination, he began his descent.

Two Hawks held his arms out to the sides, trying to balance himself on the slippery surface. Just over halfway down, his left foot wedged in between two rocks. It happened so fast he barely had time to register the jolt of pain that arrowed through his ankle and up his leg. Twisting his body in reflex, he lost his balance and began to tumble down the hill.

He couldn't stop what was happening, couldn't control it.

It didn't even seem real. It was like a dream.

At some point during what felt like an endless descent, he heard the sound of a bone snapping. He felt it pierce the skin, but there was no pain, just the warmth of blood and a deep regret for failing in his task to find Kimana.

He landed in a crumpled heap near the riverbank, his body covered in scrapes and bruises.

Something warm trickled down his face.

Then, like a dreaded promise kept, the pain finally registered and seared through his left leg that was twisted beneath him.

It was unlike anything he'd ever felt before. With a strange sense of distance, he wondered if the scream he heard was his.

His vision blurred.

A soft growl penetrated his consciousness and he lifted his head. Standing less than a spear-length away was a dark wolf, its hair raised along its spine.

It bared its teeth and snarled.

His body, cold and aching for so long, felt oddly light. In a detached, almost curious way, he acknowledged that he would die here. Closing his eyes one last time, he offered a silent apology to Kimana.

CHAPTER SEVEN

K imana woke to the screaming of her muscles. She groaned and stretched, trying to work some warmth into them. Her sleepy eyes settled on a smoke flap high above her and she stared at it in confusion, uncertain in her sleepiness where she was. Her puzzled gaze settled on the unfamiliar paintings decorating the walls, and she remembered where she was with a rush of despair.

Tossing the fur aside, she scrambled to her feet.

It was much colder than it had been the night before. Shivering, she tugged on her moccasins, grabbed a buffalo fur, and draped it around her shoulders.

Creeping toward the flap of the teepee, she watched the two sleeping mounds for movement. One of them was snoring with deep, booming rumbles that normally would have made her giggle. But not now. She had to relieve herself, and she felt dirty. She was still covered in grime and blood from the attack. Maybe she could find a stream to wash in.

She slipped through the opening in the teepee and stared.

Although it had snowed on the prairies, the Blackfoot camp had been brown and bare when they arrived. During the night, winter had crept into the valley like a white wolf, silent and stealthy. Powdery snow blanketed the ground. Aspen and birch trees sagged under the weight of the heavy snow.

Even some of the tall, stately pines stooped to the ground like weary old women, bowing under the weight of their burden.

And all around her, mountains speared up into the air, their peaks frosted in white, set starkly against a sky dotted with puffy clouds, and so vibrant and blue it hurt her eyes.

In the distance, at the far end of a long, narrow valley, stood an imposing mountain that looked unlike any of the other peaks that were visible. It was shaped oddly, almost like a pinecone. To its right was another mountain, with what looked like seven small fingers thrust upward, as if reaching for the clouds.

It was difficult to imagine evil spirits lurking in such a beautiful place, but she felt a frisson of fear just the same.

Finding it hard to tear her eyes away from the raw beauty of the scene, she headed for the trees, her feet crunching and squeaking on newly fallen snow. After relieving herself, she scooped up a handful of snow and rubbed it briskly over her cheeks and arms, washing away the filth that covered her. Her breath caught as it chilled her skin. She scrubbed it into her hair and used a twig to pull out the tangles. Trying not to wince against the pain, she combed it until it was dry and gleaming in the early morning light.

The sun was finally starting to shake off its lingering coat of clouds. It kissed the snowy mountain peaks with a soft pink glow, but it promised little warmth despite its effort. She tugged the buffalo robe tighter around her shoulders and turned to survey the quiet village. The people were still sleeping, obviously worn out from their night of celebrating. A scout squatted on the side of a mountain. She could feel his eyes boring into her. She kept her gaze carefully averted and tried to make her survey of the village seem casual. She glanced around, wondering which teepees held her people. A few dogs sniffed around the fire pit, searching for leftover scraps. One of them saw her and came forward with his head bowed and tail wagging.

"I'm so sorry, but I have nothing to give you."

She reached down and rubbed his head.

His grey fur was matted and dirty, but his eyes were friendly. He licked her hand and whined, liquid brown eyes watching her with a hopeful gleam.

Scratching him behind his ears, she grinned as he burrowed his head into her palm. The dog's ears suddenly perked up and he looked behind her toward the trees. With a low growl he crouched to the ground, and the hair on his back stiffened. Then he turned and scurried away, his tail tucked between his legs.

Icy fear crawled over her, and she spun around at the sound of a twig snapping.

An enormous dark wolf peered out at her from the trees. It bared its teeth and snarled. Her throat went dry. She struggled just to breathe, her heart thumping in her chest.

All thoughts of spirits fled as she stared at the beast.

She whipped her head around, wondering why the guard did not sound an alarm, but he hadn't moved from his crouch. She was certain he watched her, but was it possible he was actually sleeping? What good was a scout that slept while on watch? A man could be harshly disciplined for less than that in her own camp.

She backed away slowly, never taking her eyes from the wolf. Every instinct told her to run. She tried to tell herself not to be foolish. Wolves didn't make it a habit to attack people. Not unless they were starving, and even then, only children or the sick. In spite of the assurance she gave herself, she couldn't stop the terror from welling up inside of her. As she edged away, it stepped from behind the trees with a vicious snarl. With each step she took backwards, it took two toward her. She desperately wanted to run, but she refused to turn her back on the animal. Showing it fear would be the biggest mistake she could make. Pain seered upward through her leg as her knee gave way beneath her, and she fell over, landing on her back in the snow. Before she could catch her breath, the animal was upon her. Terrified, she knew she could do nothing to stop the attack, and she covered her face with her arms. She felt the wolf's hot breath as it lowered its head to her neck, and she knew her life was over. She could not help but remember that other time, so many moons ago, when she had nearly lost her life. Perhaps she had cheated death then, and now it had come for her once again.

"Makwai! Down!"

Kimana felt the weight of the wolf lift from her body and it whined plaintively.

"Are you all right, Kimana? She didn't hurt you?"

Running Wolf kneeled over her, his eyes racing over her body in concern. She stared at him. "It's a wolf!"

He chuckled as he wiped snow from her face. "Yes, I know she's a wolf."

How could he think anything about this was funny? "Don't touch me!" She shoved his hand away from her face and tried not to burst into tears. "It was going to kill me."

The grin left his face and his eyes sobered. "No, Kimana. She just didn't know you. She probably thought you were an intruder."

He must be mad!

"How can you know what a wild animal will do? She chased me. She jumped on me. Her teeth..."

Kimana watched in disbelief as Running Wolf shook his head.

"I said she wasn't going to attack you. She isn't wild. She is my companion. She has lived here with me for years."

"You have a wolf for a pet? Are you crazy? Of course, you're crazy, all of this is crazy!"

She wanted to hit him, and all he could do was stare at her with that dopey smile. She was overcome by the urge to plow her fist into his grinning face but managed to restrain herself. Then something in his gaze changed as he stared into her eyes. The intensity unnerved her.

"What are you staring at?"

Running Wolf turned and whistled softly. The great black wolf loped back to them, her tongue hanging out between her teeth, looking like some kind of huge puppy. A puppy with very sharp teeth.

"Makwai, this is Kimana. She's a friend." He scratched the creature between her ears and Kimana watched, her eyes round with fear. Then he spoke to her in the same tone one might use with a small child. "Kimana, this is Makwai. *She*'s a friend. Her name means wolf."

He continued to grin at her, but his smile faded as he watched her fear turn into anger.

"Now I know you're possessed of an evil spirit. No one makes a friend of an animal that can kill people!"

"What are you talking about? Makwai hasn't killed anybody."

"Not yet!"

She shoved his hand away and scrambled to her feet, looking at the wolf from the corner of her eyes. She looked back at Running Wolf and found him staring intently at her once again.

He grabbed her by the hand and his eyes bore into hers.

"Strange. I didn't realize your hair wasn't the colour of mud," he said.

Her mouth dropped open and she twisted out of his grip.

"Wolves are good for furs, not good for friends."

She knew her voice was high and sounded panicked, but she couldn't control it.

"Keep that beast away from me. Or if you really want to be my friend, as you called me, skin her and give me the fur so I can stay warm."

His eyes narrowed and his jaw tightened, and she sensed she had gone too far. She didn't care. He was crazy. With a last, wary glance at the wolf, she turned her back on them both.

Her moccasin-clad feet left deep furrows in the snow as she returned to the lodge to start the morning fire and prepare breakfast. The prospect of preparing a meal for this man or his father made her want to gag, but her stomach ached with hunger. She'd eaten so little in the last few days, and she was feeling weak. If she didn't prepare something, no one would. She'd be cursed before she would go another day without a decent meal.

Running Wolf watched as she stalked off toward the teepee. For the first time, he noticed the limp his father had mentioned. It did nothing to detract from the stunning image she made as she stormed away. He grinned. By the spirits, she was beautiful! Her eyes had flashed at him, and her chest heaved in anger as she lectured him on his pet. Her fear of the animal was obvious, and yet her courage was equally obvious.

The heavy buffalo hide she wore draped over her shoulders hid her upper body from view, but he could still see her shapely hips swinging as she walked. Her waist-long hair almost seemed to shimmer like copper in the sun. Realizing he was gaping after her like an untried youth, he closed his mouth and scowled.

"Well, isn't she cheery this morning," he grumbled to his friend as he scratched her ears. Large grey eyes laughed at him. "Oh, hush up, you scraggly beast."

***

Kimana swept the flap of the teepee aside. Her moccasins were caked with wet snow and a puddle quickly formed beneath her. Tossing the buffalo robe onto the ground, she held her hands in

56

tight fists and muttered between clenched teeth.

Wolves as pets.

Arrogant warriors.

What else would she have to deal with this morning?

Black Eagle glanced up from his mat and frowned. She raised her chin and her eyes held a defiant challenge.

"Breakfast," she snarled, and his eyebrows cocked at the tone of her voice.

She stomped over to a sack and pulled out a large strip of dried pemmican. She tore it in two and faced the old man.

"This is breakfast."

She flung it through the air. With a speed unexpected in one so old, his gnarled hands reached out instinctively to grab the food before it fell on the dusty ground.

Throwing herself onto her mat, her teeth tore into the meat as savagely as any wolf.

"I have only so much patience, Kimana."

The words were spoken so softly that she had to strain to hear them. The chief stood and tossed the pemmican back into its bag.

"You need to learn some manners. I think I will eat with Fire Dancer and his family. I am sure they will have some fine rabbit stew, and maybe some willow bark tea to warm these old bones of mine. They may even have some friendly talk for an old man to enjoy."

She stared at his back as he left the teepee. Looking down at the food in her hands, she realized she wasn't hungry anymore.

***

Running Wolf watched his father as he emerged from the lodge. Black Eagle looked at him and waved him over. "Come, my son. Let us see if Fire Dancer and his woman have anything hot for breakfast. It is too cold in our lodge to enjoy a meal."

Running Wolf stared at his father in confusion. Cold? But he had added more wood to the fire before he left to find Kimana. By now it should be warm. With a shrug and a glance at their lodge, he followed his father across the camp.

***

Silver Fox edged closer to Running Wolf and smiled into his eyes. It was a good sign that he was here so early. Maybe that Cree woman had displeased him and he would decide to sell her.

Black Eagle slurped up the remainder of his stew and let out a belch.

"That was fine stew, Singing Deer."

The chief smiled at Fire Dancer's woman and a light blush coloured her cheeks. Silver Fox sneered. Her mother was always blushing. It was so ridiculous. Didn't she know how stupid she looked?

Singing Deer smiled at the chief. "You honour us with your presence, Black Eagle. But I thought you had adopted the girl so she could prepare your meals. Of course, you are welcome here anytime. It is our honour to have you visit us."

Silence filled the lodge as everyone waited for an explanation. Silver Fox knew no one would ask directly. That would be considered rude, but it was expected that some explanation would be forthcoming. When none was, Silver Fox looked away from Running Wolf and smirked at his father.

"Can she not cook?"

Fire Dancer turned to his daughter in fury and cuffed her on the head. "Hold your tongue, daughter."

Silver Fox clenched her teeth and tried to suppress the savage glare she wanted to shoot at her father. How dare he humiliate her in front of Running Wolf?

Chief Black Eagle gave a thin smile. "I am quite sure she can cook, however, she is tired and I decided to let her rest. And we need fresh meat." The chief turned to his son. "Today we will hunt," he said, then turned to Fire Dancer. "You will do us great honour by gracing our lodge tonight for a meal."

"The honour would be ours, old friend."

Black Eagle nodded, burped once more, and stood to leave. Running Wolf unfolded his long legs and rose to his feet. He turned to follow his father. Silver Fox leapt up, touched his arm, and spoke softly into his ear.

"I knew that woman would be trouble. When we marry, and your father is gone to be with our ancestors, we will sell her."

Running Wolf looked at her coldly. "Do not speak of my father going to the Place of the Spirits, Silver Fox. Napi willing, that will not happen for a very long time."

Flashing black eyes at him, she pouted, knowing her lips would look full and tempting.

"I meant no disrespect. I only meant to say that she obviously does not know how to care for a man. But I do, Running Wolf. I know how to do many things that please you." She cast a quick, furtive glance toward her parents and lowered her voice to a husky whisper.

"When will we speak the vows? I want to be able to share my mat with you. I am tired of sneaking off into the trees. And now it's getting cold."

A practiced hand reached down between his legs and fondled him. Her eyes narrowed seductively, and she was sure he was tempted to carry her off into the trees and leave the hunting to his father.

"This is not the time or place, Silver Fox."

He firmly removed her hand and glanced over his shoulder, but Fire Dancer and Singing Deer were busy discussing some pelts that needed softening.

"It is never the time or place anymore."

Her voice rose in a whine, and Fire Dancer glanced up, looking at them curiously.

Running Wolf scowled at her. "I have things to do. I will see you at dinner tonight."

With a curt nod to her parents, Running Wolf was gone.

"Do not pressure that young warrior, Silver Fox. You might end up disappointed," Singing Deer said.

She turned to her mother and laughed. The old woman didn't know anything. She had forgotten what it was like to be young and beautiful, and desirable to men. She had probably never known what it was like. Her own marriage had been arranged. But Silver Fox would have more than that. She wouldn't settle for just any warrior. She would have Running Wolf, and there was nothing anyone could say about it. One day, she would be the wife of a warrior, but not only a warrior, she would be the wife of a chief.

"We are as good as wed. Everyone knows it."

Singing Deer shook her head and turned away. "Does he?"

CHAPTER EIGHT

Running Wolf smiled grimly at his father as they went into their lodge to get their bows and arrows. The sight before them brought them both to a shocked halt.

Kimana stood with her legs spread and a large stick in her hands. Her hair was in wild disarray, her lips curled into a snarl. She waved the stick around as if trying to ward off some evil spirit. Makwai crouched near the wall, looking like she was about to spring. She growled softly. Fur stood up along her spine.

Running Wolf sighed.

"Get this creature out of here!" Kimana screamed, waving the stick back and forth as if daring the wolf to come closer.

Running Wolf crossed the teepee in two short strides and snatched the stick from her hand. He tossed it across the fire, well out of her reach.

"What in the name of the spirits are you doing?" he asked.

She continued to stand as if ready for battle, watching every move Makwai made. "I said, get this thing out of here! She is stealing the food, and she stinks!"

She was starting to annoy him with this hatred of his pet.

After the scene with Silver Fox, his patience with women was at an end. "Makwai is always welcome in this lodge, Kimana, especially when it gets cold. It's been her home for years."

She turned her furious gaze on him. He stared at her, stunned again by her beauty. Her hair swirled around her waist and seemed lit from within. Her eyes snapped and sparkled like quartz crystals set in onyx. "Well then, I'm leaving! I'm not sharing a lodge with an animal!"

She whirled toward the entrance, but he grabbed her arm, holding her in a firm grip. Enough was enough. Beautiful or not, if she didn't stop acting like a spoiled child, he would be tempted to turn her over his knee. That thought gave him pause for a moment, as the image of her laying temptingly over his thighs stirred him. Somehow, he knew this wild female would fight him tooth and nail, and for some reason, that was far more interesting than her acquiescence. But he'd never laid a finger on a woman in anger in his life, and he was not about to start now. Forcing the image from his mind, he clenched his teeth and spoke slowly.

"Be very careful, woman. We will not long tolerate your disrespect. Did your father allow these kinds of temper tantrums?"

"My father did not allow stinky, vicious creatures to share his lodge!"

"No, just hard-headed, sharp-tongued ones. You'll have to get used to Makwai. Besides, she smells no worse than you did yesterday."

He watched in fascination as she sucked in a shocked, angry breath. He tried not to focus on her breasts.

"I bathed, in case you didn't notice!"

The scowl left his face and he lifted his eyes to hers.

"I noticed, Kimana."

He had indeed noticed. She was far from the wretched looking creature he had first dragged screaming onto his horse.

She was magnificent.

Liquid brown eyes, framed with the thickest, blackest eyelashes he thought he had ever seen, flashed with rage. Her cheekbones were high and sculpted. Three thin white lines followed the contour of her left cheekbone – the scars his father had mentioned, and that he had never even noticed until this moment. Somehow, they made her face all the more interesting, all the more stunning. He wanted to run his thumb over her cheeks, to find out if her skin was as soft as it looked. And her hair. It was glorious. He'd never seen anything like it. It was glossy and dark and shot through with red fire like the light of the rising sun on a river.

His eyes travelled the length of her body and came to rest once again on her heaving breasts.

Having her in his lodge was definitely not going to be easy.

His bride, Laughing Brook, had been beautiful and sweet, but she had lacked the lush curves and valleys that graced Kimana's body. He forced his eyes away.

"Come, Makwai! Time to hunt."

Makwai trotted over to Running Wolf, her tongue lolling out of the side of her mouth in a lopsided grin. Her big head swung over to look curiously at Kimana as she passed. Kimana sprung away.

Running Wolf opened the flap and looked at his father. During the heated exchange with Kimana, he'd forgotten his father was there. "I will wait outside, where it's not so hot."

Black Eagle nodded and grunted, then followed him out.

**

The north wind was cold, but the sun had pushed back the clouds and it shone warm on their faces. The mountains were blinding in shades of white, muted blues and hard greys. The snow on the ground was thick, and the top layer had melted just enough to make walking difficult. Makwai had long since abandoned them. She was, undoubtedly, searching for a meal in her own way, or had, perhaps returned to the camp to further torment Kimana.

A white rabbit skittered across their path, its long ears flopping with each leap. It paused a moment to look at them, as if shocked that they didn't pursue, then disappeared into the thick brush. Neither Black Eagle nor running Wolf showed more than passing interest.

It was deer they were after.

The sun inched its way across the sky and was almost at its zenith when his father stopped to examine a tree branch with its bark stripped away. A raw, pale green layer was exposed.

Running Wolf knelt down and examined tracks of cloven hooves in the snow. He fingered a hoof print.

It was a male, and large. The tracks were close together. The buck was moving slowly. They followed the trail and came to a pile of fresh pellets, still shiny and warm, steaming in the chill air. A rustle in the branches brought them both to a crouch. Scuttling along the ground, their heads swivelled this way and that, as they listened for another clue that would pinpoint the location of the animal they sought. Before long a clearing appeared ahead.

The buck stood at the far end, his ears quivering. His head was turned toward them, and his sides trembled. The white flag of his tail lifted, and before he could spring away, Running Wolf put an arrow into his bow. In less than a heartbeat the buck fell to the ground, just as he began to spring into the safety of the trees.

The arrow had gone straight through his heart.

"Well done!" Black Eagle said, clapping his son on his back. Together they approached the kill. Running Wolf took out a long knife and made a perfect cut through the flesh. He pulled out the heart and held it out to his father.

Black Eagle took it into his hands and lifted it reverently toward the sky.

"Great Spirit, and Spirit of the Deer, we give you thanks this day for your sacrifice. We are grateful to you for your gift."

Running Wolf dug a hole in the snow, and they buried the heart to honour the deer's spirit. He tied some cords around the buck's legs and hauled it onto his shoulders. He staggered slightly under the weight, but when his father reached out, he grinned and shook his head.

They walked together in the companionable silence that hunters share after making a kill. There was no need for words. To each man, the company of the other and the gift of the deer were enough.

They were almost home when Black Eagle broke the comfortable silence. "I know it is difficult for you, having her live in our lodge."

Running Wolf grunted. "I am certain it is no less unpleasant for her."

"That may be so. It is strange having a woman living with us after so long."

"And what of you, father? Does Kimana's presence not remind you of what we have lost? Of what you have lost?"

Chief Black Eagle stopped and looked into the distance with a thoughtful gaze. "Every day when I awake, I am reminded by the silence that your mother is not there. She is not there." He smiled sadly at Running Wolf and touched a hand to his heart. "But she is here. She will always be here. You have lost much as well, my son. I know you still blame yourself for what happened. But perhaps it is time to let go of the past. To look toward the future."

"I can't. What I did was unforgiveable."

"What you did was unacceptable. Not unforgiveable. You were young. You learned. You have been forgiven. It is time to forgive yourself."

"I can't."

"Perhaps not today. But soon."

Running Wolf watched thoughtfully as his father started walking again. After a moment, he hurried to catch up.

"I hope Kimana and Makwai have not torn each other apart by the time we return."

Black Eagle chuckled. "There is more to it than just hating the smell of wolves," his father said as they trudged through the wet snow. "I am certain her eyes held real fear."

Running Wolf snorted. "There is nothing that woman fears."

"You are right, she is very brave, but it is when she is the most frightened that there is fire in her eyes and a sharp edge to her tongue. She is much like my beloved Chepi."

Running Wolf looked at his father in disbelief. To compare the wildcat in his lodge with his sweet mother was more than absurd, it was madness.

Black Eagle looked up at the clear blue sky. He pulled his robe closer against the biting wind, nodded to himself and hurried on.

Running Wolf stood staring after him.

"Do not stand there gawking, my son. We have many mouths to feed this night," his father said without turning to look over his shoulder. "Kimana needs time to prepare this wonderful food that you have provided."

***

Shouts of laughter filled the camp. Kimana grinned at Little Otter as she watched him play. He hadn't asked her about his parents, hadn't even said a word. Her relief was palpable. She had no idea what she would tell him. She simply could not know for certain, but it seemed likely they had died in the raid. She would not tell him that. Could not. She could never face his tears. She wondered again at children's ability to adapt and accept what life threw at them. Here he was, playing with the other children as if he had known them for all of his short life.

64

They ran through the camp, making balls of snow in their hands and tossing them at each other. Their screams of laughter echoed off the mountain peaks. The women, both Blackfoot and Cree, looked on with patient smiles.

And seated together near the central fire to keep their bones warm, the old men tried to hide their own amusement behind fierce scowls. But nobody was fooled. They were as delighted with the children's antics as anyone.

Utina had come to visit, bringing her news. They had shared some willow bark tea while her aunt told her about her new lodge. She told her that Little Otter had gone to live in Fire Dancer's lodge. Kimana scowled when she heard that, worrying about how Silver Fox would treat her young cousin. But there was little she could do about it.

Now they stood near the fire and watched the children play.

"They are actually very good people, and kind too, Kimana. They are nothing like the stories I have heard. I don't mind being second woman to this warrior. His first woman treats me well. She even has small children I can help care for. I've wanted my own children for so long."

For a moment, it looked as if she might cry, but she smiled bravely. "It's not the life I would have chosen, but we are here, so we should make the best of it. It must be the will of Manitou."

Kimana tried to smile at her, but she did not agree. How could she pretend to be happy? How could she say this was the will of the Great Spirit? The children belonged with their people on the prairies, not living in the shadow of the mountains.

Utina gasped and laughed, clapping her hands as she watched the children run behind the chief's lodge and toss some balls of snow at a group of warriors. "Just look at them, Kimana! The men do not even get angry!"

Little Otter ran up to Kimana and grabbed her by the hand. "Come, Kimana! Come play with us!" His sweet face beamed with pleasure.

"I am too old for these games," she smiled down at him, but inside, her stomach twisted. His mother had been her closest friend. Rainchild had helped Kimana prepare her wedding gown and kept her company for the countless hours it took to soften and prepare the hide. She had teased her about Two Hawks, and laughingly hinted at the mysterious pleasures Kimana would encounter on her wedding night.

Now, she was gone.

Everything was gone. Her parents, her friends. Even her beautiful wedding dress. She wondered where Two Hawks was. Had he tried to find them? Or had he given up when he'd seen the slaughter? Would he even want her now if he knew she was alive? There was a good chance he wouldn't. She supposed she was lucky to have escaped rape so far, but he would never believe the murdering Blackfoot had not used her body and discarded her like leftover meat tossed to the dogs.

Little Otter stood watching her, and his eyes held just a hint of sadness, as if he suspected what she was thinking about. He gave her hand a gentle squeeze and smiled. "You weren't too old to play with me before we came here. Please come."

Not knowing what else to do, Kimana allowed herself to be pulled into the throng of shrieking children. Before long, she was laughing with them as a ball of snow shattered against her face. She turned and threw a ball at her attacker and was soon rolling in the snow as the children piled on top of her in fits of laughter.

It was good, to play and laugh. To forget, for just a while, where they were. Little Otter sat on her chest and scrubbed her face with a snowball. His giggle made her smile.

But her smile faded as she saw Running Wolf and Black Eagle emerge from the trees.

"It's time to get off, now," she told Little Otter.

He rolled off her chest and looked at her curiously. She stood up and brushed the snow from her buffalo robe.

Little Otter was still on his knees looking up at her, covered in snow from head to toe. He followed her eyes to the men she was watching. "Kimana, what's wrong? Why aren't you playing anymore? Did I hurt you?"

She smiled sadly. "I really think I'm too old for these games." She touched his face and whispered, "Will you play for me? And tell me all about it later?"

He nodded, his eyes round. She bent down and kissed his cold little nose, then ran a hand down his cheek. He looked so much like his mother. "Have fun. I won't be far if you need me."

She glanced over at Running Wolf. He still stood by the trees with the deer over his shoulders. His eyes had not left her face. She hated him. Tipping up her chin, she looked away dismissively, and strolled back to the lodge with as much dignity as she could.

***

"I will not prepare this deer! I am not your slave!"

Running Wolf took two long steps toward Kimana and grabbed her shoulders, shaking her with far less force than he was tempted to. "No, you are not a slave, Kimana. For better or worse you are the woman of this lodge, and you have certain duties you are expected to perform. You dishonour my father with this stubborn attitude. You dishonour your own father."

She stared at him, stunned, then wrenched away from his hands and pulled back her arm to slap him. He caught her wrist in his hand and glared into her eyes.

"Do not strike me, woman or you might not like the consequences."

She stared into his hard eyes and cold fear settled into her stomach. Would he really hit her? Her own father had never struck her or her mother, but she knew that many men hit their women. Had she been spared that all her life only to suffer it here? At his hands? She swallowed her fear, tilted her chin and forced a defiant tone into her voice.

"You can't threaten me."

Her voice shook, and she hoped he would think it was anger and not fear. She must not show him fear. It was a weapon too easily used by men.

He stepped closer and she could feel his warm breath on her face. "You forget yourself."

"You can't touch me. Your father would not allow it!"

She looked over at Black Eagle. He stood with a blank face, silently watching. Why didn't he say something?

"My father wants your people treated well, but he will not put up with this behaviour from you, or anyone. He won't stop me if I decide you need to be taught a lesson in manners."

She turned frantic eyes to Black Eagle, but he folded his arms over his chest and turned deliberately away.

She was alone.

"I'll send Meda to help you. Our guests will arrive when the

67

sun goes down. That will give you enough time to prepare a decent meal."

Running Wolf followed his father from the teepee. Kimana stared at the flap as it closed behind them. She sank to her knees. Frustration and sadness welled up inside of her and she tried to fight back tears. Why couldn't it be easy for her? Easy like it was for Little Otter and Utina, and the rest of her people? Why did she have such a hard time accepting their fate?

***

Meda entered the lodge on silent feet and stood over the weeping girl. She wanted so much to comfort her. She knew the pain of losing a loved one, the pain of being in a strange place surrounded by the enemy. Once, she and her sister had been prisoners here. But now she knew the kindness of these people. This had been her home for many years. Kimana would only make it harder on herself if she kept fighting them. Meda shook her head.

It would not go easily, that she was sure of. This child had too much fight in her. She wondered if Running Wolf would be able to tame her wildness. Or perhaps, she would tame him. Only the Great Spirit knew the answer to that.

She tried to make her voice gentle. "Kimana."

Kimana looked up at the voice and stared at Meda with eyes bright with tears. Meda knelt down and folded the girl into her arms, crooning softly. Her heart broke for this fiery young woman. "These tears are good, Kimana. They will help wash away your pain."

"I have done something terrible, Meda. I have disgraced my father."

Meda sat back and wiped a gnarled hand over Kimana's face, pushing her long hair behind her ears.

"How did you do such a thing?"

"I don't know what's wrong with me. I have never felt so angry. I say and do things that I would never have done in my home. Black Eagle is being so good and kind, and I act like a spoiled child!"

Meda smiled to herself. Sometimes, what was unsaid was more important than what was said. The fact that Kimana had not mentioned Running Wolf was significant. "And what of Running

Wolf? Is he also kind and good?"

Kimana scoffed. "He is like an angry grizzly bear with a sore on his paw."

Meda raised an eyebrow and a smirk touched the corner of her lips. Indeed, he could certainly seem that way. But she knew the boy he'd been and had watched him grow into a man. She knew the kindness inside of him, and the sorrow and guilt he carried with him every single day. Losing both his mother and his bride was almost more than he could bear. It would be enough to break almost anyone.

"You don't know him, Kimana. He has lost much to your people. I know I said we would not talk of it, but maybe you should know. Maybe it will help you understand."

Kimana opened her mouth to protest, but Meda laid a crooked old finger over it. The war had gone on for a long time. It was time the girl knew.

"A few summers past, our warriors went to your village to raid for horses. This is not so unusual. The people have been doing this for longer than we can remember. Not long after, a Cree raiding party came here while the men were away hunting. Black Eagle's wife – my sister - and Running Wolf's young bride, tried to stop them. They were killed, Kimana, then left to rot."

"You're not saying my people did this!"

Meda sighed and nodded her head.

"No! My people would not do such a thing!"

"Yes, Kimana. Both your men and ours have done some terrible things. It is the way of men, is it not? To war? To pillage? It's nothing we can change. They had been married for less than the time between two full moons. Running Wolf blames himself."

"Why would he blame himself? That's foolish."

Meda sighed. "That is not for me to speak of. Kimana, you and Running Wolf have much in common. You are both strong, proud people. You both have pain. Sorrow. Grief. I know this is hard for you, but please try not to judge him too harshly."

"I can't help what I feel."

"No, but what you feel can change, if you allow it. Come now. I will help you prepare the meal. You need to eat, do you not? Put away your anger. Leave the warring to the men. It's what they do best."

She smiled as Kimana nodded and brushed away the tears from her face.

"You have such a beautiful face. Lovelier even than Silver Fox. When we are finished, I will braid your hair for you, make you pretty."

Kimana scoffed. Beautiful she was not. Had it not been for her father's position, she could never have hoped to marry anyone.

"You have an impossible task ahead of you. Besides, why would I want to look pretty?"

Meda grinned and her old eye twinkled as she watched annoyance flare in Kimana's face.

"Not pretty for anyone in particular. Pretty just because you like to look pretty. Don't look so startled, I was a young woman once. I know."

***

Chief Black Eagle did his best to entertain his guests, but after a while he gave up trying to penetrate the gloomy atmosphere that had settled on his lodge. Running Wolf and Kimana sat on opposite sides of the fire staring at each other with open hostility. The tension in the air was thicker than spring mud. Even Silver Fox seemed disturbed and couldn't stop fidgeting. She snuggled as close as she decently could to Running Wolf, running her fingertips lightly on his thigh but his son didn't seem to notice. Like Running Wolf, her eyes rarely left Kimana's face, and as the evening progressed, she became increasingly agitated.

Black Eagle let out a long sigh. The night was a disaster. What could he have been thinking of? The only bright side had been the laughter and antics of Little Otter, who had finally curled up next to Kimana and fallen asleep.

With understanding smiles, Fire Dancer and Singing Deer stood to leave. After seemingly endless words of thanks and praise for the meal, Singing Deer carefully picked Little Otter up into her arms so as not to wake him, then gave a nod to her daughter, and left the lodge with Fire Dancer. Silver Fox tossed one last scowl toward Kimana, gave Running Wolf a pout that he likely did not even notice, rose to her feet and stalked out the door.

Black Eagle watched them leave and sighed again. It was a mistake to ask them here tonight. It was too soon. He wondered what had gotten into his son. He'd never allowed himself to become so angry with a woman. Not even Laughing Brook, his beautiful young bride, had ever affected him this way.

What was it about Kimana that angered him so? Was it her spirit? No, his son respected women with some fire. His own mother had plenty of fire in her. Was it the fact that she was a Cree? That they had lost so much to their enemies?

He watched as Running Wolf grabbed his arrows and began sharpening them, casting black scowls at Kimana. She ignored him, clearing away the remains of dinner before grabbing her buffalo robe and wrapping herself so tightly that Black Eagle wondered how she could breathe.

At least she had prepared dinner without more fuss. She would settle in soon, accept her new life. Black Eagle grunted.

Kimana glanced over at him, and then turned quickly away when she saw him watching her. A smile turned up one corner of his mouth. She was a good girl. One day she would be a credit to this lodge, a credit to the people.

He wondered about the man she would have married if they had not been attacked. Did she love him?

Foolish thoughts.

A woman's thoughts! He snorted. Love was not necessary to a marriage. But he and his wife had shared a love that was gentle and sweet. And they, too, had begun as enemies. He could only hope the Great Spirit would give the same precious gift to his son.

And to Kimana.

One day, he would call her daughter. One day she would find a strong young warrior, marry him and give him many children. But for now, these two would have to learn to live with each other. What was done, was done.

With another deep sigh he covered himself with his robe and fell to sleep.

***

Red embers glowed in the fire pit.

Running Wolf glanced over at Kimana's sleeping body, his fist still clenched around an arrow.

Her hair gleamed in the fire's light.

She had prepared a good meal, and there had not been another word between them. Then why was he still so angry? Why did he want to shake her, to crush her in his arms and kiss that defiant

71

look right out of her eyes?

He tossed the arrow onto the floor and strode across the teepee. He'd wake her up right now!

He reached out an arm and turned her over. Her eyebrows drew together, and she muttered in her sleep.

In sleep, her features were relaxed, and he marvelled once again at her beauty. Hair fell around her head in a shimmering pool. Long eyelashes swept her cheeks. He sat back on his heels and watched her chest rise and fall with each soft breath. Desire, so strong he could barely contain it, pulsed through him.

A strand of hair had fallen over her face. He reached out a hand to smooth it away. She sighed and turned her face toward his fingers.

He eased back with a scowl creasing his cheeks.

Without another glance he stormed from the teepee into the cold night air. He stared up at the stars and exhaled through his mouth. The mountains crouched above the camp, black and forbidding like hulking bears. The moon teased him with its presence, peeking out from behind a cloud and hiding its face again like a shy maiden.

Kimana was a fire, blazing in his mind.

He felt his need growing and he looked across the camp at Fire Dancer's lodge. Silver Fox was inside, and he knew a soft scrape on the hide would bring her out and into his arms, warm and willing. She'd made no secret of her desire for him tonight. He sighed again. No shy maiden was she, but an accomplished temptress. He wondered how many men she had run into the willow bushes with, and he was shocked to realize that he didn't even care. He knew she expected him to marry her. She always had, even when he was promised to Laughing Brook. Even marrying her had not quelled Silver Fox's obvious interest.

Rage and despair had become constant companions in the last few years.

Like his mother and his aunt Meda, Laughing Brook had come to live with them as a child, after her parents had been killed in a raid against her people. They had grown up together, and both had assumed she would be his someday.

It was too painful to think of her now, too painful to think of his responsibility for her death. And now, each day, he had to face the look in Kimana's eyes, and know that she held him responsible for the death of her people.

No, he would *not* let that woman into his mind!

He forced his thoughts to the warm body waiting for him a stone's throw away. He could relieve himself on Silver Fox without guilt. He'd rarely before taken what she so freely offered, but there was no reason not to.

And no better time than now.

He thought about her words to Kimana, her insults. A derisive laugh escaped his lips. Silver Fox, of all women, had no moral high ground.

No, he certainly would never marry her. He had no great love for Silver Fox, but he would never share his wife with other men. He refused to kill one of his Blackfoot brothers over a woman. No, she was good for only one thing. And at the moment, that that thing stirred his blood.

Long strides brought him next to her teepee. He scratched on the hide and stepped back into the trees.

Moments later, she came through the aspens like a wanton spirit and folded long arms around his neck. A buffalo robe slipped to the ground, and he could see her soft, naked flesh gleam in the moonlight. With a groan, he ground his mouth onto hers. He slid his hands around her narrow hips, held her buttocks and lifted her off the ground, pressing her hips against his own.

As he kissed her, a face formed in his mind, and his need grew stronger, throbbing through his blood like the beat of war drums as copper-streaked hair and eyes like autumn leaves appeared before him.

"I knew you'd come for me."

He opened his eyes and the image in his mind faded. With a groan he pushed Silver Fox away.

"Cover yourself."

"What?"

The word came out in a shriek that had him wincing. "I should not have come for you tonight. Forgive me."

Curse Kimana. He could not even relieve himself like a normal man without being distracted by her.

Her very presence in his mind mocked him.

***

73

Silver Fox stared after him as he stormed through the trees. She clenched her teeth and looked back toward Black Eagle's lodge. Her! It was her fault! One way or another, something would have to be done. She refused to give up Running Wolf for anyone.

CHAPTER NINE

Running Wolf rose from a crouch and stretched his back. Hours of squatting motionless on the side of a mountain was a job for the young, he thought. He looked through the pines and shielded his eyes from the rising sun. He'd better pay more attention, or he'd start to soften. He hadn't taken the watch for a couple of years, not since he started to mentor the young man who threaded his way through the trees toward him, making far more noise than he should.

He waited until Stands Alone was a little closer, then hurled his blade toward the boy's feet.

Stands Alone looked up, eyes wide in shock. The blade quivered in the hard ground, less than a hand's breadth from his toes. He raised his eyebrows at Running Wolf. "Good morning to you, too."

"You should pay more attention, pup. I could've killed you."

Stands Alone shrugged. "You wouldn't have."

Running Wolf fought a smile. In spite of the difference in their status within the tribe, Stands Alone often showed an easy familiarity toward his mentor, even fondness. It was a feeling that was reciprocated.

"That's not the point, pup. You're supposed to be aware of everything around you. Whether or not I would kill you is irrelevant. Someone else - had there been someone else - could easily have done so."

"Well, hopefully not first thing in the morning. That would be mad manners."

Running Wolf scowled. He wasn't interested in giving the boy a lesson this early in the day. And he certainly wasn't interested in arguing the point with someone who insisted on cheerfully disagreeing with everything he said. Not after spending a sleepless night perched above the camp, his muscles protesting more with each passing hour.

Running Wolf folded his arms over his chest. "What are you doing here? It's early to be out."

"If you want me to leave..."

"Did I say that?"

"Someone's cheerful today."

Running Wolf allowed himself a twinge of annoyance. The boy had gotten a lot more relaxed and friendly in recent months. Maybe it was because they were nearing the end of his formal training. Another two summers, and the boy would probably marry. It was rare for a young man to marry so young, he thought. Some waited until they had seen twenty-two or more summers so they had enough status and wealth to impress a prospective bride's family.

He didn't mind the familiarity, really. Stands Alone was the closest thing he had left to a real friend – and the closest thing he'd had to a little brother since he was a child.

"Sorry. Long night."

"Problems?"

"No. That's why it was a long night."

Stands Alone nodded. "Got it. I'm not going to miss that. So, what are *you* doing here? You haven't taken watch forever."

"I needed to get out of our lodge for a while."

"Ah." Stands Alone grinned. "Problems with the wild cat."

Running Wolf snorted. "She's the most difficult woman I've ever met."

"Yes, and a beautiful one."

He snorted again. "If you like wilful, spoiled brats, I guess you'd find her attractive."

"Come on. She can't be that bad."

"Can't she?" Running Wolf lowered himself back down to a squat. "Ever since my father decided to take her into our lodge, the place has been in an uproar. I can't find any peace there at all.

Every time I turn around, she's snarling or sneering at me. You can't even talk to the woman. And she hates Makwai."

Stands Alone crouched down next to Running Wolf and allowed his arms to dangle over his knees.

"Hmm."

"You should have seen her half a moon ago, threatening Mawkai with a stick. Demanding we get that 'stinky, vicious creature' out of our lodge. I thought she was going to tear the whole teepee down. I swear, sometimes I'd like to turn her over my knee and give her a good spanking."

Stands Alone laughed. "Now, that's a sight I'd like to see. I don't think she'd be the one nursing her wounds after."

"Watch it, pup."

"I'm just saying." Stands Alone looked away. "There must be a reason she doesn't like the wolf. Maybe she's scared."

"That's what my father said, but I don't believe it."

"Well, whatever. You know, you have to give her a chance. Let her settle in. She'll come around."

Running Wolf grimaced. "Doubt it."

The young man gave an exasperated snort. "She's gone through a lot. You have to be patient."

"You don't know what you're talking about. What she's gone through? And what, exactly, has she gone through?"

Running Wolf fought the feeling of guilt that plagued him any time he thought about the death of her father. Could she ever forgive him for that? He snorted inwardly. And why should he care if she forgave him?

Stands Alone didn't answer. It was a lucky thing as Running Wolf was running out of patience. He didn't appreciate being lectured by his own apprentice. No matter how close they'd become. And they both knew Running Wolf wouldn't hesitate to knock him on his ass if he got too impertinent.

"If you think she's so wonderful, you take her."

"Maybe I will. She's incredible. No one here can come close."

Running Wolf tightened his fist and fought back another surge of annoyance.

"It takes more than looks to make a good wife, pup."

"Quit calling me that, old man. Is that why you haven't asked Silver Fox to marry you?"

Running Wolf stared, his jaw slack. "You're pretty cheeky today. Who said I was interested in Silver Fox?"

Stands Alone grinned. "Come on. We all know you've been going off into the bushes with her."

"I certainly am not. Not since... it's none of your business, anyway."

"Since what?" Stands Alone turned a questioning glance on his mentor.

"I said - never mind. Not for a while."

Below them, the camp showed the morning's first signs of life. Children darted around teepees and women shuffled back and forth, tending to their morning chores. Kimana hadn't emerged from their lodge yet.

"If you must know, I'm just not interested in what Silver Fox has to offer. That's all. If you want her, you're welcome to her."

"No, thanks. She's a little too wild for my tastes. I want someone with a softer side. A little less brazen."

Running Wolf grunted. He set his jaw. "Well, you can forget Kimana, too. You're too young."

"We're the same age!"

Running Wolf's lips thinned, and he gritted his teeth. "I said you're too young, pup. My father would never allow it. You have nothing to offer her. Neither do I, if it came to that."

"I can ask. Nothing stops me from asking."

Running Wolf rose to his feet and looked down at his friend.

"Your friendship with me stops you."

"Why? You don't want her. You said you can't stand her."

"I said she's difficult. And no, I don't want her. She's trouble. As your friend – as your mentor - I couldn't allow you to make that kind of mistake."

Stands Alone's eyes flashed with anger. "Well, then, maybe it's time for the student to leave the teacher."

Running Wolf ground his teeth together and snarled as he watched Stands Alone wind his way back down the mountain.

CHAPTER TEN

That Injun was a dead man, sure enough. Not yet, but soon. Before the sun rose in the morning, for certain.

The old trapper tossed another stick on his small campfire and looked at the man he'd found crumpled in a heap near the river. He'd covered him with a thick, woollen blanket to try to bring some warmth back into his icy flesh, but it wouldn't matter much. He was just lying there, good as dead. His flesh was still cold as the river in the dead of winter. But he was still breathing. That was something. Who knows how long he'd been unconscious?

Jonesy had bound the Injun's wounds, cleaned him up some, and tied a splint to his leg, but if he did survive the night, it would likely need to be re-broken and set proper, or he'd never walk again, sure as the day was long.

Or short, rather.

At this time of year, there wasn't much sun to speak of.

Jonesy peered up at the sky and located Orion. That wily old hunter was just now starting his journey across the night sky, followed by his faithful dogs.

Yessir.

Just what a man needed, sure enough. A faithful dog, and good hunting. Couldn't ask for more. Other than good grub, of course. And maybe a soft and willing woman now and again. Course, that bit was optional. He'd gone without a woman for a long time and didn't much need one these days.

He reached down and scrubbed his hand over his mutt's head. Ol' Jack gave him a toothy grin, then swung his head back to watch the Injun. He stroked his chin. If it weren't for Ol' Jack and that spooky black wolf, he'd never have found the Injun to begin with. Not that it would make much difference.

Strange, that wolf. Just like the last time. Years ago, now. He'd almost forgotten.

Jonesy thrust out his jaw, scratched his cheek and studied the man. Looked just a little familiar, but he couldn't quite put his finger on it. Now the wolf, that was different. It wasn't the first time he'd seen that particular wolf. 'Course, it couldn't be the same animal, not after all this time. It didn't make sense. But it sure looked the same. Dark as night. Eerie looking. Spooky. That other wolf had led him to an Injun, too. But not a man. No, that last time had been a wee lad. Not more than a few years old. Took him to the Cree, Jonesy did. Seen him a few times over the years when he traded with the redskins. Seemed to do all right with his new home.

'Course, that was years ago. Years.

There was no way that wolf and this one were the same. He'd found this Injun next to the riverbank, buried nearly head to toe in a fresh dump of snow. He never would have seen him at all if Ol' Jack hadn't whined and pawed at the snow.

And he never would have been there had the wolf not led them straight to it.

Weird, that's what it was.

The way the wolf had approached without any fear at all, turning its head this way and that, as if it was trying to show him something. He'd tried to chase the darned thing off, but it just kept coming back. Just like the last time.

Ol' Jack hadn't even growled, useless old mutt. He'd wanted to play with the beast. And there the wolf had stood, looking just like somebody's pet.

Curiosity got the best of him in the end, it did. So he'd followed the creature. It led them right to the riverbank, and then sat down like it was waiting.

Jonesy shook his head.

Strange. Yessir, right strange.

That's when 'Ol Jack found this Injun.

Squirrel, Jonesy figured at first, when 'Ol Jack started pawing at the snow. Or something dead. Not much else would interest the mutt.

Still couldn't get over it, finding an Injun, all alone, bloody and broken like that. Well, if the man did live, maybe he could get a reward or something. Maybe the Injun's people would be grateful. Then again, maybe they'd sent him out here to die. He'd heard of things like that. Stories like than ran rife amongst the white folk. So maybe the Injun's folk wouldn't be grateful. But you never knew. There was always a chance they'd reward him somehow. Worth a chance. Yessir. Worth a chance.

Jonesy scratched at his beard and watched the unconscious man. Well, didn't make no never mind anyhow, any which way. He'd probably be dead by sunrise.

He tossed another stick on the fire and listened to it crackle and hiss. Sounded almost like coffee cooking. Couldn't remember the last time he'd had some coffee.

Well, soon enough, he'd reach the Cree camp up North. They were bound to have goods to trade. Another week or so should get him there. Unless he had to drag this Injun with him.

He snorted. Not likely. The man would definitely be dead come morning.

Stuffing a hand into his coat pocket, Jonesy pulled out a thin leather pouch. He half-filled a pipe with tobacco, and carefully lit it, then watched the Injun thoughtfully as he sent rings of smoke toward the sky. Strange as strange could be. Yessir.

CHAPTER ELEVEN

Kimana leaned against the fence and watched the horses paw at the snow in a fruitless search for grass.

It was a fine herd. The horses were sturdy and strong. She recognized many of them. Her father's horse, a stallion painted in brown and white patches, nickered to her and tossed his head. She tried to smile but couldn't. She waved a small greeting and sighed. The proud animal would never again feel the weight of her father on his back.

A dappled grey mare broke from within the throng and trotted up to the fence. She lowered her head and reached for Kimana with a soft, wet muzzle and a low nicker.

"Wind Dancer! I didn't know you were here!" She couldn't keep the joy from her voice. She held her face to the horse and rubbed its cheek with her own. "You are so beautiful."

"Yes, she is."

The mare tossed her head and her eyes rolled back in her fear of the strange man's scent. The horse whirled and retreated into the safety of the herd. Running Wolf stood a few steps away and watched Kimana with an unreadable expression on his face.

"What are you doing, Kimana?"

"I was only looking at the horses."

Feeling defensive, like a child caught touching someone's medicine bag, her chin lifted, and her eyes dared him to accuse her.

"Relax. I'm not saying you were doing anything wrong. Your

people had many fine horses. They cared for them well. The grey one, that one that you were touching, she knows you. Well."

"She was mine. Her name is Wind Dancer."

He gave her a sceptical smile. "Yours, Kimana? I didn't know the Cree gave horses to women."

"She was a gift from my father."

His eyebrows lifted in surprise.

"That is a precious and unusual gift. You like to ride, then?"

"Yes, often my father and I would ride together on the prairies. Many thought it strange to see the chief ride with a girl, but he never cared what they thought."

Sorrow threatened to bubble to the surface once again, and she forced it brutally away. Never would she let this man see her private pain.

"You miss him."

His voice was gentle and filled with sympathy. But sympathy from the enemy was the last thing she wanted. Her face clouded over, and she turned away, trying to hide the confused tears that had sprung to her eyes despite her best efforts to stop them.

He reached out and turned her chin toward him. She jerked away, but he turned her face back with a firm but gentle grip.

He was so close she could smell sage and the musky scent of buffalo from his robe. "If I told you that I regretted what happened, would you believe me?" he asked.

Her eyes flashed with fire, "You are saying you regret destroying my home, my life? Taking my father from me? Why then, did you do it? Do you regret it? Do you? And if you do, does it change anything?"

He dropped his hand. "No, the past can never be undone. But the future is not set."

"My future holds nothing."

He sighed, stared off toward the trees. A moment passed. Two. "I am going hunting. Would you like to ride with me?"

She stared at him with suspicion.

"Why would I go anywhere with you?"

"I just thought maybe you might like to go for a ride."

She watched his eyes, looking for the trap she was sure was hidden within his words. "I didn't think warriors took women on a hunt."

"Not normally. But who will stop me? It is my decision. Like your father, I care little about what others think. If you don't want to come, fine. It matters little."

"I didn't say..."

Confusion swept over her again and she searched his eyes. Ride with him? There was nothing she wanted more than to feel the wind in her hair. To forget, just for a while, that she was a prisoner here. If the price of that tiny bit of freedom meant spending a few hours in his company, she would pay it.

"I would like that."

He nodded once and strode back to the lodge, returning with two brightly coloured blankets and ropes for the horses. His bow and arrows were slung over his back.

"Ready the grey mare. She knows you. She would be the best choice."

Her eyes lit up with joy, but she quickly composed herself, took a blanket and rope from him and climbed into the pen.

It was quiet in the camp. Most of the people were still warm in their furs when Kimana and Running Wolf rode out.

The horses picked their way daintily through the snow. The only sound in the early morning was the soft swish of their tails and their gentle snorts as they blew air from their nostrils.

Kimana rubbed a hand over Wind Dancer's neck, feeling the bristly hair. She smiled as the mare tossed her head in pleasure. Being taken from her home certainly hadn't harmed her. She was as spirited as ever. The Blackfoot were legendary for their care and breeding of horses, even in the short time since they had acquired them from the Shoshone, their southern neighbours. They had learned much since the dog days and were the envy of countless tribes. There were still many who relied on dogs to move their camps each year.

Kimana glanced over at Running Wolf, watching him from beneath lowered eyelashes. He rode tall and straight and moved with the horse as if they were one. His long leggings were heavily fringed, and his moccasins were high, almost to his knees. They were covered in white weasel fur, but the bottoms were stained black. She eyed them curiously, and wondered if they dyed them, or if they were, in fact, stained from the black ashes from prairie fires, as so many people believed. It was said they set fire to the grassland and forced the buffalo into enclosures or down gradually narrowing corridors toward cliffs. Buffalo jumps were a favoured choice of many of the people. The herd, led by a few dominant males, and one matriarchal female, would stampede toward the cliff, not seeing the danger until it was too late. Then the force of hundreds or thousands of animals bearing down on the few in the front would cause most of the herd to hurtle over the cliff, landing in a broken heap on the rocks below.

The Blackfoot, or so the stories were told, used fire to frighten the animals into stampeding. It was their moccasins that had given them their name, the *Siksika*, the Black Footed people.

Her gaze moved curiously up his body. He wore a heavy buffalo robe, and his shining black hair hung loose and blew gently in the breeze. A single white feather was knotted at the top of his head. His face was lean and sharp-featured, his nose straight, and his cheekbones high and well defined. His mouth was relaxed, and did not, at the moment, have the hard line she had become used to seeing. He looked relaxed. Almost... content. A strand of hair hung past his jaw. She had a sudden urge to tuck it behind his ear. If she moved just a little closer...

With a jolt, she realized she was feeling something akin to attraction. She stared at him, and felt something strange stir inside of her, a tiny fluttering in her stomach that she had never felt before. If they had only met in a different way, he might be a man her father would be proud to call son. Warmth flooded her cheeks and she turned away, giving her attention to their surroundings. They travelled slightly north, and west, deeper into the mountains.

The trees here were different than what she was used to. They were tall and straight – perfect for teepee poles - and they swayed in the wind. She looked up and a wave of dizziness washed over her. The trees were nearly high enough to touch the sky! On the prairies, the trees were short, dense and heavily foliaged. By this time of year, they would be naked. These ones were different. They were covered in small, sharp needles, and were green. Her brows knit together as she thought about how strange and beautiful it was here. She wondered why it had never occurred to her people to venture farther into this wild place. But they had always preferred the open prairies.

"Don't you ever long for the grasslands? Do these mountains

not make you feel closed in? Trapped?"

He smiled at her and looked toward the strange, pinecone shaped peak in the distance. "No. These mountains are the heart of my people. Here we see the majesty of creation. How can one look at the sun rising on a distant peak without feeling free, without wanting to run and laugh and dance? The prairies feed our bodies, but the mountains feed our spirits."

He pointed toward the odd, rounded mountain.

"See that mountain there? We call it Raven's Nest."

"You name the mountains?"

"Not all of them. But that one is special. There's another one farther south that's similar. Not round, like that, but flat on top. We call it *Ninistako*, Chief Mountain. It's the place Thunder lives."

She looked at him curiously.

Thunder had once stolen a man's wife, he explained, because he was jealous of a human having a woman of such beauty. The man tried to get help from all the animals, but none would help him. They were afraid of Thunder and the storms he would bring. But finally, the man asked Raven for help, and Raven agreed. He flew to Thunder's home and challenged him. A horrible rainstorm blew in and lightning bolts struck the ground, but Raven flapped his wings until the rainstorm blew away and the air grew icy. As he continued to flap his wings, different clouds surrounded Thunder's home, and a winter storm blew in, blanketing everything in thick, cold snow. Thunder eventually gave up and sent the man's wife back home.

"Raven and Thunder agreed to divide the year into two parts, winter and summer. It's been like that ever since. That mountain you see there, that's Raven's home. Winter belongs to him."

"It's beautiful," Kimana said.

"Yes. It is."

"Thank you for telling me the story."

Running Wolf smiled. "You like stories."

"Yes. My father often told the ancient tales."

"My father has told stories as long as I can remember. It's good to know where we come from. The stories help us, so we don't forget. It's important to remember."

They rode for a while in comfortable silence.

A short time later, Running Wolf stretched out a warning hand. Kimana brought Wind Dancer to a stop without thinking. Many times, she had hunted with her father, and she knew it was important to be aware of his signals, to respond quickly. Their lives could depend on it.

Running Wolf pointed through the snow-covered trees, and she followed his gaze. A white-tailed doe stood nearby, a fawn, perhaps slightly less than a year old, at her side. The doe's ears perked up, and her flesh quivered. Liquid brown eyes watched them. The fawn continued to tear and chew at the pale green inner bark of an aspen tree, seemingly unaware of his mother's anxiety. Running Wolf sat unmoving, and Kimana was surprised to see his mouth turn up into a gentle smile as observed the pair.

The smile transformed him.

She stared, mesmerized. He glanced over at her and grinned. Her cheeks warmed yet again.

He looked back at the deer but made no move for his bow. Finally, the deer bunched her muscles together, and bounded into the safety of the forest, her fawn close behind. The sounds of their flight were muffled thumps in the snow. Kimana let out a sigh, and Running Wolf turned to her, a teasing smile on his face.

"Did you think I would kill her, Kimana?"

She nodded.

"The baby needed his mother far more than we needed her. There are other deer in the forest. Napi will provide our food."

"I've heard that name before. Stands Alone spoke of him."

"Napi is the Old Man, the creator of all things. What do you call him?"

"He is Manitou. The Great Spirit."

Running Wolf shrugged and smiled. "He has many names."

He urged his horse forward and Kimana sat for a moment, watching him, a soft smile settling over her face.

A tiny strand of understanding had passed between them, fragile yet strong, like the web of a spider.

She knew she would never forget this moment. He might be the enemy, but they had shared something precious. It seemed that even a man as hard and dangerous as he was could have mercy on those weaker than himself.

Obviously, he could see and appreciate the wonder and beauty in the world around them. Part of her didn't want to believe there could be anything good in this man, but the proof lay in the tracks left in the snow by the retreating deer, and in his conspiratorial smile as he turned with a questioning look in his eyes.

"Are you coming, Kimana?"

She gently nudged Wind Dancer, and was soon riding next to him again, feeling oddly comfortable and at peace with the man who was her sworn enemy.

***

Snow sparkled on the trees like bits of glittering quartz. Kimana closed her eyes and let the warmth of the afternoon sun wash over her. The day had been almost surreal. Somehow, they managed to put their mutual distrust and animosity aside for a time. They'd ridden for hours and talked about little things, unimportant bits and pieces of everyday life in her village and his. They were careful not to speak of the attack or mention anything that would cause sparks to fly between them. He seemed so relaxed and at ease, and she was reluctant to break the mood, but her curiosity had grown as she listened to him talk about his people. She watched him from the corner of her eyes. "Are you marrying Silver Fox?"

He turned to her with a startled expression, then scowled. "I haven't really thought of it."

"Well, she is very beautiful."

His dark brows arched in surprise. "It takes more to make a good wife than just beauty, Kimana. Tell me about the man you were supposed to marry."

Her eyes clouded over. "There's nothing to tell. Not now."

"Was he a good man?"

She nodded her head. She didn't know if Two Hawks was even still alive. If he was, was he looking for her? Would he find her? And if he did, would he even want her anymore? He would assume she'd been raped, used brutally by the Blackfoot. It wouldn't matter if it was true or not. No man would want her for a wife now. She thought of her people and she fought back the tears. Her mother, killed by her own hand, her father, slaughtered. Her friends. No, she wasn't supposed to think of those things. Not today. Not now.

She squeezed her eyes shut, and tears rolled down her face.

The day was too perfect to ruin. She wouldn't allow herself to think of them. Tomorrow was soon enough to remember what Running Wolf and his warriors had done. Not today. *Not today.*

Running Wolf watched her and felt his stomach twist and knot with sharp-edged disappointment. She'd obviously loved the man she was supposed to marry. Had he died on the night of the attack? Had he been one of the warriors Running Wolf had killed? He shifted his weight and scowled.

Why should he feel guilty?

He had done what had to be done. War was a part of life. He glanced down at his horse and rubbed the long neck. Would Kimana ever be able to open her heart to another man? Or would she end up like him, numb inside, unable to love or be loved? He'd treasured Laughing Brook more than anything in the world and had lost her. Never again would he let himself feel that deeply for anyone. He couldn't bear to lose someone like that again. But somehow the thought that Kimana felt that depth of emotion for her Two Hawks left him feeling empty and cold. And something more, something like disappointment.

He forced himself to look away, allowing her the privacy of her memories and her pain.

***

By unspoken agreement, they didn't discuss her people again for the rest of the ride. They found no other deer but Running Wolf didn't seem concerned. She wondered about the change in him. His mood had lightened again, and he teased her gently, slowly wearing down her reserve. He shot two white rabbits and a weasel, slinging them carelessly over his shoulder, laughing and grinning like a boy on his first hunt. She stared at him, stunned. She'd never seen him look so light-hearted, never heard him laugh. She couldn't help but respond in kind, delighting in his antics. It occurred to her that she felt happier than she had a right to feel.

Well, what did it matter? She was here until the spring, and then she would leave and find a Cree village. They would help her free her people. Nothing could be done until then.

It was nearly sunset when they rode back into camp. Kimana watched as Black Eagle emerged from the lodge and observed them with a quizzical smile. Running Wolf tossed the tiny carcasses to him and looked back at her with a triumphant grin, as if he had brought home an enormous buck.

Laughter bubbled up and out of her lips and she smiled at him, feeling oddly content. Someone cleared their throat. She looked around and spied Silver Fox standing at the entrance to her teepee, watching them with narrowed, fury-filled eyes. Kimana smiled at her, taking delight in the rage that spread over the woman's face. She wasn't sure why she enjoyed taunting the woman.

With a toss of her head, and a saucy smile, Kimana urged her horse to follow Running Wolf to the horse enclosure. He reached up to help her from her mare, and she accepted his arms with a grin, feeling strangely easy with him. As he lifted her down, her body slid against his and their eyes met with a jolt. They stared at each other for a long moment before she lowered her eyes in confusion.

What was this she was feeling?

It was so unlike anything she had felt before, even with Two Hawks.

No. This was wrong. She shoved his arms away, suddenly angry at both of them. She ran to the lodge, brushing past Black Eagle.

***

Kimana stood knee-deep in the water and watched as the current ripped chunks of ice and an enormous tree from its roots, hurtling them down the river toward her. She tried to climb out, but the tree's branches reached out and grabbed her as if hoping she could save it, and dragged her deeper into the icy water.

"No! Help me!" she screamed, but there was no one to hear her.

She was being pulled under, her body tossed upon the sharp rocks and ice like a cornhusk doll. Glacial water numbed her limbs. She didn't even have the strength to kick. Blackness surrounded her. The voice of the Great Spirit called out, whispering her name.

Kimana.

Looking up, she saw the face of her father, his eyes sad. An eagle feather dangled from his fingers, then fluttered to the ground. Tears rolled down his cheeks and he shook his head as he looked sadly into her eyes. She reached out to touch his face but he vanished. In his place stood a tall, young warrior, with long black hair and intense, brooding eyes. Beside him, stood a wolf. The warrior smiled at her and reached out with strong arms, pulling her from the freezing river.

Kimana.

"Kimana, wake up."

Opening her eyes, she stared into the face from the dream. His eyes were filled with worry as he held her shoulders and looked at her intently.

"It's all right. You're safe."

And suddenly his arms were around her, and without thinking, she slumped against him, allowing him to comfort her as she tried to sort out her thoughts. Dreams never just happened, there was a purpose, a message, maybe a warning. What did it mean? Why was her father so sad? Had she done something to hurt him? Had she failed him?

"What is it? Was it a bad dream?"

She nodded and shivered. She could still feel the icy bite of water on her flesh and the intense sadness of her father.

She thought about the tree that had smashed into her body. There was something strange about it. It was almost like the branches were moving, twisting and thrashing like arms and legs. It was almost human, and desperate for her to either save it or pull her under with it. She shuddered.

"You're safe now, Kimana. Nothing will harm you. I promise."

He ran a hand over her hair, stroking it slowly, and gently rocked her in his arms. She closed her eyes as the warmth from his body flowed into her own. It wasn't right. She shouldn't let him hold her like this. He had taken everything from her. She should despise him. Why, then, could she not push him away?

Why, then, didn't she want to?

Running Wolf held her, watching her chest rise and fall as she drifted off to sleep. She'd been so frightened. When she screamed, he'd felt utterly helpless. Had he done this to her? He frowned and lifted his eyes to his father, who sat watching from the other side of the fire.

Black Eagle reached for his pipe and filled it with willow bark. He lit it and drew in some smoke, released the sweet smell into the air. His father watched him with a thoughtful expression, and then motioned with his pipe for his son to join him.

Running Wolf lowered Kimana's sleeping body onto her mat and gently covered her with a thick fur. He brushed her coppery hair back from her face. Her skin was perfect, like warm honey dripping down a tree on a summer day. Her face was relaxed in sleep. He caressed her cheek, running his fingers gently over her scars, and a tiny smile curved her lips. He bent over her, his mouth lingering above hers.

She had lost so much. An overwhelming urge to protect her flooded through him.

But he knew it made no sense. He could never forget the hatred in her eyes when he'd captured her. He snatched his hand away as if he'd been burned by the heat of her flesh. She was not his to protect. She never could be. He'd failed to protect those he loved once. He would never again allow himself to care that much for anyone. He just could not face that kind of loss again.

Not for the first time over the years, he denied the tears a weaker man would have allowed to fall. He would never give his heart again. Not to anyone. And definitely not to this incredible temptress with her fiery hair, molten eyes and a body his own ached to touch. No. Never. He no longer thought of her as the enemy, despite what her people had done to his woman, and his mother. They had stolen the very life from his soul. They could take nothing else from him.

He had nothing left to give.

CHAPTER TWELVE

Two Hawks awoke with a jolt and stared up into a grizzled face. An ancient white man leaned over him, his mouth open in a grin that revealed both missing and blackened teeth. The stench coming from his mouth was enough to make Two Hawks gag.

The old man cackled and sat back on his heels. He slapped his knees and cackled again, shaking his head and grinning madly.

"Thought you were a goner, Injun. Sure enough did. Yessir. Thought you were a goner for sure. Didn't I say he was a goner, Ol' Jack? Didn't I?"

Two Hawks struggled to understand the words. He had learned the language of the white man but didn't use it often. When he did, it was usually to speak to the missionaries or traders that came into their camp trying to teach them about a being they said was greater even than their own Great Spirit. The missionaries' language was a bit different than this old man's, but he was able to understand most of it.

He rolled onto his side, and pain speared through his leg. He felt himself grow dizzy, and bile rose in his throat. His leg. He'd broken his leg.

"Gonna have to set that leg. Probably have to break it again. May not heal right otherwise. But you're a tough young brave, ain't you. Little pain won't mean nothing to you."

The old man slapped his knees again and shook his head. He held out a hand.

"Name's Jones. Wally Jones, but you can just call me Jonesy. This here's my mutt, Jack."

Two Hawks stared at the proffered hand until Jonesy shrugged and dropped his arm.

Jonesy hooked a thumb toward a scruffy looking dog. The dog whined and grinned, then bellied forward, looking hopeful.

"You can call him Ol' Jack. He's the one that found you in the snow. Thought you were a dead man. Yessir. Didn't think you'd wake up. Took a nasty fall, didn't you? Got a little knock on the noggin, cracked a few ribs too, I'm thinkin'. Broke that leg. Nasty. Nasty break."

Two Hawks watched as the old man shook his head mournfully then shoved himself to his feet with a dramatic groan. Jonesy hobbled over to the campfire and pulled off a steaming pot.

"Got me some beans and such here. Don't know if you like beans. But I suppose you'll eat if you're hungry enough. Can't give you no coffee, though. Out of coffee. But you probably don't drink it anyway. Probably just drink that bark tea you Injuns seem to favour so much."

The old man brought the pot over and set it on the ground next to Two Hawks.

"Don't talk much, do you? Well, go ahead and eat, boy. Then we'll set that leg and get goin'. Light won't last much longer, and we have a ways to go."

Two Hawks looked at the pot and sniffed. He couldn't decide which was worse, the old man's breath, or the stench coming from the pot. He gave Jonesy a suspicious look.

"Don't trust me, Injun? Think I'm gonna poison you? Here. Watch."

Jonesy shovelled a forkful of beans into his mouth and chewed noisily. Brown goo dribbled down the old man's lower lip, and a long tongue shot out and slurped it off. The dog whined.

A sickening wave of hunger shot through his stomach. How many days since he'd eaten? Jonesy held out the pot again, nodded encouragement. Two Hawks grabbed it and shovelled the beans into his mouth. Disgusting or not, it was food. Or something like it. If he wanted to find Kimana again, he'd need his strength.

Jonesy watched him with a grin.

The grin faded and his brows knit together as if he was trying to figure something out.

"I feel like I know you, Injun. Sure as the day is short on Yule Tide morn', I swear you look familiar to me."

Long past caring about the taste, Two Hawks continued to shovel the beans into his mouth.

CHAPTER THIRTEEN

W ind whined and howled through the mountain pass like a pack of scrawny wolves, bringing with it heaps of snow and ice to trap the people in their lodges. The solstice had come and gone. The days were short and the sun, when it shone, had little strength. For the most part, the people stayed inside wrapped in thick furs, straying no farther from their fires than necessary.

There wasn't much choice.

Kimana sat cross-legged on the floor of the teepee and glanced at the fire, fidgeting absently with a moccasin that needed repairing. Chief Black Eagle had been her only company for days. She had no idea where Running Wolf had gone this time, or when he'd be back. If he ever came back. He may be dead for all she knew. Frozen solid somewhere out there. The thought of that was terrifying.

She shivered as she listened to the wind's mournful wail. It was like nothing she'd ever heard before. It literally moaned.

It was driving her crazy.

She glanced at Black Eagle, but he seemed unconcerned.

The walls of the lodge shook under the onslaught, but the hides were thick and well stitched, and very little air crept in to chill her.

Almost two moons had passed since she'd come here. It had been days since she had been out of the teepee. It was too cold for the children to play outside, too cold to hunt. Days like these were best spent with family, warm around a fire, listening to stories.

She shifted restlessly and glanced at Black Eagle again. There was no way she would ask him to tell her a story, though there was little else to do while in the grip of the winter storm. So, she kept busy stitching and repairing moccasins and clothing.

Or trying to.

She hated this kind of work.

Her favourite pastime of late was dreaming up ways to poke at Running Wolf. But he certainly wasn't giving her the opportunity. He was never around.

It seemed the less she saw him, the more out of sorts she became. That was part of the problem. She didn't see him often. Not that she wanted to, but it would give her something to do. Something to break the tedium of these cold winter days. Look at her, she thought with disgust, acting like she wanted him around. That was the last thing she wanted. It really didn't make sense why his absence annoyed her so much and knowing that only made her more irritated.

He was rarely in the lodge these days at all, although he occasionally came back at night, and he hardly spoke to her when he did grace them with his presence.

Sometimes he didn't come home at all.

Kimana snorted. She couldn't care less.

She'd rather not speak with him, either. It didn't matter to her one way or another where he was or what he did.

A blast of wind shook the teepee.

He could freeze out there for all she cared.

Not that he would. She was sure he had found a cosy place to hole up in. A warm companion.

Probably that Silver Fox.

She snorted again. As if she cared.

Scowling at the teepee's entrance, she jabbed her wooden awl into the thick elk hide of the moccasin and straight through to her thumb. Yanking her hand out, she stared at the blood that beaded up.

Insensitive, thoughtless man!

Couldn't he see how his father was restless and bored? How much he obviously missed his son? Didn't he care? She pursed her lips and looked over at the chief. Black Eagle sat quietly, whittling away at a piece of bone he was fashioning into a pipe.

97

He took no notice of his companion.

The least Running Wolf could do was keep his father company.

Well, if he was gone, so was his foul-smelling pet, at least. It was getting on her nerves how the beast would just lay there, staring at her with her creepy grey eyes and saliva dripping from her tongue. Like Kimana was her next meal. But at least the beast had stopped growling and snarling at her all the time.

Kimana tossed the moccasin on the floor.

If she didn't find something to do, she'd go mad. She cleared her throat, but Black Eagle didn't look up. She had to find something to do. Something to pass the time. Anything. She sighed.

"What's troubling you, Kimana?" The chief's voice was soft and kind, as always. She glanced over and found him watching her with a quiet intensity she found unsettling.

"I'm just thinking."

The chief tilted his leathery face. "Would you like to talk about it?"

She shrugged off the hides, rose from the floor and started to pace. "Aren't you bored? I'm bored. I know the days are short, but they seem so long. My father used to fill the winter days with stories. I miss them." Her voice cracked a little, and she hoped he didn't notice. "I miss him."

For some reason she didn't feel uncomfortable admitting that to him.

"Would you like me to tell you a story?"

Whirling to face him, she clasped her hands together. Unable to contain her joy, she nodded. She didn't really think her father would mind, but still, it felt almost disloyal.

Black Eagle laid his pipe down and patted the floor next to him. "Come sit here. I will tell you the story of a mighty hunter and a tiny mouse."

She allowed herself to believe he had taken the decision out of her hands. Her reservations gone, she eagerly grabbed her discarded buffalo robe and settled herself next to him, snuggling into the fur. She resisted the urge to cuddle up against him. She tugged her fur up to shield her face so he couldn't see her delighted grin.

She'd heard a similar tale before, but it didn't matter. It was a favourite story for the children, and her father had told it often. It would be good to hear it again. Stories felt like home.

"Long ago, before we had horses, before my great-grandfather was born, or his great-grandfather, there lived a mighty hunter. He could catch any kind of animal. He was never hungry. For many years he played with them, hunting them, and then letting them go. He didn't kill them because he caught more than he needed. But one day he realized that he was bored."

Kimana nodded and sat up straighter. She knew exactly how the hunter felt.

Black Eagle paused and drew on his pipe. He blew smoke rings into the air, then shifted on his mat.

"It was no longer a challenge for him to hunt the animals, because none could escape him. He sat on the ground for a full moon's time and stared at the sky, trying to think of what he could do."

Black Eagle told her about the animals, and how they came out from behind the trees and watched the hunter. They began to get worried, because he just sat and did nothing, he just stared up into the sky. One night, said Black Eagle, the hunter was watching the moon as it marched across the sky, and he had an idea.

He would catch the moon!

So, he made a trap, and threw it up. The moon was caught and could not get free. Its light began to dim, and the hunter was very proud of himself.

"The people were furious because they could no longer see at night to travel," Black Eagle said. "They begged him to let the moon go. Knowing they were right, he tried to untie the moon. But it was very hot, and every time he got close, he got burned. He was a proud man, and did not want to admit this, so he kept it tied up. But soon, animals and people from all over the land became very angry."

Kimana waited in breathless anticipation.

She knew he was getting to the good part. She would never tire of hearing the stories.

The hunter called all the animals together, and threw them, one by one, up at the moon. They tried to chew through the cords that tied it, but no animal could. It was too hot. Finally, a mouse offered to try, but the mighty hunter laughed. How could one small mouse do such a big job? But, in anger and frustration, he tossed the mouse up. The mouse was small, but he was very brave. He chewed and chewed, though his fur was burning.

"He chewed through the cords, and finally the moon was free. The mouse jumped back to the ground and ran away, safe once again. But his fur was all burned and was the colour of ashes, and it remains that way to this very day."

Kimana stared at Black Eagle and twisted a strand of hair around her finger.

Was she as brave as that little mouse? She frowned, wondering if she would have both the strength and the courage to help free her people, as the mouse had possessed the strength and courage to free the moon.

A determined smile played at the edge of her lips and she gave a decisive nod. As soon as the spring came, she would leave this place and find a way to free the prisoners. Somehow, she'd find Two Hawks, and bring him back here.

A cold draft skittered over her face and movement caught her eye. Running Wolf stood by the teepee's entrance, his black hair hung over his chest, his feet planted far apart as if he was ready for battle.

He cocked an eyebrow.

A shiver chased down her spine. She felt relief that he was back, but also something like nervousness. Had he read her thoughts? Could he know what she planned? That was just foolish. There was no way he could. Besides, it didn't matter. He couldn't stop her.

And why would he want to?

He would probably be glad to be rid of her, of her people. He hated them all. And she hated him.

She didn't even try to stop the sneer that settled over her face as she looked at him.

He narrowed his eyes and she deliberately turned away, presenting him with the hard lines of her back. Maybe she wouldn't wait for spring. Maybe she would wait only until a Snow Eater came and took the snow and cold away. She was still amazed by the intensity of the warm winds that came in winter and blew through the mountain passes, increasing in speed and warmth before bursting out onto the prairies. Although her people had experienced them, they were so far away the effects were nothing like they were here, in the pass.

But more to the point, they were her best hope for early freedom. Nothing would stop her then.

Not even Running Wolf.

CHAPTER FOURTEEN

D on't curl your fingers. Hand flat so she doesn't bite you by accident," Kimana said. "Now, let her sniff you."
Little Otter beamed as a horse easily twice his height lowered her head to snuffle at his palm.

"Tickles!"

Kimana smiled and ruffled his hair.

He erupted into giggles as the mare nosed around his belly. "What does she want? She wants to eat me!"

"No, she's looking for a treat. Here, I brought some camas bulb."

Little Otter looked up and grinned. One of his top teeth was missing. She'd never seen anything cuter.

"Can I have some?"

"No, little man, it hasn't been boiled. It's hard and dry after sitting so long. Maybe later I can prepare some for you. Hold this flat in your palm. There you go."

Her cousin chortled as the horse's lips contorted around teeth nearly as big as her thumb. The mare chewed the root and tossed her head, then continued her search for more.

Kimana turned toward the sun and closed her eyes, letting the warmth caress her face. It was good to be outside after so long. She thanked the spirits for the Snow Eater. She was fond of Chief Black Eagle, but she needed a break from his company. She needed to breathe fresh air and feel the wind on her skin. When Little Otter had come to her lodge that morning, asking her to take him to see the horses, she hadn't hesitated. She'd grabbed some camas bulb, taken his hand, and run with him to the horse pen.

"You can pet her. Just run your hands down her body like this."

Little Otter's eyes were huge as he mimicked Kimana's movements, stroking the animal's neck.

"Good morning! Happy day!"

Kimana turned at the sound of her aunt's voice and smiled as Utina and the young warrior, Stands Alone, approached, their robes swirling around their legs.

"It is a good morning, isn't it? Windy, though." Kimana said.

"It's always windy here," Utina said as she smiled at Little Otter. "Good morning, Little Otter. And are you well this fine day? Are you perhaps thinking of going on a hunt?"

Little Otter giggled and ducked his head, then hid behind Kimana. He'd always been a little shy around adults, even those he knew, and the sight of the tall warrior was no doubt daunting. Stands Alone was a nice young man, but he was still a warrior, and Little Otter was young enough to be intimidated.

"We have some news we thought you'd find interesting," Utina said and smirked.

For some reason, her aunt's tone of voice made her nervous. "Why don't you run off and play," she told Little Otter. "I'll come find you later and bring some camas root."

Little Otter didn't hesitate. His little legs churned as he ran off to find some children close to his own age. She knew he wouldn't have any trouble. The village had dozens of youngsters.

She turned back to Utina and the warrior and forced a smile. "News?"

"Well, Stands Alone has some news. He was telling me about it this morning, and I thought you'd find it interesting since it could affect you."

Stands Alone blushed as Kimana gave him a questioning look. Blushed.

He was adorable. It was hard to remember he was a grown man when he did that.

"Well," he said, "I don't know that it will affect you, really. Not directly."

Utina snorted and pinched his arm. "Just tell her. Tell her what

Silver Fox told you. You're not going to believe it," she told Kimana.

Kimana stiffened. She wasn't interested in anything Silver Fox had to say. The woman was vicious and had taken every opportunity to sneer at her or make rude comments whenever they were in close proximity. Which, considering how much time they'd all spent indoors over the last few weeks, was far too often. Stands Alone shuffled his feet and looked a little uncomfortable under her gaze.

Utina rolled her eyes. "Oh for goodness sake, I'll tell her then. Silver Fox and Running Wolf are getting married."

"I didn't say getting married. I didn't say that," Stands Alone protested. "I said Silver Fox was hinting."

Kimana forced the smile to remain on her face. "And what does that have to do with me?"

"Don't you see?" Utina asked. "He'd move out. I know how much you hate him, and who could blame you? They'd have their own lodge. Then you'd have to move out because no one would tolerate you living alone with Chief Black Eagle. Even if he is old enough to be your father."

She wasn't sure what bothered her more, the idea of leaving Black Eagle's lodge – and she was enjoying his company more every day – or the thought of Running Wolf marrying that horrible woman. But why should she care what he did? He was nothing to her, even if they had enjoyed each other's company the day he took her riding. Really, the tension between them was intolerable. She didn't understand it – why she always felt she had to snipe at him or why he constantly scowled at her like he thought she was up to no good. Black Eagle did his best to keep the peace and had even insisted that Makwai stay out of the lodge during the day.

He knew she was afraid of wolves, but he hadn't asked her why. Running Wolf hadn't asked either, but she suspected he wouldn't care even if he did know. It didn't matter to him how she felt or what she thought. That's just the kind of man he was. Self-centred. Well, he and Silver Fox deserved each other. It worried her, though, that she might have to move. She'd talk to Black Eagle about it tonight. There must be some way they could manage it without too much scandal. Maybe Little Otter's new family could be convinced to let him come and live with her and the chief. It would be good to have him closer. He missed his mother, and even though there were lots of children to play with and his new family was treating him well, she knew he needed more contact with someone he knew and loved.

So did she.

"I hope they're happy together. I'll offer up a song for their good fortune." She tried to smile but couldn't quite manage it.

***

"I've been thinking."

Running Wolf looked up from the mountain lion track he was tracing with a finger and gave Stands Alone an amused glance. "Thinking. Is that something new?"

"Funny." Stands Alone punched Running Wolf on the arm and grinned. "No, seriously. I've been thinking about Kimana."

Amusement fled.

"Oh, well, that's new." He didn't even bother to try to keep the sarcasm from his voice.

He shook his head and turned his attention back to the paw prints they'd been tracking since morning. He should have known. The boy was obsessed. "Can't we talk about something else? Tell me how we know this is a mountain lion and not a lynx."

"The paw pads are bigger. A fair bit bigger. Less space between them. And there's some belly and tail drag marks. The prints are deeper in the snow. Heavier. But it's the belly and tail marks that really clinch it. Lynx walk lighter, higher. There's no drag."

"Good. Male or female?"

"Male. You never want to talk about her."

"And you never want to talk about anything but her. Can we concentrate on the task at hand, please?"

"Sorry."

Running Wolf rose to his feet and continued following the tracks toward a rocky outcropping a short distance away. Then he crouched and waved Stands Alone over to look at a steaming pile of scat.

"He's close. This is still warm. Tell me what he ate."

"Looks like he ate the organs. It's dark. Wet looking. Not much hair."

"What kind of hair?"

"Looks like elk."

"Close, but no. Mule dear. The hair's about the same length, but it's coarser. See?" He rubbed a few strands of hair between his fingers. "Even though a cow elk's hair is coarse as well, this isn't flexible enough."

Stands Alone took the hair from Running Wolf and rubbed it.

"Okay, that makes sense. But they don't really seem that much different to me, to be fair. Look, I know I overstepped myself before. At the lookout. I wanted to apologize. I've missed spending time together, you and I. Doing stuff like this. I know you were angry with me, and I've been trying to figure out why. You've always encouraged me to speak my mind with you." He hesitated. "Do you think this is the same cat we've seen before?"

"Looks like. I just don't want to talk about her. She frustrates me. I thought that cold snap was never going to end. The warmest fur isn't quite good enough when you're sleeping under the stars."

For the better part of the last moon cycle he'd slept outside when it was not bitterly cold, trying to avoid his lodge as much as possible. Seeing Kimana every day was hard enough, but seeing her sleeping face when he awoke, listening to the soft tinkle of her laughter as she listened to one of his father's stories – he just didn't know how much more he could take. It wasn't that looking at her was a hardship. It wasn't. She was, as Stands Alone said before, the most beautiful woman he'd seen, with the possible exception of his own mother. No, he thought, even his mother hadn't been as beautiful as Kimana. Or as contrary.

"You know you could have stayed at my lodge. Anyway, I think that's part of the problem. You don't have an outlet."

"What is that even supposed to mean? Outlet. What a ridiculous thing to say. You sound like an old woman."

Stands Alone ignored the dig.

"She's on your nerves. I think you should just talk about her. Get it off your chest. You'd feel better." Stands Alone pointed at the scat. "If the cat's eaten recently, and it looks like he has, do we really need to worry about him stalking the village?"

"We always have to worry when an animal this big is taking an interest in people and getting too close. I don't see how talking about her is going to help."

"Maybe it won't. I had dinner at Fire Dancer and Singing

Deer's lodge a few days ago. The day the Snow Eater blew in. Silver Fox was hinting that you and she were thinking about getting married. When I talked to Kimana about it..."

Running Wolf looked up, eyes blazing. "When did you talk to Kimana?"

Stands Alone lifted his hands, palms facing forward. "Relax. I ran into her this morning at the horse pen. It wasn't a big deal. Her aunt, Utina, was there. And Little Otter. We were just talking."

Running Wolf swallowed the fury that threatened to erupt. Why it bothered him that this young pup was getting friendly with Kimana was beyond his comprehension. But that wasn't what enraged him. The fact that he'd also told Kimana Silver Fox's lies filled him with an almost uncontrollable anger. And oddly, with something close to panic.

"You told her Silver Fox said we were getting married? Why the hell would you do that?"

"I just told her what Silver Fox said. Everyone knows Silver Fox is a liar."

"Kimana wouldn't know that."

"Why does that bother you so much? You said you weren't interested in her. Why do you care what she thinks?"

Good question.

"She's my responsibility."

"She's not, really. But I think it's more than that."

He sighed. "Let's leave it at that, all right?"

"I wonder if it's guilt you're feeling."

Running Wolf rounded on Stands Alone and grabbed the front of his buffalo robe in his fist. "You'd better explain that."

Stands Alone took a step back. Visibly braced himself.

"You're the one who ordered the attack on her people. She knows that. Every day you look at each other, and every day you're reminded of the animosity between you. It has to be tough living with someone who sees you as the enemy. She's got to get out of your lodge, it's as simple as that. She has to find a way to settle in here. I think she needs to find a husband. Silver Fox thinks we would make a good couple."

"Silver Fox does." He rolled his eyes. "Great Spirit, save me. Since when have you started listening to her advice?"

"I'm just saying. Look, that's not the only reason. People are starting to talk. They don't think it's right for her to be in your lodge. Since you're not married."

"It's my father's lodge. And I haven't touched her."

"Not the point. You could. Who would know? She needs a husband. If her reputation gets destroyed, that's it. She'll never marry, never have her own home here."

"And you think you'd be good enough for her?"

"As good as anyone else."

And better than some.

"What makes you think she'd be interested in you?"

Stands Alone bristled.

"What makes you think she wouldn't?" He spun on his heel and stalked off toward the camp. Running Wolf watched him go, the mountain lion forgotten.

It was another good question. Stands Alone was right. Kimana would never forgive him for the attack. She'd never forgive him for the loss of her intended husband or her family. It would be best for everyone if she found herself a husband and moved into her own lodge. And the sooner, the better. For all of them.

CHAPTER FIFTEEN

Two Hawks tried not to grind his teeth together as he leaned on his walking stick and watched the people bustle around the camp. The Northern Cree had been polite to him, had tended his wounds and given him shelter, but he didn't really feel welcome here. It had been different when he was a whole man with a tribe he belonged to. Now that he was nothing – with no one - it was a different story.

A Snow Eater had come, gobbling up most of the snow and ice from a recent storm that had blown in from the distant mountains. The people were enjoying the weather, spending much of the day under the warm sun. They were still wrapped in furs, but they lifted their faces toward the sky often, and smiled.

Every warm winter day was cause for celebration.

For some.

The Snow Eaters always brought hope and smiles to the people, even though they knew winter was far from over. Even though they were meticulous planners – had to be to survive - they lived in the moment whenever they could.

Dogs barked and played, and children ran after them, hooting and yelling, pretending they were great hunters with their miniature bows and arrows.

Most of the children ignored him, but the odd one spared him an occasional pitying glance as they scurried past. He would rather they ignored him totally than feel sorry for him.

He didn't need their pity.

He'd lost track of how long he'd been here. Jonesy, that ornery old trapper, had dragged him most of the way from the great river. It had taken more than half a moon's time to find this Cree village.

He wished the old man had just left him to die.

What was there for him now? Kimana was gone. There was no way he would find her now. And even if he could find her, what would be the point? He was useless, no better than a sightless old woman, hobbling around camp on one decent, and one completely useless, leg. He couldn't even mount a horse, let alone be a warrior. Or a husband.

And if the reactions of the young maidens in this camp were any indication, Kimana wouldn't want him anyway. No woman would want a pathetic excuse for a man. The young women here looked at his mangled leg in horror and revulsion.

It was twisted at an odd angle, and no matter what he did, he couldn't hide his pronounced limp.

Jonesy had done his best to set it, but the healer in this village said there was little point in re-breaking it now. It would never heal properly. He had simply given him ointments to help with the pain and ease the constant ache.

Why hadn't Jonesy just left him to die? Why!

He lifted his stick and slammed it into the ground in a rage, earning disapproving stares from a group of older women sitting around a fire nearby. One of them leaned forward and whispered something to her friends, and they snickered. He ground his teeth, turned away, and limped slowly toward his small lodge.

Didn't they know who he was?

Didn't it matter that he had once been a great warrior?

How could it matter? What he was once was unimportant. What he was now was the only thing that mattered. A useless excuse for a man.

These people had taken him in, tended his wounds, and treated him, at first, like a returning hero. But as the days went by, and it became obvious he would be more of a burden than they had expected, the attitude toward him had chilled considerably.

They assumed at first that he had been injured in battle, and when he told them he had fallen down an embankment while searching for his woman, they looked away in embarrassment. It was not the noblest way for a great warrior to get injured.

They were disgusted, but only mildly interested, in his account of the devastation he had found in his own camp. Their chief listened carefully, nodding and shaking his head in turn as Two Hawks told the tale. And then the old man told him there was nothing they could do to help him. Without knowing who had attacked, there was little anyone could do. Besides, he said, it was not their battle. War was a serious thing, something not entered into lightly. Their tribe had lost too many young warriors over the years to risk losing more over a woman.

Or a wounded man's pride.

With that pronouncement, the chief had dismissed him, and the people refused to speak of it again.

Just accept it, their eyes told him. Manitou had willed it.

He was welcome to stay, but he must contribute somehow. But how could he contribute with this mangled leg? He'd be lucky to grow old here, for the people to toss him their scraps as if he was a dog.

Two Hawks reached the flap of his teepee just as a group of children came around from behind the lodge. A little boy in front skidded to a halt and stared up at him. The other children plowed into their leader, and the group landed in a shrieking pile of tangled arms and legs. The children separated themselves and scrambled to their feet, watching him with an odd combination of fear and excitement.

They obviously thought he was a monster.

Why disappoint them?

He bared his teeth and snarled. The group tripped over each other as they screamed and ran away. He sighed. Once he was a warrior. Respected. Loved by his people. Now he was an object of scorn and pity.

An object of fear.

And a burden to people who had been good enough to take him in.

His shoulders slumped and he turned and looked west, out over the prairies, toward the setting sun. Toward the mountains.

She was out there, somewhere. Perhaps she was looking toward the east, even now. Looking for him. Wondering when he would come for her. He closed his eyes in frustration. She would never know why he didn't come. Maybe she would think he'd abandoned her. Maybe she thought he was dead.

He still had her wedding dress, tucked safely inside his bag.

How many nights had he taken it out, unfolded it, and run his fingers over the soft hide? How many times had he buried his face in it and tried to remember how she smelled?

The chance of finding her - of giving the dress to her - were slim now. With one good leg, how much could he do? How far could he go? He was tempted to toss it into a nearby fire, but he couldn't bring himself to do it. Perhaps, somehow, he would see her again one day, and give her the dress. Maybe she would find a worthy warrior for a husband, and she would want the soft hide.

The thought of her with another man made him want to plow his fist into something.

Had she already lain with someone else? Given them her body? Would she be so brazen? No, he couldn't believe that. She was pure and sweet. She would never give herself willingly to her captors. She would wait for him.

But he was afraid it would be over between them. How could she ever accept him? No woman would accept a half a man for a husband. But he had to know for sure. And he still intended to avenge the death of his people. Kimana's abductors would pay. And he had another little matter to attend to. An even more personal reason for vengeance.

He looked down at his leg.

Yes. Someone would pay.

With their lives.

With his free arm, he swept aside the flap of his teepee and hobbled inside.

CHAPTER SIXTEEN

K imana sat on a thick pile of furs in Meda's teepee, trying to stitch a robe without stabbing herself. Her fingers ached.

"I had a strange dream last night, Meda."

The old woman looked up from the moccasin she was repairing with a single, startled eye.

"A strange dream, you say? Tell me, what did you see, Kimana?"

Kimana shrugged, then looked back down at the robe. She hated sewing. Even though she'd been taught how at a young age, she'd never quite acquired the knack for it. She certainly hadn't acquired any love for the task.

"Makwai came into our lodge and tugged off my furs with her teeth. It was night, but I could see her clearly. She had a purple stone around her neck, and it seemed to be lit from within. It was glowing, like the moon."

Meda reached out and touched her knee. "A purple stone? Are you sure?"

"Yes. Is that important?"

"All things in our dreams are important. Go on."

"You know, I really hate that wolf."

Meda huffed out an impatient breath.

"Makwai has been good company for Running Wolf since his mother and Laughing Brook died. She helped him get past his grief. You shouldn't be so hard on the animal."

"She's just an animal, Meda. And she smells horrible."

"No animal is just an animal. You know better than that. And she can't help how she smells. Now tell me what happened next."

"She spoke to me. Not in words. It was like I could hear her thoughts. She said she had a gift for me and told me to follow her. I don't know why, but I wasn't afraid. Wolves scare me, but I wasn't afraid."

"What kind of gift?" Meda asked.

"That's what doesn't make sense. She led me through the trees and down a hill. There was a small river at the bottom. We followed it a while, and she kept looking back at me. I guess she wanted to know if I was still behind her. We rounded a curve and there were buffalo, pawing through the snow. Searching for food. There weren't many."

"How many?"

Kimana looked at the old woman.

"Maybe as many as two people's hands. Maybe less. Not more."

Meda stared at Kimana intently, and she couldn't quite hide the excitement in her voice. "Did she say anything else? Do anything else?"

"She told me to watch for her in my dreams." Kimana snorted. "As if I'd get excited about that."

"Can you tell me where they were?"

"Just some ravine. I don't know. It was a place like any other. Nothing special."

Meda gave an exasperated snort.

"I don't know your land, Meda."

"Describe it. What did the ravine look like?"

"It was only a dream, Meda. It wasn't real. Don't you dream?"

"Not like I used to, child. Not anymore. Do you dream often?"

Kimana laid down the robe she was working on and her eyes grew thoughtful.

"Not often. More lately. Since I came here. And come to think of it, Makwai is in most of the dreams. I guess it's because she bothers me so much. I hate having her share our lodge."

"That makes sense. Tell me what the ravine looked like. Was there anything different about it? Any landmarks?"

"It had small cliffs, not more than three men in height. The stream, of course. Landmarks. Let me think." She laid the robe in her lap, tried to picture what she'd seen. "A strange tree stood on the ridge above, twisted and oddly shaped. It was short. It looked very old. Barely alive."

Her eyes narrowed. "And there was a large broken tree laying across the river. It's like I said. A place like any other."

Kimana watched curiously as the old woman struggled to her feet and scurried out of the teepee.

***

Running Wolf looked up and scowled as Meda burst through the flap of Black Eagle's lodge, her face flushed, her breath coming in deep gasps. His father smiled with obvious pleasure at her entrance, but his smile turned quickly to a concerned frown as he looked at her flushed face.

"What is it? What's wrong?"

"Do you have men out scouting today, Black Eagle?"

"I always have men scouting, Meda, you know this."

"Kimana had a dream. She dreamt of buffalo. A small herd."

"So?" Running Wolf said. "We all dream of buffalo. Especially in the winter. Who does not dream of buffalo in the winter?"

Meda's brows drew together in an unspoken reproach, and she looked back at his father. "I think she has the sight, Black Eagle."

Black Eagle looked at her with more interest. "Why would you think she has the sight? We hardly know her. Has she had other dreams?"

"She said she's dreamed before, but we've never really spoken of it."

Running Wolf shook his head. "She has been here for a few moon's time, Meda. You cannot know her that well. How could you know? Not many have the sight." His father nodded in agreement.

Meda drew herself up to her full height and scowled at both men.

"There was a time when you would not question my opinions. A time when you trusted my intuition."

Black Eagle chuckled. "Don't be offended, old woman. I don't always trust my own judgment these days. I think the time is coming soon when I will let my son lead our people. We're getting old, Meda."

"Pah! Speak for yourself."

"All right, then."

"I can see the gift within her. She's different. I don't think she even knows."

"I-ni-i! I-ni-i!"

Black Eagle struggled to his feet and gave Meda a startled look. Buffalo! Running Wolf stared in shock. Someone had spotted buffalo.

"You see?" Meda smirked, "I am not so old and stupid as you think I am."

Black Eagle reached out and ran a gnarled hand down her cheek. He spoke softly, but Running Wolf could not help but overhear. He stood up, walked to the flap of their lodge and waited.

"The only one who is stupid is me," his father said in a low voice. "For waiting so long to insist... When will you move into this lodge and become my woman? There's no reason for you to live alone."

Meda shook her head and tried to look disinterested, but her lips curved. "We are too old for such things."

"We are never too old." He smiled again.

Running Wolf glanced back at his father and waited for his nod. If there were buffalo, and he still had his doubts, there was much work to do.

***

The black stallion shifted and tossed his head. Running Wolf ran his hand over the trembling animal's neck and whispered soothing words to calm him. The horse's ears twitched, and he snorted, his breath coming out in frosty clouds. The animal was as eager as his rider, and his sides quivered with impatience. Running Wolf stared into the distance. The winter was far from over, and though they still had plenty of stores of dried meat, every member of the tribe would welcome the taste of fresh buffalo.

If there really were any buffalo.

He glanced over at Kimana. She was seated on her grey mare, and she stared down with an odd expression as children touched her legs, and women glanced at her with a mixture of awe and excitement as they walked past. Even the warriors grunted could not hide their anticipation. Although he was eager to be about the hunt, Running Wolf couldn't quite believe the rumours that were flying through the camp.

The sight. They said she had the sight.

Running Wolf searched for the old one-eyed woman who had fired the gossip. She stood next to his father, her face filled with a smug pride. Old fool. Didn't Meda know if Kimana's dream was proven false, as it surely would be, she would suffer the scorn of every man, woman and child in the camp? No matter that Kimana herself had done nothing to encourage the talk. The people wouldn't care. They were putting their hopes in the dreams of one single girl. If they were disappointed, who knew what might happen. But then again, the scouts said they had seen the beasts with their own eyes, so maybe it was true.

Maybe.

He turned his gaze upon Kimana once again and found her watching him with a wary expression on her face. Was it confusion he saw within the amber depths of her eyes? Or was it fear? She obviously wasn't comfortable with all the attention she was receiving. It would be bad if her dream was found to be false. But how much worse would it be if her vision proved accurate? The only other member of the camp to have the sight was Meda, and her visions were rare these days. It took the people a long time to accept such gifts in other people, and those who had them were often feared more than they were revered.

The excitement was building to a fever pitch, and the hunters were ready to go. They only awaited his signal. He looked at his father. The chief gave him a small nod and an encouraging smile. Running Wolf lifted his arm. Every head turned toward him. The children fell silent, and the only sound was the snorting of the horses and the whining of the camp dogs. He let out a whoop and dropped his arm. The ground churned up beneath the hooves of the horses as man after man rode out of the camp. Some of the women would follow to help with butchering and packaging the meat. Tonight, if all went well, they would dine on fresh buffalo. Running Wolf watched as the last man rode from camp, and then glanced over at Kimana. She looked at him uncertainly, not sure if she should wait for him, or follow the other men. He pressed his feet into the sides of his horse, urging it toward her. He had a strong impulse to pull her on to his mount and kiss away the nervousness he saw within her. But she didn't need or want his sympathy. She'd likely just spit it back into his face. Still, he hated seeing her uncertainty.

"Shall we find out if you truly have the sight, Kimana, or should we go back to our lodge? Perhaps we can find something there to amuse us while the people go on this fool's errand."

The hesitation and doubt in her eyes changed to fire. She snarled at him and whirled her mare in the direction the hunters had ridden. With a kick, she spurred Wind Dancer into a gallop.

Running Wolf smiled as he watched her ride off, chuckled. Then he dug his own heels into the sides of his horse and set off to join the hunt.

***

An enormous bonfire burned in the centre of the camp, and the people sat around it, laughing and sharing stories of the hunt. Kimana watched from the shadows around the edge of the fire. Their return had been greeted with excitement, but there had been something more. Before they had left on the hunt, the women and children had spoken to her with respect and open friendliness. She hadn't been totally comfortable with it. She was starting to like these people, and that would be dangerous. She couldn't allow herself to forget who they were, and what they had done to her family and friends. But when the hunting party returned to camp, the women looked at her strangely. More than one woman had grabbed a child who had gotten too close to her, pulling them away and quietly scolding. There was awe in their eyes, and something akin to fear. Except for Meda, no one had spoken to her for hours, and as the celebration wore on, she retreated farther and farther back from the ring of light around the fire.

Meda had tried to draw her closer, but quickly gave up when Kimana pleaded exhaustion from the long ride. The old woman was obviously enjoying herself too much to bother insisting.

Silver Fox held court in the centre of a throng of young women, tossing her head and saying something that made them all look over at Kimana. Some of them laughed. Some of them looked wary. Chief Black Eagle huddled in a pile of furs, smoking and laughing boisterously with a group of elderly warriors too frail to climb up on their horses.

Kimana hadn't seen Running Wolf since the sun went down.

She shifted her weight and tugged a buffalo robe closer around her shoulders. She knew some of the women were afraid of her now. Stupid dream. She should have kept her mouth shut, but how was she to know Meda would make such a fuss, or that her dream could possibly be real? The buffalo had indeed been in a ravine, and the oddly shaped tree had stood like a sentinel on the ridge above them. They had only taken a handful of the animals, allowing the rest of the small herd to escape.

The hunt was over almost as soon as it began, and they had returned to the camp, triumphant. The women went about the business of preparing the meat. Huge chunks of it still smouldered on the fire. The mouth-watering scent filled the cold night air.

She felt more and more alienated as the evening wore on. She wanted to climb under a pile of furs, to shut out the sounds of the celebration and laughter. But her teepee was on the other side of the fire, and she didn't want to walk past anyone. Her only other choice was to go around.

She glanced nervously about, looking for any sign of the Makwai, but she didn't see her. Turning her back on the fire, she circled around the outskirts of the village until she was behind her home.

Home. When had she started thinking of that teepee – of this camp - as home? It wasn't possible. She clenched her teeth and peeked out toward the fire. No one would notice her if she slipped inside. Her robes were dark, and the fire so bright it would blind anyone who peered into the darkness.

She held her breath and crept around to the door.

It was dark inside. No one had been there since morning, and the fire had not been tended. She stuck out an arm for balance and tried to find her way to her mat.

A whisper of sound came from behind her and she whirled around, prepared to fight off the wolf. Her stomach pitched and her legs grew weak.

She made out the shape of a man and was about to scream when a hand shot out and gently covered her mouth.

"Shhh. It's only me." Running Wolf lifted his fingers from her mouth and let his hand trail slowly down her arm. "I frightened you."

She nodded, and immediately felt foolish. She could barely see him. He certainly couldn't see her nod. Because she felt silly and weak, she straightened her spine, and willed herself to speak. "You should not sneak up on people."

"No, you're right," he said, "I should not have been so rude. Please forgive me."

She wasn't sure, but she thought he might be laughing at her. It was too much. First Silver Fox and her snide jokes, and now Running Wolf. How much more could she take? She jerked her shoulder away from his hand. "Why aren't you with your people? There is much to celebrate. People to laugh with. People who enjoy your company."

He didn't answer her for a moment, and she thought she heard him sigh.

"Must you always be so unpleasant? I swear gutting a buffalo would be a more enjoyable task than trading insults with you."

"Go gut a buffalo, then. I don't care."

She wouldn't admit to herself how much his words hurt. Why should she care what he thought? He was nothing to her.

Light speared into the teepee and she lifted an arm to shade her eyes. He stood at the doorway, looking back at her. His body was lit from behind, and she couldn't see his face, but his back was rigid.

"Goodnight, Kimana."

The flap closed behind him, and with the returning darkness, she felt an overwhelming sense of loneliness and regret. It was stupid. The whole thing was stupid. For better or worse, this was her home, at least until spring, and she couldn't spend the next couple of moons in solitude. Utina and the other women from her tribe were making friends and becoming a part of the families they lived with.

Running Wolf treated her with kindness and respect, and she repaid him with insults and rudeness.

She sat down on her mat and tucked her feet under the fur robe. There was much to think about.

Curling into a ball, she pulled a pile of furs on top of her, shutting out the sounds of the people. She squeezed her eyes shut, but for a long time she saw the image of Running Wolf standing in the doorway, looking back at her. She wished she'd seen his face. She wished she knew what he was thinking at that moment. She was afraid, suddenly, that her insults had gone too far.

CHAPTER SEVENTEEN

Kimana tossed a handful of sagebrush onto the fire and smiled at Chief Black Eagle. He was telling another story, and his weathered face was animated as he thrust out his arms, showing how big the antlers were on the first deer he'd killed as a young boy.

She smothered a chuckle as his hands inched further apart. The antlers grew larger with every telling of the tale. Running Wolf sat next to his father, nodding with interest, making little sounds of appreciation and wonder. He glanced at her and grinned, his eyes dancing with amusement and obvious fondness for the old man.

Her breath caught as she looked at him. His face was relaxed, and his boyish smile turned his usually stern expression wondrously sweet. Something warmed inside her as she watched him listen to his father. He had, no doubt, heard this story many times before. She herself had heard it several times over the long winter. But he acted as if it was the first time.

The two of them had settled into a kind of truce after the night of the celebration. For a while, he seemed to avoid her, and they hadn't spoken much, but as the weeks had gone by, they started to have polite conversations. He hadn't touched her since, and she was ashamed to find herself almost wishing he would. It had been so long since she'd felt the touch of someone she loved, even if just on her shoulder or arm. She missed the easy way her father had of showing his affection and love for her, and the hugs of friends and family. Here, no one touched her. She wanted to believe the Blackfoot were cold-hearted, but the months she'd spent here had shown her it wasn't true. The people were warm and friendly with each other, and they treated one another like family, even the old and the frail. Especially the old and frail. Those ones more than any other, the people treated with the greatest honour and respect. In fact, everyone was treated with warmth and kindness.

That was true of everyone except her, apparently. Meda claimed it was because she held herself apart from the others, but Kimana knew it was more than that. Since her dream, the women had kept their distance. More than once she'd seen Silver Fox smirking at her and heard the whispers of the women. "Witch-woman," they were calling her, and though they were never openly rude, they avoided her as much as possible. It hurt, and it made her angry. It wasn't her fault she had dreamt of buffalo. Stupid dream. She never should have told Meda.

She sighed, and it took her a moment to realize the chief had stopped speaking. She looked up and saw both of the men looking at her with quizzical expressions.

"Never have my stories bored you before today, little one."

Black Eagle smiled, but his eyes were filled with concern.

"No, it's not your story. I think it's wonderful. My apologies. I guess I'm just tired of winter. I wish the Snow-Eater would come and take away the snow and cold once and for all."

"That is my wish, as well. There's not one person in this camp who does not dream of the end of winter. It will come in time. The little Snow Eaters have been rare this winter, but soon spring will be here. But what will you do then? I will have no more stories to tell until the leaves have fallen from the trees once more. It will be many moons, and you'll wish you'd paid more attention to my tales." He grinned as he spoke, and she felt an undeniable surge of love for the old man who reminded her so much of her own father. She stepped forward and dropped to her knees before him, throwing her arms around his shoulders.

"I love you."

The whispered words were out of her mouth before she realized she was thinking them. Her arms fell to her side, and she sat back on her heels, staring at him in astonishment.

He lifted a gnarled hand and touched her cheek, his eyes soft and filled with the same fond look her father used to have when he touched her that way.

Was it possible for her to love this man? Somehow, over the long winter, he had become like a father to her. Her own father had often told her there was a time for everything, and everything, in turn, had its own time, and then passed away. Yes, she decided. Her heart had room to love him. Even if it lasted only a while, she could allow herself to feel something for this kind, wise old man.

For a time.

Soon enough she would leave this place, but for now, the Great Spirit had filled some of the emptiness inside of her through Black Eagle. She turned her cheek into his hand, and felt the warmth spread through her.

A scratching sound came from the doorway of the teepee.

"Kimana?" Utina's voice came through the flap. Kimana rose to her feet and glanced at Running Wolf, embarrassed that he may have seen her moment of weakness, but he was intently studying his arrowheads, a scowl creasing his forehead, as if concentrating deeply on some unseen flaw in the material. With an apologetic smile for Black Eagle, Kimana called for Utina to enter.

Her aunt scurried through the door and gave a quick smile and nod to the chief and Running Wolf.

"Please forgive me. I wished to speak with Kimana, but I can return later." Utina seemed both excited and agitated, and looked at the men hesitantly, obviously hoping they would take her hint and leave. She darted a furtive glance toward Kimana.

Black Eagle hauled himself to his feet and shook his head. "No, my son and I will walk a while. Stay. Drink some hot tea. It's no trouble." With a nod to Running Wolf, the chief strode through the door. Running Wolf hesitated only a moment, looking curiously from one woman to the next, then rose from his mat and followed his father outside.

Utina watched them leave, then turned toward the niece who was not many summers younger than her, her face breaking into a delighted grin.

"I'm with child!"

Kimana stared, then sank to her knees. She folded her hands together and then looked up at Utina. "Meda will know what to do," she whispered.

"What to do?"

She felt the raw edges of panic racing through her. Something had to be done. "There's a plant with hooded blue flowers, streaked with white. It can bring on the moon-time, Utina. When the blood refuses to flow, the flower can cause it to flow once more. Meda will know. She may even have some. We shouldn't waste time."

"What are you saying?" Utina stared at her in disbelief, "I want this baby, Kimana."

"You can't. You don't." Kimana grabbed Utina's robe, alarm rising steadily inside her. She knew she sounded hysterical, but she couldn't stop it. If Utina was with child, then all was lost. "We have to leave this place, Utina. Spring is coming. You can't travel that far when you're with child."

"I came here to share news with you. News that makes me happy. Maybe you want to leave these people, but I do not. We have nowhere to go. Our people are gone, Kimana. Gone. You need to accept this. You need to make a new life here. With these people."

"You don't understand. I can't do this thing you ask of me. Every day I look upon the faces of the men and I see the blood of our people. I hear their laughter, and all I hear are their war cries as they slaughtered our loved ones." Hot tears began to stream down her face. "Your own husband was killed, Utina. Don't you remember? And now you share a mat with one of these monsters and tell me you will bear his child. You tell me this with joy on your face. You betray your people. You betray the ones you loved."

Utina's nostrils flared and her eyes darkened. "You dare to speak to me of betraying our people! I, at least, am the honoured woman of a great warrior. You, you are little more than a whore, sharing your mat with the son of a chief, the man who will one day lead these people. Don't look so surprised. People talk. Do you really think he will take you to wife? Why should he give you his protection when you spread your legs for him for free? Was it not enough to be the daughter of a chief, Kimana? You also need to whore for one?"

Kimana surged to her feet and slapped Utina in the face. For a moment, they stared at each other as Utina held a hand to her reddened cheek. Kimana shook her head helplessly and reached out as her aunt ran from the teepee.

"No. Please come back. Forgive me."

But Utina was already gone. It was hopeless. Now, they would never leave. She threw herself onto her mat, covered her face with her hands, allowed the hated tears to flow. They wracked her body until, exhausted, she fell into a troubled sleep.

***

The river lapped at her knees and she watched, riveted, as the current tore an enormous tree from its roots. Makwai stood on the opposite bank, watching with her strange grey eyes. The torrent of ice-choked water carried the tree toward Kimana, but she was frozen in place. The branches scraped at her legs, tearing at her body and she felt herself being dragged under the icy water. Makwai lifted her head and howled. No!

"No!"

Kimana's eyes flew open. Running Wolf knelt above her. His hands were on her shoulders and he shook her gently until her eyes focused. They stared at each other in the orange glow of the fire. She shuddered, once, and then started to shake. Turning her face away from Running Wolf, unwilling to look him in the eyes, she fixed her gaze on the chief. On the other side of the lodge, Chief Black Eagle continued to snore.

It was the same dream she'd had before. Running Wolf touched her chin, turning her toward him.

"Another dream?"

She nodded her head. He pulled her into his arms and held her.

She tensed but didn't bother to struggle against him. She was so tired of fighting. She felt like she'd been fighting for so long. Fighting to hate these people. Fighting to hate this man who held her so gently, as if by doing so he could take away her sorrow. She was tired of fighting her own feelings. Was she the only one who refused to accept their captivity? Every day she watched the Cree women and children, watched them settle into their new lives. They laughed, worked and played with the same intensity they had before the attack, before they were ripped from their homes. When she looked around the camp, they seemed to blend in with their enemies like a perfectly stitched seam. It was almost impossible to identify who was Cree and who was Blackfoot. Her

Cree sisters were the wives and second-wives of Blackfoot warriors, and soon, some of them would be having babies. Like Utina. It was unlikely she was the only one.

Would they be able to escape when their bellies grew round? When they held their tiny babes in their arms, and looked over the fires at their new husbands, would they be willing to leave? Their men were gone, and all they could hope for if they left would be to find a Cree tribe they could join. And then, the process of making new lives would begin all over again.

They wouldn't do it. She knew that now.

She didn't understand how they could accept what was done to them, but she knew they would never leave.

Were they so wrong?

This place was just a place, and these people were not so very different. They hunted and gathered, sewed and cooked, laughed and cried. They raised babies, mourned their dead. Their children ran and played, and the old men smoked their pipes. The women were women, and the men were warriors. No, it was not so very different at all.

Running Wolf still held her in his arms. It was pointless struggling against him. If she was honest, she wasn't even sure she wanted to. One day she would run, she'd promised herself that, but it would not be today. She was so tired of fighting. Tired of feeling alone. Her body sank against his, and she rested her cheek against his smooth, warm chest. She heard the rhythmic beating of his heart, and the occasional pop of an exploding stick from the fire. His heartbeat was hypnotic. For a moment, she could pretend she belonged there, in his arms. Just for this night, she could pretend he wasn't the enemy. That he was a man, just a man.

He stroked her head, running his hand down the length of her hair, and she closed her eyes, then snuggled deeper into his arms. His heart began to beat faster, thumping hard against her cheek, and she could feel her own heart speeding up to keep pace. His breath quickened, and he shifted.

She looked up at him in surprise and watched his eyes as looked at her intently, then cupped her face in his hand. She felt like she was drifting, watching the scene from a distance. Powerless to stop it, unwilling to fight it, she remained absolutely still as he lowered his head and touched his lips to hers. Her eyes fluttered closed, and her insides quivered like willow leaves fluttering to the ground in a gentle autumn breeze.

The pressure of his lips left hers for a moment, and then his mouth was on hers again. But this time, the kiss was deeper, more urgent. No longer separated from the moment, she felt every sensation as they slammed into her like the tree from her dream. His arms went around her back, and he dragged her onto his lap. She couldn't think. Two Hawks had never touched her this way, never held her, or kissed her. Part of her knew it was wrong, but she couldn't stop it. Didn't want to.

She lifted her hands and wrapped them around his neck, pulling him closer, deeper. She heard him groan, or maybe it was her? He tore his mouth away from hers, kissed her throat, her chin, her cheeks. His mouth left trails of fire on her skin. She wanted more. Needed more.

Running Wolf lowered her body onto the mat, and stretched out beside her, running his hand down her waist and over her hip. All he could think about was how much he wanted this woman. She arched her back and moaned as he moved his hand lightly over her breast, brushed against her nipple and felt it harden beneath his touch. She twisted and pressed herself against his leg. Although her body responded to his touch as if she was experienced in the ways of men and women, he knew she'd never been with a man before. She seemed lost in the experience, and he was certain he could have her beneath him before she realized what was happening. For a moment, he was tempted. So tempted. Never had the need to lie with a woman been so strong.

She was everything. Incredible. Sweet. Trusting.

Pure.

Disgust for his behaviour washed over him and he pushed her arms away, rolled onto his side, and rose to his knees. She looked up at him in confusion. She was an innocent. Untouched. Pure. She trusted him, and he betrayed that trust by touching her this way. She deserved better than this. Once again, his emotions had taken over. He'd lost control, and this time, the price would be higher than he was willing to pay, higher than he was willing to let her pay.

"Cover yourself."

He knew his voice was gruffer than it needed to be, but he couldn't help it. She had to understand how serious this was. If the people in the village found out, she would be no better than an outcast. No man would take her for a wife if they knew she had lain with him. He thought of Silver Fox, and the way she crooked her pretty finger for any man who looked at her. She would never marry. She hadn't figured that out yet, but every man in the camp talked about her with a combination of lust and scorn in their voices. The women would never dare say anything to her face, but they, too, looked at her with disdain. Running Wolf certainly wasn't the only one who'd run into the willow trees with Silver Fox. The women were polite to her face, but he knew none called her friend. She was the kind of girl you rolled around in the bushes with, not the kind of girl you took to wife. He thought of the village men looking at Kimana with that same kind of lust and expectation in their eyes.

The thought of another man touching Kimana the way he almost had filled him with cold rage. She still lay where he had left her, her hair fanned out on the soft furs, her moistened lips parted slightly, her eyes bewildered.

A bit hurt and confused.

"I said cover yourself, woman. You look like the village whore."

Shock, then anger, flashed over her face. He tossed a fur into her arms and ignored the look she shot at him. She probably hated him now. Fine. She needed to hate him. As long as her fury still burned inside her like a prairie fire out of control, it would be easy to stay away from each other.

He could feel her stare searing into his back as he stormed from the warmth of the teepee.

CHAPTER EIGHTEEN

illage whore.
It hurt more than she wanted to admit, and this morning, she was determined not to admit anything.

The sun was just now rising, but she'd already put several hours between herself and the camp. She couldn't believe she'd almost talked herself into believing she could accept the Blackfoot. She absolutely refused to even think about Running Wolf.

How could he say that to her? Hadn't he learned anything about her over the long winter? Hot tears ran down her face. She brushed them away with an angry swipe. Why had she let him touch her that way? No, she absolutely would not think of him. He didn't deserve her tears. He was arrogant and cruel. How could she have let him touch her that way? Was she possessed by evil spirits? Oh, why could she not stop thinking about him? Her own mind betrayed her!

Wind Dancer picked her way over snow-covered rocks, her neck bent, her muzzle low to the ground. The mare's breath hung in the morning air in icy clouds. They were almost through the mountain pass, and the endless prairies – freedom - lay not far ahead. From there, it would probably be a few days ride to the nearest Cree camp. She just hoped she could find one before the brutal cold returned and they both froze to death.

Kimana chewed on her bottom lip and tried not to think of the warm furs she had dumped in a heap on her sleeping mat. It was

130

warmer than it had been for a couple of moons, but the sun was still weak, and the snow lay heavy over the earth.

The silence of the morning was broken by the cry of an eagle, and Kimana looked up, shading her eyes against the rising sun with her right hand. She slowed Wind Dancer to a stop and watched the fluid dance of the bird as it rode unseen currents of air. The eagle circled three times, let out a screech and flew west. Kimana twisted around to watch its flight over the mountains. An inexplicable sadness overwhelmed her, and she lowered her eyes.

She remembered the eagle feather she had found on that sun-drenched afternoon so long ago and thought of her father's words about her going on a journey. She thought about her dream, and the look on her father's tear-streaked face as he let the eagle feather fall to the ground.

When someone finds a feather, it means they are about to leave on a journey to a new and strange land. Why else would the eagle give his feather, if not to speed you on your way?

What could it all mean? She wished she were a wise-woman like Meda, someone who could interpret dreams and omens.

And this eagle circling above her today... Was that also a sign? She snorted. If so, the eagle was confused. He was flying in the wrong direction.

She pressed her knees into the sides of her mare, urging her forward. As they continued their journey east toward the plains, she glanced back over her shoulder. The eagle was gone, but she could still hear his piercing cry. She tried to ignore the sick, uneasy feeling in her stomach.

***

Blood streamed from Running Wolf's hand and ran down his raised arm as he slammed his fist into the tree yet again. Pain spiked through his hand, and he embraced it, tried to escape inside of it. Physical pain he understood. It made sense to him. Kimana and the feelings she drew out of him did not.

He didn't know why he'd said those things to her, or why he wanted to hurt her with words he couldn't take back. And he didn't know why the look of confused pain in her eyes tore at his gut the way it did.

Why did she have to lie there looking so beautiful? So trusting? Why did her hair have to shine in the firelight? Why did her lips part as if begging him to grind his own mouth down onto hers? Didn't she know what that did to a man?

Why did she have to tempt him that way? For a moment his anger surged inside of him. She deserved what he said to her. She was no different than Silver Fox, tempting and teasing with her eyes and body, thinking she could control him through his desire for her.

His forehead thumped against the tree. He ignored the scape of the bark against his skin. Shutting his eyes, guilt overcame him. His mouth filled with the bitter taste of bile. He was such a fool. She was nothing like Silver Fox. She was innocent and trusting and had no clue what she was doing to him. She hadn't deserved what he'd said. Now she would be lying on her mat, more confused and hurt than he was. He pictured her face streaked with tears. Raising his head, he pounded his fist into the tree again.

But why did he care how she felt? And why did he want so badly to protect her, even from himself? There had been talk in the village for weeks. He knew what people were saying about her. Witch-woman. Whore. He saw the knowing looks that passed between the men. He could see the women keeping politely distant. And through it all was Silver Fox, watching Kimana with amusement, and watching him with open invitation.

She'd gotten bolder over the long winter.

He had also heard the talk. Rumours were a part of camp life, and he knew he could do little about them, but they angered him nevertheless. People were saying he would marry Silver Fox once his infatuation with Kimana had run its course, and that Silver Fox would insist Kimana be sold.

Could Silver Fox herself be responsible for the gossip? No. She might have the sexual ethics of a male rabbit, but even she would not be that cruel. Still, the rumours were getting ugly, and he didn't know how to protect Kimana from them.

Was his father blind? Couldn't he see what was happening? It would be best if the chief sent her to another family, or better still if he married her off to a young warrior in a different camp.

At the thought of another man running his hands down Kimana's golden body, possessing her as he so desperately wanted to, he let out a howl of rage, its echoes muffled by the softening snow.

He turned around, leaned his back against the tree and sank to the ground.

There was nothing to do but take her as his wife.

It was that simple.

He could no longer deny that he felt something for her. It wasn't love. It could never be love. He didn't think he was capable of that anymore, but it didn't really matter. Very few marriages were based on love. If he felt desire for the woman who shared his mat, that was more than he could have ever hoped. No one could replace Laughing Brook, and although he would have preferred never to do so, he knew he would have to take a wife again one day. He would be expected to have children. Kimana was as good a choice as any, and better than most.

He closed his eyes and allowed himself to imagine what it would be like, to have her, warm and willing. Her soft lips parted, her chest heaving with desire. Lifting her arms and wrapping them around his neck, pulling him down for a kiss. Lowering himself onto her, into her, her legs wrapping around him, pulling him deeper and deeper inside.

With a frustrated groan, his eyes snapped open and he tried to slow the blood rushing through his groin. Yes, he would take her to wife. It was the only solution. And then he would finally possess her, and the whole world would know she belonged to no man but him. It was what he should have done when he first brought her to his village.

He surged to his feet with a grim, determined smile. It was time to return to camp. She would need time to prepare for the wedding, and he didn't want to wait any longer than he had to.

***

Kimana pulled up on the reins and looked at the river. It was partially thawed, and the current was strong. It was colder in the mountain pass than it was here, and she wondered if the Snow Eater gained in strength as it burst onto the prairies. She hadn't counted on the river being thawed yet. With the flow so strong it could be dangerous to cross it alone. She turned and rode north for a while, hoping to find a spot where the ice was still solid. The sun was as high in the sky as it would be able to climb during these cold winter months.

By now, the people would know she had gone. She considered

pressing her heels into Wind Dancer's flank to speed her progress and then decided against it. She would maintain a slow, easy pace, and save her mare's strength. Besides, there wasn't much chance of pursuit. Why go to the effort of sending men to search for one woman? Especially one who was obviously held in such low esteem by the people of the village.

It was well past mid-day when she tugged on the reins and brought Wind Dancer to a stop. It was pointless. The banks of the river were still choked with ice, and the centre was running freely. She had already lost precious daylight and both she and her horse were getting hungry. She didn't want to turn south in what could be a futile attempt to find a safer place to cross.

Her choices were limited. She could continue north and eventually west back into the mountains, or she could make camp and wait until there was less ice. But the current would only grow more violent as the ice continued to thaw. Neither idea appealed to her. The only other option was to attempt to cross here, where the river was narrower. She judged the distance to be close to the length of five or six horses at most. She encouraged the mare forward with a gentle press of her heels. Wind Dancer hesitated at the bank, shying at the sound of the rushing water and the snapping of the ice as it loosened from the banks. She tossed her head in protest and snorted. Kimana pressed her heels harder into her flank, but the horse refused to proceed. Kimana's back tensed with frustration. She was running out of time. She gave the reluctant mare a solid kick with both feet. The horse snorted again and reared up slightly, then plunged into the icy current.

***

Running Wolf looked up at the sun. It climbed steadily toward its zenith. He'd been riding hard since just before daybreak but had lost time where the signs of her passing had been less obvious. He shouldn't be surprised she had left. The woman couldn't be trusted. With furious determination, he shoved away the memory of his words to her. He knew she'd reached the great river and turned north. Fear threatened to overcome him. If she tried to cross farther north she would be in trouble. The river was unpredictable deep, and sharp rocks lurked in the dark shadows of the banks. Some of the ice was still thick, but the current was strong and was slowly chewing away at it, weakening it and making it more dangerous with each passing moment. At this time of year, it was suicide to attempt a crossing alone.

The hours of riding had been filled with guilt and anger. He remembered opening the flap of the teepee and creeping quietly toward her mat. He was going to touch her face and tell her his plans for their future. And all he found when he reached down a hand in the dark was a pile of furs. He'd flung his thick robe to the other side of the fire and sat on her mat, head in his hands. For a while, he thought he would let her go. It was what she wanted. She'd made no secret of her hatred of his people. He looked up and watched the shadows dance around the lodge. A gust of wind shook the teepee. She'd be cold. Or worse. Minutes later he was on his horse, determined to bring her back, even if he had to drag her by the hair on her damned beautiful head.

He looked grimly up the river. When he found her, that was exactly what he was going to do.

The roaring of the river drowned out the possibility of hearing anything, and he urged his horse a little faster. He knew he was asking too much of the animal. It was difficult to run in the snow for any amount of time, and the hours were taking their toll. The stallion's sides were heaving, and Running Wolf knew he would have to let him rest soon.

***

Kimana's head broke the surface of the water. Her throat felt like she was swallowing shards of granite as she sucked air into her lungs. She fought to stay above the water, but the current was too strong. It sucked her down then tossed her up just to hurtle her down the river into slabs of ice and rock. Something large and dark thrashed and twisted as it came toward her. The tree from her dream.

Suddenly her head felt like it was going to explode as something smashed into the side of her skull. A strange warmth flooded her body. The water enveloped her, covered her head, and she drifted below the surface. Her eyes closed as she floated gently into blackness.

CHAPTER NINETEEN

Hands covered in worn, oiled deerskin reached into the glacial waters and dragged the woman from the river. Jonesy turned her over and looked at her face.

Her skin was so pale, he could darn near see through it. Her long, dark hair was plastered to her body, and she lay in his arms, barely breathing. It was getting to be a habit, he thought with a wry grin, this rescuing of Injuns. Maybe it was his mission in life. His uncle always said everyone needed a mission in life. A purpose, he said. Well, rescuing Injuns wasn't the worst thing he could do, though the good Lord knew, he didn't seem to be getting rich off it. His grin quickly faded as he gave her battered body a quick look-over. She'd need a gentler hand than that other Injun had. He lowered her to the ground, turned her face carefully to the side and pushed against her stomach to force out any water she had swallowed. She was a young one. Pretty as a sunrise in springtime. He hoped it wasn't too late.

***

Running Wolf stared at the sickening scene on the riverbank. Kimana's spirited mare lay broken and battered against the rocks and ice. She was still alive, but barely. Her sides shuddered with the effort of drawing breath. He slid from his horse and approached her quietly, speaking in soft, soothing tones, trying not to frighten her any more than she already was. He reached the edge, went down on one knee, and ran a hand down the contours of her head and neck. Her eyes rolled and she thrashed weakly. He murmured to her, rubbed her neck with long, soothing strokes. She relaxed against him, trusting that he would help her. There were gouges in her hide, and the ice and snow were stained red around her. Her legs twisted at odd angles, and in places, chunks of fur and flesh had been torn from her once flawless body.

What a waste of a sweet, beautiful life. He looked up the river and tried to ignore the burning in his eyes.

There was no sign of Kimana. Had he been too late to save her? Had she drowned? He refused to accept that. He had to keep looking. But the soft grunt from her horse drew his eyes back down. He couldn't leave Wind Dancer like this. He reached into his calf-length moccasin and pulled out a blade. The mare would never survive her encounter with the river. Her injuries were too great even for the healing abilities of Meda.

He had no choice.

He stroked her head once again and brought his mouth close to her twitching ear. Whispering softly, he looked into her trusting eyes. When he was certain her spirit understood what he had to do, he drew the blade in a clean, quick line across her throat, and watched her lifeblood drain into the churning river.

Unashamed, he let his tears flow freely as he held her head on his lap. He lowered his head to hers and closed his eyes. He knew he didn't have much time, but he owed the magnificent creature a moment of respect.

Laying her head down gently, he sat up, wiped his face, and searched the river with his eyes. If he hadn't left Kimana all those hours ago, this beautiful animal would still be alive. If he'd only returned sooner, instead of brooding, both of them would be safe. Now the mare was dead, and Kimana likely was, as well.

Running Wolf returned to his horse and sprung onto his back. The animal shifted restlessly. Dead or alive, he would find her. One way or another, he would take her home.

***

Noise. Horrible, piercing noise. It felt like someone was shrieking inside her head. No, it wasn't inside her head, it was coming from somewhere else. It was whistling. Someone was whistling. An ear-splitting, awful whistle. Kimana opened her eyes and squinted against the sunlight. She closed them again, winced at the sharp pain that shot through her skull.

Sick. She felt sick.

She rolled over onto her side and tensed as her muscles protested the movement. Allowing her eyes to open gradually, she tried to take in her surroundings, but her vision was blurred, and everything looked strange and out of focus. The whistling continued, and she turned her head toward the noise. A grizzled, old white man crouched next to a fire, blowing smoke rings into the air. His left hand stroked a scruffy grey dog sitting next to him, scratching behind his ear. The dog watched the man in obvious adoration and thumped his scraggly tail on the ground.

"Watch this one, 'Ol Jack. You just watch. I am the king of the smoke ring. Yessir,"

The man blew a perfect ring, and then sent a thin stream of blue smoke through the middle. He cackled.

"There! You see? Betcha can't do one that good. 'Course, you don't smoke, do you, 'Ol Jack? But even if you did, you sure couldn't do one as good as that. No sirree."

The dog seemed inclined to agree, whined once, then collapsed on the ground in delighted defeat, laying his head on his front paws. His tail continued to thump enthusiastically as he watched his master.

Kimana watched them for a while, trying to understand where she was, and who the man was, but she couldn't piece it together. She'd been running away from something, but she wasn't sure what. Was it this man? Had he caught her? No. That didn't seem right.

Had she been running, or riding? Riding, she thought. On a horse. On Wind Dancer. She turned her head, but she couldn't see the mare. The effort cost her. She felt a wave of pain and dizziness in her head. Her stomach threatened to empty itself. Closing her eyes against the throbbing, she let herself sink back into unconsciousness.

***

The powerful stallion shifted and snorted as Running Wolf hauled up on the reins. He looked down at the tracks, following them with his eyes from the trees, to the river, and back into the trees. Something had been pulled from the river, laid down in the snow, and then carried away. There was only one set of footprints and the prints of a medium-sized dog. The prints leading away from the river made deeper impressions than the ones leading toward it. It was obvious whoever had pulled something from the water had dragged it away.

There was no question in his mind it was Kimana who'd been hauled out of the river. But was she still alive?

And who had taken her?

He looked at the tracks leading into the trees. Whoever it was, they were on foot. At least, they had been when they approached the river.

He pulled the reins to the left and pressed his knee into the horse's flank. It wouldn't be long now.

***

Jonesy wandered over to the sleeping girl. Yessir, she was a pretty one. She had a nasty bump on her head, but no broken bones, near as he could tell. She was warmer, that was for sure.

Yep. She'd live.

And she'd be better off than that other one he'd rescued. Providing she had her wits about her. There was a good chance she'd be a babbling idiot, what with that lump on her head. Something must have hit her pretty darn hard. Darn shame. Darn tootin' shame. She was pretty as a freshly baked pie. Saskatoon berry pie. Yessir.

Jones cackled. He was getting poetic in his old age.

He knelt down and ran his fingers down her hair. Poor wee thing. Lucky for her old Jonesy had saved her bacon. Yessir-ee.

It was his mission in life.

But there was something about her. He was pretty sure he'd seen her before. Not recently, though. She was older. Quite a bit older. She was pretty, though, unusual looking. He knew for certain he'd seen her before. Had she been a child at the time? He'd have to think on it.

***

Running Wolf crouched in the trees, watching the white man touch Kimana's hair. His hands were ready on his bow. If the man laid another finger on her, he would kill him. The old man cackled and sat back on his heels. The dog lying next to the fire turned his head toward Running Wolf and growled, his hair standing straight up along his spine. Running Wolf gave him a quick glance, dismissed him as any kind of real threat, and turned his eyes back to the white man. Dogs didn't concern him. White men did.

"What is it, 'Ol Jack? Somethin' there? Who is it? Come out where I can see you! I've got a gun!"

The old man followed the dog's gaze to the trees. His lips puckered out and his eyes squinted. Obviously spotting Running Wolf amongst the trees, he reached into his back pocket. His hand shook as he fumbled to pull out some kind of a weapon. Running Wolf stood, legs spread, his bow stretched taut, an arrow nocked and ready to send flying into the old man's heart.

The man froze.

"Hey, ho. Now, that's not a nice way to say hello to a fella. Put that thing down, boy, before you hurt someone."

Running Wolf took a step into the clearing, but he didn't lower his bow. As long as the old man held a gun, he would be as good as dead before he even lifted it.

"Now, listen here. I ain't done nothin'. This here your woman? Pretty little thing. But I ain't touched her, I swear it. I just saved her, that's all. It's my mission in life, rescuin' Injuns and such."

He put his hands into the air and backed away from Kimana. The dog continued to growl.

"All right. See? I'm harmless. Put that thing down, boy. I don't want no trouble."

The old man edged backward toward the fire. He watched Running Wolf, and his tongue flicked out and ran nervously over his lips. He continued to back up and tripped over his dog. He landed with an audible thump and grunt next to the fire. Ol' Jack yelped.

"Dag-nab it! Look what you made me do! Jack, you all right boy?"

The dog thumped his tail against the ground again.

Running Wolf took another step forward. The man threw his hands back up into the air and his eyes widened.

"I'm all right. I'm not hurt."

The man rested his hands on the ground and expelled a breath. He sucked air in through his nose, gave his head a shake and peered at Running Wolf.

"That your woman, boy? She's hurt, but I fixed her up a bit. Wasn't me that hurt her though, I promise. Pulled her from the river. I was just ryin' to help her. Save her. It's my mission in life."

Running Wolf shot a glance toward Kimana. Her honey-toned skin was paler even than the old man's. She looked dead. He swung his head back to the old man and narrowed his eyes.

"I tell you, boy, I was only trying to help her. I won't shoot you or nothing. Do you understand a word I'm saying to you? Look here. Watch." The man tossed his gun toward the trees. His dog wagged his tail and lunged for it.

"Jack, gol-darn-it! Stay, you crazy varmint! Sit!"

The dog skidded to a stop, gave his master a questioning look, then dropped onto his belly and whined, tail thumping wildly on the ground.

Running Wolf watched the man. He had never trusted the white man, but this one seemed harmless enough, if maybe slightly mad. His hands shook, and he was out of breath. He looked old and feeble. Not to mention more than a bit witless. How the man had dragged Kimana from the river was a mystery. Running Wolf looked at her again and felt his stomach jitter. He let his bow drop to his side and ran to her, dropping on his knees beside her motionless body. He put his hand under her nose and felt the soft whisper of breath. Her chest barely moved, but she was breathing.

She lived.

Closing his eyes, he sighed and thanked the spirits. Every muscle in his body relaxed. Laying two fingers against her neck, he felt the slow, steady beat of her heart.

Thank the spirits, she was alive. Forgetting the old man, he put his hands behind her back and lifted her limp body against his own. He drew in a deep breath and let her sweet scent wash over him. She lived. Trying not to weep in relief, he buried his face into her hair.

She lived.

***

Kimana woke to the gentle swaying and soft snort of a horse. She was a child, and her father was carrying her home while she slept in his arms. She smiled. Her body was sore everywhere, but it was warm. Lovely and warm. It felt like she was wrapped in a cocoon. She heard a soft murmuring, a voice speaking words she could not quite make out, but somehow, they soothed her.

But it was not her father's voice. But who? Had she finally died and gone to the place of the spirits? She opened her eyes and looked up into the face of Running Wolf.

Yes, of course. Running Wolf. Good. She smiled and snuggled deeper into his chest.

He stared straight ahead, his eyes dark and expression grim. He held her in his arms, safe against his chest. She tried to lift her hand, to touch his face, but it was so heavy. There was something she had to tell him, something she needed to ask, but she couldn't remember. It didn't matter.

Later. She would ask him later. Her eyelids fluttered closed and she sank back into a dreamless sleep.

***

Running Wolf shifted Kimana's weight slightly and drew her closer to his chest. The old man had taken good care of her. He'd probably saved her life. You never knew with white men. Some of them were barbarians. And some of them, like the old trapper, were good, if not a little strange.

He looked down into her face. Her colour was a bit better. Her cheeks had a bit of pink in them now. At least she didn't look like a corpse anymore. She looked like a child in his arms, so peaceful and trusting. Her eyelashes swept her cheeks, and her lips were parted slightly. When he tipped his head toward her, he could feel her soft breath on his face.

His reaction at discovering her alive surprised him. It was more than just relief. He'd felt like his life would be over if she was dead. Losing Laughing Brook had been devastating, but it had filled him with anger and the need for revenge. In a way, it had given him Kimana. Losing this woman in his arms would have destroyed his soul. Suddenly, he knew without any doubts that he wanted her for his wife. Not just because she was incredibly attractive. Not just because she would make an excellent wife, not just because it was the right thing to do, but because she was more than he'd ever hoped for. Much more. She stirred something inside him that even Laughing Brook had not stirred. She enraged him, fascinated him, made him laugh and smile. It had been years since he'd done either, until she came into his life. It made him a bit uncomfortable. He hadn't ever wanted to feel anything for a woman again, but it was obvious his heart didn't know that. His father would say the spirits knew what he needed and had guided him to her. He might be right. Since Kimana had come into his life, nothing had been the same. He didn't think he could ever go back to being the way he was before. He didn't want to. He liked who he was when he was with her.

She made him whole.

He brushed her lips with his. "Live, sweet one," he whispered, "and grow strong. I will make your life so much more than you could imagine. We will ride through the hills and sit by a stream. We will swim in the warm, bubbling pools of water, hidden deep in the mountains. We will watch the eagles soar overhead, and we will make love under the stars. You will never be alone as long as I am alive. And you will always be safe in my arms. That is my promise to you."

She sighed against his lips but did not awaken. Shifting slightly, she turned her face toward him and snuggled more deeply into his chest. Running Wolf stared down at her trusting face. With a certainty he had never felt about anything before, he knew he loved her.

He would never let her go.

His horse was sure-footed and knew his way home. They had travelled this way many times before. It would take days at this slow pace but Running Wolf didn't care. If the weather turned bad, he would build a shelter. If she woke up and wanted to ride alone, he would walk beside her. However long it took, he'd get her home, to the place she belonged. He would have Meda tend her injuries and make her strong once again. He'd announce his intentions to his father and the rest of the people. And then they could begin their lives together.

CHAPTER TWENTY

K imana opened her eyes and looked up at the stars. The sky was clear and black, and the stars twinkled and danced in the heavens. The air was crisp. Cold. She could see her breath. Yet she felt oddly warm. Something heavy lay on her stomach, and she became aware of a pressure against the left side of her body. She turned to look and saw Running Wolf staring at her. He lay motionless, his dark eyes staring into hers. His expression was serious, but a small smile touched the corner of his lips.

"How do you feel? Do you have pain?"

She shook her head, and a pain pierced her skull. "Yes. My head hurts. And my back, I think, but I'm not sure."

"Do you remember what happened?"

She looked back at the night sky and tried to remember. She'd been running away. From him. She glanced at him and looked away again. A river. She'd tried to cross the river. She narrowed her eyes, trying to remember what happened. The current was strong. Cold. Wind Dancer lost her footing. She remembered falling into the icy water and desperately trying to reach the embankment, but the memory wasn't clear. Something had hit her. A tree? That was all she remembered. From that point, it was just darkness.

And then a strange man. Whistling? Wind Dancer. Where was she? A dog. Old Jack? And nothing. Nothing.

"Where is my horse? Is she safe?"

Running Wolf stroked her head and tucked it onto his shoulder. "Tomorrow. You need to rest."

"No. Now. Tell me."

She shoved his arm away and sat up. Dizzy. So dizzy. She closed her eyes and took a deep breath. The sick sensation passed after a few moments. She opened her eyes and looked around. Running Wolf's horse stood nearby, one leg lifted. He slept. Wind Dancer wasn't with him. She wasn't there at all.

Terrified, she turned to Running Wolf and demanded an answer. "Where is she? Don't try to protect me. I need to know. Please."

He sat up and wrapped his arms around his knees. He sighed, then looked her steadily in the eyes. His face was grim, but his voice was gentle. "She's dead."

Kimana's breath hitched.

"No," she whispered.

"I found her on the edge of the river. She was barely alive. I couldn't save her. No one could have saved her."

She turned away so he wouldn't see her tears. It was her fault. If she hadn't been so reckless... Wind Dancer hadn't wanted to cross the river, she'd known how dangerous it was, but she had forced her.

"Tell me," she tried to keep her voice even, but she choked on the words "Tell me if she was in pain."

"I don't think so. The water would have numbed her. It was very cold." She felt him touch her shoulder and she jerked away. "Kimana, it's not your fault."

"How can you say that? I sent her into the water. I killed her. Me."

"Stop. It's done."

How much more could she lose before it broke her? When would it end? She wanted to blame Running Wolf. If he hadn't attacked her people and stolen her from her home, Wind Dancer would still be alive. If he hadn't called her a whore, her beautiful mare would be safe in her enclosure, huddled next to her companions for warmth. But she knew that was foolish. He hadn't made her force Wind Dancer to plunge into the river. It was her choice. She alone was responsible.

"You said she was barely alive. Then you were with her when

she died?"

She thought she saw something cross his face. Regret? Pain? Guilt? It was as if he hadn't wanted her to ask that question. He looked away. Just when she thought he was going to refuse to answer, he turned back. "She would not have survived. I did what had to be done."

The tears were flowing freely now, and she didn't care. "Did you hurt her?"

With the speed of a wild mountain cat, he was on his knees before her, holding her cheeks firmly in his hands. "Do you think I would cause her to suffer more than she was? No, Kimana. I did not hurt her. She knew, maybe more than I did, what needed to be done. I released her spirit, eased her suffering. Will you blame me for that? Will you scream at me? Hit me? If that's what you need to do, then do it. If you can't forgive me, I will accept that. But don't accuse me of causing suffering to such a brave and beautiful animal. Never do that."

Sobbing, she let herself be pulled against his chest. He ran his hands down her hair, and down her back, murmuring against her ear, soft, meaningless words that were meant to comfort.

Running Wolf held her close, rocking gently. He knew the pain she was feeling, the confusion and anger. He knew she blamed herself. And he knew nothing he could say would change that.

Only time would heal her.

No, he knew better than that. Not even time could take away the pain. At best, it would only dim it somewhat. But it would stay with her always. Grief was like that. You never healed from it. No matter what people said, time did not heal grief. You just learned to live with it, that was all. He stroked her back as she cried in his arms. Her tears undid him. She was always so strong. A fighter. Through everything she'd been through, he'd never seen her really give in to her heart ache. A few stray tears. The ghost of sorrow in her eyes. Never more than that. But now she leaned against him, crying against his chest, broken by the death of a beloved mare.

He hadn't wanted to tell her, had hoped she would assume the horse was dead when he found her, but when she looked him in the eye, he knew he couldn't lie to her.

If he hadn't been so harsh, she never would have run. He knew it, but he couldn't change it. Eventually, she grew quiet, and only an occasional shudder went through her body. He wished he could erase the last couple of days. See her smile. Hear her laugh. He wanted her to trust him, to see what he felt for her, and discover if she could feel the same.

He loved her.

He knew that now.

He wasn't sure at what point his feelings had changed. It was possible he had loved her from the moment he hauled her up off the ground and looked into her haunted eyes so many moons ago. There had been something about her, even then, that touched his soul, made him respect her. Made him want to protect her, care for her, be her friend. And more. He loved her spirit, her defiance. Her strength and determination not to give in to her enemy. Her sense of duty and honour. The responsibility she felt for her people. All of these things spoke to him. But now, at this moment, it was not the strength he saw within her that touched his soul, made him ache deep inside to show her he loved her. It was her sorrow, her softness, her sweet vulnerability that called out to the deepest place in his heart. His heart ached for her. If only he could take away her pain, he would. Before today, he'd wanted to find a way to make her forgive him, to somehow make up for the past, for what he had stolen from her. But now, all he wanted was to protect her, to give her some of the joy he had stolen away, to make her smile and laugh again. All he wanted was to love her. And hopefully, for her to love him in return.

He ran his fingers down her back, feeling the heat of her body through her robe. By all the spirits, he wanted her so much.

Kimana didn't know how long she leaned against him, or when her tears finally stopped. She wasn't sure at what point his soothing, comforting strokes changed in their rhythm, their intensity, but she suddenly found her heart pounding in her chest, her body responding to his touch, craving it. He whispered against her ear, but she didn't know what he was saying. She didn't care. She wanted to forget, just for a while. She wanted him. His body was warm, but his hands felt hot, so hot. She shuddered and snuggled closer to him, desperately needing more.

Turning her head, she lifted her arms and wrapped them around his neck. Pulling his head down, she laid her lips against his. She felt his body tense against hers, then his arms came around her back and pulled her closer. His mouth was hot, insistent. She wondered briefly what she was doing. Just days ago, he had called her a whore for responding to his advances. It had been like plunging into an icy stream in late spring. It had hurt, embarrassed her. Angered her. But now, she was the aggressor. She was the one demanding, and he was the one responding to her touch.

It terrified her.

It empowered her.

He lowered her onto the soft fur and untied her robe, stopping to stare with a helpless expression at her naked flesh. She shivered as the night air caressed her skin. His eyes changed as he looked at her, darkened. And then, for a moment she was overcome with shyness. Never before had a man looked at her this way. Would he think she was beautiful? Would he compare her to other women? To Silver Fox? Then he raised his eyes to hers.

"I'm sorry. This isn't right. I want you more than anything, Kimana, but not like this."

Fear and shock settled into her stomach in a cold, brittle ball. She reached over and yanked a fur on top of her. He sat back on his heels and watched her as she tried to hide her humiliation, but her feelings were not as easily covered as her body. She knew she couldn't keep her shame from his eyes.

"Get away from me."

"Don't be angry. Please."

"You're saying you don't want me."

"No. I do want you. But not like this. Not here. Not now. This isn't real. You don't want to make love. You're looking for a way to work off your anger and pain over Wind Dancer."

Furious because she knew he was right, at least in part, enraged because he had the gall to say it, she stoked the fires of her anger in an effort to stop the tears. She glared at him. "Don't tell me what I want. You don't know me."

"I think I do, but that's not the point. You're angry. You're hurting. I'm available." His voice was so reasonable. So infuriatingly calm.

"Available? How dare you. Would I let your father touch me this way? You're saying I'd lie with anyone who was convenient."

"That's not what I'm saying."

148

"Then what? I know you've gone off into the bushes with Silver Fox. And that's okay? That's all right. Why? Because you're a man? Or maybe you think that I'm a whore, too, and that's why you don't want me. Well, maybe you're right. Maybe I did want you just because you were available. Thank the spirits we stopped when we did. I must be mad. I'd never let you touch me if I were in my right mind. Maybe that bump on the head addled my wits."

"Don't. You're nothing like her. I never should have said that. I'm sorry."

He reached out to touch her, but she jerked away.

"Listen to me, Kimana. I just don't want to do anything to dishonour you. Something you might regret. We've already done too much, gone too far. I don't want to make love to you, Kimana. Not yet. Not until we're married."

She went still as she stared at him in disbelief. Married! He assumed she would marry him? Without even asking her? That might be how the Blackfoot did things, but it wasn't her way. If he thought he could take her by the hair and drag her into his teepee, pound his fists on his chest and announce to the world she was his woman, he could forget it. She had the right to refuse. And she would.

"I won't marry you."

"You will."

"I won't!"

"Kimana think about what we've done. We have a duty..."

"Duty? Duty! I will not marry you. I will never marry you! How could you think I would ever be your wife? I would rather eat fresh moose dung than marry you. Don't ever touch me again."

She flopped down onto a fur and shut her eyes, willing him to go away. How could she have been so brazen? Why had she let him touch her like that? She could feel her cheeks flaming.

For a long time, there was no sound. Then she heard him stand up and walk away. His stallion snorted softly, and she thought she could hear him murmuring to the animal. She strained to hear what he was saying, but his voice was too soft. Maybe he would leave her here, ride off into the night, and abandon her.

Then she heard him lay down a short distance away. She

listened to him breathing, and to the sounds of the night until her eyes grew heavy.

She didn't understand why she felt so sad.

***

Jonesy stared at the fire. Something was bothering him. Something just wasn't right. He couldn't quite put his finger on it, but it bothered him just the same. He rubbed his thumb over the stone he held in his hand and continued to watch the flames. 'Ol Jack whined and thumped his tail.

"I know. I feel it too. There was somethin' about that girl. Seems to me I should remember, but I can't. It'll come to me. It'll come."

The dog rested his head on his master's knee, stared up into his eyes and thumped his tail. Jones shivered. It was getting cold again.

***

Running Wolf opened his eyes to a world that sparkled and shimmered in the cold light of the sun. Spiky hoar frost clung to the trees and fresh snow glittered on the ground. He tugged his fur closer around him. Overnight, the temperature had plummeted.

The sky was clear, but it seemed washed of colour. In the trees to his right, a small herd of elk was busy tearing strips of bark from the aspen trees, exposing the sweet green flesh beneath. Their winter coats were thick and heavy, and their tails flicked rhythmically as they went about their morning meal. Their bellies were getting heavy with pregnancy. In another two or three moons, their babies would be taking their first wobbly steps.

A massive bull stepped through the trees and stared at Running Wolf, his head erect and majestic, his large eyes soft and liquid brown. He had an impressive rack of antlers, with several branches, and at least seven points on each side. Soon, the bull would shed them, and about the same time his babies were born, the antlers would start to grow back, covered in a soft, dense fur. By fall, they would be even more impressive than they were now, having shed most of their smooth covering.

Running Wolf smiled in admiration. The bull was magnificent, the undisputed lord of his forest.

They watched each other for a while, the bull twitching and turning his ears as he stared at Running Wolf. Perhaps, deciding not to risk staying any longer in the presence of the humans, he snorted loudly, tossed his head and whirled back toward the trees. His herd bolted away, churning up clumps of snow. The bull gave Running Wolf one last look before following them.

Running Wolf raised himself on one arm and watched as the herd of elk fled into the forest. Seeing them like that was a gift. He turned toward Kimana, wondering if she was awake, hoping she had been fortunate enough to share the experience, but she was still asleep, her coppery hair falling like water over her face.

As if sensing his stare, she sighed and rolled onto her stomach, turning her face away. It was cold, but clear, and traveling would be good today. He hated to wake her. Give her a little longer, he thought, and laid back down, resting his head on his arms.

He had almost taken her last night. In her grief, she would have been willing, but he knew she would regret it. And if she did, there was no way she would ever accept him as her husband. That tweaked his pride a little, he had to admit. Maybe more than a little. Some part of him had been sure she would say yes. That she would have been grateful to have his protection and the honoured position as the wife of the chief's son.

He rolled his eyes. Meda would say he had an exceedingly high opinion of himself. She would probably say it while boxing his ears, just to show him put him in his place.

He chuckled. She was a feisty old thing, but he adored her. He'd never tell her that, though. Her head might swell and burst open, and what good would she be then?

The old woman was more like a mother to him than an aunt. He wondered if his father would ever talk her into sharing a mat with him on a permanent basis. The chief would probably be shocked that his son knew about their interest in each other, and their regular, albeit clandestine visits to each other's mats. They had been very discreet, but there were some things you couldn't hide.

Kimana moaned in her sleep.

So, she'd rather eat moose dung than marry him? They'd see about that.

CHAPTER TWENTY-ONE

Kimana's back ached. The ride back to the Blackfoot village was long and tedious, and once again she was forced to be on a horse with this insufferable man. But at least this time she wasn't in the humiliating position of being held in front of him like a child.

Not that being behind was much better. In order not to fall off, she had to keep her arms around his waist.

It was awkward.

Somehow, she had to hold on to him without leaning her chest against his back. Some of her soreness was due to her ordeal in the river but sitting like this for hours at a time certainly didn't help.

Her head still hurt. Her bottom was sore. Her nerves were raw. If they didn't stop soon, she was going to shove him right off his damned horse and leave him to rot in the snow.

As if he sensed her thoughts, he brought the stallion to a stop and vaulted off, turning to her with his arms outstretched and a small smile playing at the corners of his mouth.

"I thought we could rest a while."

"I don't need to rest."

Stupid! Stupid woman. Why did she allow him to bring out the worst in her? She wanted nothing more than to climb down and stretch her legs, but his smile was so infuriating, as if he knew she was sore all over and needed to stop. She refused to give him that satisfaction. She could ride as long as he could.

Longer.

By all the spirits in the mountains and on the plains, she was so sore.

"Well, you might not need to rest, but I could use a break. Stay up there if you want to." He shrugged, an annoying, who cares sort of lift of the shoulders that had her gritting her teeth. He flashed a smile - all teeth and charm - and turned away, sauntering into the trees as if he was going on an afternoon stroll.

"Fine!" She yelled after his retreating form. She looked at the ground. It seemed so far away. Did she even have the strength to climb off this massive horse? Maybe she'd just slide off, drop onto the snow. Roll over. Get onto her knees and try to stand that way. Maybe she'd just crawl. It would be easier than trying to walk.

Her shoulders slumped as she considered her options. Too exhausted to give it much thought, she stretched out and lay on her stomach, dangling her arms down the horse's flanks.

"Here. Let me help." He'd come as quietly as a lynx and was lifting her off his horse before she could protest. "Hold onto my arm. We'll walk a while. Try to get some warmth into your legs."

She let him lead her around the horse in ever-increasing circles, his steps shortened to match her own. Why was he being so nice all of a sudden? Maybe he thought she was addled, her brains scrambled by the bump on her head. It didn't matter. It felt good to walk, and she was warming up a little. She looked down at his hand, and for the first time, noticed signs of a recent injury. His knuckles were raw and bruised. She grabbed his fingers and gave him a suspicious scowl.

"What happened?"

He looked at her in surprise, then glanced down. "It's nothing."

Why were men so infuriating? Why did they refuse to answer simple questions? "It's not nothing. You're hurt."

He refused to meet her eyes and tucked his hand into his robe. She dug her heels into the snow and refused to move another step until he answered. "What happened? Tell me."

He paused, looked at her, then nodded. "All right. When I left you the other night, before you ran away, I sort of... ran into a tree."

"You what?"

"I hit a tree."

"Weren't you watching where you were going?"

A corner of his mouth twitched, and she could swear he looked embarrassed. "I hit the tree. With my fist. The tree won."

"Why would you do something like that?" She stared at him, not understanding. Then she thought about his words, and realization hit. "Oh. Never mind."

"It's not what you think."

"Isn't it? You were furious with me when you left."

"No, Kimana. No, I wasn't. I was furious, but not with you."

"I don't understand."

"I treated you badly. Said things I shouldn't have said. I'm sorry. I was angry. But not at you. I was angry with myself."

"But, you said I was acting like... like the village whore."

His hands came up and cupped her cheeks. He turned her head so she was looking directly into his eyes. Her breath caught.

"I didn't mean that. I mean, I meant it, but I didn't. I don't want people talking about you. You deserve better than that. You deserve to be treated with honour. If I had lain with you, you would be dishonoured, and I can't let that happen. Won't."

He turned his right hand and ran the back of his fingers down her cheekbone and over her chin, then back up again. He swept her hair off her face and tucked it behind her ear.

"You were meant for me. No, don't say anything." He laid his fingers gently over her lips. "Just listen. I know you're angry. Confused. I don't want to see you get hurt. I want to marry you. Then no one can ever say you're anything less than respectable."

So, his offer of marriage had been just a gesture. He was trying to be honourable. Save her reputation. She didn't know why that hurt so much, why it made her want to cry. Two Hawks had wanted to marry her for reasons more acceptable than that, though that hardly mattered now. He may not have loved her, but it would have been a good match for both of them. Few people married for love. Most married for convenience. But everything had changed. She was no longer expected to make a good match. She didn't have a father to answer to. If she married - if she ever married - it would be for love, not because it was the right - or expected - thing to do.

"I'm sorry. I won't marry you. I don't want to marry anyone."

"Damn it, Kimana. You will marry me. You can't continue to live in our lodge and not get married. People are already talking."

"I don't care. I'll move out. I'll speak to your father. He'll understand. He'll help me find another family who could use an extra pair of hands. And you can't tell me what to do."

She was only vaguely aware the tears forming in her eyes. She couldn't deny she had feelings for him. Feelings that confused and frightened her. But she knew he didn't share them. He cared about her, but that wasn't enough. She wanted to be loved. Needed. Respected. She wanted him to feel the same passion for her he had once felt for Laughing Brook. But that wasn't possible. He'd made it very clear how he had felt about his young bride. And he'd made it clear he would never give his heart again. Not to her. Not to anyone.

"Damn it, Kimana. You're not listening to me."

"No. Please don't say anymore. I just want to go home now."

She pulled out of his arms and walked back to the horse, her back straight. She didn't bother to wipe away the tears that now spilled down her cheeks. She'd let him see too much already.

155

CHAPTER TWENTY-TWO

K imana and Running Wolf rode into the village and were greeted by silent, curious stares. No one spoke to them. It was a marked contrast to the first time she had ridden into the village. Her own people stopped what they were doing and gave her openly disapproving looks, their mouths turned down in displeasure. Were they angry she'd left, or disappointed she'd come home? She knew she hadn't made things easier for them, with her talk of escaping. And Utina was particularly furious with her. Had she told the other women what Kimana had said the other night? Had she shared her opinion about the morality of Kimana sharing a lodge with Running Wolf?

If so, it was no surprise the women looked so disgusted. It wouldn't matter what the truth was. All that mattered was what they perceived as truth.

She hated gossip.

Maybe Running Wolf was right about her reputation. She would have to speak to Black Eagle right away and ask him to find her a new family to live with. But as she watched the way the people looked at her, she knew it would be difficult to find anyone who would take her in.

She wanted to bury her face in Running Wolf's back, to hide her shame from the people. But what did she have to be ashamed of? She straightened her back and looked the women boldly in the eyes, one by one, as they made their way to the horse enclosure. Each woman turned away as her eyes met theirs. All except one.

Silver Fox watched from the flap of her lodge with a narrow, hostile expression. When their eyes met, she smirked and tossed her head, then went inside her teepee.

Running Wolf brought his stallion to a halt, climbed down and offered his arms to Kimana. She glanced around, feeling self-conscious. Running Wolf lifted his eyebrows and turned his head to see what she was looking at. The women whipped their heads around and busied themselves with their tasks. She took his arms and let him lower her to the ground with as much dignity as she could. She knew the people still watched her, though they were being a little more subtle. Antagonizing her was one thing. Making the chief's son angry was another. Maybe she should consider his offer after all. No. That wasn't the answer. It might be the easy thing to do in the short term, but she wouldn't be happy. Not knowing that he ached for Laughing Brook. That every time he looked at her, he would be thinking of someone else. It was best to get out and away from his constant presence as soon as possible. She looked at him for a minute, letting her eyes take in the details of his face, his strong chin and sculpted cheekbones, his straight nose and sensuous lips. His eyes. She could lose herself in them if she wasn't careful.

"Thank you. I must speak with your father."

"Kimana..."

"No, please don't. I have to go."

She hurried toward the chief's lodge, but she could feel his stare.

***

Chief Black Eagle puffed on his pipe and blew fragrant smoke into the air. He sat on a mat, legs crossed, with one arm resting on a knee.

"Hmm," he grunted.

He took another puff, blew out the smoke and watched it swirl up toward the smoke hole.

"Hmm."

Kimana kneeled on the floor and watched him, silent, waiting for a response to her request. So far, he had said nothing, only grunted thoughtfully, and kept his eyes on the blue eddies of smoke that drifted through the teepee. She was usually comfortable in his presence, but she felt as nervous as a young girl on her first vision quest. Black Eagle said nothing, but she was worried she'd offended or disappointed him.

Just when she thought her knees would go numb if she didn't move, he laid his pipe down and turned to look at her.

"This thing you ask of me is not an easy thing to grant. Why do you run from your problems, instead of facing them like the little warrior I know you to be? Why do you not stand and fight? You came to us, a frightened girl, but you stood proud and tall. Your months with us have turned you into a woman, but now you kneel with head bowed and beg for me to take away your suffering. Do you not remember the story of the little mouse? If the mouse had run away, the moon would still be bound, and the Earth's creatures would not be able to travel by night. Do you not have the courage to face the words of other people?"

She stared at him, mute with shock. She'd expected understanding, not judgment. Not a lecture on courage.

"Is it true, then? Has my son dishonoured you?"

"No. We have not lain together."

"Then you must hold on to that truth. What others believe matters little."

"Not to me. And not to Running Wolf. People are talking. He told me this himself. Please. Please let me go to another lodge."

"Hmm." He picked up his pipe and turned it over in his hands, examining the intricate carvings. "I will order a meeting of the council. I will ask if anyone will take you into their lodge." He paused and gave her a sharp look. "But you must be prepared. I will speak to the men, but it will be up to their women. I can not order any one to take you into their home."

"I understand. All I want is a choice. The right to make my own choice."

"And have you given thought to your choices? Right now, you have a choice. You may stay, hold your head high, and have the freedom of being an honoured member of my household. If you are taken into another home, you may lose the freedoms you have become used to. I will no longer be able to offer you my protection or the benefits that come from living in my lodge. Do you understand?"

She bent her head. "Yes. I do. Thank you."

"You are like the butterfly. You like to live in the moment.

That's obvious by this quick decision. But, like the butterfly, you also need your freedom. What will you do if you no longer have it? Your spirit will be crushed. This is what I fear for you."

"I would rather lose my freedom than my pride."

He grunted. "Yes. It is unfortunate. Pride alone will not give you peace." He waved his arm, dismissing her. "Go now. I have much to consider."

***

Running Wolf struggled to contain his fury as he listened to man after man tell the chief they were certain their women would not take Kimana into their homes. They gave no reasons, just expressed their doubts in a way that left no doubt they had no intentions of even asking. It didn't make sense to him, this rage. He should be glad no one wanted her. Instead, he felt offended. Warrior after warrior shook their heads, often after glancing his way. What were they thinking? Did they share the opinions of their women? Did they think Kimana was disgraced, used by him, discarded, and willing to spread her legs for any man who looked at her?

It was his fault.

He should have insisted she marry him. Just by doing this, asking these men to take her into their homes, it sent the wrong message.

They would think he had grown tired of her and was casting her off.

They couldn't be more wrong.

But it was not the sort of thing men spoke of. They did not engage in the same kind of gossip that seemed to occupy so much of the women's time. Instead, they watched silently, and kept their own counsel. At times like this, he wished they could be more like their women. Speak their minds and get it all out into the open where he could dispel them of whatever misconceptions they had.

But he could not approach it openly. It just was not done.

The silence grew uncomfortable. Fire Dancer cleared his throat and reached for the talking stick. He thumped it once on the ground. Every eye turned toward him as he began to speak.

"Chief Black Eagle. My respect for you is great. If you would have the girl in your own lodge, she is worthy to live in mine. My woman has often said she likes the girl's spirit. Perhaps Singing

Deer would allow her to come into our home. I will make your request known to her."

Running Wolf caught his breath as his belly jerked. The last thing Kimana needed was to be taken into Silver Fox's lodge.

Why was she so stubborn? Why would she not marry him and have done with this foolishness?

Stands Alone stood and took the talking stick. He looked around nervously and thumped the talking stick on the ground.

"I was wondering..." He cleared his throat. "I was wondering, Chief Black Eagle, if I might ask for her to be my wife. It seems no one else wants her, and I could use a woman in my lodge. Besides," he continued, his face turning pink, "It is time I got married. And she is very beautiful. I would be honoured to do this thing."

Running Wolf's vision went blurry. He wanted to slam the impertinent little whelp into the ground and pound on his face until it no longer resembled anything human.

"May I ask your permission to ask her to marry me?"

***

Black Eagle shot a quick glance at his son. It was obvious his son was enraged. It looked like it was taking all his strength not to attack the young brave.

He looked thoughtfully at the young warrior. Stands Alone was a good man. Young, but eager to prove his worth. He had done well in recent battles and hunts and would be a good provider. But he was young. Inexperienced. Eighteen summers was not long enough for maturity. And Kimana needed someone mature. Someone who could accept and appreciate her wildness, but not crush her spirit. Someone who was her equal.

Stands Alone might acquire those qualities eventually. Black Eagle looked at him critically. Would Kimana find him acceptable? He was tall and strong. Good-looking, he supposed, if that was important, and it seemed to be, to the young women these days. What could it hurt? He would give his permission for the young man to court her and see what came of it. If Running Wolf didn't like it, he could court her as well. Ultimately, Kimana's future would be in her own hands.

So, it seemed that she would have a choice after all. He nodded his head. That was good.

"You have my permission to court her, Stands Alone, but the final decision lies within her own heart. In the meantime, if Singing Deer will allow the girl to go into her home, that is what will happen. Now, it is time to smoke."

Stands Alone blew out a breath and looked around the lodge, grinning like a fool.

Running Wolf scowled fiercely.

Black Eagle hid a smile behind his pipe.

CHAPTER TWENTY-THREE

Jonesy shuffled over the stream bed, yanking on his mule's reins.

"Get a move on, Bessie, ya ornery old coot. I said move!"

The mule stretched her neck forward and set her hooves firmly into the ground, nearly sending Jonesy flying onto his backside.

"Dang it! Dag nab it, Bessie!"

He flung the reins onto the ground and set his hands on his hips. "We ain't got all day ya know. I want to catch them Injuns before they move camp. Might be too late as it is."

He marched up to the mule and took the sad looking face in his hands. The more determined he was, the more stubborn she became. Maybe he'd try something different. Maybe he'd bribe her. That was one way to get a female with her mind all set to come to your way of thinking, sure enough. "Come on, Bessie. It's not much longer. Look at 'Ol Jack. He's not complainin'. Just a while longer, and I promise, I'll give ye a nice treat."

The mule brayed, tossed her head, and still refused to budge.

"Well, paint me purple, I ain't seen a mule as stubborn in all my live long days." Jonesy spit on the grass and plopped himself down, holding his head in his hands.

"We've got to get movin'. I got to talk to that Two Hawks fella. Whoo-ee, won't he be surprised! I just might get me a reward after all!"

'Ol Jack barked delightedly and wagged his tail. He loped around behind the mule and gave her a nip on the hind legs.

Bessie's left leg shot backwards, but 'Ol Jack scooted out of the way just in time to avoid being brained. The old mule was crankier than a bear fresh out of hibernation, but she lurched forward. Jones scrambled to his feet and grabbed the reins just as she shot past him. He had to run a little to get ahead of her, but he grinned and hooted. They just might make it after all. 'Ol Jack tore past them, his tongue lolling out, grinning.

CHAPTER TWENTY-FOUR

The people bustled around the camp, preparing for their first move of the season. Spring was right around the corner, and soon they would need to hunt for buffalo. The people were treating her differently. Or maybe she just felt different. She was still living in Black Eagle's lodge. She knew the council had met, and that no one had offered their home. Silver Fox's mother had said she would consider it for a while, but no invitation had been extended yet. In a way, nothing had changed, and yet, nothing was the same. She glanced up at the young warrior who strolled next to her. Stands Alone looked at her every now and then, blushed, and looked away.

She'd never seen a man blush before. He was very sweet.

Since the council meeting, he'd been openly courting her. Before that day, he'd spoken with her only occasionally, but there had been many times over the winter she had felt his eyes on her. Running Wolf ignored her completely, which suited her very well. His proposal had obviously been made in some moment of madness, and he was glad to be rid of the responsibility of defending her honour. It didn't explain the black looks he gave Stands Alone when the young man rapped on the hide of their lodge. It didn't explain why he snarled at him.

It was almost as if he was jealous, but that was ridiculous. She really didn't want to think about why his moods bothered her. And she definitely didn't want to think about the fact that her eyes sought him out every time she walked about the camp.

It was just that he was so annoying.

Anyone would give a lot of thought to someone who made their lives unbearable. Yes, that was what it was. She wasn't looking for him. She was just trying to know where he was so she could stay out of his way. She smiled to herself. That made perfect sense. As for his moods, well it didn't matter. He was obviously in a mood about something, and it was no concern of hers. She continued to walk with Stands Alone, circling the perimeter of the camp. Tomorrow, the village would be completely torn down, and they would begin their migration into the foothills. There was much to do, but for now, she was enjoying the company of this handsome, attentive young brave. It was nice to be in the company of someone who was cheerful. Someone who obviously wanted to be in her company. She'd been lonely for so long. Utina still wasn't speaking to her. Most of the other women weren't either. But at least they weren't whispering about her anymore.

That was probably thanks to the young man who walked next to her. His interest in her - the fact that he was courting her - and Running Wolf's complete and utter lack of interest, gave her more respectability than she'd had before. She didn't think she was really interested in Stands Alone in that way, but it was a nice feeling to be wanted.

And it was good to have a friend.

It had been almost a week, and they'd walked together every day. Sometimes, they just walked around the camp, and sometimes, they walked into the forest. He didn't talk very much. He was obviously painfully shy.

It didn't bother her.

She liked the quiet. And she liked him. She knew he wanted to marry her, but she wasn't ready to make that commitment. She needed time to get to know him. Chief Black Eagle said she could continue to stay in his lodge until she made a choice. There was no hurry. She cast a quick glance at Stands Alone and smiled. He was strutting. Actually strutting. Like a pheasant for his hen. His shoulders were straight, and his back was erect. His arms swung back and forth, and he looked inordinately pleased with himself as he looked around the camp.

His arm brushed against hers and she looked up at him as he came to an abrupt stop. He stared down at her, his lips parted, his eyes a little dreamy.

"Is something wrong?"

He jumped a bit at her question, blushed again, and shook his head.

"No. I just wondered... may I, would you, is it all right if I held your hand?"

He was so sweet when he stammered. So much the warrior, and so much the little boy still. She smiled at him and nodded, holding out her hand. His face went scarlet, but he reached out and took her hand firmly in his. As they continued to walk, he swung their arms. A grin spread once again over his face. She looked away and smiled, thinking how adorable and sweet he was, and allowed him to set their pace.

***

Running Wolf stood just inside the trees, watching Kimana and Stands Alone. His hands curled into fists. He felt a little ashamed, lurking in the trees, spying on them as they sauntered around the camp like two love-sick pups. When Kimana smiled at the boy, Running Wolf wanted to hit the nearest tree. It was sickening. Pathetic. Stupid.

He'd watched them for almost a week now, walking back and forth, talking, smiling. He was so annoyed by their display that he'd hardly eaten for days.

Stands Alone reached for her hand. Running Wolf chuckled. Now he'd find out. Kimana wouldn't stand for that nonsense. His mouth dropped open as he watched her smile and let the young man tuck her hand into his. Fickle, faithless woman!

He wanted to burst through the trees and knock the impertinent pup flat on his back. Little troublemaker. He was barely a man. He had no battle scars, no glory, hardly any feathers at all. What could she see in him? He sneered. Was it his pretty face? His soft lips? The boy had a face like a woman, all smooth and perfect, as unblemished as a newborn babe's bottom.

Kimana didn't need a child. She needed a man. She needed him, Running Wolf.

What was his father thinking of?

Rustling in the trees took his attention away from the young couple. He felt tugging on his arm. He looked down into the face of a little boy. What was his name? Small Beaver? Little Beaver?

Little Otter. That was it. He was one of Kimana's people. The boy looked at him with huge eyes.

He was used to children, but not really comfortable with them. It had been a long time since he was that young, and for many years he had focused on hunting and warring, not on playing with children. But he knew enough to realize his scowl might seem frightening. He made an effort to soften his features and tried out a smile. He was afraid it came out more like a grimace, but it was something, anyway.

"What can I do for you? Little Otter, isn't it?"

The boy nodded, but he didn't speak.

"Well?" He sounded gruff. He knew it. But the child didn't shy away from him, he just kept staring up with those guileless eyes. Running Wolf lowered himself to one knee and looked the child in the eye. Maybe his height intimidated the boy.

"What is it?"

"Why is Kimana holding that man's hand?"

Running Wolf's mouth twisted. Count on a child to ask a question no adult would. He flicked a glance toward the two and grunted. "I suppose because she wants him to."

"But it's you she likes best."

Running Wolf looked at the child in surprise. "Why would you... how do you know that?"

The child smiled at him, an innocent smile that promised unwavering truth. "She looks at you all the time. Even when you aren't looking at her. I've seen it. I have. That's what grown-ups do when they like each other best."

"Do they now?" He looked at Kimana again. She was holding the pup's hand, but she certainly wasn't looking at him. She was craning her neck all over the place as if she was looking for something, for someone, else.

He grinned, suddenly feeling a whole lot happier. And a whole lot hungrier. Hungrier than he'd felt for days. Weeks, maybe.

He laughed, and swung the boy into the air, depositing him on his shoulders. Little Otter squealed and giggled. He patted the boy's leg. "Come on then, let's find something to eat. With all the women in this camp, there must be someone cooking something."

***

Kimana turned at the sound of the giggling. She stared in

167

disbelief as Running Wolf and Little Otter came through the trees, grinning like crazy fools. Little Otter perched on Running Wolf's shoulders, hanging onto the top of the warrior's head. He swung his legs madly as if he were urging on a horse. But what amazed her the most was Running Wolf himself. He was smiling. Really smiling.

It transformed him.

She stared, stricken by the sight of the man and the boy, stricken by the joy that was all over Running Wolf's face. He had never looked so glorious. His rare smiles always transformed his face, but this was different. He was beaming. Positively beaming. She didn't think he even liked children, and here he was giving Little Otter a ride on his shoulders like they were old friends. And he looked so - amazing.

She watched their journey across the camp, even more astonished when Running Wolf broke into a trot and let out a whinny like a horse, tossing his head as he galloped around. Little Otter shrieked with laughter, delighted with the antics. Running Wolf laughed as well and grinned up at the wee boy.

Kimana felt a tugging on her hand, and she looked down, confused. She fought a surge of annoyance. Stands Alone was trying to pull her away, but she dug her heels into the ground and refused to move. Couldn't he see she was busy?

"Kimana, come on."

She frowned and shook her head, never taking her eyes off Running Wolf and Little Otter as they crossed the camp, seemingly oblivious to their audience.

"Kimana."

She yanked her hand away from his and swung around, placing her fists on her hips. His whining was getting on her nerves. He didn't own her. How dare he insist she come away?

"What is wrong with you? I'm busy. Can't you see that?"

He looked so shocked, so devastated, she felt a little guilty. She was, after all, out with him for the afternoon. He deserved her attention. But his pleading had to stop. "I'm sorry. I was distracted."

He stood stiffly now, and his features hardened a bit. His boyish face looked more like a man's suddenly, and she knew she'd offended him. She really didn't want to hurt him. She just didn't know if she was ready for a commitment, or ready for the possessiveness he was already displaying. She needed time.

She placed a hand on his chest and gave him a gentle smile. "Please forgive me. I'm tired. That's all. I still haven't fully recovered from the river. I think I need to rest."

He glanced toward the retreating figures of Running Wolf and the boy and nodded. "I understand. I shouldn't have kept you out so long. May I escort you back to your lodge?"

She nodded, glad he seemed to understand.

They walked back to her teepee, but this time, she kept her hands folded in front of her. She didn't want to hold his hand. She didn't want him to assume more than she was ready for. They reached the flap, and she turned toward him with a smile.

He shuffled his feet, looking as if he wanted to ask something. She waited.

"May I walk with you tomorrow?" he asked. "During the move?"

"Is that allowed?"

He gave her a sheepish grin. "Not really. But no one will say anything. Hopefully."

If he wanted to risk being chastised, it was up to him. She looked away and nodded. It couldn't hurt, as long as she kept some distance between them. He bent his head as if to kiss her cheek, and she backed up. His eyes seemed to darken and he tipped his head, then spun on a heel and strode away. She stared after him, afraid she had just given him his final lesson on becoming a man.

CHAPTER TWENTY-FIVE

Kimana pushed a strand of hair from her face and glanced up at the sun. They'd been on the move since daybreak, threading their way through thick stands of forest, emerging onto the prairies a short time ago. Wind chased them from the west. It was a good thing they were going east. At least they weren't walking into it. That would have made the long journey unbearable. Prairie grass bent in submission to the wind, flattening against the still damp earth.

With the strength of the wind, it wouldn't take long to dry the land.

Her hair whipped around her. She regretted not braiding it before they left. Perhaps, when they stopped for a rest.

Makwai loped along a short distance away from the procession. So far, she kept pace with them, never coming closer, but never going farther away either.

Kimana still wasn't comfortable with the wolf, but she was getting used to her. She couldn't remember the last time Makwai growled at her, but she was unnerved by how closely the animal watched her - especially since the incident in the river. It was unnerving.

As if sensing her thoughts, Makwai swung her head toward Kimana and gave her a huge, canine grin.

Earlier in the day, Meda told her it would take several days to reach their destination – a buffalo jump used by the Blackfoot since the beginning of time. Scouts had already been sent ahead to search for a herd to coax into the drive lanes.

Overhead, the sky was bright, dotted with small, puffy clouds that stretched endlessly toward the horizon. Two black ravens hovered in the air, their wings outstretched and perfectly still as they road on unseen currents. It reminded Kimana of the eagle she'd seen the day she'd fled the Blackfoot camp, and how it seemed to be telling her to turn back toward the mountains.

Toward the Blackfoot people.

The ravens rose and fell in an endless dance, following the people as they made their way toward the buffalo killing ground. A four-day journey, Meda had told her, longer if the wind shifted and was no longer at their backs.

The Blackfoot didn't waste a single step. They knew exactly where they were going and how to get there. Kimana had never seen such organization.

The camp had been torn down that morning with speed and precision. Now, the people walked in three long lines toward their destination. In the first were the wives and older women. They carried packs on their backs, and escorted travois filled with teepees and other camp possessions. Many of the women were fortunate enough to have dogs or horses to pull them, but some didn't. The smallest children sat upon the contraptions, too excited to fall asleep. Soon, she was sure, their little heads would start to nod, and they would snuggle deep into their soft furs.

Kimana wasn't married, but as the only woman of her lodge, she was required to walk with the married women, guiding a horse-pulled travois laden with the trappings of their home. She was glad she had a horse to help with the work. Pulling a heavily laden travois for hours was exhausting. She was already sweating, and they'd only travelled half a day. In the second line were the young men and unmarried women. In the third line, older children giggled and laughed, accompanied by the old men.

The warriors brought up the rear, sitting tall upon their horses, carrying only their weapons and solemn faces.

Singing Deer walked in front of her, her shoulders slumped as she guided her horse. She carried a large pack across her shoulders, and her back bent under the weight of their belongings.

Kimana glanced toward the middle line and located Silver Fox. She laughed and chattered with the other young women, sparing not a single glance for her overburdened mother. Kimana pulled her horse out of the line and dropped the rope. She hurried up to Singing Deer, ignoring the curious stares of the other women. When she reached Singing Deer's side, she touched her on the shoulder.

The older woman looked at her in surprise, then guided her horse out of the formation.

"What is it? I'm tired. Now I have to catch up to get my place again."

Kimana hesitated, wondered if she would be insulted. "May I carry your pack? I'm young. My shoulders are strong. You have enough of a burden already."

Singing Deer's mouth dropped and she stared. Kimana watched a number of emotions cross the woman's face. Shock. Annoyance. And then understanding and gratitude.

The older woman smiled.

"I won't take offense at your offer. If I were younger, I might. I'd ask you why you thought I was not capable of caring for my own belongings. I'd be insulted. But I am far too old, and far too weary to be angry. Thank you, Kimana. You are kind."

Singing Deer shrugged out of her pack and handed it over with a smile.

"Meda said you have a kind, sweet spirit. I see she's right."

Kimana pulled the straps over her arms and hoisted the bag onto her shoulders. By all the spirits, the woman must be transporting rocks! She watched Singing Deer run and pick up her horse's lead rope, scurrying forward to regain her place in line.

She stood to the side for a while, watching the long line of women pass, nodding and smiling at her with more friendliness than she'd ever received from them. She didn't notice the happy tears streaming down her face until Running Wolf galloped up and reined his stallion to a stop. The horse snorted and tossed his head, his legs prancing in protest.

"Is everything all right?"

She turned away so he wouldn't see the tears in her eyes. She nodded. Yes, everything was all right. For the first time in several moons, everything was all right.

CHAPTER TWENTY-SIX

Two Hawks stared in disdain at the rumpled old trapper sitting across the fire. Jonesy tore strips of pemmican with his chipped and crooked teeth and chewed loudly enough for the people in the next lodge to hear him.

It was all he needed. One more reason for everyone to cast disapproving looks his way. He was getting tired of being treated like an unwelcome guest. Like a bother. And now this. No one had seemed pleased when Jonesy stumbled back into camp, bellowing rudely for Two Hawks. The old man was lucky he hadn't ended up with his throat slit open or his tongue cut out.

If he didn't stop babbling soon, it might still happen.

Jonesy burped and swiped the back of his hand over his mouth. Somehow, he'd managed to get chunks of the dried meat and berry mixture in his very thick, very tangled beard.

Two Hawks looked away in disgust.

"So I was sayin'," Jonesy said once he'd swallowed the bulk of the food that was crammed into his mouth. "I think it's my mission in life to save Injuns. After grub, I went to the river to wash up, and I saw the strangest thing. First, there was this wolf, sittin' on the other side of the river, looking at me with eyes that seemed to know what I was thinking. Spooked me. Wasn't expecting it. To look up and see this beast just sittin' there lookin' at me like I coulda been its next meal. But that coulda been a dream, come to think on it. I'd been drinkin' a little bit, I have to admit. Well, I just sat back down on my haunches and waited some. To see what it'd do. Next thing I know..."

He burped, thumped his fist on his chest, and burped again.

"'Scuse me. Next thing I know this thing comes hurtlin' down the river. Now, I knew right away somethin' was odd, what with the fact that the thing seemed to be wearin' clothes and all. Higgerty-jiggerty, you Injuns sure make good pemm-ee-can."

His lips almost disappeared when he grinned. Two Hawks smiled thinly. He wished the old man would get to the point. He didn't want to be rude, but he was getting tired, and the man's endless stories were beginning to bore him. The trip they'd made together after his accident had nearly driven him crazy, having to listen to the man's constant, relentless blathering.

Two Hawks wasn't sure how the trapper had tracked him down. They'd moved twice since the time they'd first arrived at the Cree village.

"Well, I forgot all about that wolf, see? All that was on my mind was getting' whoever or whatever that was outta the river. Turned out it was an Injun woman, just like you."

Jonesy looked a little panicked. "Not that ye look anythin' like a woman. I just mean she was an Injun, is all. I laid her on the ground and pushed on her tummy, 'cause I figured she swallowed more'n a passel of water, and that ain't good. Didn't think she'd live, an' that's God's truth."

Two Hawks tried to paid attention but found his mind wandering.

Jonesy loved to talk.

Why should he care about the man's mission in life? Why should he care who he rescued and who he let die? As far as he was concerned, Jonesy was nothing but a meddlesome old man.

"... just as pretty as Saskatoon berry pie with her hair all afire..."

Two Hawks smothered a yawn with his hand. If he didn't come to the point soon, he'd toss him out and let him harass someone else. If Jonesy thought he owed him something for saving his life, he was going to be in for an unpleasant surprise.

Yes, he acknowledged to himself, he was bitter. The last few months had been the worst of his life. He'd finally cornered the old healer in the Cree village. Threatened to kill him if he didn't re-break and set his leg. The healer had threatened to curse him, but Two Hawks guessed he valued his skin enough not to find out who was more serious.

And he didn't believe in curses. He'd survived worse.

When he felt his bone snap under the man's hands, he'd almost come straight up off the ground and wrapped his hands around the healer's neck. It was just as well he hadn't. He hadn't made any friends here, that was for certain. Killing off their healer would have guaranteed him a painful death. Listening to Jonesy babbling now almost made that memory seem pleasant.

"... and I remembered what ye said about yer woman getting taken and all."

Two Hawks straightened up, his eyes sharp and focused on the trapper's face.

"What did you say?"

"I said, somethin' bothered me. Somethin' about her hair. It lit up like the sun. Wasn't 'till later I remembered ye sayin' yer woman had all that fire in her hair. And I thought ye might be grateful to know I saved her life. At least, she was alive when that other Injun took her."

"What other Indian?"

"The one that came and took her. The Blackfoot fella."

Blackfoot. Of course. "How do you know he was Blackfoot?"

Jonesy clucked his tongue and shook his head. "I been workin' my trap line longer'n ye've been alive. Met more'n my share of Injuns. Speak their language right good, too, if I do say so. I recognize them by the way they tie their feathers on, and the way they decorate their clothes. I gotta know how to recognize what Injun I'm jawin' with. Otherwise, how can I trade goods with 'em?"

"Did she go with him willingly?"

"Well, now, she weren't exactly awake when he carried her off. I weren't sure she'd wake up, and that's God's honest truth. But that Injun, he picked her up like she weighed nothin' at all, held her to his chest. Kissed her, right tender like."

Two Hawks felt rage warring with relief. And a sudden gratitude toward the man he'd been cursing for months.

"It wasn't for a couple of weeks that I made the connection. I was movin' down my line, clearing out traps and resettin', and it occurred to me, just like that. Yessir. I thought maybe she was yers, like I said. Otherwise, I'd have been here sooner. Plus, old Bessie was bein' ornery. That held me up some."

Two Hawks reached over and grabbed the bag of pemmican, then tossed it at the old trapper. "Tell me everything you know."

CHAPTER TWENTY-SEVEN

Dust choked the air. Thick clouds of it billowed up and the ground vibrated unnervingly as dozens of buffalo stampeded through an ever-narrowing corridor toward their death at the buffalo jump. Almost as if sensing their impending death, their eyes were wild with panic and terror. It was a nursery herd, a group of females and yearlings, with a handful of bulls. The older, larger bulls were conspicuously absent. It was a small group by any standards, but that was fine. The men had already culled them, allowing the majority of the pregnant females and a few of the younger males to escape several hours earlier, chasing them far from the rest of the stampeding mob of deadly hooves and savage horns.

It was imperative to drive them far away from their parent herd. It was said the doomed creatures could communicate the danger from a distance and any escaping animals would warn others away from the trap in the future.

As a rule, they liked to kill the herd as a whole, so they could be reborn together as a complete herd in their next lives, but that would be wasteful at this time of year.

Kimana had never been allowed to be this close to a hunt, and she'd never been next to a corridor. She knew she'd soon have to be down at the bottom of the jump, helping the women prepare the meat, but for now, she watched in awe and wonder as the beasts thundered past. She knelt a healthy distance from the western edge of the drive lane. It was dangerous to get too close, especially for a woman untrained in the hunt. It was possible for one of the charging animals to get out, and if that happened, it could be deadly.

It was fascinating to watch the Blackfoot drive the grunting animals. Her people tended to hunt on horseback or using special corrals. This way seemed far more dangerous, but she had to admit it was exciting.

The air seemed to spark with energy, and she grinned as she covered her nose and mouth with a piece of hide. It was terrifying. It was amazing.

They would need close to a hundred head if they wanted to have enough to last through summer. She knew the Blackfoot depended on the buffalo more than many tribes, but to all the people everywhere, the buffalo were sacred - their lifeblood.

She laid her hand on a pile of rocks, one of hundreds of stone cairns that lined each side of the corridor. Warriors stood on the edges, waving their arms and working the terrified animals into a frenzy. Others rode inside, expertly weaving around the beasts.

The v-shaped drive lane was long and narrowed gradually until it finally led to a blind cliff. The lead cow, an old, wise looking creature, barrelled toward the jump, oblivious to the fact that she was leading them to their deaths. Soon it would be too late to stop the momentum of the herd behind her. Warriors yelled and waved hides, keeping the group in a tightly knit pack.

And in a panicked frenzy.

She watched Running Wolf as he thundered past on his horse, yelling and waving a colourful buffalo skin.

Her interest in the buffalo momentarily forgotten, she watched as he twisted this way and that on the horse's back, observing the animals with a confident and practiced eye.

He really was every young maiden's dream, she had to admit. Strong, tall, heart-breakingly handsome. His bare chest glistened with sweat. Legs hugged the sides of his stallion, muscles flexed as he steered the animal with his knees.

Warmth flooded her face. She looked down at her hands, trying to concentrate on something else, but she couldn't stop her eyes from wandering back to him. She almost wished his offer of marriage had been sincere. Although Stands Alone was sweet, he didn't inspire anything inside her except friendly amusement and affection. But Running Wolf was a different story. He annoyed her, enraged her, but she never felt so alive as when she was arguing with him. Or being held by him.

She realized she'd never really known what it meant to feel alive until the day she'd met him.

Resigned to the fact that her mind would betray her if she tried to stop, she allowed her eyes to roam freely over him. Maybe it was just infatuation. In time, she would tire of staring at him, of watching him ride with such beauty and grace.

They moved as one, horse and man, the stallion seeming to anticipate his moves. Together, they leaned into a sharp turn, and she caught her breath, terrified the horse would lose his footing in the churned-up earth and send them both flying.

She sighed as they maneuvered into a safer position. He was more than an impressive rider. He was a natural leader, and it showed. His ability to lead his men on a hunt and in battle guaranteed him the position of chief when his father grew too old or died.

She didn't want to think about Black Eagle dying.

She hoped Singing Deer would refuse to allow her to move into their lodge. If not, she might have to ask the chief to withdraw the request. Although being that close to Running Wolf was dangerous, she knew she would miss his father terribly.

He wheeled his horse around and glanced at her. Laughed in delight. Grinned. White teeth gleamed against the dusty surface of his face. He only spared her a brief second. Any more than that, and his life could be in danger. One misstep, and he could disappear beneath the great hooves of the buffalo.

What must he think of her, kneeling in the dirt, watching him like that, like some silly, smitten girl?

She felt heat flood her cheeks once again.

How many times had she replayed that night in the clearing, when she had offered herself to him? Did he still think of it? Did he still want her?

Disgusted with herself for allowing her mind to wander where she had forbidden it, she turned her thoughts back to the hunt.

Earlier that morning, Meda had performed a ritual with her sacred *Iniskin*, her 'buffalo stone'. The stone was oddly shaped, with a large spiral on one side. It was smeared with ochre, and she raised it high above her head, gripping it tightly as she chanted the words that would bring the buffalo to them. When she was finished, she dropped it to the ground, and the whole tribe sat in silent awe. She told them the story, and they listened in respect, though it was obvious they had heard it many times before. She spun the tale of the first *Iniskin*, and how it had revealed itself to a Blackfoot woman - a great honour to be sure. The woman had been poor, the second wife of her husband, and very old. Her buffalo robe was full of holes and her moccasins were worn. She had found the stone in the fork of a cottonwood tree and held it in her hand as it sang like a chirping bird. The songs, Meda said, cast a spell over the buffalo. The people held the stones in great reverence and prayed to them before each hunt.

Kimana wasn't familiar with the *Iniskin*, and she had found the ceremony and story fascinating. It just added one more brilliant facet to what she was learning of these people. They were not the brutal warriors she had always believed. They laughed, cried, loved and mourned. They had a rich and beautiful history and customs that touched her soul. They were worming their way further into her heart with each passing day.

The first day of their move, for the first time since coming to the enemy's camp, she'd felt accepted. Watching the women walk by, smiling and nodding at her after she took Singing Deer's pack, she'd been overwhelmed by a feeling of belonging. In her own tribe, the people treated her with respect, but even there, she hadn't truly belonged. The Cree women thought she was a spoiled child, pampered by an indulgent father and ignored by an indifferent, and often crazed mother.

It was true.

But here, with these people, she was just a woman, no more or less than anyone else. And they were finally accepting her. Especially now that she was keeping her dreams to herself. She felt like she belonged.

Turning her thoughts back to the hunt, she craned her neck to look for the warrior who now occupied so much of her thoughts, but he was out of sight. A flash of movement caught her eye.

There was Makwai, having the time of her life, dancing back and forth between the snorting beasts, snarling and nipping at the flanks of any buffalo that skirted too close to the edge of the drive lane. The wolf swung her head around and grinned at Kimana before trotting off to harass another frantic buffalo. But she never went too far away or was out of sight very long. Kimana was getting used to her constant presence. And unlike the terror she'd once felt at the sight of the wolf, she now found it oddly comforting.

Over the pounding of hooves Kimana heard a faint scream. She whipped around, trying to find where it was coming from. Her heart seemed to stop as she saw Stands Alone lying on the ground just outside the drive lane. One leg twisted beneath his body at an odd angle, obviously broken. He dragged himself across the earth, calling out to his horse, but the painted mare had galloped off, leaving him defenceless and alone. His whole body shook. He was more than just injured. He looked terrified.

He stared at a point slightly west, shaking his head, still trying to drag his body across the dirt. She turned to see what he was looking at.

One of the buffalo, a young bull, had escaped the corridor. He stood a short distance from Stands Alone, breathing heavily and blowing great clouds of dust from his nostrils. His sides heaved, and he turned his mammoth body toward the young warrior. The boy yelled again, and the bull snorted, tossed his head and began to charge, tearing up the ground beneath his massive hooves and bending his head so his lethal horns were pointed straight at Stands Alone.

Kimana scrambled to her feet and started to run, fumbling at her belt for her blade. Not that a blade would help against such a huge animal.

No one else seemed to notice he was in trouble, and if she didn't help him, it would be too late. Too far. He was too far away. There was no way she could reach him. She stumbled across the ground. Called his name. Screamed for someone to help.

The sound of approaching hooves had her spinning around in terror.

Running Wolf.

She blew out a shaky sigh. He'd heard the scream as well. Bending over at the waist, she tried to catch her breath as sharp pains shot through her right side. There was so much dust. It clogged the air. She choked and coughed, all the while praying to the Great Spirit that Running Wolf would reach Stands Alone in time. The stallion galloped hard, but she knew it was going to be too late. He would never make it.

She fell to her knees.

Watched helplessly as the bull bore down on Stands Alone.

Running Wolf was still too far away. The young warrior yelled one last time, let out a strangled scream as the bull struck him in the chest with his deadly horns, throwing his body through the air like a child's toy. He crumpled to the ground and fell silent.

Covering her face with her hands, Kimana closed her eyes and wept.

***

Kimana lay curled on her side, weeping long after the hunt was finished. She knew she should be helping prepare the meat, but she couldn't bring herself to move. All she wanted to do was sleep.

Running Wolf had ridden back and lifted her off the ground. He carried her in his arms to the area below the buffalo jump where they'd set up a temporary camp and laid her gently on a robe. He sat with her a while, stroked her hair, murmured words she didn't even try to understand. Finally, when she refused to respond to him, he'd covered her with a hide and left her to grieve alone.

Oh, why had she been so cruel?

She'd treated Stands Alone like a child. Just because she didn't want him was no reason to hurt him the way she had. She'd seen the unhappiness in his eyes, the way he'd hung back during their move, even though she'd said he could walk with her.

She'd felt his eyes on her a hundred times that day, and each time, she'd looked away, trying not to feel guilty for leading him on. She hadn't meant to give him false hope. For a while, she'd even thought she might find a way to love him. Had he been trying to prove something by chasing that bull alone? Had he been trying to prove he was a man, worthy of her attention and respect?

She couldn't think about it anymore. It was just too hard.

When her body was exhausted, just when it seemed the tears would never end, she quieted. It was a tragedy, but she knew she was not responsible. It didn't matter what she felt. If Manitou chose to take him to the place of the spirits, it would have happened no matter what. It didn't make it any easier, though. If she'd pushed him to being reckless, she would always live with that knowledge, and part of her would always feel the weight of knowing.

Unfolding her legs, she rolled into a sitting position, and watched the women work. She wrapped her arms around her knees. No one paid her any attention.

The women bustled around the killing ground, skinning the hides as quickly as possible. Even though the air was cool, the stench was almost unbearable. Ribs popped and snapped as they were broken in order to clean out the entrails. Some of the carcasses were hauled down to a stream where they were cleaned and butchered on the spot.

Kimana watched as the married women cut out the sacred tongues and ate them in thanksgiving, offering the other, still steaming organs to the warriors. The best hides were scraped clean and stretched on drying racks. Soon, they would be rubbed with a special ointment made from herbs and buffalo fat to make them soft and pliable. The meat wouldn't keep long, so most of it was pounded into a paste to be made into pemmican with last-year's chokecherries and Saskatoon berries, and fat rendered from the carcasses. Some of the meat would be eaten freshly cooked, though, and was a treat everyone would be anticipating after the long winter.

Her stomach pitched and rolled at the thought of food.

Groups of women carved sweet tasting marrow out of the bones. In a while, it would be preserved in bladders made from stomachs and kept for a special occasion, eaten as a delicacy. The people worked hard, but they all smiled, laughing and joking amongst themselves.

She wondered bitterly if they even cared that Stands Alone was dead.

But that wasn't fair. She knew it.

Later, there would be time enough for grief. But for now, the meat and hides must be cared for, or the hunt, and his life, would be for nothing.

She rose to her feet and sighed. If she wanted to be part of this tribe, she'd better do her part. They would work long into the night.

CHAPTER TWENTY-EIGHT

K imana sat near the edge of a stream. A breeze carried the lonely sound of a flute from the direction of the camp. She wrapped her arms around her legs and laid her head on her knees, turning her face sideways so she could catch the haunting sounds. The grass around her was lush and green, the tender spring shoots giving way to a richer, fuller grass that would cushion their feet for months to come.

Tendrils of hair defied the loose braid she had woven it into and billowed around her in wisps, like a rich, coppery cloud.

The music rose and fell, weaving a story without words. A story of love and loss, joy and sadness.

It had been weeks since the buffalo hunt, and still Kimana could not forgive herself for the part she'd played in Stands Alone's death.

His funeral had been quiet and thoughtful, but very little mourning accompanied it. He had no family, no one to really grieve his death as his body was put on a travois and lifted high into the trees. She'd been presented with his possessions, as it was assumed they would have married had he lived. She hadn't had the heart to refuse and clutched his robe to her breast with an intensity she knew only served to confirm the assumptions of the tribe. They couldn't know it wasn't heartbreak she felt, but intense guilt.

Laying her forehead on her knees, she sighed as the music wept and wove its tragic tale.

Running Wolf approached on silent feet. Grass swayed around his legs. He didn't want to disturb her, but he couldn't stay away any longer. He had to know, once and for all, how she really felt. He had to know if there was any hope of a future between them. He'd given her time and distance, knowing she was struggling with the death. He didn't want to pressure her or impose on her mourning, but he couldn't stay away.

"Kimana."

He watched as she lifted her head and looked over her shoulder, her eyes hooded and sad. At least she wasn't crying. Many times in the last few weeks he'd wanted to take her into his arms and soothe her pain, but it was the wrong thing to do. And the wrong time to do it. He crouched beside her, dangled his arms loosely over his knees.

"Would you rather be alone?"

"No, not really." She stretched out her legs and leaned back on her arms, closed her eyes for a moment then stared across the stream. "I was just thinking."

"About what?"

"Stands Alone."

He'd been afraid of that. She'd kept to herself since the young warrior died, speaking only when directly addressed. More than once he'd watched her wiping tears from her cheeks. He hadn't realized she'd felt so deeply for the boy.

"It's difficult for you."

She turned and looked away, her eyes troubled.

It upset him more than he wanted to admit. The possibility that she'd truly loved the young man was like a blade through his heart. But he had to know. If she loved Stands Alone, really loved him, then he'd seriously misjudged her feelings, and there was no hope for them. There would be no point in attempting to go any further.

"Of course it is." She sighed. "Oh, Running Wolf, I'm just so tired. Since you took me from my home, I've felt nothing but guilt. I've done nothing but let people down. Stands Alone, he was just one more person I failed."

"How was it your fault?"

"If it wasn't for me, he never would have left the safety of the corridor and gone after that bull."

"He made the choice. He acted foolishly. You didn't make him do it."

"No. But if he hadn't been trying so hard to impress me, he wouldn't have."

"It's not your fault." He reached out, took a strand of her hair in his fingers, let it glide over the palm of his hand. "Listen to me. It is not your fault. Tragedies happen. You have to let him go."

"How can you say that? Let him go? Have you let Laughing Brook go?"

His hand jerked back.

"You don't know anything about her. Or what happened."

"I know more than you think. I know you blame yourself."

He came up from his crouch and scowled down at her. "The blame lies exactly where it belongs."

"Oh, on my people?"

"On the ones who hurt her. Killed her. Your people, yes. My enemies."

"It always comes back to that, doesn't it? Your enemies. My enemies. Your people. My people. You and I will never get past that."

"You got past it with Stands Alone."

"He wasn't to blame for the attack on my people."

"But I am?"

She looked away.

He was responsible, he knew that. He took full responsibility, and always had. But to blame? If her people hadn't attacked his village, he wouldn't have needed vengeance. None of this would have happened.

But he wouldn't have met Kimana, either. And he couldn't be sorry for that. Still, though, it didn't answer the question he had come to find the answer to.

"Just tell me this. Did you love him?"

Kimana sighed again.

Did she love Stands Alone? Yes, she thought. Like an aunt loves her nephew. Like a sister loves her brother. But not like a woman loves a man. She didn't know how to answer him, what he wanted to hear. She was tempted to say yes, just so he would leave her alone, but when she looked into his eyes, she could see that only the truth would satisfy him. And suddenly she knew she had to tell him the truth, even if it meant laying herself open to be hurt once again. Nothing was more important than honesty between them.

"I loved him, yes. But not the way you mean. He wanted more. I couldn't give it to him."

"Why?"

How could she tell him? How could she say it was him she really loved? Him she dreamt of when she lay on her mat at night. Him she looked for when she awoke. He was the first thing she thought of in the morning, the last thing she thought of before she went to sleep. And the guilt of that, of thinking of him, and not of Stands Alone, ate at her every day. But how could she tell him that?

He lowered himself to his knees and took her shoulders in his hands, turning her body toward his.

"Kimana, tell me why. Please."

"Because it's you. It's you I love."

Saying the words, knowing she meant them, felt a little like tossing off a heavy, winter buffalo robe and thrusting her bare arms toward the summer sun. He stared at her, and she tried to steady her breathing. Was he angry now? Appalled? It didn't matter. She wouldn't lie to him, no matter how humiliating it was. It had taken her months to realize how she felt for him, and now that she had, she couldn't change it.

Had telling him been a mistake? Just as she was ready to turn away, he wrapped his arms around her back and pulled her against his chest.

His mouth wasn't gentle this time. It was hot and insistent, demanding, almost rough. She found herself draping her own arms around him, meeting him halfway, more than halfway, demanding the same thing from him that he asked of her.

Here, in this warrior's arms, in the arms of the enemy, she had finally found what it meant to love, to want, to need.

To be loved.

Wanted.

Needed.

Here, in this warrior's arms, she knelt by the side of the river, no longer hearing the sound of rushing water, or the sound of the distant flute.

188

No longer did she feel the grass beneath her knees or the aching loneliness that had gripped her for months.

She barely noticed when he stood up, lifted her, held her against his chest, her legs draped over his left arm. She barely noticed when he walked into the privacy of a stand of cottonwood trees and laid her down on a soft mat of grass.

But when he laid down next to her and ran his long fingers up the inside of one calf and then down the other, when he ran his fingers over her stomach, and outlined her breasts, when he kissed her neck and whispered against her skin, she felt her entire body come alive.

"Love me, Kimana."

"I do. I do love you."

"Let me love you."

She arched her back, pressing herself against his chest, feeling his hands between her legs. Her lower body seemed to explode with sensations as his fingers explored and probed her flesh, separating the folds and sinking deep within her liquid depths.

Her body tensed, stiffened as pleasure washed through her in wave after wave. And when he rose above her, lowered himself gently into her, she arched again, offering herself to him. A tiny cramp ran through her abdomen as he eased himself inside, but the pain passed quickly, so quickly it was gone before she was even sure it was there, and soon she was filled with a new sensation, a fullness and rightness that she never knew could exist.

Lifting his body weight off her, he held himself up with his arms, he looked into her eyes as they moved together in an ancient dance. He watched her face as he poured himself inside of her and whispered her name. Finally, spent, he lowered his forehead onto her own, and closed his eyes.

"Love me, Kimana," he whispered as he pressed his mouth against hers.

"I do."

CHAPTER TWENTY-NINE

Storm clouds bulged and churned overhead. A flash of sheet lightning lit the sky, followed closely by the crack and boom of thunder. Two Hawks tugged a hide over his head as rain pelted him in the face.

Evidence of a recently abandoned encampment was all around him. Traces of buffalo carcasses, stripped of everything useable, lay in a heap at the base of a small cliff. Rings from teepees dotted a small area on the plains below the cliff. And a short distance away, in a stand of trees, a lone travois swayed and creaked in the wind.

He shivered.

He knew the Blackfoot lifted their dead into trees, but he'd never seen it for himself. It obviously wasn't a usual burial ground, though, as there were no other platforms in sight. The body was shrouded in a buffalo hide, and a collection of objects lay on the ground below.

Two Hawks wasn't particularly interested in going any closer, even though he was curious.

Some, he knew, would rob the dead of whatever jewellery or possessions had been left with the body, but he wasn't amongst them. He had respect for the dead. And a healthy dose of fear as well that came of a lifetime of teachings.

He wasn't about to invite the enmity of the spirit world just to satisfy his curiosity.

In spite of that, he sat on his horse for a while and watched the travois sway. Listened to the wood creak in protest as it swung from side to side in the wind.

He was grateful for the horse. Without it, the search would have been impossible. The price had been higher than he wanted to pay, and in the end, all he had to trade was Kimana's wedding dress. He knew how hard she'd worked on it and dreaded telling her he'd traded it for the beast, but he hadn't had much choice.

She could always make another one.

If he found her. If she was still alive.

He was fairly certain the Blackfoot he sought had been here recently. The burial platform looked fresh, and the hide was undisturbed on the body. It was tightly wrapped, and the body obviously hadn't decomposed enough to draw the carrion birds. He urged his horse a few steps closer. Something in the pile of possession laying on the ground had caught his eye.

In a flash, he leapt from his mount.

There, amongst the scattered possessions, was a neck ornament.

His fear of the dead forgotten, he snatched the necklace off the ground. A chunk of pink quartz glittered in his hand.

Kimana's. It was the necklace he'd given to her the week before the attack, the day he'd left on his vision quest. He'd wrapped the stone himself with bits of sinew and attached it to a strip of leather. He'd placed it around her neck before giving her a chaste kiss on the lips.

"Don't forget me," he'd smiled.

"How could I forget?"

He'd taken the memory of her gentle smile with him on his long journey and had replayed it in his mind countless times since he found her gone and his village destroyed.

The hope of finding her was the only thing that had kept him alive. The only thing that kept him going.

He sank to his knees and held the stone to his chest, rocking back and forth, his keening moan drowned out by the boom of thunder. Tears streamed down his face as he lifted his eyes to the platform above.

He'd come too far to find her dead. She couldn't be dead. It wasn't possible.

Knowing he was inviting the wrath of spirits, not to mention

191

the bad luck that was guaranteed to follow one who disturbed the dead, he knew he had to see her face for himself.

He had to know for sure.

CHAPTER THIRTY

K imana kneed her horse out of line and stared down into the coulee. She knew she must look ridiculous with her mouth hanging open, but she couldn't help it. And she didn't care. She'd never seen anything like this before. Countless brightly painted teepees crammed the land on both sides of a slow moving, milky river that carved its way through the landscape. Hundreds of them. No, thousands. On either side of the river, hills dotted with sage bushes and cottonwood trees sloped upward, and in the distance, across the prairie, was a huddle of blue-tinted hills.

She'd known there would be a lot of people here, but she had no idea it would be this many. Long before the gathering place had come into sight, she'd heard them. She couldn't make out individual voices, just the dull roar of many thousands of people talking and laughing.

It was the Time of All People Coming Together - the summer gathering of the Blackfoot. Weeks of travel had led them here, to this place.

She continued to stare as her tribe hurried past, chattering with excitement in finally reaching their destination, in finally getting to see old friends. Children scrambled off their travois perches and tore down worn pathways, squealing with delight. Many of them remembered other summers spent here, but for some, it was the first year they were old enough to participate in the many of the events at the gathering.

The day before, they'd met up with two other large groups of people, all heading toward the canyon Where the Drawings Are.

She, too, was excited to see the sacred place. Two Hawks, in years past, had told her about the strange mushroom-shaped sand and rock formations called hoodoos, and the sandstone cliffs carved with drawings made both by people and by spirits. Although she could not see them yet, she knew they were just ahead. It was the place he'd travelled to for his spiritual quests, the place he'd gone before the attack on her people. Although it was known to be Blackfoot territory, many people from tribes all over the land considered it a sacred and mystical location and journeyed there each year, singly or in groups.

She wondered where Two Hawks was now. Had he ever made it to this place for his vision quest? Had he found what he was seeking? Had he returned to their village and found them all gone? Had he searched for her at all, or had he given up? She hoped he had not searched very long. In a way, she hoped he hadn't looked for her at all. She shoved away a twinge of guilt. Wherever he was, she hoped he had moved on with his life. Just like she'd finally decided to move on with hers.

As the last of the women hurried past, she tugged on her horse's lead rope to slip back into line in front of the warriors. As she moved forward, the hoodoos came into sight, and she came to an abrupt stop. Her horse snorted softly in protest.

Nothing she had ever heard could adequately describe the strange formations. They were like miniature mountains, not much taller than a man, some narrowing near the top and some widening. Most of them were capped with large, flat rocks. Some were peppered with small holes that allowed daylight to shine through and speckle the ground beneath them with light.

There were so many it would be impossible to count them.

A chill shivered over her skin as the impact of the place hit her. Here, for more years than could be counted or remembered, people had come to meet with long-dead ancestors and other spirits. It wouldn't have surprised her if, at night when no one was around, the sound of their voices, chanting and singing, could still be heard echoing off the cliffs.

Overhead, an osprey glided on a current of air against a blindingly blue backdrop, whistled *chook, chook, chook,* and dove with a piercing scream toward the river.

In spite of the massive number of people, the osprey would have no competition for the fish it sought. Unlike the Cree, the Blackfoot did not normally eat fish. Meda said it had something to do with the underwater people they believed lived in rivers and lakes. Because the fish interacted with the mystical people, they were considered unfit for consumption. It seemed a little odd to her, but she accepted the fact that she would probably never eat fish again. It didn't bother her too much. She'd always preferred the meat of buffalo and other land creatures.

"So? What do you think?"

Running Wolf reigned his horse to a stop and grinned down at her, his face radiant with the delight of finally reaching this special place.

They shared a smile.

"It's incredible," she said.

"Yes. It is."

Together they watched children jumping from one hoodoo to another. Laughed when they heard Little Otter calling them from the top of yet another hoodoo, waving his hands like mad. It hadn't taken him long to run off with the other children.

"He's happy," Running Wolf said.

"Yes." As happy as he could be after losing his parents, she thought bitterly.

Where had that thought come from? She hadn't had such an unhappy thought in weeks. In fact, she'd been happier and more accepting of her situation than she'd ever believed possible.

"And you, Kimana? What of you? Are you happy as well?"

She lifted a hand and touched his leg, resisted an urge to run it down the outside of his calf.

"Very happy."

Days ago, they'd decided to get married, but they still hadn't told anyone. Not even Meda or Chief Black Eagle knew their intentions. It was, for now, their secret, their own private joy, and they weren't ready to share it. The time would come soon enough, and they would be under the constant gaze of their people until their marriage took place. She wondered if there would be any traditions or customs she needed to learn before the marriage took place.

She'd have to ask Meda.

"Have I told you about the rattlesnakes, Kimana?"

Her brows creased together, and she shook her head.

"You may not have those where you come from. We have none in the mountains or foothills, but here, in this place, there are many. And they're dangerous."

He explained how to recognize their sound and told her if she heard it to stop and look around. Chances were, the snake would be lying somewhere ahead, and she should back away slowly. It frightened her a little, but he said the snakes were more afraid of her than she would be of them.

"This place isn't just prized because of the drawings. Many different types of birds and animals gather here, as well. They don't seem to mind us coming. They know we respect both them and the land."

Kimana nodded and wiped sweat from her brow.

During the weeks they had leisurely wended their way across the rolling plains toward the gathering place, summer had descended fully upon them, along with an almost unbearable heat.

Now that they were nearing the summer solstice, it would be hot all across the prairies, but the temperature here seemed even greater. She lifted her deer skin dress away from her clammy skin and turned to ask him the question that had been increasingly on her mind as they travelled but hadn't wanted to ask. She hadn't wanted to break the spell that seemed to be cast around them.

"Will my people be sold?"

His face darkened. "I don't know. Why are you asking me that?"

It was still a sore point between them, the way her people had come to be with his own, so as a rule, they didn't discuss it. But now that they'd arrived, she had to know. She wasn't sure what she would do if the answer was yes. She knew he didn't like talking about it, but she decided to press him about it anyway. It made her a little angry that he obviously still thought he'd done nothing wrong. She understood now, about the woman he'd lost and his mother. How deeply he'd been hurt, and how much he'd needed revenge. She tried to accept what happened, but sometimes, it was hard. And it annoyed her that he avoided talking about it.

"I need to know. We have a right to know." She tried to keep her voice light but was afraid the fear crept into it. The fear – and the anger.

"Kimana, I can't answer you. I don't know. It will be up to my father and the elders."

"Don't you even care? And what of me?"

"You will never be sold. You are mine. As for the rest, there are things you can change and some things you can't. You have to learn to accept that."

With a sigh, he pressed his knees into the sides of his stallion and galloped after the rest of the tribe.

She watched him go and struggled against the feeling of resentment that bubbled up inside her at his words, and the unshakeable fear that something bad was about to happen - and would destroy the love that had developed between them.

***

"How long will we be here, Meda?"

The old woman looked up from the pole she was attaching buffalo hides to and grinned. "Shame on you, you impatient girl. Are you ready to leave already?"

Kimana smiled.

"No, I just wondered. I've never been at a gathering like this, and I don't know what to expect."

She'd been feeling unsettled since her conversation with Running Wolf. The excitement she'd felt upon arriving had soured with the possibility that she wasn't going to like the decision the elders would make about her people, perhaps had already made. Not knowing was the worst thing.

Meda shrugged. "We'll be here less than a single moon's time, then we'll leave to gather the summer berries so we can start to prepare for winter. It's only because the gathering is so important that we take the time away from harvesting. I thought I'd explained this to you."

"You did. I just need to ask you something. Has Chief Black Eagle told you what will happen to the prisoners?"

"The prisoners, Kimana? They have never been treated like prisoners, not since you arrived in our camp."

"Were we free to go?"

"No."

"Then we were prisoners. We still are."

197

"So that's how you think of yourself. You should be ashamed." Meda softened her words with a pat on Kimana's knee. "I thought you'd grown in wisdom and understood that we are all the people. We are all one."

"Running Wolf obviously didn't think so when he dragged us away from our home."

Meda cocked her head and looked at Kimana with a single, speculative eye. "I thought that was settled and left in the past where it belongs. Tell me what is really troubling you, little one. You've been so happy these last weeks."

Kimana sighed.

"I don't know. I guess I'm just a little nervous."

"Why?"

"Being here. All these people. I didn't know I'd feel so unsettled."

"It's more than that. What are you not telling me?"

"I don't know how I feel about being surrounded by the Blackfoot. It feels so strange to have the enemy – what I've always thought of as the enemy – all around me. It's just hard to accept, that's all. And I'm still not sure Running Wolf can accept our differences."

Kimana looked around at the circle camp the people were forming around a bare, central area on the plains overlooking the canyon. Only the chiefs, elders and medicine men and women were allowed to camp in this area. The rest of the people camped down below.

"Are you sure it's not you who can't accept the differences, Kimana? No, don't answer yet. You don't give Running Wolf enough credit. He has more reason than you think to be accepting of an enemy in his camp. So, you're uncomfortable, are you? You think it's not possible to fit in? I think you're just being stubborn. How do you think I felt the first time I attended a Blackfoot summer gathering?"

"The first time? What do you mean?"

Meda sighed and flexed her gnarled fingers.

"Oh, these old bones don't work the way they used to." She dropped the hide onto her lap. "Let's take a minute to rest. I'll tell you about how I came to be with the enemy, as you call them."

Meda gently folded and laid the hides on the ground next to

her and settled herself into a more comfortable position, grunting softly as she adjusted her body.

"What did you mean how you came to be with the Blackfoot?" Kimana asked. "I thought you were Blackfoot."

"No. I was Shoshone. I still am, but now, I am Blackfoot also."

"My mother was Shoshone. She was captured in a raid by my father."

"Ah," said Meda. "That explains your name."

"But if you are Shoshone, how could you be the Blackfoot Medicine Woman? I thought..."

"I earned my position, Kimana. Now don't be so rude. Let me tell my story."

Kimana felt her face grow warm. It wasn't often Meda scolded her. A far-off look settled onto Meda's face as her brows lowered.

"Long ago, my village was attacked. My sister and I were taken prisoner. This was back in the day when the Blackfoot and Shoshone warred often, and bitterly. Before the Blackfoot drove them farther south, beyond this sacred place we are now. Taking prisoners was common in those days. Chief Black Eagle was a strong young warrior. He led the attack. He was handsome and powerful, and full of life. He was also arrogant and proud. Like his son. He took one look at Chepi and decided to make her his woman."

"Chepi? Running Wolf's mother."

"Hush now and let me tell my story. You are such a rude girl! As I said, Black Eagle wanted Chepi the moment he saw her. It was hard to blame him. She was beautiful. She had a voice like a flute. The first time he heard her lift her lovely voice in song, he called her She Who Sings. In my language, Chepi means to sing."

She paused and adjusted a leg.

"Chepi fought him for a while, like you have fought Running Wolf, but she learned to accept what happened. It was hard for us to fit in, just like it's been hard for you. She was a dreamer of dreams, and I was a seer, and interpreter of dreams. The people were suspicious. An abundance of gifts in anyone was uncommon. For two women, two sisters, to have such gifts... well, they saw this as both a blessing and a curse. They weren't comfortable. Because I was a healer, they accepted me more quickly. With Chepi, it was different. She had another gift they could not understand. Here, pass me my bag. I want to rub some birch bark salve into my fingers. They don't work the way they used to. Some days I think the ache will never leave."

Kimana rose, hurried over, and grabbed Meda's herb bag.

Meda took the bag and pulled out a carved bone bowl, big enough only to fit into the palm of her hand. A piece of hide was stretched taught over the top and it was tied with a thin strip of buffalo sinew. She removed the cover and dipped her gnarled fingers into the thick, sweetly odorous paste, then massaged it into her hands.

"Thank you, little one. Ah, that's better. Thank the spirits for the gift of the birch trees. So, I was saying. Chepi had a gift. She could talk to animals. Hear their thoughts. As much as the people understood that all the world is connected, that animals are both the spirits of those who have gone before us, and also those who are to come, no one hears the thoughts of animals unless they are on a vision quest. But she could. Since she was three or four years old, she had that gift. One day while she was playing, a wolf came out of the forest and talked to her. The wolf told her to always listen carefully to the animals, because they would lead her. Wolves, especially, were special to Chepi, even sacred. They are fierce protectors of their young. She always respected that. Identified with it."

Meda wrapped the scrap of hide back over the bowl and tied the sinew around it.

"In time, the people accepted her. Partly because she was a good wife to Black Eagle, even though she didn't love him at first."

"She did not love him?"

"Not at first. Now hush and listen. In time, she grew to love him, but first, before love came, she respected him. She gave him two strong sons. Like a mother wolf, she was intensely protective of her children."

"Two sons? But Running Wolf has no siblings. I thought he was the only child. He's never spoken of a brother."

"He would not. He blames himself for what happened to Two Birds. But that is another story. Don't distract me, Kimana. I'm getting old and forgetful. I'll forget what I'm trying to tell you, and then my breath will be wasted. For now, I will tell you about

Chepi. And about me. Although it didn't seem so at first, Chepi was blessed by the Great Spirit when Black Eagle chose her as his woman. He loved her. Treated her well. I was not so lucky," she said with a grimace. "The warrior who took me for a wife was a hard man. Daily, he beat me and told me I was ugly and useless. But he found something about me useful, it seemed. My gifts as a healer and an interpreter of dreams brought much wealth into our lodge. He both loved that and hated it. That a woman should bring more wealth to his home than he did was a very sore point for him. It did not, however, stop him from appreciating it. Like Chepi gave Black Eagle two sons, I gave my husband two sons as well. I was blessed enough to see them grow up, but both were killed in battle a few summers ago. My husband died in battle as well, a number of years before that. They all had honourable deaths. Black Eagle offered to take me in to his lodge as the sister of his wife, but I refused. There was no need. As medicine woman, all the people give me a share of what they have. I didn't have to worry about having food to eat or hides to stitch into robes. My point, Kimana, is that we had every reason to hate the Blackfoot, and we did, for a while. But eventually we accepted what happened, and both of us found great joy, despite the hardships. You can, as well."

Kimana looked down at her folded hands. "I wish I didn't have a gift. I wish I didn't dream. Things would be easier."

"Whoever said anything in life would be easy?"

"I'm getting them more often now. I try to think of happy things when I go to sleep at night, but the dreams always come."

"Tell me about them."

"It seems like my father is in every dream. He always seems a little sad."

"Do you know why he's sad?"

"No. He just drops an eagle feather on the ground, and tears run down his cheeks."

"What do you think he's trying to tell you?"

"I don't know. I don't know. And the wolf is there. Makwai. She's always there. I can not escape her, even in my dreams."

"What is she doing?"

"That's the thing. Sometimes she's snarling. Sometimes she looks at me and I feel a kinship with her."

"Is Running Wolf in these dreams?"

"Yes, and Two Hawks, the man I was to marry before the attack on my village. They stand, Running Wolf and Two Hawks, facing each other, Makwai between them. She snarls at each one in turn, and they circle around her, like they're trying to find a good angle to launch an attack. Waiting for the other to let his guard down."

"And do they attack?"

"I don't know. I never see it. The dream changes. They disappear, and there's only Makwai, looking at me with her strange eyes. She's crying, too. What do you think it means?"

"I think she's trying to give you a warning. What the warning is, only you can decide. There are some things I can not give you the answer to. It's up to you to find the meaning. But why didn't you tell me you were still dreaming?"

Kimana flung her braid over her shoulder in impatience. "Everyone dreams, Meda. We've talked about that before."

Meda reached out and curled her hand around Kimana's fingers. "Yes. Everyone dreams. But your dreams are different. You know this."

Kimana shook her head. "I don't want to be different. Look what happened last time. The people acted like they were afraid of me."

"People need time to adapt. You are what you are. They will accept this. You will, too. Tell me what happens then, in your dream."

"At the end of the dream, my father is crying again. I'm crying. I feel like someone has died, but I don't know who, and I'm crying. I wake up with tears on my face."

"Have you told Running Wolf?"

"No." There were still things she couldn't share with him, even though she loved him. And he might misunderstand and think she was unhappy.

"Why not?"

"Why would I tell him?"

"A better question is why would you not tell him. Kimana, you think we don't see what has happened between you? The love that's grown? It's there for everyone who has eyes to see. At least for those who want to see."

A group of women hurried past, pausing only long enough to smile and nod.

"Does Black Eagle know?" Kimana asked.

"Yes, he knows."

"What does he think?"

"He's happy for you. Happy for his son. It's been many years since he's seen joy on Running Wolf's face. Neither one of us was surprised that you would bring that joy to him. When will you marry?"

"I'm not sure. At the end of the gathering, I guess. We don't want to make a fuss. We weren't going to tell anyone yet. We wanted to just keep it between us for a while."

"I understand that. Some things are best savoured slowly, like a good rabbit stew."

Kimana looked up, startled, as a little boy, barely old enough to walk, stumbled over her legs in his hurry to get wherever he was going. She smiled and watched him run off on his chubby little legs, his arms flapping like a bird.

"It's not that we didn't want you to know. We just – weren't ready to share it. I thought we did a good job of hiding our feelings."

"There's not much you can hide from someone who loves you."

Kimana smiled and squeezed Meda's hand. The old woman had become more like a mother to her than her own had ever been.

"Let's get back to work. Help me up," Meda demanded.

Kimana helped the old woman to her feet and pretended not to see her stretch her back and groan in obvious pain. Then they continued tying buffalo hides to the teepee poles.

"We'll have to put together a lodge for you."

Kimana looked up, startled. "But I thought we'd stay with Black Eagle."

Meda chuckled and shook her head. "You will need your own place."

"But what will Black Eagle do? With no woman to care for him, and his son gone?"

"Don't worry about that. Things have a way of working themselves out." Meda lashed on the last hide then nodded to Kimana. Together, they raised it up, drove in the pegs, then laid the stones they had gathered earlier around the base to firmly anchor it to the ground.

"The wind whips through the canyon, though not as strong as near the mountain pass," Meda said. "Still, we don't want it to blow away."

The rings were one thing the Cree and Blackfoot had in common. At each place they had stopped and put up their lodges during their journey, they left behind rings of stones. It was simply easier to gather new ones than to try to lug the rocks around with them as they travelled throughout the year. The teepee rings served as markers as well, though the people knew the land well enough not to need them.

Kimana stared thoughtfully at the throng of people around them. It wasn't the only thing they had in common. There were many things. So many things.

It was something to think about. *We are all one*, Meda had said. All one.

"There," Meda said and nodded. "Now, we will go and put up my lodge. Then we'll have something to eat. And tonight, all the people will gather together, and we will sing and dance, and give thanks for the opportunity we have been given to meet again, healthy and whole. And we will mourn our dead together. Tomorrow, we will make plans for your marriage."

CHAPTER THIRTY-ONE

Kimana chewed her bottom lip as she examined a pair of moccasins. The stitches were far from perfect, but maybe no one would notice. She was getting better at stitching, but it was still one of her least favourite tasks.

She bent her head and tied off a thin strip of hide.

It was a Cree tradition for a woman to give a pair of moccasins to her future husband. She'd have to explain it to Running Wolf, tell him he needed to accept them in order to accept her as his wife.

Acceptance.

That's what it all came down to. Whether or not she could accept her new life, her new home. Whether she could accept him. Accept that they were, as Meda said, all one.

Well, she thought, and smiled, she might be expected to adapt to Blackfoot traditions, but there was no way she was going to give up important traditions of her own. He would take the moccasins and he would appreciate what they meant. If they were going to live together, both of them would have to learn to adapt and accept each other's differences.

Maybe even learn how to celebrate them, like Meda said.

She allowed herself to drift back in her mind to the day at the river when he'd first made love to her. When they'd walked along the riverbank afterward and found a waterfall. She'd shaken off his hand and run into the small pool beneath the falls. Laughed and lifted her hair in the spray, then sunk into the water and swum across to the other side. Climbed out and onto the far bank, her deerskin dress drenched and clinging to her body.

He watched every move.

"What are you going to do, Running Wolf?" she had laughed and grinned. "You don't want to ruin your new breechcloth. I spent hours stitching those seams, hours making the hide perfect. If you ruin it, you'll insult me."

Her eyes dared him to dive in, her smile teased. She was certain she was safe from him on the other side of the water. Then he dove in, and a moment later he appeared near her feet. Wrapping his arms around her legs, he'd dragged her back into the river.

She remembered how he peeled off her dress and laid her down in the sunshine. Her whole body shivered as the droplets of water evaporated from her skin. He held her and stroked her until she was warm, and aroused, and needed him all over again.

She waved a hand in front of her face to cool it down from the memory then bent again to her stitching.

Someone scratched at the entrance to her lodge.

"Come in."

Hoping a smile would hide her flaming cheeks, she looked up. The smile froze on her face as Silver Fox lifted the flap. The woman had excellent timing.

"I hope I'm not disturbing you."

Kimana stared. It was the first time Silver Fox had spoken directly to her in months. She'd probably come to see Running Wolf.

She mentally rolled her eyes. Big surprise. That she showed up now, right after they announced their upcoming marriage ceremony, could only mean she hadn't given up her obvious infatuation with Running Wolf. Well, she'd have to get over it. Nothing was going to change it.

Still, Kimana couldn't very well tell her to go away. That would be rude.

But inviting her in didn't mean she had to offer her any willow bark tea, that was for sure.

"No, I was just finishing some stitching. Come in."

Silver Fox stepped inside.

"Those are lovely." The woman waved a hand at the

moccasins. "Are they a gift?"

"Yes." Kimana didn't want to be rude, but she didn't feel she needed to explain what she was doing. She waved a hand and invited Silver Fox to sit down.

Couldn't very well kick her out.

"I just thought we could chat for a little while," Silver Fox said.

"You're not looking for Running Wolf?"

"No, I was looking for you. I thought you'd be in here, getting out of the heat. I don't blame you."

Kimana shrugged and tried to smile politely. "Looking for me?"

"Yes. I thought we could get to know each other a bit better. Since you're marrying Running Wolf, and he's practically my brother."

"Your brother? He never told me you were that close." She took some guilty pleasure in seeing a look of annoyance flash in the woman's face.

"Well, Laughing Brook was my best friend."

"He never told me that, either."

"Do you really think he's told you everything?" Silver Fox couldn't hide the sneer in her voice, and they both knew it. Kimana lifted an eyebrow.

"I'm really pretty busy right now. If you'd like to talk with Running Wolf, he should be back before nightfall. He's meeting with the elders."

"No, he isn't."

"Yes, he... "

"No, he's left the camp." Silver Fox sat back on her heels and smirked, obviously pleased she knew something Kimana didn't.

"He must be hunting."

"No, he's left. He won't be back now for four days. Oh, didn't he tell you?"

Kimana's stomach pitched. "You obviously have something you want to share. So why don't you?"

She must be dying to. Kimana took a deep breath to steady herself for what she somehow just knew was going to ruin the rest of her day. If not longer.

"He's on his spiritual quest before the Sun Dance."

"Sun Dance." Kimana's voice was a hoarse whisper.

"Didn't he tell you? He and the other men who are performing the ceremony will move camp for four days before coming back here. Then they'll fast and dance for another four days. I just can't understand why he didn't tell you. Why he wouldn't. As close as you are, I mean. It's hard to imagine him keeping anything that important from someone he actually cares for. Don't you think?"

Silver Fox was obviously taking a great deal of pleasure in sharing her information, but, in truth, Kimana hadn't heard too much past the words *Sun Dance*. She'd grown up hearing stories of the practice, and how brutally dangerous it was to those men who participated.

"Do you know of it? The Sun Dance? The men skewer their chests with wooden spikes and are lifted into the air to twirl from the top of the Sun Lodge for hours, even days sometimes." Silver Fox said. "He's done it before, of course, but he's doing it again for some reason. I can't imagine why." Her hands fluttered to her chest. "But when I ran into the Vow Woman this morning and she told me he would be performing again, well I..."

"Leave."

"What?"

"I asked you to leave."

"Well," Silver Fox said as she rose to her feet, then placed her hands on her hips. "How rude. It's obvious you haven't learned any manners since coming to live with our people."

"I've learned all I need to learn."

Kimana watched while Silver Fox sashayed outside, trying to look offended, but far too obviously pleased with herself.

She turned her head and stared, unseeing, at the ground. He was doing the Sun Dance. She didn't care that he'd done it before. She didn't like it, but she accepted it. It was in the past. She'd thought. And now, he was doing it again. Without telling her.

When had he planned for her to find out? The day of the dance?

Brutally shoving away the sorrow that threatened to spill from her very soul, she focused on the one thing she could allow herself to feel.

Disappointment? No, what she felt wept inside of her even now.

What she felt was fear. Even if they survived the ordeal, all too often men died from the dance, their wounds festering and filling their bodies with poison. The best medicine women in the land could not always save them.

She surged to her feet and lurched through the teepee flap, holding it open in a clenched fist. The elders' circle camp surrounded a bare central area with a large ring of stones. The place where the Sun Lodge would be erected. He'd be gone for another four days, but maybe she could convince Chief Black Eagle to stop him. Otherwise, their dreams of a life together could disappear like smoke through a smoke hole.

***

Running Wolf dropped to his knees, exhausted. Four days of fasting and dancing had taken its toll, and still, he had another four tortuous days ahead of him back at the gathering. Not to mention the day of the Sun Dance itself when his body and mind would be tested and tortured in the final stage of the dance. He'd done this before, but he had been younger then.

He stretched out his legs and rolled onto his back. He'd forgotten what it felt like, to do the final leg of the ceremony, and though the days of fasting and endless dancing had jogged his memory, he still couldn't allow himself to think about the pain he knew would come.

Women said childbirth was like that. After it was over, you knew it was painful, but you couldn't quite remember how intense the pain actually was. It was probably a good thing, he thought, or women would stop after only one child.

He glanced down at his chest, ran a hand over the scars that still remained from the last time he had performed the dance, four summers ago. A few short months after his mother and Laughing Brook had been killed. He'd performed that dance as a way to purge himself of his pain. It hadn't worked. It had toughened him, though.

He realized now that his reasons for doing the Sun Dance before had been almost selfish. When he'd hung suspended in the air, the hot sun beating down on his aching body from open flaps above, all he'd thought about was vengeance.

Not exactly the spiritual reasons a young man should do the dance. But he hadn't exactly had the good of his people in mind, had he? No, he was focused on one thing. And it had led him to do something he knew he should regret. Knew it, but spent every day thanking the spirits he had done it anyway.

Because doing it had given him Kimana. A woman he knew was strong enough to love him, someone whose spirit wouldn't be crushed by his. A woman he could allow himself to feel something for. Someone who challenged him, made him laugh, and made him forget the images that plagued him each night when he slept.

He creased his brow. Come to think of it, he hadn't dreamed about the those things in several weeks.

Not since around the time he made love to Kimana.

Well, she was good for him, that was all the explanation he needed. So, he would dance again, and hope it went better this time. Better for him, for her, and for his people. The people needed strong leaders. Whether or not they chose him for their chief after his father stepped down was not important. They needed men who could make sacrifices for the good of all. It was time to prove to himself, and anyone else who needed to know, that he had matured, that he was ready for whatever might come. That he was ready to commit to his people, to make any sacrifice necessary for them. For the woman he loved. It was not strictly necessary that he do it. Not as far as everyone else was concerned. But it was necessary to him. To purge himself of any lingering resentment toward the Cree. To prove to himself that he was truly ready to move on to the next phase of his life.

He stretched his arms above his head and looked up at the open flap high above. The sky was starting to darken, and soon, the stars would appear above him. But he wouldn't see them. He knew he'd drop into an exhausted sleep before long and be up before the sun rose in the morning. Tomorrow, they would return to the gathering and set up the Sun Lodge for the final half of the ceremony.

He wished he'd be able to spend some time with Kimana, but it wouldn't be possible. He couldn't have any physical contact with anyone until after the ceremony. He couldn't see any woman except the Vow Woman, and she was in full ceremonial dress when she was in the lodge.

But it was Kimana who would tend his wounds after. He had

that to look forward to. Being in her arms was all he really wanted.

He turned his head and looked at the other men who had joined him on this spiritual quest. Most of them were sleeping already, regaining their strength for the long days ahead.

Looking back at the open flap above, he thought he probably should have told Kimana he was doing the dance, but he had a feeling she would object – and he hadn't wanted to fight about it. She didn't understand, that was all. But she would.

When she saw how important it was, not only to him, but for their people, their future, she'd understand.

CHAPTER THIRTY-TWO

Two Hawks crawled on his belly, dragging himself forward on his elbows through the tall grass that rippled and swayed around him.

He'd spent the last two days scouting the Blackfoot gathering place, looking for some sign of Kimana, but so far, he hadn't found her. He had no reason to think she might be in the circle camp on the plains above the river, but it was the only place left to look. Of course, it was possible he'd just missed her. The number of people was staggering. His lips twisted into a wry grin. There was nothing like crawling right into the enemy's camp. Literally.

He'd seen Little Otter and Kimana's aunt, as well as a dozen other Cree women, so he knew he'd found the right place. But there was no sign of Kimana.

So far, since arriving at the place Where the Drawings Are, he'd managed to go undetected, and he was grateful he'd been to this place before and knew his way around. In fact, he might know it better than the Blackfoot themselves.

Annoyance pricked at him as the dark wolf that had been dogging his steps for the last week loped toward him, her tongue lolling out. She sat on her haunches and grinned at him, then swung her head toward the camp.

He was used to her presence by now, although he wondered why she insisted on following him from the buffalo jump. She wasn't hungry, that was obvious. She hadn't been aggressive at all, just curious. Even friendly.

He shook his head and looked back at the camp as a dog yipped.

If he did find Kimana here, he still didn't have a plan for getting her out, but he'd deal with that when the time came. For now, he just needed to know she was here, alive and safe. The memory of thinking she was dead when he'd found her necklace at the buffalo jump still haunted him. Why she'd left it there was a mystery he wasn't sure he wanted to solve. The thought that she'd given her heart to someone else was too much to bear.

He let his gaze drift over the camp. Then his eyes sharpened. Just when he was beginning to think he'd never find her, there she was, coming out of a lodge on the south side of the circle camp.

His heartbeat quickened.

***

Kimana paused outside the entrance to her lodge. Nearby, a dog barked. She lifted a hand to shield her eyes from the glare of the sun and scanned the prairie grass. There was nothing out there except for Makwai.

Odd that she showed up now. She'd disappeared not long before they arrived at the gathering place. Running Wolf would be glad to see her.

Something fluttered in Kimana's stomach, some nervousness she couldn't quite identify the cause of. Although Chief Black Eagle had assured her that her people would not be sold, she still felt unsettled.

Maybe it was his response to her objections to the Sun Dance. Even the Cree sometimes did the dance, he'd said, so what was the problem? Leave it alone, he'd warned. Running Wolf would do what he would do, and there was nothing she could say about it.

They'd see about that. The minute he returned, she intended to tell him exactly what she thought.

She'd spent the last three days stewing over the issue and had only decided to confront Black Eagle that morning. She was still a little intimidated by him, even though she'd started to think of him as a father. The way he'd thinned his lips when she voiced her concerns told her she was stepping over a line it would be best not to cross. Traditions were traditions. Custom was custom.

If she was a timid woman, she might drop it and let Running

213

Wolf do what he wanted to do. But timid was the last thing she was. And this was too important to her. She could not risk losing him. Her determination of the other morning to accept Running Wolf and his ways seemed like a childhood memory, innocent and naïve.

Well, he'd be back tomorrow, and they'd have a serious talk about what differences they could accept, and which ones they could not.

Dropping her arm, she hurried down the trail toward the coulee. A group of women were going out to beat bushes and collect berries. There was always something to do.

CHAPTER THIRTY-THREE

Running Wolf spun around and glared at Kimana. She had no right hauling him out of the Sun Lodge, no right making a scene in front of the men.

After they'd retired for the night, no less.

He dragged a hand through his hair. The night air was close, hot on his skin. Even the breeze was warm and drenched in the scent of sage and wild prairie roses. This was the last thing he needed. There were only three days left before the final part of the ceremony, and he had to rest. Already his body was strained beyond belief.

And his mind.

"Do you have any idea what you could have done?"

A less controlled man might grab her shoulders and give her a good shake. "Any idea how much bad fate you can bring on a Sun Lodge by being there before the final ceremony? Besides the men, only the Vow Woman is allowed inside."

Not just bad luck on the lodge, but also on the dancers. It was a good thing he'd seen her just as she started to step through the flap.

"I won't be at the final ceremony. And, to speak frankly, neither should you," said Kimana.

He snorted. She was upset. He understood. But there was no point in talking about this now. There'd be time enough to argue about it later. Why they even needed to argue about it was beyond him, but she obviously thought it was an issue, and she wouldn't let it go with a civilized discussion.

"Not now, Kimana."

"Yes, now. I won't be there. In fact, if you insist on going through with this I'm going to have to do something. And you won't like it."

"Do what? Like what?"

He grabbed her arm and dragged her down a trail toward the hoodoos, away from the eyes and ears of the people. She wanted to talk about it? They'd talk about it. "Don't squirm."

"Let go of me."

"Not on your life. I wouldn't take a life's worth of buffalo hides to let go of you. Do you think I'm crazy? You're a little wildcat."

She yanked on her arm again as they approached the river. He kept his grip firm, neither loosening or tightening. Not for the first time, he was convinced that her father had obviously let her do whatever she pleased.

But he had always been forced to admit he liked her spirit. Something about this wild Kimana he found appealing in a dark, sensual way. Yes, he liked her spirit. But only as long as she wasn't being foolish.

She yanked again.

Foolish like she was now.

He glanced back and scowled.

"You'll pull it out of its socket if you do that."

She gave a harder yank. She dragged back on his arm and pulled him to a stop.

"Then. Let. Me. *Go!*"

With each word she yanked her arm a little further out of his grip.

No, he wasn't going to do this. He wouldn't be dragged into a fight by a woman.

And he didn't want to hurt her.

He dropped her arm and put up his hands.

"Done."

Facing each other, they watched opposing sets of dark eyes and heaving chests. He glanced around at the hoodoos rising around them into the night. They looked otherworldly with the light of distant fires dancing on them, creating black shadows outside of the light. They'd come far enough. And they were alone.

He took a deep breath. Had to get his irritation under control. Otherwise, he might be tempted to teach her the manners her father had neglected. He snorted a little in amusement at himself. He'd likely end up on his own ass if he tried.

"All right. Now talk. What do you mean you won't be at the ceremony? What in blazes are you talking about, woman? And what do you mean I won't like what you're going to do about it?"

She stepped forward and titled her chin up toward his. The outrageous little wildcat was challenging him!

"I told you once before how I felt about this," she said. "I told you I didn't believe in it."

"You don't believe in it?"

"No. We've talked about this once before."

"When?"

She waved a hand in dismissal.

"Once when we were comparing rituals and traditions that both our people share. I just don't believe in it."

"What foolishness. Your own people do the Sun Dance, Kimana. You've admitted as much."

"Yes, but never with mutilation! Not anymore. You could die!"

"That's not true. We don't mutilate. It's just piercings."

"In my tribe we considered that dangerous. My father didn't believe in it. Our elders agreed. Most of them. Some of them."

"Well, here we do it, and you're going to have to get used to it."

"Get used to it? I've been doing nothing but get used to things since you dragged me from my home eight moons ago. I've done nothing but adapt."

He winced. It was true. All of it. No, he shook his head. She'd been a prisoner. It was the way. "It's up to you to adapt to me and my ways, not the other way around."

He winced again. Hated how it sounded coming out of his mouth. Knew it was the wrong thing to say. And he knew it wasn't true. She'd already given so much. Changed so much. He was certain there would have been a better way to say that.

She stood staring at him, in obvious shock.

"I see. Then we have nothing else to say."

As quickly as she twirled around to go back to the camp, he grabbed her arm.

"I think we do."

He tried to turn her but she twisted out of his grip.

"Don't. Let me go. Just, please, release my arm. Let me go."

He was sure there were tears in her voice. Tears were one of the only things that could bring him down. And because he'd only rarely seen her anything but strong, her tears ripped him apart inside.

"Never. Turn around, Kimana."

"No."

"Turn around. Please."

They'd fix it. They'd make it better. Find some way to get past this one thing. He just needed her to stop crying. He should never have said that.

And now her shoulders were shaking. He closed his eyes and sighed. All right. She won. No Sun Dance.

He gave her a gentle tug.

"Look at me."

He half expected her to fold herself into his arms and let him croon away her tears. The last thing he expected was the see her eyes glittering, not with tears, but with rage unlike anything he'd ever seen in battle. Or anywhere else.

"I've adapted all I'm going to adapt. And you. You probably won't even wear the moccasins I made you."

"Moccasins?" He couldn't stop the grin. She'd made him moccasins. She hated making moccasins. He leaned back against a hoodoo and tucked his thumbs in his breechcloth. "Of course, I'll wear them."

"Yes, you will." She punctuated each word with a stab of her finger in his chest.

By all the spirits, she was gorgeous when she was angry.

"But you don't even know why, do you? No. No, you won't wear them. I won't let you." she said, narrowing her eyes. The firelight on the hoodoos reflected in their depths. She had no idea how utterly and completely beautiful she was. He reached out and cupped her chin.

"I will wear them. I want the moccasins, Kimana. And I want you."

She tugged her face away from his hand, grunted and cocked a hip. Folded her arms across her chest. "Well, too bad, Running Wolf. I don't want you."

"Yes, you do." He grinned.

"I certainly do not."

"Oh, I think you do". He stared into her eyes, then lifted his hand to her face again, running the backs of his fingers down her cheek. "Tell me. You want me. As much as I want you. I've missed you, Kimana. Missed touching you. Missed being with you. Come with me. Let me love you."

He started to reach down to lift her into his arms, but she held out a hand and stuck it on his chest.

"What about the Sun Dance? Do you still intend to go through with it?"

"I don't see how I can, now. The Vow Woman won't allow me to do it after leaving the lodge the way I did tonight. Besides. It means that much to you. So, no. No Sun Dance."

He reached down yet again to scoop her up into his- arms, but she put a hand on his chest again, and shook her head.

"Oh no, you don't. You're not carrying me into the bushes again."

Then she surprised him by stepping forward, brushing her breasts against his chest as she wrapped her arms around his neck. "This time we'll walk side by side."

And she kissed him.

And the world started to spin.

"Take me somewhere no one will find us," she whispered against his neck.

***

Kimana sighed as he lowered her body onto the smooth, sandy surface of hoodoo large enough to hold the Sun Lodge and a thousand spectators. High overhead, a moon that was not quite full hung in the sky. She clung to his mouth, gripped his shoulders.

She wanted him.

Needed him.

He was right, it had been too long. Weeks since the day at the river when he'd rained kisses over her flesh and made her ache for more.

She trailed her fingers down a wide chest that narrowed

temptingly at the waist. He was pure male. All hard muscles and sun-kissed skin. She let her fingers trail up his arm, then over his hair. It billowed black around his shoulders and onto his chest. The hard lines of his face were softened by desire.

"I want you inside me," she whispered, and tugged at his breechcloth. "Take me."

"Not yet, little wildcat. I want to look at you, first."

She lifted her arms and let him pull off her dress.

Leaned back on her elbows and smiled. Gave her hair a little toss and smiled a purely feminine smile at the power she had over him. But he also had power over her. Just look at him.

He was magnificent. His skin had a slight sheen of sweat from the hot night air. It glistened like liquid gold in the distant firelight and under the waxing moon. They were far enough away from the people, but if someone was out for a stroll, they would probably see their silhouettes on the top of this hoodoo. But that just made it more exciting. Wilder, somehow. If someone did see them, they'd never know who they were, so it didn't really matter. And she didn't think she could wait any longer to have his hands on her.

"I want to touch you," he said, his voice husky and gruff.

She lifted a hand, and his gaze fell to her breasts. Her breath caught in her throat as he devoured her with his eyes.

She clamped a hand around his neck as he lowered his mouth to her nipple, nibbling gently, suckling with an exquisite and maddening gentleness. She felt her breasts tighten and the nipples harden with a strange but wonderful ache.

"Oh, yes."

His tongue flicked out, and he drew ever-widening circles around the nub.

A breeze danced over her skin. Tingled where he left moist trails with his mouth. She arched her back, wanting him to take her breast inside his mouth. To suck hard, deep. As if sensing her need, he turned his lips toward her and tugged gently on her nipple with his teeth. She moaned.

"I want you, Kimana." He nuzzled between her breasts, kissing in the valley between them, and then up either side, sucked lightly on her nipples again, each one in turn. This was what she'd craved all these weeks, the feel of him touching her, waking up her body and setting it on fire.

He rolled onto his back and pulled her on top of him. Her hair fell over her shoulders and she tipped her head back as he ran his hands down her body and over her hips.

"Do you have any idea what you do to me?" he asked.

Then he inched her back and sat up, pulling her chest toward his mouth. Her legs straddled his hips, and she could feel herself growing hotter. Wetter. Aching with need. She rocked her hips, rubbing against him. Nothing anyone had ever told her had prepared her for this feeling.

Somewhere far away a wild cat roared in the night.

He rocked them for a moment, then lifted her up and settled her onto his hardness. A moan escaped her lips and she threw back her head again as he lowered her gently onto him.

She'd never known it could be like this.

So wild.

Primal.

Two bodies merged into one - a single being throbbing in the night. She moaned as he rocked her against his body, his hands caressing her hips up to her waist and back again. He made her feel so alive.

"Beautiful," he murmured. "So beautiful."

He wrapped his arms around her back and pulled her chest against his, taking her lips with a savage groan, rocking harder, deeper until one, then the other cried out into the night.

When they were both spent, she lay on top of him, her heart pounding in time with his.

***

Two Hawks clenched his fist around the handle of his blade and stabbed it repeatedly into the ground as he watched the two lovers embrace on the top of the hoodoo. His relief at finding Kimana alive was overshadowed by his rage at seeing her in the arms of another man.

Willingly in his arms.

He'd almost revealed himself when he saw the Blackfoot warrior drag her away from the Sun Lodge and down the path toward the river. He couldn't hear what they said to each other, but he could tell they were arguing. The fact that she seemed only angry, and not frightened, had been enough to keep him from killing the man on the spot. Instead, he'd followed them upriver to the hoodoos.

He didn't want to watch, but he couldn't stop himself. The more intimate the scene became, the more rage built up inside of him.

What he did want to do was hurl his blade right into the heart of the man who touched his woman. His woman. His. No man had a right to take what belonged to him.

What was his by right.

By promise.

By vow.

No man had a right to touch that body.

A strangled roar of rage burst from his throat as he watched Kimana throw her head back in passion as the man ran his hands up her waist and over her breasts.

He couldn't watch.

Couldn't stop watching.

Something rustled in the sage bushes and cottonwood trees that concealed him. He turned his head to catch the sound. He rose from his knees to a low crouch and crept through the brush, careful not to disturb any branches and give away his position. He didn't know if his presence was known or not, but he wouldn't be taken without a fight.

Under the light of the moon, he caught a gleam of flesh. He froze, ready to stab with his blade. Then, less than an arm's length away, a woman came to an abrupt stop. But she didn't seem to notice he was there.

He could hear the rush of sharply indrawn breath. She stared, lips slightly parted, through the trees at the same scene he had just witnessed. His own breath caught as a thin stream of moonlight lit her face. She took a single step forward and fisted her hand around a thin branch. He cringed at the sound it made as the leaves brushed her arm.

Was she alone? He glanced around. Nothing moved. Her breathing and the quiet rustle of leaves were the only sounds in the night.

He looked back at the woman.

Smirked.

Blackfoot weren't too observant, were they? He could slice her throat before she even knew he was there. It would be a shame to end the life of someone as stunning as she, but that wouldn't stop him if he thought she'd give him away. He tucked his blade into a strap around his waist and reached out and to wrap his arm around her neck.

She turned her face casually and stared into his eyes. He could see the gleam of teeth in the moonlight.

"There you are," she said, and trailed a finger down his chest. "I thought I'd lost you. Now, I want to know exactly who you are and what you want, or I'm going to scream."

CHAPTER THIRTY-FOUR

Kimana's eyes snapped open and she stared in confusion at the moonlight streaming through the smoke hole. She strained to hear the sound that had awoken her but heard only Black Eagle's rumbling snores. She glanced over at Running Wolf's mat, then remembered he had gone back to the Sun Lodge after walking her back to their lodge so he could officially withdraw from the ceremony. So, who had called her name?

Or had she been dreaming?

Since returning with Running Wolf from the hoodoos, she'd slept restlessly, flipping from side to side in an effort to find a comfortable position. His insistence on speaking to the Vow Woman about the dance that night irritated her a little, and warred with the sweet memory of making love under the moonlight.

Kicking off the light hide that tangled between her legs, she rolled onto her side and closed her eyes. It must have been a dream.

"Kimana."

Not a dream. A voice, barely discernible. Someone was outside the teepee.

"Running Wolf?"

"Shhh. Come outside," came the whispered reply.

Draping the hide around her shoulders, she slipped out through the entrance and looked for Running Wolf, but a cloud had passed over the moon, and the camp was shrouded in darkness. Then an arm snaked around her waist, pinned her arms and pulled her back against a hard chest. She knew, instinctively, that it was not Running Wolf.

"Let me go!" She arched away from the man, but he tightened his grip and covered her mouth with his other hand.

"Who did you think it was, Kimana," a man's voice whispered harshly into her ear. "Who have you given yourself to?"

For a moment, she froze in shock. Then she struggled against him, and the arm that held her trapped against his chest jerked, causing her to draw in a sharp, startled breath. "Are you in the habit of meeting men outside the lodge at night?"

She couldn't quite make out his voice, but there was something familiar in the whispered words. Something just familiar enough, just safe enough, to make her stop struggling.

"Be quiet, and I'll uncover your mouth. Will you be still?"

She nodded.

The hand disappeared, and he turned her around to face him. Moonlight lit his face. She gasped.

"Two Hawks!"

"Shhh."

"Where did you come from? How did you find me? You have to leave before someone sees you."

She looked around in a panic, but no one was about this late at night.

"Did you really think I wouldn't find you?"

"No, I... I hoped, I thought, I didn't know."

"So you did hope I'd come. I'm glad of this. Let's walk. We have much to talk about, and I'm not in the mood to fight off the blade of the Blackfoot scum I saw you with tonight."

He grasped her arm and dragged her away from the lodge, past the outer edge of the circle camp.

Apprehension snaked through her belly as the impact of his words hit her. He had seen her with Running Wolf. Something in his tone made her want to yank her arm out of his grip and run back to the lodge, but she owed it to him to give him an explanation, so she let him lead her away from the camp, toward the path that led to the river.

Part way down the trail, he paused as another cloud passed over the moon, temporarily stealing away the light.

"Where are we going?" she asked.

LISA REANEY

"Somewhere we can talk without being heard. I've made camp close by."

He led her down the path and along the river, past the hoodoos where she and Running Wolf had made love. She was surprised for a moment at how well he knew where he was going, then remembered he'd been here before.

"How did you know we'd be at this place?"

"I've been tracking you. And it's no great secret the Blackfoot come here for their annual summer gathering. We spoke of this many times. Quiet now. We'll talk shortly. We're almost there."

They followed the twisting river far from the throngs of people camping and rounded several bends before coming to a tangled mass of buffalo berry bushes. He released her arm, parted the bushes and waved her ahead of him. In the wall of the cliff, she saw a dark slit, wide enough for a man to walk through, and maybe a horse. A cave. And one she hadn't seen when she was out beating the bushes for berries with the women just the day before.

"How long have you been here?"

"Come inside," he said. "I'll answer your questions, but only after you answer mine."

She felt uneasy, didn't want to go in, but that was silly. He would never hurt her. And she knew she owed it to him to give him an explanation. Inside the cave, she strained to see through the blackness, and heard the sharp sound of flint snapping against flint. Then a spark. She smelled the earthy scent of dried moss catching fire. An orange glow appeared in the dark. The flames grew and she saw him crouched in front of a small ring of stones.

"Sit down, Kimana. Are you thirsty? I have water."

"No, I'm fine."

She hugged her arms to her chest and turned back to the entrance of the cave. She couldn't sit down, she was too jittery. She felt his eyes on her back. She grew uncomfortable, knowing he would want an explanation for Running Wolf.

"Who was the man I saw you with tonight?"

She turned around, tried to soften her voice, soften the blow she knew her words would be. "He's to be my husband."

Two Hawks surged to his feet. "Did he force himself on you? Were you raped? I'll rip his heart from his chest and feed it to the

226

dogs."

"No. I gave myself willingly."

His silence filled the cave. She looked down at her feet, then lowered herself to the ground.

"You are promised to me."

She sighed. "I was. But that was before. A lot has changed, Two Hawks. I'm not the person I was."

"How could you give yourself to someone else when you were vowed to me? Didn't you know I would be searching for you? That I would expect you to fulfil your promise?"

"I didn't know what to think. So much time has passed. After the attack, I looked for you. I watched for you, but you didn't come. I didn't know if you were alive or dead. I could only assume you'd moved on with your life, and all I could do was move on with mine."

"By giving yourself to the enemy?"

She winced. "I'm sorry."

"How could you accept this? You've spent your whole life hating the Blackfoot, and then I come here and find you living amongst them like you've been with them forever."

"It's complicated."

"Complicated. You'll have to do better than that. There's no excuse for accepting a life with the enemy. You should have fought them. Didn't you even try to escape?"

"Once."

"Obviously you failed. And what of the other women? Have they settled into their new life just like you have?"

The sarcasm in his voice hurt.

"You don't know what it was like."

"No, I don't. Why don't you enlighten me?"

"Have you ever thought about how similar we are to the Blackfoot?"

He spat on the ground. "We're nothing like them."

"We're more alike than you know."

"And you've been deceived by their lies."

"I've lived with them. I've watched them."

"And now you think you know them. You forget, Kimana. You forget how they have warred against our people since the dawn of time. You forget how they butchered our warriors, stole our women and children, left our village in ashes."

"I haven't forgotten," she whispered, and the pain of losing her father washed over her again.

"But you've forgiven it."

"Yes. No. No, but I understand why."

"What is there to understand?"

"I can't explain it."

"Try."

She turned her face to the slice of light streaming through the opening to the cave and sighed again.

"When they first took us from our village, all I thought about was escape. And vengeance. What they did was horrible, but our people have done horrible things, too. They were only doing what we would have done. They were seeking revenge for wrongs committed against their own people. By ours."

"And you think that justifies what they did?"

"It explains it. It's not an excuse. It's a reason."

Two Hawks rolled his eyes and shook his head. "You're not thinking rationally. You're thinking like a woman."

"Of course, I'm thinking like a woman," she snapped. "That doesn't mean I'm not thinking rationally."

"It means it's a good thing I got here when I did. I can save you from the biggest mistake you'll ever make."

"I don't need saving."

"I think you do."

"Since when are you in charge of my life? You're not my father."

"I'm your mate."

"No, you're not."

"Close enough."

"We never spoke the vows."

"Not yet. But we will."

"Two Hawks, you don't understand. I can't allow you to make decisions for me. I'm not an innocent maiden anymore. I've had to learn how to survive in a strange place. I've had to make decisions on my own and learn to live with them. I'm sorry, but I can't marry you."

His lips thinned as he stared at her, his face a mask of fury.

"I didn't come all this way to be told you want someone else."

"I'm sorry."

"What makes him better than me?"

She hesitated. Knew she could not hurt him more than she already had. "Nothing."

"Then tell me why you want him."

"I love him."

"Love." He sneered.

Silence fell between them like heavy snow, muffling even the sounds of their breathing. Had she ever told Two Hawks she loved him? No, she realized, she never had. They'd played together as children, grown up together, laughed and cried together. She loved him, yes, but she realised now it was the kind of love you feel for a brother or a friend, not a mate. She'd never loved him in the way a woman loves a man she wants to spend her life with. Not like she loved Running Wolf.

She looked up at Two Hawks, hoping he could somehow see into her heart and understand what she found it almost impossible to explain. She'd grown up knowing she would marry for all the right reasons. What she thought were the right reasons. Security. Status within the tribe. Companionship. Other people's expectations. She'd never hoped to marry for love. It hadn't even occurred to her. But now, that was more important than anything else.

He stared at her in disgust.

"Love," he said again. "What does love have to do with anything?"

"Everything."

And saying the words, she realized she meant it. All the anger she'd felt over the attack on her people, the annoyance over the Sun Dance, none of it mattered. She loved Running Wolf. Somehow, they would find a way to get past their differences.

"If love is what you need, then I can give that to you."

"You don't understand."

"No, you don't understand. Since you were a little girl, I wanted you. I've always wanted you. I can't let you go."

"You'll have to. I'm sorry. I have to go. Morning will be here soon, and Running Wolf will be looking for me."

She stood up to leave, turned toward the entrance. And felt his arms coming around her again. Pinning her to his chest.

"Then he'll have to keep looking. You're not going anywhere except with me."

CHAPTER THIRTY-FIVE

W here's Kimana?"
Running Wolf stood just inside the entrance of the lodge, staring at the cold fire pit. A feeling of dread skittered through his belly. He looked up at his father and repeated the question.

Black Eagle shrugged.

"She wasn't here when I woke up a few moments ago. I know she came in late last night. I assumed, when I awoke, that you and she had gone off together somewhere again. I should probably scold you for that."

Running Wolf grimaced but looked the chief directly in the eye. He wouldn't apologize for being intimate with Kimana, not even to his father.

Black Eagle waved his hand toward Kimana's mat.

"Her sleeping hide is gone. Maybe she went for a walk. It's feels chilly today. The summer sun must be weak this morning."

"It is. But still, it's not like her to leave without starting a fire. Especially on a morning like this."

His father grunted and nodded, his eyes filled with concern, then he lifted an eyebrow. "Did you argue again last night?"

Running Wolf looked at Black Eagle in surprise, then looked away. He'd prefer people didn't know their private business, but it was hard to keep a secret in such close quarters. When he and Kimana argued, it seemed the whole village knew about it. But then, no one's business was secret. It was a fact of life he had always lived with, but it still grated.

"We had words."

"Maybe she needed to walk off some anger. Better than arguing again this morning. Why aren't you at the Sun Lodge?"

"I will not be doing the dance. I have already spoken to the Vow Woman."

"Ah. And that would be because you went off last night?"

"It was my choice. It's not Kimana's fault." Running Wolf said, trying to keep the annoyance out of his voice.

"Did I say it was Kimana's fault? It seems you have some anger to walk off, as well."

"I'm not angry."

"No, I can see that."

"I said I'm not angry."

"You've said that twice, my son. A more perceptive man than I might wonder why you felt you had to convince him. Don't worry about her. I'm sure she'll be back soon."

He wasn't angry. He was worried. Leaving this way was not like her. Running Wolf left the lodge and wandered through the elder's circle camp, stopping at the edge of the cliff to look down on the larger camp below. Maybe it was like his father said, she was still angry about the Sun Dance and needed to work it off. But he couldn't shake the feeling there was something more than that.

She'd rather confront him than keep her anger to herself. He'd learned to appreciate that about her - her directness, and the fearless way she stood up to him. It wasn't like her to avoid him after an argument. Besides, that argument had ended in the most delightful way. For both of them. Anger was the last thing either one of them would be feeling today.

And yet, she was nowhere to be found.

The sun washed the landscape with golden light and sparkled on the murky water. Upriver, the hoodoos seemed to glow as if lit from within.

It might be cool now, but by the time the sun reached its zenith, it would be unbearably hot.

He scanned the camp on both sides of the river, but he couldn't see her. It didn't mean she wasn't down there. But finding her might prove a more difficult task than he was in the mood for. With thousands of people milling around, it would be like trying to find a chunk of quartz in a dry riverbed full of rocks.

On a cloudy day.

"Good morning, Running Wolf. It's a fine morning, isn't it? The hoodoos look beautiful this morning, and the sky is such a bright blue."

He turned to find Meda standing a few steps away, her hand shading her eye from the bright sun.

"Yes. Have you seen Kimana?"

"Not since yesterday. She's supposed to come by my lodge this morning so we can finish your new teepee. But why aren't you at the Sun Lodge?"

"I'm not doing the dance."

"Oh? So Kimana talked you out of it, did she? I thought she might."

He didn't answer. The reason for not doing the dance was not the old woman's business, although he was sure his father would fill Meda in when they talked later. There was little the two didn't share.

"Well, if you see her, tell her I'm waiting for her at my lodge. I'll start without her, but she really should be there. Be a good boy, and tell her to hurry, would you? These old hands can't sew for long."

"I'll do that," Running Wolf said.

He spent the morning wandering through camp. He lifted his hand in acknowledgement more times than he could count as people greeted him by name. He would have liked to stop and chat with some of them, renew old acquaintances, but the longer he looked for her, the more disgruntled, the more worried, he became.

Finally, when the sun was high overhead and he was wiping the sweat from his brow, he turned toward the hoodoos. Maybe she really was in a pout and had returned to the place where they'd made love the night before.

By now, he was seriously annoyed. He was tempted to put her over his knees just for making him waste so much time looking for her.

He snorted and couldn't quite stop a grin. That would be a sight to see. Not to mention an invitation for bruises and possible broken bones. His. The little wildcat would never tolerate such manhandling.

But if he didn't find her soon, he just might take the risk.

***

Jonesy watched the young Injun woman rub the soft hide between her fingers.

It was a good idea coming to the Blackfoot gathering to sell some of his hides and such. Shoulda thought of doing that last year. He mostly went to the Cree gatherings, but there were more people here than he could sneeze at. He'd remember that in the future. Opportunity, yessir. Lots and lots of opportunity.

He wondered if Two Hawks had made it this far, or if he'd found his woman already. At least he hadn't had to go on foot. Trading Bessie for that crazy horse he'd ended up with had been a big mistake until Two Hawks had traded the beast for the dress.

But then, the dress hadn't been able to haul his stuff. Maybe he'd finally get it off his hands. Be a shame to part with it, though. It was like some kind of art.

The pretty young thing in front of him held out the dress and gave it a shake, letting the hide unfold. She smiled at the musical sound the beads made as they trembled. Yessir, she was smitten, that was for sure. He rubbed his hands together, and grinned.

"How much?" she asked him.

"Well, now, young lady, that's the thing. A hide as fine as this has gotta be worth at least a pony or two, I'm thinkin'.

She looked confused.

"Horses," he said, and held up two fingers. "Two horses. And not wild ones, either. Gotta be tame. Tame. Understand?"

"Tame, yes, of course. Two? Not two. One."

"Sold!" He cackled. "Been a pleasure doin' business with ya."

***

Running Wolf stood on top of the hoodoo and surveyed the area on each side of the river. He was starting to worry. Even if she was furious, she wouldn't just disappear, and he'd looked everywhere. Of course, it was possible he'd missed her. More than possible, it was likely. Angry with himself for spending the better part of the day searching for her, he turned to climb down off the hoodoo.

A bit of white caught his eye against the sandstone.

He bent down, picked up a feather and twirled it thoughtfully between his fingers. He couldn't shake the feeling his feisty little bird had flown from him.

***

He climbed the trail back to the circle camp. It was the third time he'd made the climb since morning. No one had seen her. It was like she'd vanished. At the top of the path, he stopped and looked around. Silver Fox was scurrying toward her lodge, carrying something in her arms.

Without thinking, he broke into long strides to catch her before she disappeared inside.

Running Wolf took hold of her arm and swung her around.

"Have you seen her?"

"Oh, Running Wolf. You startled me." She clutched her burden to her chest.

He gave her a little shake. "Have you seen her?

"Seen who? What are you talking about? Seen who?"

"Kimana? Do you know where she is?"

"Why would I know where she is? I'm not her keeper. I'm just as happy never to see her again, if I'm totally honest with you."

Damned woman was becoming more waspish all the time. Especially since word had gotten around about his and Kimana's wedding. He supposed he should have expected her to be angry, especially since she assumed they would speak the vows together. But he didn't have time for that right now.

"I just wanted to know if you've seen her today."

Silver Fox smirked. "Lose her already? She'll be a tough one for you to keep track of. You'd better establish some rules, or she'll treat you like a young boy at your mother's knee."

Running Wolf bristled.

"No one treats me like that."

"Well, not someone who truly cares for you. But only you know that." She shifted the pale hide in her arms. "You know, I wanted to speak with you about Kimana. As a friend. I'm not sure if you know what you're really and truly getting yourself in for."

A pained expression settled over Running Wolf's face.

"Thank you for your concern. But I don't think I have anything to worry about. I just want to find the woman."

"Are you sure she came back?"

"Came back? From where?"

"I saw her by her lodge last night, after dark. But she wasn't alone."

He turned to leave. She couldn't tell him anything useful. She'd seen the two of them when he'd walked Kimana back home.

Silver Fox grabbed his arm.

"Wait. That's what I wanted to tell you. She was with a man. That's all I meant about knowing what you're in for."

He shook off her hand. "She was with me. I was taking her home after a walk."

"No. No, she wasn't going back to your teepee. She was leaving. And I think I know you well enough to be able to recognize you, even in the dark. The moon's almost full, you know. It wasn't you she was with, Running Wolf. I can tell you that for sure. She was with some other man. I thought you knew. I thought you'd finally come to your senses and decided not to marry her, cast her out."

He sensed the sincerity in her words, and it tore at him.

"Impossible. She'd never betray me."

"No, it's not. I should have told you this, too, but I ran into a man I didn't know yesterday. I was out for a walk. Last night. Evening. He asked about Kimana. He didn't say his name."

"What man?"

"A stranger."

"Blackfoot?"

"No. His words were a little too different to be Blackfoot. I'm sorry, but he sounded Cree. How long have you been looking for Kimana?"

He looked up at the sun. It was halfway between its zenith and sunset.

"All day," he growled.

"Well, there you go. I'd be willing to bet it was that man she was supposed to marry before she – you know, came to our village. She's probably long gone by now. You always knew she'd try to escape the first chance she got. You can't forget the fact that she's tried it before. If he came here and found her, she'd go. Of course, she'd go. The Cree are different, they don't have our values, but it's what I would do if I was her and the man I loved showed up."

His palm went numb from the pressure of his fingernails.

"How late was it you saw her?"

"It was the middle of the night. I'm sorry to say this, but I told you not to trust her."

Fear and anger chewed their way through his gut. He had no reason to believe Silver Fox, but he also had no reason to doubt her. She might be known to lie, but she'd always been honest with him.

He shot her a look. That he knew of.

But if she was telling the truth - and the sick feeling in his stomach told him she was – where would Kimana have gone?

Suddenly, he wanted to lash out, slam something. He ground his teeth together and tightened his fists again, fought back a sneer.

It was more likely Silver Fox would be out with a man late at night than Kimana.

"What were you doing out wandering that late at night?"

"Jealous?" She smiled, then laughed, almost sweetly.

"Unfortunately for you, Running Wolf, it's not any of your business. We both know that if it was, I'd certainly not go wandering off in the middle of the night. And not with another man. I know exactly where I'd lay my head and spend each night. Whose arms I'd spend them in. We both know."

He looked away, uncomfortable.

"If you really insist on knowing, I was out to relieve myself."

"Are you sure it was the middle of the night?"

"Quite sure. Everyone was sleeping by that time. I couldn't even see the scouts, but then they're farther out on the plains, away from the camp, aren't they?"

"Yes."

"Running Wolf?" She laid her hand upon his arm again and looked into his eyes, her own eyes soft with invitation. "I'm sorry this has hurt you. Please let her go. She'll just hurt you, and you don't deserve to be hurt again. You've lost so much already."

CHAPTER THIRTY-SIX

She was tired of men making decisions for her. And she was tired of being picked up, tossed onto a horse, and taken off to wherever a man felt he had to take her. Kimana glared over her shoulder, eyes narrowed into slits, lips curled back into a snarl.

Two Hawks raised an eyebrow. "Don't do that, Kimana, you look really unattractive. It makes your scars stand out."

Unattractive? How dare he!

"I'll show you unattractive."

"Please don't," he said.

"Release me immediately."

"I don't think so. I've learned my lesson."

"Not well enough."

"If you think I'm going to let you go so you can jump on me again you're wrong. My bones ache more than enough these days since the accident."

"You've said that twice, now. What accident?"

"I'll tell you what," he said. "Ask me later, when you actually seem to care."

"Don't wait for it."

"Don't worry."

She faced forward and let her lips settle into a scowl. "Who said I don't care?"

"Please. I'm finding this really tiresome."

"You'll find it a lot more tiresome if you don't let me go."

"Where is the sweet girl I used to know? You've turned into some kind of wild animal."

"A wild *cat*. And don't you forget it."

"What's gotten into you?"

She turned her face away and shook her head. What had gotten into her? She didn't know. Since meeting Running Wolf, she really was like a wildcat.

And for some reason, rather proud of it.

Fighting with Two Hawks just didn't give her the same thrill fighting with Running Wolf did. He didn't seem to light the same spark in her.

But she did care about Two Hawks no matter what he said. That hadn't changed. She always would.

"Please tell me about your accident. I want to know."

"Suddenly you care, Kimana?"

"Of course, I do," she said, exasperated.

"All right. It happened when I was looking for you after the attack on the village. That's why I couldn't find you sooner. I lost my footing going down the side of a bank near a river and fell. Broke my left leg, banged up the rest of my body pretty well. An old trapper found me and took me to another Cree village, farther north."

"An old trapper?"

"Yes."

She stared off into the distance, not seeing the endless prairie stretched out before them. It was just a fog, like a dream, but she remembered a grizzled, old face. And a crazy cackle.

"An old trapper rescued me, too."

"I know."

That snapped her back. "What do you mean you know? How could you know?"

"He told me."

"But how..."

"He found you, he told me, floating in a river. He said you almost died. That he pulled you out, got you warm. How do you think I knew where to look for you?"

"But what are the chances..."

"I know. Strange, isn't it?"

Kimana shifted her weight and rolled her neck. By all the

spirits, she hated this endless riding. It played havoc on the muscles.

"At least untie me until we stop again."

"If I do, do you promise not to try to fly off the horse?"

"I value my neck, thank you."

He slowed the horse to a halt with his knees, and quickly untied her wrists. Then, before she could open her mouth, or even think about pushing herself off, he kicked the animal back into a slow gallop. She swallowed a sigh, flexed her fingers and stretched her arms in front of her. They started to tingle. Better that than being tied.

"The trapper told you to look for me at the gathering?" she said over her shoulder.

"Yes. But that wasn't the first place I looked. I travelled well into the mountains before heading back down the river toward that big buffalo jump. You'd been there," said Two Hawks.

"How do you know?"

"Wait a moment. I'll show you."

She felt him fumble around at his chest.

"Remember this?" he asked, bringing his hand around her, holding it in front of her face.

A neck ornament with pink quartz dangled from his fingers.

She gasped.

"You stole from the dead?"

"You can't steal something that belongs to you. Where did he get it, Kimana? Who gave it to him?"

"Obviously, it was me."

"Why? I gave that to you as a promise. Why would you give it away, and why give it to a dead man?"

"He was special to me."

"Special enough to give away my promise to you? Just how many men have you been special with since you disappeared?"

"How dare you!"

"You forget. I saw you last night. With that Blackfoot. Were you with that boy as well? The dead one?"

"No."

"But you gave him the gift I gave to you."

"I had an obligation to him. Of sorts."

"Well. First you had an obligation to me, and I intend to see you keep it. Even if I have to tie and gag you."

***

Running Wolf nodded his thanks to the scout, then turned his horse in the opposite direction, back toward the summer village. To the gathering. The place he'd started from.

And the place he was returning, empty handed.

None of the men on sentry duty out on the plains had seen them.

That left only one possibility. They'd taken the river. Which meant it was going to be very hard to pick up their trail. And the sun was setting. Which meant it would be impossible to continue the search until tomorrow.

Which meant he might not find her at all.

***

"Can't we stop for a while? It's almost dark. I'm thirsty. Hungry. We haven't eaten for hours. My hind end is getting sore."

"Kimana, that was rude."

"It's not rude. It's true."

"You're not supposed to say so."

"I will if it's true."

Two Hawks was silent for several minutes.

"We can stop for the night. We've come far enough for one day. Anyone who is searching for us won't be able to follow the trail at night, anyway. But I'm going to have to tie you, I'm deeply sorry."

"Oh, please. Don't be sorry," she said, not bothering to hide the sarcasm.

He brought the horse to a stop next to a stream, vaulted off, and held out his hands to help her down. She accepted his assistance with a slight thinning of the lips, expecting him retie her immediately.

"No," he said. "I think I'll leave you free for a while. You can relieve yourself, then we can have something to eat. But Kimana, I'm warning you, don't even think of trying to escape."

She nodded curtly, then waded through the tall prairie grass to crouch behind a small group of Saskatoon berry bushes.

"Tell me about the boy you gave my stone to," Two Hawks called out.

"I'm a bit busy here."

"My apologies. I'll wait."

"There's really nothing to tell."

"Must be something. You wouldn't have given my stone to him if you hadn't felt something for him."

No, that much was true. She'd cared about Stands Alone. But how did she explain the guilt she had over his death? How did she explain that she'd allowed the young warrior to believe she was interested in him, when all she really wanted was Running Wolf? And how could she possibly explain all of that to Two Hawks?

"He courted me for a while," she said, and walked back to the stream.

Two Hawks looked up from his crouch beside the water where he was filling a water bag.

"You allowed it?"

"I didn't discourage him."

"You were vowed to me, Kimana."

"I didn't know if you'd ever find me, or if I'd ever escape. Besides, you could have been dead, for all I knew."

"I'm not. Obviously. And what about this other one? The one you were," he paused for a moment to give her a disapproving scowl. "*With* last night?"

"Running Wolf."

"The one you say you're going to marry."

"I am going to marry him."

"We'll see about that."

She thrust her arms out to the sides in frustration. "Why can't you understand that I moved on with my life?"

"I didn't."

That shook her. Here it was again. All over again. More guilt. More responsibility for yet another man's pain. She couldn't take any more of this. They watched each other for a long moment in the fading light.

"I'm sorry. I truly am so very sorry, Two Hawks. I wish there was something I could do to make it up to you."

"There is. Honour my claim. Your father wanted you to marry me. You owe that much to me." He gave her shoulders a quick shake and looked deep into her eyes.

"Honour my claim, Kimana."

CHAPTER THIRTY-SEVEN

Running Wolf slid off the stallion and ran his fingers across the grooves left by a set of hooves in a mud bank. He looked up at Makwai and grinned.

"Good girl, Makwai"

He stood, nodded to the men he had gathered before beginning his search of the river, then looked east. The moon was full and the sky above was covered in thin, wispy white clouds, the kind that diffuse the light and spread it all over the landscape. Just over the horizon, the clouds parted for the briefest of moments, and he could see the stars painting the sky. All too soon, when the weather grew cold and winter descended upon the land, the mighty hunter and his faithful dog would once again shine brightly, making their nightly trek across the sky.

He scratched Makwai behind the ears. Not every hunter was lucky enough to have such a faithful companion but Running Wolf and the hunter who crept across the sky during the cold winter months knew the value of a good friend.

"Don't we, Makwai? Yes, we do."

He'd known it was the right thing to do, to follow Makwai. She had appeared just as he and his small war party had been about to leave the camp.

She growled and whined, running in half circles, dashing back and forth in the tall grass.

Trusting the wolf as much as he trusted his men, he decided to follow her.

243

Together, they travelled with Makwai heading north along the edge of the river until the wolf began to fuss on the east side of the bank where the river curved.

He glanced back down at the hoof prints. The animal carried the weight of more than one body. Its prints sunk deep into the muck. They wouldn't be far now. Even though it was slow going along the river, they would make faster time going across the plains than the Cree horse could carrying two people.

The last thing his enemy would expect was for any pursuers to find them during the night, along unfamiliar terrain.

Well, the enemy warrior would get a surprise.

Running Wolf smiled, his lips thinned with determination.

***

"Kimana, wake up. It's time to go."

She rolled over onto her back and opened her eyes a crack. The sky was that odd shade between black and purple.

"It's not even morning. The sun's not up."

"It's time to go. The sky's getting light. Come on, we have to get moving."

She rolled back onto her stomach.

"Don't want to. Tired. Sore," she mumbled. And cranky. He'd probably try to tie her up again, and that meant she was going to have even more aching muscles fighting him off. She'd rather delay that little battle for as long as she could.

"Sleep. Let me sleep."

"No, you have to get up. You'll feel better after you eat something."

"Not hungry."

She heard the crack of his knees as he crouched beside her and laid his hand on her shoulder.

"Come on. I promise I won't tie you today."

"Is that supposed to motivate me?"

He chuckled. "No. But maybe this will."

She whipped her head around and glared at him as she felt the crack of his hand on her backside.

"If you put your hand on my woman again, I'll kill you."

They both turned to stare at the sound of the voice. Running Wolf straddled his stallion, his face set in a murderous scowl, hair loose and flowing around his shoulders. He looked every inch the warrior. A furious warrior.

He spared her a brief glance, before locking eyes with Two Hawks.

Two Hawks whipped a blade out of his calf-length moccasin and stood up, legs braced as he faced Running Wolf.

"So, you found us. I commend your tracking skills. And your stealth. But I really didn't expect you so soon. I thought you wouldn't catch up to us until later in the day. If at all," Two Hawks said.

"We rode through the night." He waved his hands toward a spot behind Kimana and Two Hawks, where three more warriors sat upon their horses. "And I had a little help from a friend."

He nodded toward Makwai, who sat on her haunches next to the stream. Her tongue lolled out in the delighted grin she wore more often than not.

Two Hawks looked at the wolf and bristled. "Wait. That's *your* wolf?"

"She's mine. As is Kimana."

"No," said Two Hawks, the wolf forgotten. "She belongs to me."

Kimana looked back and forth between the two men, then pushed herself to her knees.

"I don't belong to anyone. I am not property to be haggled over. And I won't allow you to fight."

"Stay out of this, Kimana," warned Running Wolf.

"Stay out of it? How can you ask me to do that? I'm in the middle of it."

She turned her face toward Two Hawks. Maybe he'd have more sense.

"Two Hawks?"

"Leave it, Kimana."

"I don't believe this."

She thrust herself to her feet, placed her hands on her hips and scorched both of them with her eyes. "I will not be fought over like some sort of prize. This is ridiculous. I refuse to be the spoils of battle."

She'd had enough of battles and vengeance. And she didn't want either one of them hurt. She laid a hand on Two Hawks' arm.

"Please. Don't fight."

He covered her fingers with his hand. "You're mine, Kimana. You've always been mine. I won't let you go without a fight."

Running Wolf angled his horse closer to Two Hawks and narrowed his eyes.

"I told you not to touch her."

"I'll touch her if I want."

"No, you won't!" Kimana said. "Neither one of you is going to touch me. You sound like children."

"Did you take her?" Running Wolf demanded. "Did you lay with her last night?"

Two Hawks stiffened. "What if I did?"

Running Wolf snarled. "If you put a single finger on her, you're dead."

"Yes, you said that before," Two Hawks said with a sneer.

Kimana's jaw dropped open in disbelief. She looked between the two warriors and shook her head.

Oh, this was too much. How dare they insult her this way? She wasn't the village whore!

"What is it with you men? You act as if I don't have any morals. Like I can't make my own choices. You act like I'm some brainless little thing who can't think for herself. I decide whose hands are on me. Who makes love to me. I decide if. I decide when." She turned a determined face to Running Wolf. "And I decide who. Me. I decide who marries me. I will not allow you to fight over me. And that's the end of it. I decide. Me!"

He threw down the reins, swung his leg around and dropped to his feet.

"You made a promise to me," he said.

"I made a promise to Two Hawks as well."

"Well, then." His eyes turned to ice. "You have a problem."

Kimana stared at Running Wolf for the space of a heartbeat. Two. Three. Then she thrust her finger toward each of their chests in turn.

"If either one of you touches the other, there will be no wedding."

She left the two men facing each other and stalked away, stood at the stream bank and watched the sky turn to pink and purple over the horizon. What she wanted didn't seem to matter to either one of them.

She pressed her fingers into her temples.

Running Wolf was right. She had a problem. She had two men ready to fight, both of whom had a legitimate claim on her. Her heart told her to go with Running Wolf, but Two Hawks was right. She had made a promise to him. A promise her father had approved. But she'd also made a promise to Running Wolf. And she had no doubt her father would approve of him as well.

She needed time to think. She needed to talk to someone. She wished her father were still alive, and that he could tell her what to do. She would talk with Chief Black Eagle and Meda. They were the only ones who could give her the advice she needed.

Kimana turned around and faced the two warriors who stood, side by side, and watched her, eerily similar expressions of anger and determination on their faces.

"If I make a choice, will you both agree to honour it?"

The men exchanged glances. They both looked annoyed. And worried.

"There will be no fight," she said. "Not here. Not today. I want to go home and talk to Chief Black Eagle. And Meda. And I need time to think. Then I'll make my decision, and both of you must agree to honour it. Otherwise, I'll walk away from both of you. Right here. Right now."

Curt nods indicated their acceptance, however reluctant. Good. That, at least, was settled, and there would be no blood shed. Not yet. And not ever, if she had anything to say about it. And she'd see that she did.

Running Wolf turned toward his men.

"Tie him."

"Really, Running Wolf, that's not necessary," she said.

"It's absolutely necessary," Running Wolf said. "I will honour your decision, but I will not allow him to ride freely into our camp. And as for you..." He moved toward her, tucked his arm around her waist, and tossed her over his shoulder. Then he dumped her onto his horse.

"You're riding with me."

CHAPTER THIRTY-EIGHT

Running Wolf glanced down at the top of Kimana's head and scowled. She'd hardly spoken during the long ride back to camp. The way she held her back rigid told him she was furious.

He probably shouldn't have tossed her onto his horse like that.

He winced, thinking again about the outraged shriek and the whoosh of exhaled air that accompanied the thump of her body against the stallion's back. She'd definitely be making him pay for that one.

He'd almost smiled at the enraged glare she'd fired at him after she wriggled into a seated position.

Lucky for him he hadn't.

Then again, he didn't mind baiting her.

He loved the sweet side of Kimana. But he adored her hot, fiery side as well. Teasing her was the most fun he'd ever had. Next to making up after the inevitable argument that followed, of course.

He snuggled his chest against her back, squeezed her gently with his arms. Felt her stiffen. Her hair flamed in the setting sun, tempting him to run his fingers through its length. He hadn't wanted to believe what Silver Fox said, that Kimana had willingly gone with Two Hawks, but now, after saying she had made a vow to the man, he was less certain. And after what she said about choosing between them, he was feeling almost as irritated with her as she was with him.

They rode ahead of the scouts and Two Hawks.

He didn't even want to look at the man. What he really wanted to do was kill him. Aside from the fact that he was a Cree and could have been one of the men responsible for the deaths of both his bride and his mother, he had stolen Kimana right from under his nose.

And there was a chance Running Wolf wouldn't get her back at all.

***

Word spread quickly as they rode back into camp. Droves of people came out to see the Cree prisoner. It reminded him of bringing Kimana and her people to their village before last winter.

From the way she stiffened, he was fairly sure she was thinking about the same thing.

Except this time, the people weren't excited. Their faces were stony, their voices silent. There would be no celebration tonight. The summer gathering was no place for enemies. He had no idea if Silver Fox had told anyone about Kimana leaving with the Cree, but if she had, he would be faced once again with the displeasure of his people.

He squared his shoulders and looked one man after another in the eye, offering no apology with his glance, expecting no approval of his actions. One by one, they nodded respectfully and watched the war party ride past.

In front of his father's lodge, he brought the stallion to a stop and watched the chief step outside. Black Eagle lifted an eyebrow as his eyes travelled over the small group. Then he reached up, gave Kimana's arm a gentle squeeze and smiled.

"You've found her. Come along, little one. We'll have some willow bark tea. Help her down, Running Wolf."

"I have a prisoner," Running Wolf said.

"I can see that. Find him a warm lodge to spend the night and set some guards. Then come back and join us for some tea. You can tell me the story."

***

"So, who is the young man you ran off with?" Chief Black Eagle asked as he patted the mat, inviting Kimana to sit next to him.

She dropped onto the mat and crossed her legs. "I didn't run off with him."

"No? Well, that's good to know. But a mark against him. We can't have men walking into our camps and walking out with the women we love, now can we? Not if they don't want to go. Did you want to go?"

"No."

"But something still troubles you. Do you want me to call for Meda?"

Kimana smiled at Black Eagle. Her heart swelled with love. How did he always seem to know the right thing to do, the right questions to ask, the right way to soothe her spirit when she was all knotted up inside? She was thankful for him. For his love, the kindness he had always shown, and his endless patience. Adapting to the Blackfoot would have been much harder without him. And without Meda.

"Please."

At that moment, the flap of the teepee lifted and Meda stepped inside, her worn face lit up from the fire's warm glow.

"There you are, we were just going to send for you," Black Eagle said.

"I thought you might," Meda said. "So, the boy found you, did he? Not surprised. Resourceful young man. And determined, I'd say. Running Wolf isn't going to let you go without a fight, that's for certain."

Meda piled a stack of furs into a mound on the floor and settled herself onto it with a contended sigh.

"That's exactly what I'm afraid of," said Kimana.

Meda ignored her for a moment.

"I don't know how you can sit, practically on the floor, Black Eagle. These old bones cringe at the thought."

"You're just softer than me," he said with a gentle smile. "As you should be."

Meda blushed. Actually blushed. Kimana looked between them in wonder. What was it between these two? It was more than just friendship. It was more than the warm relationship between a man and his wife's sister. But she would never ask. It was their business. But if they did have something special between them, Kimana couldn't be happier. They deserved some extra joy in their lives.

"So," Meda said. "Tell me about this young buck you ran off with. Is he handsome?"

Black Eagle snorted.

"Legitimate question. I'm not too old to notice and enjoy a handsome young man. And neither is Kimana. So? Tell me everything."

Kimana glanced back and forth between them. How did she explain why she had left with Two Hawks? How could she explain that he had taken her forcefully from the camp but that she had gone willingly with him in the end? It would only get him into deeper trouble. But these two deserved her honesty. She knew they would be fair in dealing with Two Hawks.

"It's Two Hawks."

"Yes," said Black Eagle. "We assumed that."

"He just wanted to rescue me."

"Can't blame him," Meda said.

"And he wants to marry me."

"Still?" asked Black Eagle.

"Yes."

"Can't blame him," Meda said again with a nod.

"Well. He's out of luck," Black Eagle scowled. "I can't see Running Wolf letting you go."

"I told him - I told them – I would choose."

They stared at her.

"They are both laying claim. I don't know what to do. I told them I had to speak with you."

"You went willingly?" Meda asked.

"No. Yes, to the cave, I needed to help him understand. But then, when I told him I was marrying Running Wolf, he wouldn't let me come back."

"Then, Kimana, I'm afraid the answer is simple," Black Eagle said. "He will have to go before the elders. They will determine his fate."

"I don't want him hurt."

Black Eagle exchanged glances with Meda.

"There will be some form of punishment. I'm sorry. An enemy can not hope to just walk in and then walk out again, taking someone unwilling with them. Such a thing must be answered. Even he would expect nothing less. He will go before the elders."

Kimana stood up and stared unseeing at the entrance to the teepee.

"I need to go for a walk. Meda, may I sleep in your lodge tonight?"

"Of course."

***

Hoodoos stood like sentries in the waning light, surrounding them on both sides. Running Wolf edged his horse closer to Two Hawks as they wound down the wide path toward the main camp.

Two Hawks sat quietly on his horse with his hands tied in front of him. Ahead and behind, leads ropes kept him firmly between two warriors. He knew Two Hawks could have thrown himself off the horse at any time. He was tied without a great deal of effort to restrain him. He wouldn't have made it far, but it would at least have shown some kind of courage.

Running Wolf hadn't quite decided if it was courage or cowardice that kept the man sitting there like a docile girl. If he had tried to run, it would have been somewhat more entertaining.

As it was, it was hard to tell what kind of a man he was. But if the man was gutless, he didn't understand what Kimana had ever seen in him.

"If it weren't for her, you'd be in the place of the spirits by now," he said, hoping to get a rise out of the man.

Why he hoped for that, he didn't know. He guessed it was because he assumed Kimana would only want the best in a man. The best in a husband. He ignored the thoughts that had been gnawing quietly at him for many moons - and had been chewing loudly ever since he'd caught up with them out on the prairies. That Kimana might not really think he was the best man for her. That she might not want him at all, now that Two Hawks had shown up in her life again.

"I said, you're lucky to be alive."

Two Hawks' upper lip twisted. "As are you, Blackfoot."

Running Wolf gave a snort of laughter.

Perhaps not such a meek little girl after all. He couldn't say why that made him feel better.

But the feeling quickly fled as he eyed the man who had tried to take away the woman he loved.

"I asked you before, and I didn't get an answer. I'll ask again, now that she's not here to object or get offended. Did you touch her?"

Two Hawks turned a scornful gaze on Running Wolf. "I would never dishonour her that way. Unlike you."

The fact that he had taken her before marriage had never bothered him before now, but somehow, knowing this man knew about it – the only living male member of her tribe knew about it, let alone the man who was originally supposed to be her husband – it unsettled him somewhat.

More than somewhat.

It pissed the hell out of him.

"I never dishonoured her," he said, gritting his teeth.

"You laid with her two nights past. I watched you myself."

He stared, slack-jawed, then narrowed his lips. "Hope you enjoyed it. That's the closest thing you'll ever get to making love to Kimana."

"You should never have touched her," Two Hawks snarled.

"You should never have come for her. As for touching her? I'll touch her again. Any time I want."

They stared at each other will equal amounts of fury and hatred. Then Two Hawks launched himself off his horse, his arms held up in the air before swinging them to the side like one large arm. He hit Running Wolf squarely across the face and knocked them both to the ground.

Running Wolf was ready to hurl Two Hawks away when his weight was lifted from his body. He swiped a hand across his lips, looked down at the blood, then up at Two Hawks who stood quietly, restrained, between two warriors, his arms held behind his back.

The grin on Two Hawks' face quickly faded. "The only reason she's with you is because you forced yourself upon her."

Running Wolf surged to his feet.

"Is that what she told you?"

"She doesn't have to tell me," Two Hawks said. "She would never touch the likes of you."

"What, a Blackfoot, you mean?"

Two Hawks spat in the dust. "A dirty, Blackfoot dog."

"You're the dirty dog."

"And you probably can't even hide your tracks in the snow."

Running Wolf snorted, both offended and amused by the insult.

"Kimana would say you sound like a child. But she's not here. So I can tell you that obviously you weren't able to hide your own tracks."

Two Hawks smirked and shook his head. "You said yourself the wolf helped you."

"She did."

"You say she's yours."

"She is."

"Then keep the cursed animal away from me, because I've had just about enough of her."

"What the hell do you mean by that?"

"That crazy beast led you to me? She led me to Kimana in the first place. She's playing with both sides of the same stone."

Running Wolf stared at Two Hawks, stunned into momentary silence.

"If she did, it was because she wanted me to kill you."

Running Wolf gave a signal to his men to reload their prisoner on a horse, and this time, to tie his arms behind his back. Tightly this time.

They rode to an empty guest lodge, one of a handful that were always erected at the summer gathering just in case. Running Wolf gave orders to his men to untie Two Hawks then set a watch. He stood by the entrance and looked at his enemy in the dim light of the teepee while one of the warriors untied his hands.

"I'll send someone with food."

"Don't bother," Two hawks said, rubbing his wrists.

"You'll eat."

"If you send Kimana with the food, I'll eat. And then I'll taste her sweet nectar on my lips again."

Running Wolf held himself very still. "You're lucky I don't kill you now."

Two Hawks took a step forward.

"You want to give it a shot? Let's do it. Let's settle this. Here. Now."

"If my father hadn't said to put you under guard, that's exactly what I'd do."

"Hiding behind an old man, now? Just like you hid behind

Kimana?"

Running Wolf turned around and faced the entrance of the lodge. Then he swung around and hit Two Hawks on the jaw, sending him sprawling to the ground.

"For that, I'll be sure to send an old shrew with your food."

***

Running Wolf stood outside the lodge and stared off into the distance, fuming. He shouldn't have lost control like that, shouldn't have allowed himself to be baited. It wasn't the accusation of hiding behind Kimana or Black Eagle that irritated him. It wasn't even the allegation that he had used Kimana unfairly. He knew it wasn't true. She had come to him willingly, both times. He refused to regret what they'd done. How could he ever regret it? She was the best thing that had ever happened to him.

He fingered his already swollen lip and scowled. The metallic taste of blood still filled his mouth. No, it was the fact that he actually admired the man he'd just knocked to the ground. He had courage, and determination, even for a Cree.

And he obviously loved Kimana, or he'd never have come this far to find her. He admired that, too.

Well, too bad. He wouldn't have her.

Passing the reins of his horse to one of his warriors, he decided to walk back to the elder's circle camp. Work off some of his anger.

He had been so sure Kimana wanted him, but now he was uncertain. After finding her with Two Hawks, and hearing that she considered her promise to him to be as valid as her promise to Running Wolf, suddenly nothing was certain anymore.

Thank the spirits the elders would not allow his claim to be heard.

That was one less worry.

He hurried up the path, eager to see Kimana. It was actually a good thing he'd missed the Sun Dance. Tonight, he'd spend the night in his own lodge, where he could keep an eye on her.

As he entered the circle camp, he passed by a group of women, huddled together, chattering about the prisoner. Silver Fox separated herself from the group and rushed forward.

He sighed.

The last thing he felt like doing was chatting with Silver Fox.

"Was that the man? The one Kimana ran off with?"

He bristled. It still wasn't clear if Kimana had gone willingly, but he'd heard nothing to contradict what Silver Fox had told him about Kimana's departure with Two Hawks.

"What of it?"

"Why didn't you just let them go?"

"Why would I do that? And why is that your concern?"

"You are my concern. You're my friend. You deserve better than to have a woman run off with some other man. I'm just concerned for you. That's all. I'm not trying to interfere. No matter what, we've been friends for a long time. I care, that's all. I just want you to be happy."

She was right. He ran a hand through his hair, trying to sort it all out in his mind. Maybe he shouldn't have followed them. Maybe Kimana hadn't wanted to come back. Maybe she wanted to be with Two Hawks. It made sense. More sense, anyway. He was Cree. She was Cree. She'd been promised to him. She knew him.

Loved him.

Loved him?

Maybe. Maybe not. Who knew?

Maybe he should have let them go and found a way to live without her. He'd been happy enough before she came into his life.

"Running Wolf?"

Silver Fox laid her hand on his arm and gave him a tentative smile. "Is there anything I can do? I hate seeing you like this."

There was nothing she could do. Nothing anyone could do.

"No, not really. Thank you."

"I just want to help."

He smiled at the young woman he'd grown up with. Run into the bushes with more than once over the years. She really cared, and right now, he needed a little understanding from someone.

"Please tell me what I can do to help," she said.

"There is something. Could you find a woman to take the prisoner some food? I would appreciate it."

"I'll take care of it. You need to get some rest. You've had a long couple of days."

"My thanks. You are a good friend, Silver Fox."

She smiled. "I just want to help."

***

"You failed."

Two Hawks looked up at the sound of the voice and stared at the woman standing just inside the flap.

"I beg your pardon?"

"I said you failed. You were supposed to take her away."

"That was the plan."

"And you failed."

"I haven't failed yet."

Silver Fox strolled forward, her hands on her hips. He rose to stand before her and braced himself as she stabbed a finger at his chest.

"You can't get far with no weapon. You had enough time to get away. Didn't you follow the river?"

"Why are you here?"

"I couldn't believe it when I saw you ride into camp, all trussed up like a grouse. Didn't you fight?"

"There are times when fighting is not the answer."

"Even when there is something worth fighting for? Or is Kimana not worth fighting for?"

He stared at the Blackfoot woman. How someone so beautiful could be so vicious, he didn't know. She had to have a reason for wanting Kimana gone.

"Why did you help me?"

"I told you. Kimana doesn't belong here. She belongs with her own people. She's not happy."

"She didn't say anything to me about not being happy."

"Well, she shouldn't have to say it. Would you be happy? Surrounded by your enemy day and night? Knowing they had killed your people?"

No, he certainly wouldn't. But why should she care if Kimana was happy?

"Running Wolf said he was sending an old shrew with food."

Silver Fox laughed. "Did he? Well, you got me."

She tossed him a small skin sack.

He grabbed it out of the air and watched her closely. "You don't like her, do you? Kimana."

"It's not that I don't like her. But since she's come to our people, she's done nothing but cause trouble for Running Wolf. He doesn't deserve that. He deserves better."

"Ah. So now we get to the heart of it."

"We're at the heart of nothing."

"Do you love him?"

"That's not your business."

"Maybe not. But you said you wanted to help me. I'm trying to understand why you would risk doing that."

"He's gone through enough. He's my friend. Kimana is wrong for him."

"Isn't that up to him?" he asked.

"He can't think straight where she's concerned. She's cast some kind of spell on him."

"Well, if she has, she's cast the same spell on me. It's not hard to see why."

"What is it about that woman? She's nothing special. She's spoiled, opinionated. And those scars. She doesn't have the first clue how to treat a man or how to care for his needs."

"Careful."

"This is pointless," she said. "I just want her gone. My reasons are my own business. You want her, you should just take her and go. I don't see what the problem is."

"The problem is that she's out there, somewhere, and I'm in here. There's not much I can do about that at the moment."

"Yes, there is."

She slid a blade out of her moccasin and pressed it into his hand. "There's one guard. He's out front. You should be able to figure out what to do about it. Though if I were you, I'd cut a slit in the back of the teepee and slip out unseen. If you get caught, they'll probably kill you. The Cree aren't too popular around here."

"Now, that's a surprise."

"Don't be sarcastic. You don't have time for that. If you stay, tomorrow, you'll go before the elders, and if you're lucky, the worst thing that will happen is you'll be sent through the sticks. But you'll probably be killed. And then your precious Kimana will be trapped here, living with the enemy, for the rest of her life. If I were you, I'd do something tonight. If you wait until tomorrow, I won't be able to help you."

Two Hawks angled his head as he listened to her. It made a certain amount of sense, but he knew Kimana, and he knew she'd be furious at being taken off without her consent, yet again.

There was a good chance he'd die tomorrow. But there was also a good chance the elders here would respect his claim, and the fact that he was willing to take her away quietly. If he could talk to Kimana and convince her to leave with him, to honour her promise to him, they could walk away unharmed.

And if they decided he should die, so be it.

Without Kimana, he really had nothing to live for.

"I'll tell you what," he said, and tossed the blade at her feet. "We'll see what tomorrow brings."

***

Running Wolf lifted the teepee flap and stepped inside. He gave his father a questioning glance. Kimana was gone.

"Where is she?"

"Well, that's a nice way to greet your father. You've forgotten your manners."

He allowed himself a brief grin. Since Kimana had come into their lives, his father had become more light-hearted, and more inclined to tease. It was good to see.

"I apologize. Good evening, father."

"Good evening to you."

"Where is Kimana?"

"Afraid you've lost her again? Not to worry. She's gone to Meda's to sleep. How is our prisoner?"

"Difficult." He ran a finger over his swollen lip. "I asked Silver Fox to arrange some food for him."

"Good. We can't let him think we aren't a hospitable people."

"No, we certainly wouldn't want that." He tried to keep the sarcasm out of his voice.

Chief Black Eagle barked out a laugh, then patted the ground.

"Come and have a smoke. I've hardly seen you since we arrived."

"I've been busy."

"Yes, yes. Preparations for the Sun Dance. Then chasing your heart across the prairies. All very exhausting. You'll sleep well tonight."

Running Wolf lowered himself onto a mat, accepted the pipe from his father and tried not to think about tomorrow. "Kimana says – she said Two Hawks has a legitimate claim."

"He does."

"Do you think the elders will consider it?"

"Why would they? He's not Blackfoot."

"No. But you agree his claim is legitimate."

"It's not really debatable. If he was Blackfoot, that would be different."

"But she feels differently."

"And that's the problem."

"Yes. If she tells them she thinks his claim is legitimate, they may consider it."

"And you're worried about that?"

"Of course."

"Do you think she doesn't want you?"

"I know she does. Or did. But her sense of duty, her honour is strong. Very strong. He had claim to her first."

"There's nothing you can do about it tonight. Get a good sleep and see what tomorrow brings. And don't worry."

"Easier said."

CHAPTER THIRTY-NINE

Makwai visited Kimana in her dreams again. The wolf lifted her legs high, trudging through snow so deep, her black belly was frosted in white.

Follow me, a voice whispered in Kimana's head.

Makwai turned her strange grey eyes to look back, making sure Kimana was following. *Follow me.*

She followed the wolf alongside a frozen river, their footsteps muffled by thick, fresh snow. Around a bend, an icy waterfall sparkled blue and white, its rushing water frozen in time.

Near the waterfall's edge, Makwai stopped, then swung her head toward a dark lump in the snow. A child. Alone. Eyes closed, whimpering, body shivering in the cold. Makwai laid down and curled her body around the child, then turned to stare at Kimana, her steely eyes glistening with tears.

The child turned to look at Kimana, watching her without fear. His shivering ceased, and he turned to snuggle his face into the wolf's chest, wrapping thin arms around her neck. Makwai nuzzled him gently and laid her chin upon his head.

Mist curled up from the frozen river and filled the air, engulfing Kimana in a thick fog. She looked around, confused, but not afraid.

A woman walked out of the mist, long black hair flowing around her hips.

Pale, silvery eyes shone with unshed tears.

She held out her hand and unfolded her fingers. A rose quartz

261

stone glittered in her palm.

"Bring my people together." She didn't speak, but Kimana heard the woman's voice clearly in her head.

"I don't know what you mean. I don't know what you want me to do."

"Bring my people together."

The mist churned and rolled, enveloping the woman until she was completely shrouded from view. Then the mist cleared, and the woman was gone. Kimana turned to look at Makwai. The wolf watched her, then nudged the boy's shoulder. His robe fell away. On his small, frail shoulder, she could clearly see a birth mark.

Two birds in flight.

***

Kimana stood at the entrance of the teepee and greeted the rising sun. In one hand, she held a smoking braid of sweetgrass. With the other, she brought the smoke toward her face and let its scent fill her nostrils.

She couldn't stop thinking about the dream. She'd woken early, had been unable to get back to sleep. She was used to seeing Makwai in her dreams, but she didn't know who the woman was or what she wanted.

As for the boy, she had no doubts. She'd seen that birthmark before and knew exactly who it belonged to. But why he would appear in a dream with Makwai was beyond her understanding. Why he appeared as a child was even more confusing.

"Good morning, Kimana. How did you sleep?"

She turned and smiled at Meda, letting the flap flutter closed behind her.

"Not so well. You?"

"As well as these old bones will allow me. Tell me what disturbed your sleep."

"I dreamed."

"Oh? Anything interesting?"

Kimana chewed her bottom lip and shrugged her shoulders. "I don't know."

"Tell me."

Kimana gave a weary sigh.

"I'm so tired of trying to understand the dreams. Just when I think I understand them, I don't."

"Was Makwai there again? You said she seems to be in most of your dreams."

"Yes, and a woman I don't know."

"Tell about her."

"She had long black hair, and strange eyes."

Meda's lips parted and her eyebrows furrowed together.

"Strange? How so?"

"Her eyes were pale, almost grey."

Meda went very still for a moment, then stared absently at her hands.

"Grey eyes, you say? That is odd."

"Yes."

"And did she say anything to you?"

"She told me to bring her people together."

Meda stared at the floor and mumbled the words to herself, then shook her head in confusion.

"Was that all? Just Makwai, and this woman?"

"No, Two Hawks was there."

Meda's eyebrows shot up. "Two Hawks?"

"As a little boy. I'm sure it was Two Hawks. But he was very small."

"How do you know it was him?"

"He has a birth mark. I've seen it so many times over the years, I'd know it in an instant."

Meda froze, then reached out and grabbed Kimana's hand, her single eye intense.

"The birth mark. Tell me about it. What does it look like?"

"Two birds flying. They look like hawks. That's where he got his name."

"Two birds. Two hawks."

"Yes."

"Kimana, we have to speak to Chief Black Eagle. We have to speak with him right now."

"Why? What's wrong?"

"The woman in your dream. I know who it was."

"Who?"

"Chepi. Running Wolf's mother. My sister."

"But that makes no sense. Why would Chepi be in a dream with Two Hawks?"

"Because she's his mother."

CHAPTER FORTY

I mpossible."

Kimana watched Running Wolf advance on them. His bare chest gleamed in the morning light that streamed through the open flap behind them. He gave her a withering glare.

"You're only saying this to save his life. So that his claim can be honoured."

It was like he'd slapped her.

She stared back at him but said nothing.

She'd known he wouldn't believe her, but she hadn't thought he'd accuse her of being dishonourable enough to lie. And of wanting Two Hawks more than she wanted him.

"Don't be impertinent," Meda snapped. "She's not saying it. I'm saying it."

"She's the one who claimed to have the dream," Running Wolf said, jerking his head toward Kimana.

"It's true," Kimana said.

"He's no more a Blackfoot than I am a Cree."

"Neither am I," she said softly.

"That's buffalo dung."

"No. It's true."

Meda stepped forward and poked Running Wolf in the chest with a gnarled finger.

"That boy is every bit as Blackfoot as you are," Meda said. "We can prove it."

"None of this makes any sense," Running Wolf said, turning

265

away and facing his father. He spread his arms. "Does this make sense to you?"

Black Eagle sat cross-legged on his mat. He scratched the back of his head and grunted.

"You see? He doesn't think it makes sense, either."

"Then neither one of you is listening. The boy in the dream, he had a birth mark. Two Hawks has a birth mark. Your brother had a birth mark. The same mark. The same place. On the shoulder. Why is this so difficult to understand?"

"I don't remember any birth mark. And none of this make sense!" Running Wolf said, crossing his arms over his chest. "Two Hawks is Cree. And my brother is dead!"

"Kimana?" Meda turned toward her. "Tell us about Two Hawks. Has he always lived with your people? Was he born there?"

"I think so. I don't know."

"How old is he?"

"As old as me. Twenty summers."

"Twenty summers," Meda repeated and stared triumphantly at Running Wolf.

"And how long ago did your brother disappear?" she asked him.

"More than fifteen summers ago."

"Seventeen. And don't argue with a medicine woman when she tells you how long ago something happened. We have minds like a rattlesnake's jaws. Once something gets inside, it's trapped. Your brother disappeared seventeen summers ago. When he was but three summers old."

"And?"

"And now, he'd be twenty. Kimana? How old were you when Two Hawks came to live with the Cree?"

"I don't know. I really don't remember. I just know he's always been there, at least since I was a little girl. My first memories of him were when I was about three summers old." She and Running Wolf stared at each other.

"Three is a young age to remember, Kimana. How do you know he was there when you were three?"

"Because that was around the time my older brother died. We had snuck off together into the woods. He wanted to kill rabbits with his new bow. We stumbled upon an old wolf, drinking from a stream. It was injured. It looked old. When it saw us, it attacked us. Clawed my face, my leg. I think that's when he shot it with an arrow. Suddenly I was free, the wolf had turned toward him, and in that moment, he told me to run. So, I ran. I thought he was behind me. But he wasn't. He wasn't. He was just seven."

Running Wolf knitted his brows together.

"So that is why you are so frightened of wolves."

"Yes. So, yes. I was three. I'm certain."

"Who else would know? Who amongst your people would remember?"

"Utina. My aunt. She was older than me, but not yet a woman. She should remember."

Meda turned to Black Eagle and folded her hands in front of her stomach. "I'd like to speak with Utina. And then, I'd like to see Two Hawks for myself. And you," she said to Black Eagle. "You are going to come with us."

"I'm not arguing," said the chief as he unfolded his legs and followed them out of the teepee.

***

Kimana and Meda walked down the path toward the main camp, trailing Running Wolf and his father. She leaned closer to Meda and lowered her voice.

"What happened to Running Wolf's brother? Why hasn't he ever told me about him?"

"It's hard for him to talk about."

"Why?"

"He blames himself."

"But why? Was he responsible?"

"He thinks so. He carries much weight on his shoulders, even if it is not his burden to carry."

Kimana glanced at Running Wolf's rigid back. He strode swiftly ahead, then slowing down until the older man caught up. He tapped his fingers against his legs until Black Eagle came abreast of him, then nodded curtly and continued the pattern all over again. He was like a stallion, barely restrained.

"He's upset."

Meda blew a breath from between pursed lips.

"Looks like a little boy on his way to watch someone else's

beating. Sort of agitated. Sort of excited."

"Excited! He's not excited, he's angry." Kimana said.

"That boy has been waiting for this day since he was seven summers old. He's mad as a buffalo bull during a stampede, sure, but he's also hopeful."

"I don't understand. What do you mean? What do you mean he's been waiting for this day? Why would he be hopeful?"

"He always hoped we would find his brother, always believed we would, long after everyone else had given up. He only gave up hope after his mother and Laughing Brook died. It was as if all hope died inside him that day."

"But we can't be sure Two Hawks is his brother."

"I am sure. Two Hawks is Two Birds, all grown up. The birth mark will prove it. We don't even need to talk to Utina."

"But if it's true," Kimana said, "Then that means Two Hawks is a Blackfoot. And that means..."

Meda stopped and took Kimana's arm gently in her hand. "It means Two Hawks' claim is legitimate, Kimana. His claim on you must be honoured. That's what's got Running Wolf's robe in a twist. He is torn."

Kimana looked at Running Wolf. He was standing on the side of the path, several long strides ahead of his father. He looked back at her with an annoyed scowl. But she could see worry in his eyes as well. And something more. So many feelings warred inside of him.

"I understand how he feels."

***

Running Wolf stood motionless, his arms hung loosely at his side, betraying nothing of the turmoil raging inside him. Dozens of people jostled past, but he noticed none of them. He was only vaguely aware of the wind that whipped through his hair, tossing it in long strands across his face and neck.

He felt strangely detached as he stared across the milky river. Numb.

Kimana's aunt had confirmed what he both feared – and prayed - was true. Two Hawks had come to live with the Cree when he was just three or four summers old, said Utina, they could not be sure of his exact age, but he and Kimana had been very close in size and ability, so she assumed he had been her age.

Brought to them by an old trapper who'd found him lost and alone in the icy depths of winter.

He'd been delirious when he was found, the old man had told the Cree. Near death. He'd saved him. The trapper had kept him alive, but the boy couldn't tell him anything about who he was.

He hadn't even known his name. The Cree had taken the boy in, Utina said, adopted him into a family, and named him for the birth mark on his shoulder. Two flying birds. Two Hawks.

Running Wolf scowled. He didn't remember any birth mark.

But something niggled at the edge of his memory. He closed his eyes, trying to see that little boy that had disappeared so many years ago. Did he have a birth mark?

And if he did, was it the same one Kimana claimed Two Hawks carried on his shoulder?

He glanced at the little group of people standing outside Utina's lodge, no doubt discussing what they had just heard. His father's arms were crossed over his chest, and he listened with a scowl to something Meda was saying.

Running Wolf ran his hand through his hair, brushing it back from his face. Kimana stood slightly to the side, watching him quietly. If she was listening to what Meda and his father were saying, she gave no indication. Her gaze was direct and a little sad.

He turned away. He couldn't stand to look in her eyes and see his own sorrow and confusion reflected there.

Looking down the river toward the edge of camp, he wondered what Two Hawks would say when they spoke to him. If it was true, and he wasn't prepared to admit it was even possible yet, did Two Hawks remember anything about what happened? Did he even remember his real name, or anything about where he'd come from? Did he remember his family? Did he remember him, his brother? And if he did, did he blame Running Wolf for what happened?

He thought he would never see Two Birds again. For a long time, he'd hoped somehow his little brother would come back to them. But as the years passed, his hope had lessened, and then when his mother and Laughing Brook had died, a bleak despair had settled over him. Despair and guilt.

He remembered his mother looking at him many times over the

years, her strange grey eyes staring intently into his.

"It is not your fault."

"I left him."

"When it is time for him to come home, the spirits will guide him. Don't despair."

She had comforted him so many times over the years, assuring him that Two Birds was where he was destined to be, and it wasn't Running Wolf's fault. But how could it not be his fault? He was the one who had left his little brother alone in the forest, while he ran off to hide. He was responsible for his disappearance. Him. No one else. Their childish games of hide and find had cost him a brother.

But there was no proof that Two Hawks and Two Birds were the same person. This birth mark they claimed Two Hawks had. It meant nothing.

He looked back at Kimana. Her eyes were lowered, and her hands were clasped together.

Did she know what it meant if all of this was true?

Suddenly, Meda broke away from the little group and hobbled toward him. He watched his old aunt approach.

"Your father is being his usual, obstinate self. It's obvious where you get it from. He wants to speak with the trappers and traders who've come to the gathering to see if they know anything. He insists on trying to find more evidence before we go and see Two Hawks. I don't know why he can't just accept..."

"I agree with him."

"Of course, you do," she said. "Well, we'd better get a move on. Do you know any of the traders or trappers?"

"No, but I know someone who does."

***

Kimana listened quietly as Chief Black Eagle explained the situation to Silver Fox. The woman's eyes gleamed as she shot quick glances toward Kimana. She seemed all too eager to help them find out the truth.

"Well, but that means Kimana has to honour her commitment to him."

"We don't know yet what it means exactly," said Meda. "The elders will have to decide what's to be done. But that's not the important thing right now. We need to find out if Two Hawks is really Two Birds."

"You know, I don't really remember what happened to him. I've heard the story once or twice over the years. He was lost in a snow storm, wasn't he? Or while he was playing in the woods? Something like that? Didn't he run off?"

"We don't need to discuss this," growled Running Wolf.

"I'm sorry. I didn't mean to bring back painful memories," Silver Fox said, and laid her hand on his arm.

Kimana bristled.

The woman never hesitated to show that she knew Running Wolf as well as anyone else did, and certainly better than Kimana. Kimana folded her arms over her chest. She wasn't going to let Silver Fox get to her.

"So, you need to speak with the trappers? I just dealt with one the other day. I bought a beautiful dress. A wedding dress. I don't really need it yet, but you never know," she said, casting a sweet glance toward Kimana.

Kimana looked away. Why couldn't she understand that Running Wolf didn't want her? The woman obviously wasn't too bright. Kimana almost felt a little sorry for her, but the woman's blatant behaviour grated enough that feeling sorry for her was not an option. Not at the moment, anyway.

Running Wolf seemed at once eager and hesitant to find out the truth about Two Hawks. She watched him, understanding his conflicting feelings. Part of him probably wanted to believe Two Hawks really was his brother. But part of him would hate to find out it was true.

Because it meant Two Hawks had as much claim on her as he did.

And she was honour bound to accept it.

***

Jonesy saw them coming. Five of them, and they didn't look happy. He spun on one foot and scuttled into the crowd. Dang Injuns. He never shoulda traded the crippled horse to that little boy for his father's quiver. Now he was in for it, sure as night was black.

He huffed and puffed from the exertion of trying to lift his knees past his hips as he ran, dodging people as best he could.

"Dag-nab it," he said as he staggered to a stop, leaned over and rested his hands upon his thighs. "Dag-nab it! This 'ol body ain't what it used be. Can't catch my breath. Whoo-ee."

Before he could get his wind back, a pair of moccasin-clad feet appeared in front of him. He lifted his head and saw a well-muscled pair of legs.

"Gol-darn! You Injuns is fast." He lifted his hands in surrender. "All right, all right, I'll give it back, but I want my horse, ya hear? Just don't cut off any fingers or toes or any such thing. Gol-darn! Shoulda left yesterday. All right, don't poke me!"

The warrior stood in front of him, arms crossed and looking as fierce a winter thunderstorm. Strong as one, too. He'd best step lightly around this one.

"Now, see, I didn't mean any harm. I didn't know the beast was crippled. I didn't know the boy took his old man's quiver, I swear."

The warrior cocked his head and narrowed his eyes.

Jonesy swallowed. He'd best shut his mouth.

"You cheated a child? A child who took something that belonged to an old man? You are in a great deal of trouble, white man."

"No. No." Jonesy held his fingers up to his lips. "We can settle this without involvin' the old folk. Yessir-ee, I'm thinkin' we can work somethin' out. Just quiet like."

He steepled his fingers in front of his mouth. "Shhh."

"You sold a wedding dress to a woman here?"

Jonesy looked at the warrior in a panic. Lordy, how much trouble was he in? First the boy, then the woman. He never shoulda come to the gathering. Shoulda skipped it and gone down to the Shoshone's gathering instead.

Never shoulda traded that dress. Never shoulda traded that horse. Or that stupid mule to begin with. Dag-nab it, he wasn't too bright.

Why he ever thought he could make it as a trader as well as a trapper, he'd never know.

He shook his head, then looked the Injun in the eye. The warrior seemed more curious than angry. Maybe that was a good sign. Maybe he wasn't in trouble after all.

Well, if he tried to broach the topic – delicately speaking, of course – maybe he'd get out with his skin intact.

"I'm thinkin' I did sell a dress, yessir."

"The woman you sold it to, is that her there?"

The man pointed behind him to the same small group of people he'd run from minutes before. The pretty little thing he'd traded the dress to was standing there looking like she thought the whole danged thing was funny. He gnawed on his bottom lip. Well, he sure as shooting hadn't cheated her. She'd cheated him with that useless nag. If he hadn't been so eager to get himself another beast, he'd have seen right off what a rickety old creature it was. 'Course, he was sort of distracted by her curves, too. Whoo-ee, she was a fine one. And that other one, standing next to her, she looked an awful lot like the pretty little thing he'd hauled out of the river. Sure looked better now. Just look at that hair. He could swear there was red in that hair.

Wondrous.

"Is that the woman?" the warrior asked again. Jonesy looked back at the other one. The one with the laughing eyes. Pretty as a Saskatoon berry pie. She sure enough was. They both were.

The warrior gave his arm a little shake.

"I'm getting' to it! Don't pinch. That's the one. Yessir. She gave me a crippled horse. Cheated me. I want the dress back. So, if we can just clear this all up..."

He looked up, startled, as the warrior yanked his arm. He half led, half dragged Jonesy over to the group. This wasn't looking too good.

"Silver Fox, is this the one you spoke to yesterday? He speaks our language, like you said. Although badly."

The warrior gave him a smirk. Jonesy drew himself up in outrage.

"Yes," the woman said. "He's the one. I've met him before. He comes here sometimes for the gathering, but not every summer."

The pretty one with the dark, flaming hair stepped forward and laid her hand gently upon his arm.

"We need to speak with you."

He peered a little closer. Familiar. He shook his head. Why did she look so familiar, both this time and last? He knew she belonged to that boy, that Two Hawks fella. So, she was a Cree. The one he'd rescued. And the one Two Hawks had been looking for. Stands to reason he'd met her when he traded with the Cree

273

over the years, he thought.

He glanced back at the warrior. Well, she wasn't with the Cree now. Sure enough wasn't. She was with this Blackfoot, and he looked big and mean and downright scary. Jonesy cringed and shied away.

"Tell him I won't hurt him," said the warrior, sounding exasperated.

"Do I know you?" the girl asked, drawing his eyes back to her face. "I think I know you."

"Well, I pulled ye from the river, remember? Back in spring. Didn't think ya'd make it. Glad to see ya did."

"Yes, that's right. Did we ever meet before that? I'm sure I recognize your face."

"Well, now, I traded with yer people from time to time. Come to think of it, I think I remember yer father. But ya were a young thing last time I saw yea. All fiery and bright-eyed. Pretty as pie. Yessir. Not as pretty as now, though, I'm thinkin'. You grew up real good. Real pretty. Pretty as pie, yessir."

"Did you know Two Hawks?"

"Two Hawks? Well, yes I did. Saved his bacon, too. Last autumn. Late. Near on winter. Come to think, it was snowin' 'round then."

The young woman looked at the warrior with worried eyes. Something wasn't right here. He pressed a hand to his jittery stomach.

"Did you ever know him before that? When he was younger? A boy?" she asked.

"Well, now, that's the thing. When I found him last year, I was sure I knew him, and the way I found him reminded me of the first time I found an Injun like that, in the snow."

Both the girl and the warrior stiffened.

"I found him when he was a youngster. Barely up to my knee, he was. Out in a snowstorm. Alongside that big' ol river you Injuns like crossin' so much. Rescued him. Yessir, I surely did. Took him to the Cree folk. Watched him grow up whenever I visited yer tribe. Watched you, too, I'm thinkin' now."

"How did you find him?" asked an old woman with one eye. "When he was a boy. How did you find him?"

"Wolf led me to him. Just like last time. Just like it led me to you," he said, nodding at Kimana. "Strange black wolf with the weirdest eyes ya ever did see. Spooky."

CHAPTER FORTY-ONE

H ave him brought to my lodge. And say nothing of this to him. I want to speak with him first."

Running Wolf gave Chief Black Eagle a nod and watched as he and the women walked up the path leading back up to the elders' circle camp. Silver Fox had been thanked and dismissed, and, fortunately, she'd made herself scarce. He couldn't deal with her right now.

He stood for a few moments after they disappeared into the throngs of people. Then he spun on his heel and strode toward the lodge where Two Hawks... no, Two *Birds* was being held.

Better not to think about it. Better not to wonder what his brother had gone through all these years. But how could he not wonder? If it was true, and he wasn't yet ready to say it was, what kind of life had his brother led? Had he been happy as a child? Had his adopted parents loved him like their own parents would have? Had he had a sister? A brother? Someone to play with, look up to?

Running Wolf was certain of one thing. If Two Birds... Two <u>Hawks</u> had grown up with a Cree brother, that boy probably wouldn't have left him alone in a storm.

He stopped a few steps away from the teepee and pressed his fingers against the bridge of his nose. Sighed. Looked up at a guard and jerked his head to the side.

"You can go. My thanks."

The guard nodded and left.

Running Wolf stared at the opening of the lodge. He took a step forward. Another. It felt almost like trudging through a mud bog. He stopped and gave his head a shake, trying to clear the images from his mind. Images of his brother as a little boy. Barely big enough to reach their father's knees. Small enough that Running Wolf, then seven summers old, could pick him up and put him on his shoulders.

He gripped a teepee pole in one hand, and laid the other against the dull hide, then dropped his head toward his chest.

"Count on all my fingers and toes. Twice!" said Two Birds.

Running Wolf nodded at his little brother. "That's right. Now close your eyes! No peeking. A mighty warrior never peeks."

"I'm not a warrior. You aren't, either."

"Am too.

"Not! Are not!"

"I will be one day."

"Me too! Then we'll fight together. And capture horses!"

"Yes. Now, close your eyes and count."

"One finger, two fingers, three fingers--"

Running Wolf sighed again.

They'd never had the chance to fight together or capture horses. They'd never gone on a raid or leered at women together. They'd never had the chance to just be brothers, all because he'd thought it would be funny to run back to camp instead of hiding nearby in the forest. And he'd been too scared to turn back once the wind picked up and the snow started pelting his face, blinding him and nearly preventing him from finding his own way home.

He'd had to live with that every day since.

He'd had to live with the sound of his mother weeping and calling out to the spirits. With the way his father would stand at the teepee entrance each night and look out into the darkness, waiting for a son who would never come home.

Impulsive, that's what he was. What he'd always been. And his impulsivity had caused the death – nearly caused the death – of his own brother. As it had caused the death of his bride and mother four summers past.

No matter how they looked at it, they'd both been cheated out of a lot.

But Two Hawks had lost more than he had.

He'd been abandoned. Lost. Alone. Had he been afraid? Had he cried? Running Wolf wasn't sure he wanted to know.

Part of him wanted to reach out and pull Two Hawks into a hug, tell him he was sorry, but he couldn't quite get his mind around the fact that his enemy – and his rival – was also his brother.

And if he couldn't get his mind around it, how would Two Hawks?

It was time to find out.

With one arm, he swept the entrance open and let the sunlight wash the teepee in warm light. Two Hawks sat cross-legged on a mat, his hands resting on his thighs. He looked the picture of ease and confidence. He gave Running Wolf a sardonic smile.

"Have you come to kill me? At least fight with honour and give me a weapon."

"I haven't come to fight."

"What, then? Is it time to go before your elders and hear that my punishment will be death by some cruel torture?"

"No, my father wishes to speak with you."

"Is Kimana with him?"

Running Wolf stiffened. "She is."

"Well then," said Two Hawks. "Let's get moving. Don't want to keep my beautiful bride waiting."

Running Wolf struggled against frustration and rage. He held out a hand and stopped Two Hawks in mid-stride. Turning his head sideways, he looked into his brother's eyes.

"First. Your word. You will treat my father with respect."

"He's my enemy, just like you."

Running Wolf shrugged. He still hadn't seen the birth mark. But, he had to admit, at this point, it was hard to argue with the facts, no matter how hard it might be to accept them.

"Maybe. But you will still give him the respect befitting a chief. Your word. Warrior to warrior."

Two Hawks hesitated. "Agreed."

"Second. Kimana is not yours yet."

Two Hawks looked at him in surprise.

"Yet? You mean my claim is being honoured?"

He fought back a surge of anger. "It has not been decided."

"But there's a chance?"

Running Wolf scowled. He didn't want to even think about this. If Two Hawks really was Blackfoot, then his claim on Kimana was as valid as his own, maybe more so. And Kimana would be honour-bound to accept it. They would all be honour-bound to accept it.

"You will talk with my father first. He will decide if you still need to go before the elders. And they will decide what is to happen to you. They will decide if your claim is valid. And you will accept their words."

"We'll see about that."

"Yes. We'll see."

***

Kimana sat quietly, her hands folded in her lap, trying to find some shred of serenity to help her get through this. Running Wolf and Two Hawks had still not arrived, and an uncomfortable silence had settled over the lodge. Chief Black Eagle puffed lazily on a pipe, looking at first glance as if he was unconcerned about the impending visit of his long-lost son, but his eyes betrayed his eagerness and agitation as they darted back and forth between the entrance and the long pipe that rested on the floor in front of him. Meda watched him closely but said nothing.

Kimana twisted her fingers together. She didn't want to think about what it would mean for her if Two Hawks was Running Wolf's brother. Her feelings seemed almost trivial, in a way, compared with what Black Eagle and Running Wolf must be going through.

But there was no denying her feelings, she knew that. When she'd stood defiantly beside the river and told them she would choose who she married, she hadn't really thought it would come down to that. She didn't know what she'd been thinking. When she was younger, she'd imagined how amusing it might be to have two men fighting over her, but the reality was far more unpleasant than some silly little girl's dreams.

What was taking them so long? She glanced at the entrance again and hoped they hadn't let their emotions get the better of them and ended up sprawled on the ground, fists flying.

Black Eagle cleared his throat.

"Should have been here by now," he said.

She hummed a wordless response.

"Well," Meda said, and rose awkwardly to her feet. "I'm going to go look for them. Make sure they haven't killed each other. You never should have left them alone together, Black Eagle. That was foolish. Just asking for trouble, that's what I think."

"I don't recall asking what you think."

"Well, now, that's the problem. If you'd asked, I'd have told you it was foolhardy, but you didn't bother asking. Stubborn old man." Meda blew an insulted breath through her nose.

"Go and look for them, then," Black Eagle growled and puffed deeply on his pipe.

The smell of sweetgrass filled the lodge.

Usually, Kimana found the smell soothing, but today, it was cloying. Too sweet and heavy. She covered her mouth and coughed.

Black Eagle scowled and puffed again, allowing huge billows of smoke to fill the air.

"I think I need some air," she said, and turned toward Meda who still stared at Black Eagle in outrage.

"I'll look for them, Meda. You just sit and rest."

"Hmph. As if I need to rest. Are you saying I'm feeble, girl?"

"No. I'm sorry. I meant no offense."

Meda sank back down onto a thick hide and frowned. "You didn't offend me. *He* offended me." She jerked her head toward the chief.

Kimana left the lodge with the sound of their bickering following her through the flap. She kept walking until she couldn't hear them anymore, then stopped and laid her hand on her forehead. If she hadn't escaped when she did, she probably would have ended up with a headache.

She looked up and caught her breath.

The two warriors walked toward her, side by side, their steps in perfect unison. She'd never noticed how alike they were. The way they walked, and even the way they carried themselves was similar. Except Two Hawks had a slight limp these days, and his build was, perhaps slightly narrower. Both of them were magnificent specimens of manhood, but when she compared her reactions to them, she realized that Two Hawks just didn't inspire the same depth of emotion. Or passion. She knew she loved him still, but it wasn't the same way she loved Running Wolf, and it never could be. Her heart had never pounded when he lowered his lips to hers. Her flesh had never broken out in gooseflesh when he touched her hand. She felt an intense loyalty, and a deep responsibility toward him, but it didn't make her want to rush forward and thread her fingers through his hair and kiss him until they were both gasping for breath.

Not like Running Wolf.

She watched them advance and looked between them questioningly as they came to a stop in front of her.

"Is everything well?" she asked.

Running Wolf glanced toward Two Hawks, then gave her a mystified scowl.

"Did you think we'd kill each other?"

She smiled. "I would hope not."

"Tomorrow," said Two Hawks.

The smile on her face flickered, then went out.

"I don't think that's funny."

"It wasn't meant to be funny," he said.

She lifted her chin and gave them both a withering glare. "Your father is expecting you," she said to Running Wolf, and cast a quick glance at his brother. "He's annoyed it took you so long."

"We were arguing over whether or not he needed to be tied," Running Wolf said.

"Are you serious?"

"No," he said, his lips turned up on one side as he let his gaze rest on her face. "I trust him enough to let him walk untethered."

She stared at Running Wolf. Did he realize that he'd just admitted to trusting his brother, the man he had called enemy just that morning? Did he realize he'd already accepted Two Hawks as his blood? She wondered what had passed between them and why they seemed almost at ease in each other's presence. Tension still sparked between them as they looked at each other, but it was tempered with something close to respect. Grudging respect, but still respect.

If by some chance, they were truly able to accept each other as brothers, if they were able to put their natural – no, learned - enmity aside, was there any way they could survive her being forced to choose between them?

"Well," Running Wolf said, "Let's get this done."

***

Two Hawks watched the old chief lay his pipe aside and wave them in. He looked at Kimana and took a step forward, then accepted a mat from an old woman. He looked at her curiously for a moment. She had a kind face, a warm smile, and somehow her face didn't seem to need the missing eye. There was something vaguely familiar about her, but he shrugged it off.

After everyone was settled around a cold fire pit, he turned his attention toward the chief.

"I am called Black Eagle," the old man said. "And this is Meda. She was sister to my wife, Chepi. A woman I lost a few summers past. Meda is a wise woman, our medicine woman. She is a seer. Like her sister was. But her gifts are different. My woman had the gift of dreams and the ability to speak to animals. Meda has the gift of interpreting dreams. You can imagine the team they once made," he said with a smile filled with both sorrow and pride.

Two Hawks grunted and watched Meda with more interest. The old woman smiled and nodded. He turned back to Black Eagle as the chief began to speak again.

"I would tell you a story."

A story? He raised his eyebrows. He had been brought before the chief to be told a story?

"Long ago, many winters past, there was a chief who had two sons. They were both fine boys, both strong. They had a bond that was unusual for children so young, boys who were several years apart in age. They played together often, running in the forests, swimming in pools of water. They were inseparable. When they weren't playing together, the younger brother followed the older everywhere he went. It was believed that they were destined to be great friends. But the spirits decided otherwise. At least, for a time."

Two Hawks glanced back and forth between Running Wolf and the chief. Running Wolf seemed uncomfortable with the tale, but his face was set as if carved from granite, and he looked as if he had no intention of interrupting. His demeanour was both respectful and resigned.

"One day, in the dark of winter, they went out to play in the woods. They ventured too far from home, and they got – separated."

He watched Running Wolf shift uncomfortably and send a scowl toward his father.

"When a storm hit, there was no way for the younger brother to be found, although the people spent several days looking. But the storm lasted for half a moon's time, and any trace of the boy's steps were lost."

"Did they find him?" Two Hawks asked.

"Not for many years."

A tingle ran along his spine as his eyes settled on each face in the teepee. Each one of them watched him closely. He suddenly felt warm. Too warm. He shrugged his shoulders and decided to ask the question he sensed he didn't really want to know the answer to.

"Why are you telling me this?"

"That little boy had an unusual birth mark. On his shoulder."

Two Hawks went absolutely still as he watched the chief's face. Then he turned toward Kimana. She watched him quietly, her posture straight and tall as she sat on her heels with her hands folded in her lap. Her eyes were sympathetic, and a little sad, and he saw the truth mirrored in their depths.

"I ask again. Why are you telling me this?"

"Kimana has dreamed dreams. She is the first one to do so in our village since my wife lost her life."

"And?"

"She dreamed of that little boy. Saw him in the snow, freezing, but alive. In the dream, she saw his shoulder. Saw his birth mark."

"Lots of people have birth marks."

"Yes," said the chief. "But no two are the same."

His headed started to spin. The lodge walls felt like they were closing in around him.

"Are you all right?" Kimana asked.

"I'm fine. Fine. Just - need some water. Air."

He staggered to his feet.

"I'll go with you," Running Wolf said and rose from the floor.

"No," Kimana said. "You stay. I'll go with him. Let me go with him."

Two Hawks didn't wait to hear Running Wolf's reply. He just

needed some air. It was the smoke, that was all. Just the smoke. It was too thick. Too heavy. Cloying. Sweet. Sickening. He stood in the sunshine and shook his head, trying to clear the fog out of his mind.

"It's not true," he said as Kimana came to stand beside him.

She laid a hand on his arm. "It's true."

"It can't be."

"I've seen it for myself."

"It was just a dream."

"You forget, Two Hawks. We've played together since we were little children. I've seen your birth mark. It is the same."

"It can't be." He shook his head again. "It's not possible."

"It's more than possible," she said and gently squeezed his arm. "It's true."

"I'm Cree. I've always been Cree."

"You're Cree," she agreed. "But you were once Blackfoot. Do you remember anything about before you came to live with us?"

He looked at Kimana, stunned. He'd forgotten.

"I guess I wanted so much to believe that I belonged, somewhere, that I convinced myself I'd always lived there."

"But you didn't."

"No."

"Do you remember anything of your life before?"

He grimaced, trying to recall. "I remember snow. And cold."

"And a wolf."

His eyes snapped back to hers. "How do you know about the wolf?"

"I dreamed."

"You never used to dream." He tried not to sound like he was grumbling, but he didn't have much luck.

She smiled. "No. But that was before. A lot has changed for me."

"For both of us."

"Will you go back in and talk to them?"

"No."

"Please. You have a father in there. And a brother."

"I don't have a brother."

"You do."

He closed his eyes. "I can't do this right now. I need time to think. Tell them I went back to the lodge. Where I was earlier. I won't leave. I just need some time."

"I'll tell them."

"Kimana?"

She lifted her eyebrows in silent response.

"If I am Blackfoot, it means my claim on you should be honoured."

"I know." The words were whispered, but he heard them clearly. He also heard the regret in her voice.

"Is it him you want?"

"I gave you my word."

"Yes, you did."

He gave her one last look before striding off toward the path that led back down to his teepee.

CHAPTER FORTY-TWO

Kimana had a decision to make, and she hoped the spirits would guide her. She needed their wisdom now more than ever before.

She glanced over her shoulder yet again at the two brothers who stood together, watching her leave the camp as the afternoon sun began its slow descent toward the horizon.

Two Hawks looked defiant, expectant. Confident.

Running Wolf's face was inscrutable, but she could feel his eyes burning into her. It was the same expression he'd worn when he squeezed her hand in his and wished her a good journey, good visions.

Her deerskin dress fluttered around her legs as she continued to walk, the long fringes tickling her shins. The wind was gentle, the day still unbearably hot.

She turned to look at the men one last time before threading her way through the hoodoos.

Two Hawks still stood where he had been, watching her leave, but Running Wolf had already started to walk away. She felt a twinge of regret, of disappointment as she watched him stride back toward camp without turning to look at her.

As she looked at him.

Had he given up, then? Was he already prepared to let her go? Tears stung her eyes, but she forced herself to take a deep breath. She wouldn't allow a single tear to fall. They still didn't know what would happen, and she refused to let sorrow overtake her before a decision was made. She would need her strength for the days ahead. She turned away and followed a worn path that had been travelled by generations of people who came here looking for answers, for the guidance of their ancestors.

She didn't know how long she'd be gone. It could be a single day. It could be a week. It was for the spirits to decide.

As they would decide whose arms she would lay in as wife.

The elders had been adamant in their decree. She would fast and pray and seek her answer from the spirits. She would allow them to come to her in visions. And she would allow them to decide her fate. Honesty and honour were expected. Assumed. She must not make a decision without the ancestors' approval.

It was the way, the elders said. It was only for her to watch and listen, and to trust that they knew what was best for her, for them all.

She'd always respected the words of the elders and the guidance of the ancestors and spirits, always obeyed them. Now would be no different, no matter how much the result might hurt. If they chose Two Hawks for her, it would be Two Hawks. If they chose Running Wolf, it would be Running Wolf.

But would the spirits take her own feelings into consideration? Did they care where her heart lay?

A grey jay chattered to her as it hopped along the mushroom-shaped cap of a tall hoodoo, his silvery, glossy feathers nearly the same colour as Makwai's eyes. Her footsteps slowed as she watched him fluff out his feathers and listened to him scold her. Kimana smiled. She wished she knew what he was saying. The spirits wouldn't speak to her yet, so the jay's words were his own. She was sure he would have his own, unique wisdom to impart as she took her spiritual journey, and she was sorry she couldn't understand him.

Or maybe he was just hungry.

"I have nothing to give you," she said.

The bird cocked his head as if listening, then chirped and angled his head to the other side. She reached into a deep pouch that hung from her waist and drew out her hands, showing them to him.

"There's nothing. I have no treats for you."

The jay chirped again, then tensed his muscles and flew away.

She watched him until he disappeared from sight, then continued down the winding path.

Before long, the hoodoos gave way to the sandstone cliffs of the narrow canyon. Carved and painted drawings appeared on the rock walls with increasing frequency. She stopped and ran her fingers over one of the line drawings. Two men, locked in battle, an eagle soaring overhead. The next image showed a buffalo hunt in all its glory. Hundreds of buffalo, and dozens of men running along beside them, herding them toward a cliff. Perhaps the buffalo jump they had visited before summer. Or another jump. She hoped their hunt had been successful.

The people had made these.

The people, and the spirits.

Thousands of Blackfoot, but not only Blackfoot. Cree. Shoshone. Blood. Piegan. Gros Ventre. Many had visited here and left their mark on the high stone cliffs and hoodoos. Many had come to do what she was doing. To let the spirits guide them. Teach them. Show them the way.

A shiver crawled up her spine as she took in the awesome power and majesty of the place. It seemed to seep out of the rock and ooze out of the very ground she stood upon. This was, by far, the most sacred place she had ever been. The magnitude of what she both saw and felt overwhelmed her. The tears she had fought before streamed down her face. Of all the places she had ever been, this place had more power than any other. She could feel the presence of the spirits all around her. Hear their moaning as the wind picked up and howled through the canyon. Feel their breath upon her flesh. Ripple the fringes of her dress.

One thing she knew for certain, she would not be alone here while on her vision quest. She was surrounded by everyone who had ever come before her. She walked a while farther, through the tall grass between the cliff and the river, looking for a place to spend the night.

She would not sleep.

She would wait for the visions to come.

Startled, she stopped to watch a flurry of sharp-tailed grouse burst from the grass in front of her. Fire birds. So-called because their habitat depended totally on fire to keep trees and bushes clear. It sounded just like they were cackling as they flew away from her, their rounded wings flapping furiously. She stepped more carefully, knowing their large nests could be hidden in the thick grass and amongst the sagebrush that seemed to grow everywhere, not wanting to step on one of their precious young. She angled away from the river, closer to the cliffs, hoping to avoid disturbing any more birds. They didn't like the presence of humans any more than they liked the presence of the white-headed eagles that soared overhead in the orange and pink-splashed sky, looking for a quick and easy meal.

She'd better hurry or she wouldn't find a place to spend the night before sunset.

Her footsteps quickened, and she searched the cliffs for a ledge she could sit comfortably on through the night. She didn't want to spend the night on the ground. She didn't feel like dealing with snakes and other crawling things.

Her eyes continued to scan the cliffs. The idea of climbing so high off the ground bothered her. It wasn't like climbing a tree, and that was bad enough.

Then she'd have to sit up there. For hours.

Well, it was better than rattlesnakes. She was just grateful it was one of the longest days of the year. The night would be blessedly short.

She wasn't afraid to be alone - she just didn't know what to expect on this quest.

Her gaze settled on a deep impression in the rock wall. It wasn't too high off the ground, she thought, maybe the height of two men. Digging her fingers into grooves in the wall, she began to climb, her soft-soled moccasins allowing her toes to grip against the rock. Half-way up, she hesitated a moment to catch her breath. Looking down, she felt a wave of dizziness. She snapped her eyes closed and laid her cheek against the cold rock.

"I'm okay. I'm okay."

She let herself breathe. Just breathe.

"What in the name of all the spirits did I think I was doing, climbing this cliff? Am I crazy? I must be crazy."

Forcing herself to open her eyes and confront her fear, she looked down at the ground. Took another deep breath.

"I'm okay."

The breath shuddered out of her chest as she blew out through her mouth. The dizziness receded. Her heartbeat slowed.

"I can do this," she said, and continued her climb.

Once she reached the ledge, she hauled herself up and quickly planted herself firmly on the smooth outcropping, scuttling backwards towards the small opening in the rock behind her. She let out another long breath. Forcing herself to inch closer to the edge, she let first her feet, and then her calves, dangle off. She gave her toes a wiggle.

"I made it, I'm here, I did it," she said in a sing-song voice and grinned. That was one challenge she had met head-on. It felt good, conquering her fear like that. She hoped the spirits had taken notice and would grant her a vision tonight. She peered over the ledge and fought back another wave of dizziness. No, she would not be afraid, she told herself firmly.

Then she looked up and her breath caught in her throat. Her fear was forgotten as she stared across the canyon at the sun that rested in the sky just above the cliffs on the other side of the river. Clouds rimmed in golden fire flirted with the edges of the sun, and vibrant streaks of purple and pink slashed the sky. The sun lit the sandstone cliffs around her, and they glowed with a golden light as if lit from within.

She couldn't hear the sound of the huge summer village upriver. No voices reached her here at all, except the voices of the land, the whispers of the spirits, an osprey screaming as it flew above the river, the rustling of sage leaves far below. And the sound of the wind, rushing through the thin valley.

She brought her knees up to her chest and wrapped her arms around her legs as she let her emotions wash over her.

This moment would never come again, her father would say.

Live every second.

And remember.

The wind rippled through her hair as she watched the sun set. In the morning, she would be here, still. And she would watch the warmth of a morning sun turn the cliffs on the other side of the river to fire.

***

Running Wolf wandered around the circle camp, watching the people pack up their belongings so they were ready when it was time to break camp. Some would leave today, others tomorrow,

290

and still other tribes would be here another week. But it wouldn't be long until the echo of their voices was just a memory in this place, as they left to begin their berry and herb gathering and prepare for the final buffalo hunts of the year before autumn came once again. It was a busiest time of the year.

He tried to tamp down on a burst of irritation and impatience. The elders had given their decree yesterday, and by today, they were getting ready to leave. Just like that. While Kimana was off, alone, waiting for some vision to appear. It wasn't that he disagreed with the elders' edict. He understood the wisdom in allowing Kimana the chance to find out from the spirits what her destiny would be.

But it frustrated him that he would have no say in the outcome. And that the ones who would have the say weren't able to sit down and have a reasonable conversation about it or roll in the dirt and fight it out. How could you reason with spirits? Argue with them?

He would have no one to blame if Two Hawks was the spirits' choice.

No one to rail and rage at.

Normally, he respected the spirits of the land too much to argue with their will, even though he may question their wisdom on occasion. But this time, they held something precious in their hands, and he wasn't sure he could accept their choice if their will and his didn't line up.

Running Wolf nodded and smiled thinly at a group of young women who hurried past in a tight-knit, giggling group. From the hesitant looks on their faces as they passed, he wondered if his smile and grunted greeting had come out more like a snarl.

He wouldn't be surprised. He felt like a tethered wolf.

He paused. Looked around. Speaking of wolves, where was Makwai? He hadn't seen her since the day he'd found Two Hawks and Kimana out on the prairies.

He shrugged and kept on walking. It certainly wasn't unusual for her to take off like that. She'd disappeared for months at a time over the years. When he thought about it, he had to admit it was strange how she'd appeared in his life right after his mother had been killed.

Were they right?

Did Makwai carry his mother's spirit? His eyes narrowed as he thought about the wolf leading Two Hawks to the Blackfoot camp.

And the trapper. He'd said a wolf had led him to Kimana when she'd tried to run away and been swept down the river. A wolf had also led the trapper to Two Hawks, after the raid on Kimana's village. He shook his head in confusion and irritation. A wolf had supposedly also led that same trapper to Two Hawks when he was a little boy, when he was still Two Birds. How could that be if it was really his mother? She had still been alive then.

If Makwai had his mother's spirit now, he understood her bringing Two Hawks back home, but did it also mean Two Hawks and Kimana were destined to be one with each other, that his own mother had a part in bringing them together?

Scowling, he paused again. Looked up. And saw his brother striding toward him.

Two Hawks certainly was making himself at home. All it took was a few words by the elders, and he was treated like a returning hero. It was good, Running Wolf grudgingly decided. No matter what else he may feel, he was glad to have his brother back home.

Even if he was still a Cree.

Bring my people together, his mother had told Kimana in her dream. Was this what she meant? Uniting the Cree and the Blackfoot? Uniting all the people who lived on the great prairies? That would probably never happen, no matter how similar they may be in their lives and beliefs. Maybe one day. She had always said that all are one. Maybe this is what she meant.

But for now, he and his brother needed to find common ground, even if Kimana stood unwillingly between them.

"Good morning," Two Hawks said.

"And to you."

Together they continued to stroll around the camp, neither one of them speaking.

"Will she be all right out there?" Two Hawks asked suddenly.

"I hope so."

"As do I."

They shared a look of quiet understanding. It was one thing they easily agreed on.

"Have you ever been to the cliffs?" Two Hawks asked.

Running Wolf nodded. "Many times over the years. It is a very spiritual place, and many Blackfoot go there for their vision quests."

"As do the Cree."

Running Wolf snorted. "And if they're caught, they have their tongues ripped out and fed to the coyotes."

Two Hawks laughed, but there was something good-natured about it, rather than cynical. They both knew it wasn't just the Blackfoot who came here, even though it was undeniably their territory. They had fought back the Shoshone more than once over the years but had eventually come out victorious. None could argue about whose land it was.

But no one owned the spirits. And this was a sacred space, where the spirits lived.

Running Wolf looked at his brother. "Have you ever been there? To see the drawings on the stone?"

"Many times." Two Hawks grinned.

"Of course you have. Why does it not surprise me. So, we have that in common, too, it seems."

"You'd expect us to have things in common, wouldn't you?"

"And I'd expect there to be serious differences. Do you think you can accept a life amongst the Blackfoot?"

"I don't know. I don't think so. I don't really have a place now, do I? Nowhere to belong. Born a Blackfoot. Raised a Cree. I guess it will depend on Kimana. Where she wants to be."

"You assume the spirits will choose you."

"I guess I do. I hope." Two Hawks stared off toward the distant cliffs.

"As I hope they do not," Running Wolf said. They exchanged glances again. "No offense is intended."

"And no offense is taken," said Two Hawks. "I guess we'll have to wait and see what happens."

"I am not fond of waiting. I prefer to make my own destiny."

"We have that in common, as well."

"But this time, your future and mine is in Kimana's hands. And in the hands of the spirits."

Two Hawks grunted in agreement.

"Can you accept the will of the spirits if they choose me, instead?"

Two Hawks took a long time in answering. "I will accept it. I don't know if I'd be able to stay if I can't have her. And what about you? Can you accept it if I am the one chosen?"

Running Wolf looked at the river below, and down the river toward the sandstone cliffs. Towards Kimana. One way or another, he faced a loss. He would lose either Kimana or lose his brother. Again.

For the first time, he was glad the decision was in the spirits' hands.

"I will accept what the spirits tell her. She would expect nothing less."

CHAPTER FORTY-THREE

The visions did not come.

Stretching her legs, she once again watched the sun set over the cliffs and wondered - not for the first time - if the visions would come at all.

"Speak to me, Great Spirit," she murmured as the vibrant colours of the setting sun washed over her, turning everything around her to gold, for the second day.

Maybe she was trying too hard. Maybe she wasn't open enough to let the spirits speak to her.

Or maybe they had nothing to say.

She pressed her fingers against her stomach, and deliberately ignored a pang of hunger.

On the other side of the river, a doe and her fawn stepped out of a thick stand of cottonwood trees and approached the water. The fawn moved eagerly forward, plunging its nose in the slow-moving river to drink. Its mother turned her head from side to side, her huge ears twitching, testing the air as she looked for danger. Sensing nothing, she joined her fawn at the water's edge.

Kimana watched them until they'd drunk their fill and picked their way through the rocky shallows along the riverbank, finally disappearing around a bend downriver.

Somewhere in the distance a coyote howled and was soon joined by a chorus of yipping voices. A great horned owl warbled nearby.

She tucked her knees against her chest and listened to the

sounds of dusk. Nature was never quiet. But it called to her, and her response throbbed deep inside her chest.

Gradually, she became aware of the feeling of being watched. Turning her head, she scanned both sides of the river, trying to see in the darkness that had gradually fallen as she listened to the sounds of the wilderness.

All she could see were dark shapes where bushes and trees had stood moments ago. Then one of the shadows moved, skulking along the edge of the river.

A wolf stopped directly opposite the ledge she sat on and turned its head toward her. She could almost feel its stare.

And somehow, she knew its eyes were grey.

"Makwai," she whispered. "Did you come to see me? To talk to me? Speak to me, Makwai. What is it you want me to know?"

The wolf sat down, cocked its head. Kimana could just make out the shape of her erect ears. Kimana smoothed her fingers over the heavy pouch of Chepi's medicine bag that Meda had gifted her before she left on her vision quest.

"Are you her? Are you Chepi?"

She didn't expect the wolf to answer – she probably couldn't even hear her whispered voice - so she wasn't surprised when Makwai just continued to stare.

"What is it you want me to do?"

She continued to stroke Chepi's medicine bag. Narrowing her eyes, Kimana untied the bag's strap and pulled it from her waist. She cupped the pouch in her hands, and looked at it for a moment, its shiny, worn surface all but invisible in the dark.

"Is this what you want me to do? To look inside?" she asked and looked back at the wolf.

But Makwai was gone.

Startled, Kimana quickly scanned the shoreline, but couldn't see anything moving, no shadows out of place.

"But I can't see," she said. "How can I look inside this bag if I can't see?"

She opened the bag and let her fingers run over the contents. Something thin and long. Something rough to the touch that she couldn't begin to guess at. Something cold and smooth, like a river stone. There were at least a dozen objects inside the bag.

It could be any one of them.

"Speak to me, Chepi. Tell me what to do."

No answer came. No inspiration.

She tied the straps of the medicine bag into a knot and slipped the pouch around her neck. It nestled between her breasts, next to her heart.

"Speak to me, Chepi."

The night seemed to stretch long in front of her.

***

Makwai grinned at her from the other side of the river. She shook her head, fluffed out her fur and grinned again. Moonlight sparkled on the river and reflected in her eyes.

Are you listening, Kimana?

"I'm listening. Tell me what to do."

Her voice seemed to come from inside her head.

You know where your steps lead you. Follow the eagle.

Kimana shook her head. She didn't understand. Follow the eagle? What eagle? Light shifted and danced around her.

Her father stood before her, his eyes moist with tears, an eagle feather in his outstretched hand. The white tip glowed silver in the moonlight.

Follow the eagle.

Her father unfolded his gnarled fingers and let the eagle feather drift slowly to the ground. He smiled, and tears flowed through the creases in his cheeks like autumn rains through a parched streambed.

She reached out to touch his hand, but he faded into the night.

"Father? I need you to tell me what to do."

Follow the eagle, Kimana.

She looked down at her feet. The eagle feather rocked in the breeze, barely lifting off the ground before it settled and rocked again. She bent down to pick it up. The beating of wings distracted her, and she glanced up to see a hawk gliding toward her, its wings snapping in the air. She covered her face with her hands, thinking it meant to attack her, but the bird only swooped down and scooped the eagle feather into its beak.

It flapped its wings, screamed and soared upward into the night. Somewhere, far away, a wolf howled. Just as the hawk appeared in the sky against the moon, she saw the feather fall from the bird's beak and spiral toward the ground.

It came to rest at her feet.
The wolf's stare drew her gaze.
Follow the eagle, Kimana.
She sat down and cried.

CHAPTER FORTY-FOUR

She came to him in darkness. Poured herself on top of him, stretched her body over his. His breath caught and held as she slid between his legs and nestled her chest against his own, nuzzled her face against his neck.

"I love you," she whispered beside his ear.

Taking his face in her hands, she laid her lips on his mouth and gently breathed the words again. Then her mouth captured his.

His heart pounded. Throbbed in his chest.

She consumed him.

Undid him.

When had he fallen so completely and utterly in love with her? When had she become his very reason for breathing? Running Wolf captured her head in his hands and threaded his fingers through her hair. Wild, tumbling hair. Like fire in the night - shifting embers of midnight and copper. He breathed in the scent of her. She smelled of wilderness and wind. Tasted of sweetgrass - and something wild and sweet. He ran his hands over her back and pulled her close. Tasted her lips, her tongue. Felt himself twirling out of control.

She kissed him with a passion matched only by his own. Ran her fingers over his chest, his hips, his thighs. And back again. Lifted herself up on her elbows and looked down into his eyes. Her hair flowed over her shoulders and brushed against his chest.

"I love you," she whispered again.

She shifted and placed her hand between his legs. Passion

flared. He grew harder, firmer at her touch. He throbbed. Wanted. Needed.

Her.

He needed her.

She was everything he could have hoped for in a woman and more. She challenged him, made him ache and yearn.

She'd shown him that all he really needed was to have her love.

And to give it back.

"I love you, Kimana. I need you."

"And I need you."

"Love me."

"Always."

She shifted again and settled her hot, moist centre against him. Moaned. Rocked against his hips, her head thrown back as the fire raging between them consumed them both. She took him to a place he'd never been, to a height he could never have imagined. Soared and swirled with him there like an eagle on the wind.

Hot tears spilled onto his cheeks.

"I love you. I'm sorry. So sorry."

He went still.

Didn't even take a breath.

Couldn't.

He looked at her in sick shock as the meaning of what she was saying finally penetrated. She ran her fingers over his cheeks and smiled brokenly through her tears.

"I'm so sorry," she whispered. "I wanted it to be you."

CHAPTER FORTY-FIVE

He was gone.

Her fingers splayed over the hide she and Running Wolf had lain on through the night, as they held each for the last time, neither one of them wanting to let go, but knowing there was no choice. No warmth from his body remained on the thick fur. Nothing to indicate she had laid with him there, except the scent of him on her body.

She glanced across to Chief Black Eagle's mat, but he was gone, as well. Her cheeks warmed at the thought he might have heard them. It was impossible to have any real privacy when others shared a lodge, but most people wouldn't ever dream of saying anything. She was grateful for that.

She probably shouldn't have come to Running Wolf last night, but once she realized the meaning of her vision, nothing could have stopped her from running through the moonlight and threading her way blindly through the hoodoos. Nothing could have kept her from him. Not even her own conscience. She had no shame over going to her wedding mat an experienced woman. Two Hawks already knew she'd been with Running Wolf. It didn't seem to bother him enough to release her from his claim.

She supposed she was grateful for that.

At least it would not be an issue between them.

Cold dread settled into her belly at the thought of laying as wife with Two Hawks. It would be like sleeping with a brother. She couldn't imagine it. Didn't want to. But soon she'd have no choice.

She'd promised the elders, as well as Running Wolf and Two Hawks, that she would honour the will of the spirits, no matter what her heart told her. But she didn't know how she was going to live with it.

With duty, at least, she thought with a wry twist of the lips. With honour. And honesty.

Would she ever be able to look at Two Hawks and accept him in her heart? Could she love him in the way a woman should love a man? Could she ever let go of the memories of Running Wolf, of being in his arms, held by him, possessed by him?

No, she knew she never would. She could never release those memories. They were the only things she had left of him, and she would never let them go. She had no regrets about being with him. And if, by chance, she carried his child, she would carry it without shame.

Her breath shuddered out as she fought back tears. Since realizing what the vision meant, she hadn't been able to stop them from flowing. But soon, she would have to face Black Eagle and Two Hawks and tell them her vision. She wanted to face them with dry eyes and a straight back. With dignity. With courage. With honour. She would not allow them to see her pain or to know how desperately unhappy she was with what the spirits told her.

What her father had told her.

And that, she thought, was the thing that convinced her. With each dream she'd had of her father since he died, he had looked at her with tears in his eyes and dropped the feather to the ground.

Follow the eagle.

The hawk had taken the feather.

And she faced a future without the man she loved.

***

Hair whipped around his face as he rode his stallion hard over the prairies, urging him faster, harder. But Running Wolf knew that no matter how hard, how fast, or how far he rode, he wouldn't be able to escape the emotions that raged inside of him.

He tightened his hand on the reins as his horse reared upward and sideways to avoid something skittering across his path.

A brown rabbit made a frantic retreat through the grass.

Bringing his stallion under control, he leaned forward and

stroked the horse's neck. They both panted heavily.

He looked back at the distant circle camp. Even now, people were tearing down their lodges, preparing to leave the gathering. And Kimana would be telling his father her vision. Telling Two Hawks. He should be there, he knew. But he didn't think he could bring himself to listen to the soft rise and fall of her voice as she shared the vision she said destroyed any hope they had of a future together.

He knew Kimana would not want him there when she shared her vision. It would be too painful for them both. Besides, he really didn't want to know what the spirits had said. It was enough that she'd had the vision. Enough that she knew what it meant. And he would accept it.

He didn't have a choice.

He'd known this could happen.

Had refused to believe it.

In fact, if he'd thought for one minute that the vision would show her what it had, he wouldn't have let her seek the spirits in the first place. He'd have swept her up onto her horse and taken her to a place where there were no elders, no seers.

Spirits, be damned.

He winced, instantly regretting the thought.

Kimana didn't feel that way. She believed strongly in knowing the will and wisdom of the ancestors. She believed in destiny. Honour. Duty.

As did he, if it came down to it. But it didn't mean he liked it when destiny tore his heart from his chest and trampled it into the ground like a blade of grass under a stampeding herd of oblivious buffalo.

He gave his stallion another stroke on the neck, then slid off and landed softly on the balls of his feet. He paced through the grass, stopping only long enough to scoop up a stone and hurl it toward the sky.

When she'd told him it wasn't him that the spirits chose, he'd nearly come undone. He'd refused to even listen to the vision.

He'd wanted to argue with her.

Tell her she was wrong.

She'd misunderstood. Misinterpreted.

But the way she'd looked at him in the dim, dim light of early morning, the way her tears had spilled onto his face, the way she'd cried in his arms had convinced him that there was no undoing what was done. The spirits had spoken, and they had all agreed to honour their words.

And so he would. He'd do it for her, for her beliefs.

Kimana and Two Hawks would likely stay with the Blackfoot. They had no reason to leave. It was Kimana's home now. Two Hawks' home, as well.

As much as it pained him, he knew he wouldn't be able to stay and get to know his brother better. Watching him with Kimana would be too much to bear. They'd all be shocked when he told them he was leaving, but he just couldn't stay. Maybe one day, he'd be able to return for a short visit, but he didn't think he could ever be around her without it tearing him apart.

So, he would leave. Travel to other Blackfoot camps. Maybe even visit the Cree, if they didn't kill him on sight. He had to find a way to make a life apart from her. All he could do was wish them well. Wish them happiness.

He could never hope to wish the same things for himself.

He walked back over to his stallion and swung up onto the animal's back.

He would go soon, gather his things, and say goodbye to his father. But not yet. He didn't think he could face anyone right now.

CHAPTER FORTY-SIX

Kimana hesitated outside Meda's lodge and stared off toward the prairies. The image of the hawk, swooping down to carry off the eagle feather, weighed heavily on her mind.

She didn't have to tell them. She could easily relay the vision in such a way that it seemed as if Running Wolf was the one the spirits chose for her. She could leave out the hawk completely. No one would know. Except Running Wolf.

But that would be dishonourable. Wrong.

He wouldn't let her do it, anyway.

She owed it to all of them, including her father, to be honest – like she'd promised she would. But how could she just walk in there and announce that she was giving up what she wanted the most? How could she turn her back on Running Wolf? Give up everything they had together?

***

Two Hawks turned to watch Kimana as she stepped inside the teepee and greeted him, Meda and Chief Black Eagle. His breath caught as he watched her. She was beautiful, as always, but her face was drawn. The usual sparkle in her eyes was missing. She looked tired.

Visions quests could be like that, he knew. Exhausting. Demanding. Draining both on the body and on the mind. She'd only been gone for two days, but that didn't mean anything. The last two days had been hard on him, and he hadn't faced what she faced. Meeting the ancestors might be exhilarating, but it was never easy. But nothing worth having was ever easy.

He knew that for a fact.

He didn't doubt she'd had a vision. He knew her well enough to know she wouldn't come back until she did. And she would share what the spirits told her no matter what she thought of it. Or how she felt about it. If there was one person he knew who understood duty and honour, it was Kimana. She believed in it the same way he did. She'd never consider being dishonest or holding something back.

He knew she was in love with Running Wolf. That much was obvious. But she loved him, too, and she would eventually care for him as much as she did his brother.

His brother.

Two Hawks still had trouble getting his mind around that. Just a single moon past, he'd had no one. He'd been alone in the world, with only the hope of finding Kimana keeping him going. Now he had a brother. And a father. An aunt. And a people. They weren't Cree, but they were his. He didn't know if he could get used to that idea. He'd distrusted and hated the Blackfoot since he was old enough to shoot an arrow. But there was no denying his blood.

He glanced impatiently toward the teepee's entrance. Where was Running Wolf?

Two Hawks had wasted no time coming to Meda's lodge when he heard Kimana was back. No matter what the result of her vision, he was ready to face it. But he wasn't worried. Did Running Wolf know he was about to lose her, so he stayed away? Was he that weak? Afraid?

He sneered inwardly. Though Two Hawks had grown up hating the Blackfoot, he'd always believed they were strong, fierce warriors who were unafraid to face their destiny. He couldn't help but admire them, even as he detested them. His brother, on the other hand – well, he didn't know him well enough to know how he would react. The fact that he wasn't here said something.

Had she already told him her vision?

He watched Kimana lower herself to a mat and tuck her legs to the side. She spent a few moments arranging her dress around her legs, straightening the fringes over her golden calves. Then she looked up and met the eyes of each one of them, in turn. Meda. His father. Himself. Her gaze gave away nothing. He'd never seen her look so composed.

Serene.

Kimana was his destiny. He knew it. From the time they were children, he'd known she was for him. He'd wanted her even on the day when she'd embarrassed him in front of the elders. He'd announced, in their presence of course, that he was a man and could no longer play foolish little games with foolish little girls. He hadn't been more than ten summers old.

He grinned as he remembered the look on her face when she stomped her foot squarely down onto his own and marched over to the men, planting herself defiantly in the middle of the amused group of aging warriors. She'd been furious. Glorious. She'd made him see the strength a female could have. And he'd wanted her with a passion ever since.

"Where is Running Wolf?" Meda asked.

"I saw him earlier this morning. He went riding. He should be here soon," Black Eagle said.

"He should be here now." Two Hawks looked the chief in the eye. "He knew we were meeting immediately on Kimana's return. I don't want to wait any longer."

Black Eagle shifted and looked a little uncomfortable. Meda pursed her lips and gave Two Hawks a disapproving look.

"I've spoken with him already," said Kimana. She tilted her chin. "I don't need my vision interpreted. It's clear what the spirits told me."

She lowered her eyes to her clasped hands for the space of two heartbeats. Three. She took a deep breath, straightened her spine, and looked Two Hawks straight in the eye.

"You are the spirits' choice."

Silence settled over the teepee. Meda and Black Eagle looked shocked, almost comical with their mouths hanging loose. But there was nothing funny here. Even as his spirit soared hearing Kimana's words, he fought back a wave of guilt. She looked like a warrior who found his best friend lying dead after a battle.

Defeated.

It wasn't serenity he'd seen in her. It was resignation.

"I accept that you say you know the will of the spirits, my daughter, but I would hear the vision for myself," Black Eagle said, and smiled gently.

"I'd like to hear it, too," Meda said. "After all, we do not know that you have the gift of interpreting visions. I'm not saying you're wrong. Just that for something like this, it's important to have it confirmed. You do want it confirmed, don't you, Kimana? I know I would."

"Please."

Kimana nodded.

Two Hawks saw a spark of hope enter her eyes. He lowered his brow as he watched her. Was she that unhappy with what the spirits said? Did she love Running Wolf that deeply?

"My father was there," said Kimana. "I've told you before, Meda, how I've dreamed of my father, and he is holding a feather. The one I gave him the day our village was attacked? He told me I was going on a journey."

"I remember."

"In the vision, he was holding the feather. He cried, and he let it fall from his fingers, as I've seen him do in dreams before. Makwai was standing on the other side of the river, and she told me to follow the eagle. The feather. An eagle's feather. He dropped it. He told me...", she stopped and looked at him, then glanced down at her lap again. "He told me to follow the eagle."

"And what happened to the feather, Kimana?" Meda leaned forward.

"A hawk came out of the sky." Kimana looked at Chief Black Eagle again. "It took the feather."

"Was that all?" demanded Meda. "Did the hawk fly away with the father?"

"No, he dropped it. It fell and landed at my feet, and Makwai told me again to follow the eagle."

"Did you tell Running Wolf your vision?" asked Chief Black Eagle.

"No. I just told him that the spirits had chosen Two Hawks."

Chief Black Eagle lowered his eyes and nodded.

"I see." He looked over at Meda. "Do you agree with her interpretation?"

"Certainly not. I don't think the vision gave her a definite answer. Or if it did, I don't think the meaning of the vision is clear, yet."

Two Hawks shot a glance at the old woman. Her single eye blazed with indignation.

"Girl, you've done us all a disservice. Interpreting your own vision without consulting an elder. Without consulting me." Meda huffed and crossed her arms over her chest. "You should be ashamed of yourself."

"What do you mean?" Two Hawks asked, then kicked himself mentally for asking. He looked back at Kimana. Her lips were parted as she stared at the old medicine woman, waiting for her reply. She looked so expectant. Hopeful. He turned away, unwilling to see it.

"It's clear enough to me. The hawk took the feather. That's the important thing," he said.

"It dropped it. And there was only one hawk. Not two," Meda said.

"That means nothing."

"It did drop it," said Black Eagle.

"I don't understand," said Kimana.

"You were told not once, not twice, but three times, to follow the eagle. Your father dropped the feather. A hawk picked it up. A single hawk. But the hawk dropped the feather. And that is the third time you were told to follow the eagle. Kimana..." Meda leaned forward to touch Kimana's knee. "The feather did not lead to Two Hawks. The answer you seek is within you. But I believe the spirits will give you a sign, just to confirm it. And when they do, you will know it. The hawk dropped the feather at your feet. It is up to you to pick that feather back up. The spirits will show you when."

Meda looked at him. "I'm sorry, Two Hawks."

Two Hawks stared at Kimana. Her willingness to share her vision, even though she was sure its meaning wasn't what she wanted, astounded him. But her reaction to Meda's words was what really mattered. He didn't think he could take away that light from her eyes. Meda was right. The vision didn't lead to him. Only one hawk. And it dropped the feather. It took it, then dropped it. It willingly gave up the prize it had worked so hard to win.

Just like he had worked so hard to find Kimana and have her as his own. But could he give her up? Could he drop the feather at her feet and fly away?

Two Hawks made a decision.

He unfolded his legs and rose to his feet, then offered a hand to Kimana.

"You promised to honour the will of the spirits," he reminded her.

She nodded.

"Then come with me. It is decided."

Behind him he could feel Black Eagle and Meda bristle, but he ignored them. Kimana's eyes were lowered, and her shoulders slumped in defeat. Then before him, she seemed to transform. Her shoulders straightened, and she looked up into his eyes.

That fierce little girl who was unafraid to face anything was still inside of her.

She nodded, then stood and placed a warm hand in his. His fingers closed over hers, and he squeezed. He had loved her since the beginning of time. And he would love her until the end.

With one last glance at the chief and the medicine woman, Kimana allowed Two Hawks to pull her outside.

CHAPTER FORTY-SEVEN

She wished he'd given her time to gather her things, to say goodbye properly. To find Running Wolf and tell him one last time how much she loved him. But he was practically dragging her across the plain and down into the coulee.

A mist filled the river valley, making ghosts of the hoodoos.

She knew Meda and Chief Black Eagle did not believe her interpretation of the vision, but she saw no other possibility. *Follow the eagle,* Chepi had said.

She did not love Two Hawks, not in the way a woman loves a man, but she knew she could make a life with him if she had to. Her father had taught her to be strong.

She tugged on his hand, then, and brought him to a stop.

"You don't need to force me. I gave you my word."

"Yes. You did."

"Then why are you dragging me?"

He looked at her quietly for a moment, his eyes dark and hooded. He glanced over his shoulder toward the hoodoos, toward the place where countless men and women had sought the guidance of their ancestors. He stared intently for several minutes as she watched him. Then he turned back to her and laid a hand upon her cheek.

"I love you, Kimana. Always have. Always will. But it is not me the spirits wish for you. You must follow your heart. Follow the eagle, Kimana."

He leaned down and kissed her cheek, then looked up into the

311

sky as the sound of a screech pierced the air. The mist was starting to lift around them, and then cleared suddenly, and in the sky, high above, an eagle circled.

A shiver coursed through her, and she watched it, catching a current to soar for a moment, then twisting and turning like a warrior at a victory dance. The eagle screamed again and flew upriver, toward the west.

"Go. See where it leads you," Two Hawks whispered.

She looked back at him, her insides churning. She wasn't sure what she felt. Was it fear? Anticipation? Gratitude.

She watched the eagle as it continued its journey along the river, past the hoodoos.

"Go. Follow the eagle."

A tingling coursed through her. Standing on her toes, she kissed his cheek, then took a few, hesitant steps along the riverbank.

Glancing back, she saw that he was already climbing the banks of the coulee.

The eagle was a small dot in the sky now. She took a few more steps, then hitched up her hide dress and started to run.

The mist that shrouded the riverbed parted before her. She ran, twisting and turning around the hoodoos that dotted the river's edge, keeping her eye on the eagle.

Then the bird seemed to stop and hover high above as if waiting for her. It screamed again, and in ever decreasing circles, spiralled downward and alit on the top of a nearby hoodoo. It looked straight at her then, cocking its head to the side piercing her with its gaze.

She continued toward it, slightly out of breath.

"What is it," she whispered. "What do you want me to do."

And then, on a distant hoodoo, she saw him. A man crouched on the top, looked westward along the river, toward the mountains.

Toward home.

"Running Wolf," she whispered. The eagle fluffed out his wings, shot her a final glance, and then flew back up into the sky. She heard another scream and turned to watch as a second bird joined it, and together they circled and danced on unseen currents of air, before turning as one toward the distant mountain peaks.

She whispered again, "Running Wolf."

As if he could hear her, he turned.

Tears of joy bubbled up inside of her as they stared at each other. Then she started to run. He jumped down from the hoodoo, and as she reached him, he scooped her up and into his arms, twirling her around.

"Take me home," she said.

Looking down into her eyes, he smiled. Her hand tucked inside of his, he laid them first on his heart, and then on hers.

"We already are."

THE END

Acknowledgements

I want to thank the following people for their help in making this book possible (in no particular order):

Denis, who put up with my constant talking about this book and the research I was doing, who helped me with brainstorming sessions over Greek food, and who retyped my entire manuscript (over half of the completed book) when my computer crashed and I lost everything, and I was in tears. Thank you.

Sasha, who encouraged and inspired me, in so many ways. You contine to amaze me, every day. I am lucky to have you as both a sister and a friend. Thank you. I love you.

Kent, who is one of my greatest cheerleaders and best friends. And for this last year - the most difficult of my life - for being my rock. (And to Barb, who put up with his nightly calls to me to make sure I was okay.) Thank you, little brother. I love you.

My children, **Justin and Michelle**, who watched this book take shape for a good chunk of their childhood, and who I always wanted to make as proud of me as I am of them. You were my raison d'être, and still are in so many ways. I love you. So, so much.

Sam, the best friend/honourary brother I could ever ask for. You've been there for me for so long, through so much. Thank you for everything you've done for me, for your love and support, and for continuing to be there for me every single day. Thank you. I love you.

Elizabeth, daughter of my heart and precious friend. Your Dad would be as proud of you as I am. Losing him was the hardest thing either of us has ever experienced, but I am so grateful for how closely it has brought us together. You are such a bright light in my life, and I love you.

Mom, who believed in me and encouraged me from my childhood to be the best I could be. I, too, miss the porch swing days, our picnics, our barbecues, our coffee dates, our countless hours talking and laughing. I'm so sorry you had to wait so long to see this book get published, but I'm so grateful that you did. I love you, my mother and my angel on Earth.

And finally, to **Brian**. For being the hero of my own real-life love story, and the inspiration for every hero of every book I will ever dream up. I miss you. Every single day.

Printed in Great Britain
by Amazon